Bitsy's Bait & BBQ

Bitsy's Bait & BBQ

PAMELA MORSI

MIRA®

ISBN-13: 978-0-7783-2423-2
ISBN-10:   0-7783-2423-0

BITSY'S BAIT & BBQ

www.MIRABooks.com

Printed in U.S.A.

First Printing: February 2007
10 9 8 7 6 5 4 3 2 1

For Matt
Fisherman and reel repair entrepreneur
research advisor and
college student
May the bass be with you!

Bitsy's Wisdom 1

Bitsy's Wisdom 1: You choose your bait for the fish that you want. But once you drop it in the water, you get what you get.

Emma had let her sister, Katy, be in charge of the map, never a good idea.

Field note, she thought to herself, *Once leaving the commercial trade route between St. Louis and Springfield, the mountainous roads become increasingly rougher and directional cues more tricky. Without a guide or compass, reliance upon mass-produced cartography is a necessary challenge.*

"It looks like we stay on this road for just a little way and then we turn," Katy said.

"Left or right?"

"Huh?"

"Do we turn left or right?"

Katy glanced back down at the map uncertainly. "Oh, I'm sure we'll figure it out when we get there," she said.

Emma managed not to roll her eyes, but it was a struggle. Katy was far too willing to just figure things out as they went along.

Her plans were willy-nilly and rarely thought through. Her decisions were made on the spot and the outcomes not always what she'd hoped. It was no way for a twenty-five-year-old single woman, mother of a five-year-old, to behave. Emma would have gladly explained all that to Katy, *again,* but her lecture was forestalled by a convenient road sign.

"There it is!" Katy cried out. "Warbler Lake Recreational Area, two miles."

Emma made the appropriate turn with only a couple of sputtering hesitations of the aging Geo's tired engine. The old car, so dependable on her little inner-city commute, had never made such a journey. And it had never towed a rented trailer with all the worldly goods of Katy Dodson in its wake.

"Warbler Lake," Josh repeated from the back seat, though the way he said it it sounded more like *Ogler Lake,* which was something completely different. Emma hoped he wasn't being prophetic.

"We're almost there, Josh," his mother told him. "In just two miles we're going to see our brand-new home."

"Yea!" the little guy said, and pumped his fist triumphantly, like an end zone celebration at a football game.

Katy giggled. It was a sound that Emma hadn't heard enough lately. "I'm so excited," her sister confessed needlessly.

Emma nodded. "Now, don't be disappointed if it's not quite how you think it will be," she warned.

"It will be perfect," Katy declared.

Emma was not quite so sure. Experience had taught her that life had a way of not working out the way you planned. And Katy was so hopeful, so trusting, that she could be her own worst enemy. But this was too important. Katy had bet her entire future on it.

Her sister clutched the sales page printed from the computer listing. Katy treated the grainy photo on thin paper as if it were a priceless artifact. In fact, it wasn't even a very good snapshot. It was too far away and the house was practically hidden behind a large outbuilding and the huge, fifties-era roadside marquee that read Bitsy's Bed & Breakfast. Because of the shade of a huge oak tree on the corner, the actual words were not completely visible. "Bitsy's" was clear. And the two big red *B*'s in the words below it. The rock house in the distance had a wide front porch and a gleaming metal roof. Its actual condition was not described in the listing.

"What does it say again?" Emma asked, and then wished that she hadn't. Katy had read it to her a hundred times, and although it did sound good, there was something missing. Something that Emma couldn't quite put her finger on.

"Ozark Mountain B & B. Great opportunity to own your own business!" Katy read aloud. "Live where you work. Turnkey operation on beautiful lakefront has long-time reputation and repeat clientele. Three-thousand-square-foot building on well-lit intersection at the end of main street. Kitchen renovated to meet all health department standards. In top condition, includes all furnishings, equipment and recipes. Open year-round with seasonal customers and local patrons. Only such business in town. Combined revenues very healthy. Charity-bequeathed estate to sell at low price."

Katy punctuated the last with her own words. "And we bought it!"

"We bought it!" Josh cheered again, clapping.

Emma shook her head. It was hard to be cautious against their enthusiasm. "There is just something…something about the description that just seems odd."

"It's such a bargain," Katy said. "That's what's amazing."

Emma shrugged. "Maybe it's just the whole setup," she said. "I mean, who buys a business on the Internet?"

"Apparently a lot of people do," Katy answered. "Why else

would they have them for sale? It's so easy and convenient. I thought it was totally cool."

Katy would. It was a perfect setup for her homebody, single-mom sister. She would have a house of her own to raise Josh in and a small, steady income. It sounded almost too good to be true. And that was exactly what Emma feared.

"What do you think *combined business* means?" Emma wondered aloud.

Katy shook her head. "Beats me. The thing about the recipes, that's weird. Of course, I'll use my own recipes. I want to make that egg-and-sausage casserole. And then have fresh fruit and popovers, or do you think I should stick with muffins? Muffins might be easier."

Emma glanced over at her sister and smiled. "Whatever," she answered. "Katy, everything you bake always tastes good."

"It's 'cause everything is made with love," she answered.

"Mama made me," Josh piped up from his car seat. "But I'm not a muffin."

Katy half turned in her seat and grabbed his sneaker-covered foot. "You're no muffin, you're a sweet sugar cake and I'm going to eat you up."

She pretended to take a bite out of his shoe and Josh shrieked with delight.

Emma just shook her head. She and Katy were so different. She was three years older, but she might have easily been another species. It was far more than just their physical differences; Katy being blond and Emma being brunette. Emma was tall and lean, rangy on the way to muscular, serious, perfectly put together, in control of her own destiny and completely confident of making her way in the world. She kept her hair clipped short, her nails natural and her makeup sparse.

Katy was soft and curvy, more so since Josh was born than

when she'd been a young single. Her hair was long and thick and pulled back from her face in a haphazard fashion that was always attractive. Her clothes were the latest fashion from the big-box stores. And her makeup was a bit more than strictly necessary. She was a woman filled with laughter, despite a life of tough luck. Katy was warm and appealing, with a vulnerability that was somehow irresistible. All the guys were crazy about her.

Katy had only been crazy about one guy, and unfortunately, that had turned out badly.

"This is it!" Katy said, taking a deep breath as they encountered the first few buildings of the little lakeside community. Emma slowed the car to a crawl as they put-putted through the tiny town, silently, expectantly checking it out.

The area was not the most desirable vacation destination in the state. It was not equal in middle-class tourist dollars to places around Branson and Table Rock Lake. That made it more affordable for Katy. It was pretty, though maybe not the most beautiful part of Missouri. Of course, with a state like Missouri, even the lesser landscape was wondrously scenic, and Warbler Lake, nestled into a secluded valley along the edge of the Ozark Plateau, was a pleasure to behold. It was not a stereotypical small town made ordinary by its familiarity. Its disjointed business district ran partway around the edge of the lake and the rest along the highway. And the architecture ran the gamut from Victorian elegance to modern metal warehouse. Strangely, Emma found the mixture appealing. Warbler Lake wasn't some stodgy Christmas card, it was a real place with real people. Maybe it would be a place where her sister could find her home in the world at last.

"Should you try to call Mr. Westbrook?" she asked Katy.

Her sister forced her attention away from the sights to dig into her purse for the phone. The man's number was on her speed dial.

Evidence of several calls back and forth in the last few days since her decision to purchase the B & B.

"Real estate is not my principal occupation," Westbrook had joked. "Rather, my occupation is Principal."

The little semantic reverse was not particularly funny, but it effectively conveyed the fact that Westbrook served as principal of Warbler Lake Elementary. When Bitsy McGrady, who'd owned the B & B for fifty years, passed away, she left her entire estate to the small-town school system that provided classes for kindergarten through sixth grade. The local board had put him in charge of finding a buyer for the business and he had turned to the Internet to make the sale.

Katy continued to punch numbers into her phone, but with no success. Finally she stared at it and shook her head.

"Shoot!" she said. "No towers."

Emma nodded. "We're probably too far back in the hills."

"I told Mr. Westbrook that I'd call when we got to town," she said. "He's supposed to meet us. He said he'd walk over from school. Isn't that great, Josh? The school is close enough to walk to."

"I could walk to school?" Josh exclaimed.

"Next year," Katy assured him with an excited grin. "Next year you can go to kindergarten. What should we do?" she asked Emma.

She shrugged. "The place is about as big as a postage stamp," Emma pointed out from the perspective of a lifelong city girl. "I'm sure we can find it on our own."

"Oh, look, Mama! Look!"

Both Emma and Katy followed the direction that the little boy was pointing. Warbler Lake, a blue jewel encased within gorgeous green hills, sat out before them.

"It's beautiful," Katy said in an awed whisper.

Emma said nothing, but nodded in agreement.

"Boats, Mama, there's boats and ducks and there's everything!"

He was right. Out on the glistening water, the scene was as pristine as a picture postcard.

As they neared the shoreline, Emma tried to tear her attention from the water to the buildings on dry land. They needed to find Katy's place. Emma needed to help her get moved in, set up and open for business. She loved her sister and adored her little nephew. The past three years, since Katy's marriage fell apart, Emma had helped to pick up the pieces. She was glad to have done that. But she was secretly longing to be on her own again. Next fall, after two starts and stops, Emma would be back in college, at last. Third time's a charm, she reminded herself thoughtfully.

"Mama, there's a park!" Josh exclaimed.

To their right, a huge expanse of land was neatly manicured. Beneath a canopy of tall oaks was a spattering of shaded picnic spots and an old-fashioned gazebo, large enough for summer band concerts or an outdoor wedding. Emma felt certain that for Josh, it was the brightly colored playground area that caught his attention. It featured a high red-and-yellow tower with a spiral-slide escape. She imagined that the little boy was already planning his future there. The road came to an end as the park widened onto a public beach and boat dock. A circular drive around a statue of a giant fishhook facilitated a turnaround.

"Pull in here," Katy said. "There's a pay phone next to the building. I can call Mr. Westbrook and get directions to the house."

Emma eased the car and trailer lengthwise into the pitted asphalt driveway in front of a deserted, miserable-looking, square box of a building, its paint peeling and both of its mismatched door screens hanging precariously.

"Wait for Mama while she makes a call," Katy said to her son.

"I'm ready to get out," the child responded.

"Use the phone," Emma told her sister. "Josh and I will take a minute to stretch our legs."

While Katy ferreted out a couple of quarters, Emma got out of the door and opened the back seat child lock for Josh. The little boy had already released himself from the car seat harness, and he leaped out of the vehicle with the panache of a pirate boarding an enemy ship.

"I like this place!" he declared wholeheartedly.

Emma smiled. Her nephew was always like a little ray of sunshine, his disposition inherited from his mother, no doubt. What he'd inherited from his father was the curly brown hair that resisted the most determined comb and the razor-sharp intellect that Emma hoped would eventually help keep Katy out of trouble.

As Josh hopped and skipped around the deserted, potholed parking lot, Emma could hear her sister on the phone.

"Mr. Westbrook, please. Tell him that it's Katy Dodson."

Josh made his way to a line of old rail ties lining a walkway in the front of the building; he traversed them as if they were a tightrope.

"Watch me, Auntie Em!" he called out.

Auntie Em had been Katy's idea, a joking nod to the frumpy, good-hearted mother figure in *The Wizard of Oz*. The character was a far cry from Josh's real Aunt Emma, but the name had stuck and she was stuck with it.

"You are amazing!" she assured the little guy.

"Yes, we made it fine," Emma heard her sister say. "No, I guess we need more directions." She hesitated, listening. "That's the road we came in on…I can see the fishhook from where I'm standing."

Josh had run out to a signpost and Emma followed, keeping a close eye on him as he neared the street, even if there was no traffic. She could still hear Katy's conversation.

"What do you mean this is it? I'm looking in every direction and I just don't see it."

Josh was hugging the signpost as if he were going to attempt to climb the pole, then leaned back, way back, and glanced up for a moment. His gaze was momentarily quizzical and then alive with excitement.

"Look, Mama, look, Auntie Em, it's the place, the place in the picture."

Simultaneously both the women followed the direction of the young boy's eyes. The faded old fifties-era sign with three red *B*'s was immediately familiar. Emma felt an instant of surprised elation before she actually read the words before her eyes.

Her jaw dropped in shock only an instant before she heard her sister's stunned voice.

"Bitsy's *Bait & BBQ?*"

Bitsy's Wisdom 2

Bitsy's Wisdom 2: To barbecue is to smoke food slowly over smoldering wood.

Field note: In dealing with cultural complexities, it is always dangerous to assume that language can be understood in all contexts. Colloquialisms vary tremendously and important details may be lost in translation.

In high school, Emma Collins had discovered Margaret Mead's book *Coming of Age in Samoa* sitting dusty on the library shelf. She'd picked it up and her life had changed. Or, at the very least, her expectations for her life had changed. A career in anthropology had become her goal. She wanted to travel to exotic locales, to become immersed in unfamiliar cultures, and to document her observations of the human condition. So far her treatise might be entitled, *The Foibles and Missteps of My Sister, Kate.*

"Don't say it," Katy ordered firmly as they stood inside the shabby little lakeside restaurant that smelled rather unpleasantly fishy. "I know you're thinking it, but just don't say it."

"What's Auntie Em thinking?" Josh asked.

"Nothing, sweetheart," Katy answered him.

He looked at Emma for confirmation. The little guy could always pick up on tension between the two. Deliberately his aunt softened her expression and winked at him.

The truth was she had plenty to say, but she'd said it all before, time and time again. Her sister was always making some kind of quick, quirky, impulsive decision, and more often than not they turned out badly. But even with Katy's track record, buying a business she thought was a bed-and-breakfast that turned out to be a bait and barbecue was a gigantic screwup.

Emma felt like Ricky Ricardo, wanting to shake a finger and say, "Lucy, you got some 'splaining to do!"

She managed to resist temptation.

"This place is just different from what I thought," she told Josh with a determined smile. "It may not be the place for you and your mom."

"I like it," the little boy told his aunt.

Emma nodded. She could see how the place would look like an adventure to a five-year-old. She could only hope that Katy would take a less daring view. But her sister was not above being impetuous.

Years ago, Katy had voluntarily left their mother and stepfather to live with her scholarship-student sister. A few years later she'd fallen in love with the boss at work, who was out of her league in every way. She'd married him against his family's wishes. And shortly thereafter she had a baby that apparently nobody wanted but her.

Katy had made some big doozy mistakes and Emma was certain that buying this place, sight unseen, was another one of them.

Glancing around the room Emma managed, with great forbearance, not to sigh and shake her head. Bait and barbecue? She'd never heard of such a thing.

Westbrook, who was to meet them shortly, had encouraged Katy to look around.

"The place isn't locked," he'd said on the phone.

A cursory glance at the ancient decor, worn tables and dusty floor suggested to Emma that there was a reason locking up wasn't strictly necessary.

Josh was exploring excitedly. "Look at this, Mama! Look at this!"

A swinging door separated the kitchen from the dining room, and the five-year-old had discovered immediately that he could ride it like some version of playground equipment.

"Be careful on that," Emma warned him. "The hinges are probably two thousand years old."

"Two thousand!" He stopped in midswing, awed by the gravity of the number.

"Auntie Em is just joking," Katy told him.

The little guy eyed Emma speculatively.

"She doesn't look like she's joking, Mama," he pointed out correctly.

Emma was rereading the sales page. Hoping that somehow, someway, the seller had misrepresented himself and that they could easily break the deal. Unfortunately, there seemed to be no glaring lie. Was there a lemon law that applied to commercial real estate? She glanced around the room. If ever a business qualified as a lemon, this one did.

Along the windowed walls to the east and south were ancient booths upholstered in faded olive-green. Three small square tables with four chairs each and one long narrow table that seated six took up most of the rest of the space. In the back corner stood an upright piano so worn and weathered the ivory was worn through on the center keys, and the wood looked more like something you'd see on a barn door than on a musical instrument. There was a Formica bar, and each one of its four vinyl-and-chrome bar stools was greatly in need of seat-cover repair.

Behind the bar was a wide pass-through window to the kitchen, flanked by a multitude of containers and bins storing everything from the ordinary—jelly packets and sugar cubes—to the outrageous—a giant jar of pickled eggs. There was a heavy layer of dust on everything, but the smell of barbecue lingered as if it had leached into the walls and timbers.

"Don't worry, Katy," Emma told her sister. "It'll all work out."

The words were familiar to both of them. Emma had been making things work out for Katy for a long time now. Vividly she recalled the day in her sophomore year of college when she'd gotten back to her dorm to find her sister sitting in the middle of the room surrounded by luggage.

"Katy? What are you doing here?" she asked, shocked.

"They sold the house," her sister answered.

"What?"

"Mom and Larry, they've sold our house," Katy told her. "They're moving to Arizona. I didn't want to go to Arizona, I wanted to be with you."

Emma was sure her jaw must have dropped nearly to the floor. She had only been keeping up with the soap opera that was her mother's life in a cursory manner, finally thinking herself out on her own, but she'd never expected this turn of events.

Emma was the "smart one" of the sisters. Schoolwork had come easily to her. She'd always made top grades and spent her teenage years with her nose stuck in a book. When she graduated from high school, she managed to secure a full scholarship at University of Missouri. Leaving home had been freeing, almost thrilling. She'd loved the cocooned college atmosphere of Columbia almost as much as the carefree weekends in St. Louis. She'd chosen anthropology as a major and pictured a future that looked very different from her past.

It was a golden time. Emma had read somewhere that the average human was only truly happy about ten percent of their lifetime. She thought of that first year away as all ten percent days. Emma used the physical distance between herself and her family to disguise the emotional distance that was growing broader every day. If she never saw her mother again, she would be okay with that.

Then one afternoon, unexpected, Katy was there. And she was not someone Emma was willing to throw away.

What's a college student supposed to do when faced with the challenge of supporting her seventeen-year-old kid sister?

Emma did the only thing she could think of to do. She dropped out of school, moved back to St. Louis, got a job and an apartment that the two could share while Katy finished high school.

It was only a minor setback, Emma had assured herself. Once Katy graduated, they could go to college together and pursue a better future for themselves as a team.

There was just one detail that Emma hadn't counted upon. Katy was not like her—she was more like their mother. Chaos, drama and the fallout from bad choices followed them both around like a pet poodle. It had sniffed out their whereabouts here in Warbler Lake and they were now disappointedly seated in the doghouse.

"Here comes somebody," Josh announced.

Both sisters directed their attention to the door. A man nearing his midsixties, overweight and with a significant comb-over dutifully wiped his feet on the mat as he opened the door.

"Well, hey! Look at you two young girls!" Spurl Westbrook greeted them. "Pretty things like you are sure going to brighten up this old place."

Katy smiled, offering a polite thank-you for the compliment.

Emma managed not to roll her eyes and object to the designation of "pretty thing." Her forbearance was based less on generosity than on the necessity of keeping him on friendly terms. It would be Emma, of course, who would need to get Katy out of this deal, and she wanted to do it without her sister losing so much as a nickel of her precious settlement money.

She stepped forward and offered her hand, cool, professional, attempting to set a businesslike tone. "Good afternoon, Mr. Westbrook. I'm Emma Collins, and this is my sister, Kathryn Dodson."

"You can call me Katy, everybody does," her sister chimed in. "And this little guy is my son, Josh."

The boy stepped forward with a dignified handshake, aping Emma's formal lead, rather than his mother's chummy welcome.

"Nice to meet you, sir," he said.

Westbrook shook the boy's hand, grinning. "And it's nice to meet a young gentleman like you," he said. "You're going to fit in real nice at our school. You're in first grade? Second?"

Josh proudly stood a little straighter.

"I'll be in kindergarten in the fall," he corrected with great seriousness.

"My goodness," Westbrook said, smiling. "Well, you're mighty grown up for your age."

Josh was beaming, completely won over. Emma glanced at Katy and saw that she was, too. That wouldn't do at all.

"Mr. Westbrook, I have to be perfectly frank with you," Emma said immediately. "This place is not at all what my sister expected."

The man grinned broadly and nodded his head as if delighted at her words. "It *is* unique," he agreed. "That Bitsy, God rest her soul, she had a knack of making the place something special. Nobody who's ever been here on a Saturday night ever forgot the experience. Did you see her here?"

The man directed their attention to a framed photo near the doorway. The image of a smiling woman in swimsuit and bathing cap was definitely 1950s vintage. She was holding up a huge fish.

"She looks happy," Katy said. "Very happy."

Westbrook nodded. "She loved this lake, this town, this business," he said. "She always said that owning her own restaurant was a dream come true."

Emma glanced around and imagined the place as a recurring nightmare.

"Um…yes, I'm sure the place was—"

"Lot of memories have been made under this roof," he continued. "Plenty of joy and laughter and just plain fun."

Westbrook directed his words to Katy. Emma could hardly fault him for that—her sister was, in fact, the actual buyer. But Katy couldn't be trusted to keep a rational and prudent head on her shoulders. She was far too impulsive and optimistic.

"I had my first date with my wife at that booth in the corner," Westbrook told her, pointing to the spot.

"Oh, how sweet!" Katy said.

"It was," Westbrook admitted. "I was seventeen years old and too shy to even talk to her. I just sat there, moon-eyed. Old Stymie Wilham was playing piano, soft and romantic, and everybody in the place stopped by to make conversation. It sure saved my biscuits. I would have only seen the back of that girl from that day forward if the whole gosh darn settlement hadn't just won her over for me. We've been married forty-one years."

"Oh, that is wonderful."

Katy's voice was sounding wistful and dreamy. Emma expected that. Her sister, with only the tiniest of provocations, could start meandering down the Yellow Brick Road. But this place was no sidewalk café on the Champs-Elysées, no historic tavern on the Concord to Lexington Road—it was a dusty, dirty, falling-down barbecue place with a smelly little bait shop attached.

"Come on, Miss Katy, Emma, Josh, let me show you around your new home and business," Westbrook invited. "You're just going to love it here."

He took Katy's arm as if he were leading her out at a cotillion.

Josh followed along behind them full of curiosity and enthusiasm. Emma trailed last, barely feigning interest. She considered her options. She could state up front that Katy wanted out of the deal without ever looking anything over. Or they could seem to inspect it and find fault—that would get her off more easily. Emma decided the latter was the better choice. Let Katy charm the old guy, she thought. It'll make it easier when I have to twist his arm to get her money back.

Westbrook filled his tour of the facilities with dining room stories that made Katy laugh. He showed her the cramped little kitchen and she oohed and aahed as if being trapped in those narrow confines full of rusting restaurant equipment was a thing to be aspired to.

Outside the back door the yard boasted several picnic tables and a tire swing hanging from the branch of a huge old oak. Josh went running to it immediately, while Katy stood with Westbrook by the huge red brick barbecue pit. The man was waxing with undue solemnity on the innate superiority of pit barbecue over ordinary grilling. Emma considered her sister to be a pretty good cook. And Katy had certainly had plenty of experience working in restaurants. But as for outside cooking, Emma was pretty sure that Katy had not so much as scorched a hamburger on a hibachi. Still, her sister listened intently as the man spoke.

Unexpectedly it brought to mind the year that Katy was married. When Sean Dodson had spoken, Katy had listened as well. Nothing good had come of that. Except Josh, of course, she mentally corrected herself. Josh was something very good for Katy, and for her, too.

The little guy called out challenges. The tire swing he'd mounted had miraculously transformed into a spaceship and he was fighting off alien invaders with what looked like a broken tree limb, but was undoubtedly a magical light saber.

Emma allowed her gaze to roam to the lake vista. The green mountains rose majestically in the distance. The place was so quiet. It looked just as Josh had said, "pretty." But what was more exceptional was the silence and the sense of solitude. Of course, it wasn't really soundless. The wind whistled through the leaves on the trees. She could hear the lap of clear blue water against a rocky limestone beach.

She had no doubt it was easy to be seduced by the tranquillity. It called to her as well. But the drumbeat of the bigger world outside still pulsed through her brain. She couldn't leave Katy in a place like this. They needed to get back the money and get themselves back to St. Louis. If Katy was still stuck on the idea of running a bed-and-breakfast, Emma was certain there were plenty to be pursued down regular real estate channels.

Emma turned from the view to peruse the house next door. It was a pleasant, fairly well-kept Victorian with a grape arbor in the yard. This was the house that Katy thought she was buying, not this run-down old wreck of a restaurant. From a rocking chair on the front porch, an old woman waved as if to say hello.

Emma waved back.

"Come on upstairs," Westbrook said, finally moving away from the barbecue pit. "I know you both must be anxious to see the living quarters."

Emma followed them as they climbed the staircase attached to the end of the building.

"These steps are good and sturdy," Westbrook announced. "I had Hiram Gouswhelter, our local carpenter, check them out. He said they'd hold up a thousand-pound gorilla. You don't have one for a pet, do you?"

Both Katy and Josh laughed. And Josh liked the joke so well, he kept repeating it as he climbed the stairs. "A thousand-pound pet gorilla. A thousand-pound pet gorilla."

At the top of the stairs, Westbrook felt around the door frame until he located the key. A minute later he'd opened it up.

"It's probably a little stuffy inside, being closed up and all," he said. "It's exactly the way Bitsy left it."

That didn't exactly recommend it to Emma.

The apartment was dark and musty and smelled unpleasantly of stale tobacco smoke. Westbrook wove his way through an obstacle course of furniture to draw up the blinds. What the light revealed Emma thought might have been better left hidden. The long living room/dining room was filled to capacity with an eclectic collection of not-quite-antique furniture. And on each and every possible surface of these were cutesy knick-knacks, dusty lace doilies and faded plastic flower arrangements. Everything was covered with a thin veneer of greasy yellow nicotine.

"P.U.!" Josh said, voicing the thought in Emma's own mind.

"It just needs a little airing out," Westbrook said optimistically. "Nothing that a little soap and water won't take care of. Come look at the kitchen."

Single file they followed the path through the furniture, the hardwood floors creaking with every step. The kitchen was a half century out of date with dark wood cabinets, Formica counters and green appliances.

"This range has hardly even been used," Westbrook said, pulling down the door so they could peruse the oven's interior. "Bitsy did nearly all her cooking downstairs."

"Nice," Katy said.

Emma didn't really think so.

The kitchen was roomy and well lit with one whole wall of narrow, aging glass doors. They walked across the goldenrod-with-avocado linoleum to step out onto the upstairs roof garden. Outside, a tired metal glider faced the lake surrounded by an abundance of plants in terra-cotta pots, all of which were either over-grown or wilted from lack of water.

"This place is a pure pleasure," Westbrook told them. "On the hottest night of summer you can sit up here and the breeze comes in off the lake. It's nice. And in daytime it's one of the best views in the community."

"All that's missing is the shadow of the fishhook statue," Emma stated sarcastically.

No one else seemed to get the joke.

"Wow! I can see forever," Josh said with childish enthusiasm.

Back inside, a door off the living room led to a small hallway where two bedrooms were separated by a narrow bath. Westbrook helpfully turned on the light switch, which caused one naked bulb to shine above a scratched mirror.

"All this tile work is original and it's in pretty good shape," he said. "The plumbing is a little temperamental, but it's still working."

The larger bedroom had a nice thirties-vintage veneer bedroom suite with a huge chest and a vanity with a big round mirror. The smaller one was obviously used mostly for storage. The narrow cot was pushed up against the windows. Every square inch of the walls, almost floor to ceiling, was covered with ancient framed photographs. The portraits were of every size and description, ranging from the end of the nineteen century to the middle of the twentieth.

"These are all family pictures," Westbrook explained. "Bitsy's husband died in World War II, but she had lots of aunts and uncles and cousins. In the end she outlived everyone. There was no one left to take anything, so we just left it all here for the new owners."

"Okay," Katy said, sounding a little bewildered by the logic.

As he stepped back into the hallway, Emma leaned close to her sister and whispered jokingly, "You know how on the Decorating Channel they give theme names for all the rooms."

"Uh-huh."

"I think they'd call this one, 'I See Dead People.'"

Katy didn't laugh, but instead shot her sister a look of reproof. "They're Bitsy's family," Katy said sternly. "They must have meant the world to her."

Emma thought about pointing out that if they meant that much, she wouldn't have displayed them in the storage room, but decided against it. She didn't want to get Katy stirred up. They'd already spent too much time in this place. Emma needed to get Westbrook aside and begin negotiating for a way out of the deal.

They walked back out onto the roof garden. Probably because it was the only place to draw a decent breath of air. With the beauty of the lake stretched out before them, Westbrook spoke with great affection about the community. He talked about the school, the church, the seniors' center, the volunteer fire department, the rescue squad and the annual fishing tournament.

Emma was waiting, not too patiently, to try to get a word in edgewise. Deciding that was not likely to happen anytime soon, she wandered back into the living room, gazing at the knick-knacks, but fastidiousness kept her from touching anything. She examined a small collection of glass cherubs for a few minutes. Then moved on to a shelf full of ceramic woodland animals, complete with a small fake tree and tiny rug of miniature pine needles. There were vases and bottles of every size and description. Colorful planters crowded with dusty roses and gummy mums. Ancient figurines of elves and horses and mermaids vied for shelf space with crocheted bells and decoupaged bread dough.

Emma surveyed the room and shook her head.

"Where's a gallon of gasoline and a book of matches when you need them?" she mumbled to herself.

Outside a horn began honking…and honking and honking. It

was not the rhythmic blasts of an overenthusiastic car alarm but long, impatient blaring intent on attracting attention.

She glanced back at the others.

Westbrook just kept talking. Katy kept listening. Outside the car kept honking. Finally, Emma stepped out the door and onto the landing. A beat-up, rusting, twenty-year-old van was backed up to the building. A man stood beside it, one arm thrust through the open window so that he could lay on the horn.

"What do you want?" Emma called out to him.

The guy glanced up. He was some old hayseed farmer in muddy overalls and mucky boots. His countenance was weathered from age and sun, and his mostly gray hair was pulled back in a pony-tail. He smiled.

At least the old coot has all his teeth, Emma thought uncharitably.

"Stop honking," she hollered.

"Okay, Bitsy," he said. "So get your backside down here and help me unload."

"My name's not Bitsy."

"If you own this place, you'd better get used to the handle."

"I don't—"

"Walk while you talk," he interrupted. "This van's not air-conditioned and these critters don't do well in the heat."

With huge arm gestures, the fellow was motioning Emma in his direction. Rather than stand there, yelling, she headed down the stairway.

By the time she reached the storefront, he had the rear doors to the van opened wide only a few feet from the building's alternative entrance. Within the dark recesses of the van was a motley collection of boxes, crates, coolers and buckets. The fishy stench was strong enough to be unpleasant. The only relief from it was from the man himself who smelled strongly of licorice. It wasn't a perfect combination.

"Open the door, I need to get this stuff inside."

He already had both hands full, but when Emma just stood there, mutely staring at him, the man sighed heavily and set one of the buckets back into the van. He put his right hand under his armpit to draw off his glove, then held it out in greeting to Emma.

"Good afternoon, ma'am," he said, his diction surprisingly formal. "I'm Lattimer Meicklejohn, your source for fresh live bait. Now, let's get this load into the shop. I hope you have cash."

Up close the guy wasn't quite the repulsive hayseed she'd taken him for. His eyes were bright blue and intelligent. His speech was crisp and clear with none of the hillbilly cadence of the school principal/real estate salesman.

"There's some mistake," Emma replied, not bothering to give her own name. The man wasn't going to need it. "I'm sure we never contacted you or ordered anything," she said.

"You didn't need to," Lattimer informed her. "In a town this small news simply floats on the breeze."

He seemed to think that was funny. Emma did not.

"We're not opening the place," she said.

The man's brow furrowed. "You have to," he said. "The bait store helps the restaurant and the restaurant helps the bait store. You're going to need both of these to make a go of Bitsy's."

"We're not making a go of either," Emma explained.

His frown wavered into sarcastic humor. "Don't tell me!" he teased. "You're knocking the place down to build a ninety-story resort hotel."

"No," she said. "My sister is not buying."

"What?" Meicklejohn's eyebrows went up in genuine surprise.

"It's just…well, this is not the business that we, I mean, that my sister thought she was purchasing."

"I thought it was a done deal," he said. "An online auction, all sales final."

"Well, it was, but…" Emma hesitated. This was not the man with whom she should be having this conversation. "Actually, with all due respect, sir, it's none of your business."

He set down the other bucket he held and folded his arms across his chest in a manner that appeared clearly confrontational. His voice, however, softened almost too much.

"Young lady, this is exactly my business," he said. "I've been providing product to this bait store for the past ten years and intend to do it for the next ten."

"That's fine with me," Emma said. "Just don't expect my sister to sell it for you."

"Hey, Latt!" Spurl Westbrook, along with Katy and Josh, came around the corner of the building. "I figured all that insane horn honking had to be you."

Josh came running up to the back of the van, as if drawn to the stink like a gull to a fish.

"What's all this stuff?" the little boy asked.

"It's bait," Westbrook answered for him. "Do you want me to help you unload?"

"I don't know if I'm going to unload," Meicklejohn announced. "The young lady here tells me that this sale is not a done deal."

Emma had not planned to bring the subject up quite so abruptly. Westbrook gazed at her shocked and slack-jawed.

"What do you mean? The papers are signed, the money's already in the bank."

"It's not at all what we thought it was," Emma explained.

"But—" Westbrook's response was interrupted. Katy, looking unusually pale except for her bright red cheeks, stayed his words with a trembling hand.

"Emma's mistaken," she said. "This place is exactly what Josh and I want."

Bitsy's Wisdom 3

Bitsy's Wisdom 3: When the weeds in the shallows begin to die off, the fish move out into deeper waters.

Katy hated to go against Emma. If she could have had all her wishes come true, one of them would be that she would never cross her sister, that not a harsh word would ever pass between them.

She'd learned, unfortunately, by the time she was a teen, that her wishes did not usually come true. That she only kept her worst nightmares at bay with hard work and a positive attitude. And that she and her sister, Emma, would never agree on everything.

"What do you know about running a barbecue place or a bait shop?" Emma asked her barely a half hour later when they were alone again, surveying the grimy, nicotine-stained apartment that Katy intended to make into a home.

"Well, I don't know anything," Katy admitted. "But I'm not too stupid to learn."

"I never said you were stupid," Emma stated firmly.

It was an old conversational rut for them. One of the advantages or disadvantages of two sisters living most of their lives together. Normal discussions had typical valleys and pit-falls, well-worn directions that could never completely be avoided.

"Maybe I don't make decisions the way that you make decisions," Katy said. "But that doesn't mean I'm always wrong."

Emma sighed with great long suffering. "You're not *always* wrong," she said. "But you're wrong about this."

Katy ignored her sister, not an easy thing to do. She'd changed into her tackiest work clothes and tied her hair up in an old dish towel.

"Sometimes things don't turn out exactly as you thought they would," she said. "But that doesn't mean that they turned out bad."

Josh was sitting in the little kitchen devouring a peanut butter sandwich and a box of juice.

"Mama, can I get a tent and put it out on the terrace as my room?" he called out to her.

"No," Katy answered without explanation.

She began unloading a shelfful of knickknacks into a laundry basket.

"What are you doing with those?" Emma asked.

"I'm going to soak them in some hot water and vinegar," Katy said. "That should get the sticky yellow off, I think. For the walls, I guess the only thing that might really work is rubbing alcohol."

"You're actually going to try to clean this place up?"

"Yes, because I'm actually going to live here," Katy answered.

Emma was shaking her head. "Katy, Katy, listen to me. You don't have to do this. I'll make them give you your money back. Or at the very worst, we'll put the place back up for sale ourselves. You guys come back to my place in St. Louis and we'll figure out our next move."

"I've already made my next move," Katy said. "I've moved here. I bought this place and I intend to keep it. I'm not going to try to welsh on the deal. The money from this sale went to the local school. That's a good thing and this is a good place."

"It's no place."

"That's not true. It's my place. Now, are you going to help me get it clean enough to unload the trailer, or are you just going to stand around and argue with me? The sooner I get moved in here, the sooner you can get on with your life."

"I never said I wanted to get on with my life," Emma stated defensively.

"I know you never said it," Katy told her. "But I also know that you do."

Katy had been responsible for stopping Emma's life in its tracks, not once but twice. For the first time she didn't really blame herself. She had been seventeen. Her mom was uprooting her again and she felt as if she was in the way. When she'd suggested that she stay with Emma, her mother thought it was a great idea. So, she went to Emma to be taken in. She thought that she could just live in Emma's college dorm and it would all be fun. Her mother should have known better. But Katy was young enough and stupid enough not to realize what a crimp she was putting in her sister's life. She forgave herself for that.

But the second time, after Sean left her, she knew exactly what a burden she was, but she hadn't known what else to do.

She remembered showing up at Emma's little basement apartment with a grocery bag full of clothes and Josh in his baby carrier. It was all she could carry on the bus. Emma had opened the door surprised to see her. The memory was as vivid today as it had ever been.

"Sean left me," she'd said. "It's been a week, and I don't think he's coming back."

Emma didn't ask questions or make accusations or offer advice. She'd opened the door and let Katy screw up her life all over again.

That was then. And this was now. It would be so easy to just go back to St. Louis and let Emma try to fix things for her. This time she wasn't going to let that happen.

"I think this place will be great for me and Josh," she told her sister. "If Bitsy McGrady could make a life here after losing her husband, I ought to be able to make one after losing mine."

"It's not the same," Emma said.

Katy shrugged. "Nothing ever is."

"I'm finished!" Josh called out from the kitchen as he got down from his chair. "I want to go outside and play on the tire swing."

Katy turned to him and shook her head. "Not until we have time to keep an eye on you. Besides, you've had a really busy day. You could probably use a nap."

"I'm too old for naps, Mama," he insisted.

"Nobody is ever too old for naps. Emma, could you dig out some sheets from the boxes in the trailer?" She turned back to her son. "Maybe if you help Auntie Em change the bed, she'll take a few minutes to read you a story."

"Okay," Josh said, though he had little enthusiasm for the whole idea.

He followed Emma out the door and down the stairs. With those two out of the way, Katy could concentrate on the considerable task before her. She was not afraid of hard work and this place was going to take plenty of it. Just getting the apartment in shape was formidable. But that was nothing compared to getting a business up and running, a business that she didn't know anything about.

"Just begin with the task in front of you. If you look too far ahead, you might lose your nerve."

That's what Sean had told her on her very first day she went to work for him. He was a good supervisor, a patient boss and a nice guy. He was also smart and funny and good-looking, and he seemed immediately smitten with Katy. She knew she should probably resist him. And Emma warned her that he was out of her league. But with tickets to the theater and dinners at elegant restaurants downtown balanced by hot dogs and peanuts at baseball games, she'd fallen head over heels.

"Just when you thought you were getting *ahead,* he turns into a *heel,*" she muttered to herself.

With a sigh she carried the basket of dusty knickknacks into the kitchen. She filled the sink with hot water and vinegar and put them in to soak. She didn't know what she would do with them, but getting them ready for something seemed like progress.

The afternoon was a long one, filled with heavy, back-breaking work. She pulled down all the curtains and blinds. The former went into the trash, the latter she washed down with a hose in the backyard. She and Emma scrubbed the walls and the windows, dragged the rugs out to the clothesline. They picked out the best, most useful pieces of furniture and moved the rest of it down the stairs and out of the way. They scoured the bathroom fixtures and disinfected the kitchen cabinets. It was nearly ten o'clock at night when they were finally ready to unload the trailer.

"See, this place is not so bad," Katy told her sister.

Emma made a tutting sound. "No, it's still bad," she said. "It's no longer totally horrible, but it's still bad."

Katy laughed. "Come on, let's get those boxes up here before we both collapse from exhaustion."

Fortunately, or unfortunately, Katy didn't have that much stuff. After a life on the move with their mom, both sisters had learned to travel light. And she'd never had enough extra cash to accumulate a lot. But she'd brought every toy that Josh owned. She knew how jolting a move could be for a child. She didn't want him to have that sense of having left something behind.

Boxes with clothes and toys weren't that heavy, and she and Emma had everything piled in the living room in no time.

"I think that's enough for tonight," Katy said. "We can get up in the morning and unpack this stuff and you will still have time to be on your way home by early afternoon."

Emma didn't respond. And the hesitation was long enough that Katy finally looked at her.

"Emma?" she asked.

"I'm going to stay down here this summer," her sister said.

"What?"

"If you're determined to try to make a go of this," Emma said, "then I at least want to help you get the place off the ground."

"This is not your problem," Katy said. "I can do this myself."

"I'm sure you can," Emma said. "But it will be a lot easier with an extra pair of hands. And I'll just feel better about helping you make a go of it."

"No," Katy said firmly. "You've got to keep working. You're going back to school in the fall."

"Don't worry about that," Emma said. "I've got enough money to start and I always intended to work myself through. Besides, being here I'll save on rent."

"You'd give up your apartment?"

"I was leaving in three months, anyway," Emma said. "And there was a new girl at work last week looking for a nice cheap place. I'm sure she'd jump at the chance to take over my lease."

"What about your job?" Katy asked.

Emma shrugged. "That's the great thing about temporary work," she answered. "Everybody knows you're here today and gone tomorrow."

Katy shook her head. She didn't want her sister to make the sacrifice, but she was too much of a realist not to comprehend how much she needed Emma's help.

"I don't know," Katy said.

Emma folded her arms across her chest, looking deliberately stubborn. "Hey, it's not like it's your choice," she told Katy. "If I say I'm going to stay here this summer, you have to take me in. That's the way our sisterhood thing works, remember?"

Her words coaxed a reluctant smile out of the corner of Katy's mouth.

"Besides," Emma said. "If ever an anthropologist had a built-in laboratory for the study of unfamiliar human tribes, I think Bitsy's Bait & BBQ might be it."

Bitsy's Wisdom 4

Bitsy's Wisdom 4: No matter how you ordinarily like your other meat, barbecue has got to be well done. It's impossible to overcook it.

Gwendolyn Dodson barely looked up as Myra, her secretary, placed a fresh cup of coffee on her desk.

"Thank you," she said, as she continued to shuffle through the reams of paper that showed up on her desk every day demanding her attention.

When Myra didn't immediately walk away, Gwen looked up curiously. "Yes?"

Myra swallowed as if she had a bad taste in her mouth. Her gaze didn't meet Gwen's eyes.

"I got a call from Khaki," she said, not bothering to offer further explanation. "So, do you want to do the Carlisle meeting, or do you want me to ask Pete or Randy to do it?"

Gwen deliberately kept her face devoid of all expression. It was one of the first things she'd learned about having a family busi-

ness—keeping your family problems camouflaged from your business associates was always good policy.

"Randy's all tied up with the franchisers," she said. "Ask Pete
what his schedule looks like. If his looks worse than mine, try to
see what you can nudge around. Put the packaging presentation
off until next week if you have to."

Myra nodded and made her way out. Gwen tried to get back
to her paperwork, but couldn't. Dressed in her standard gray business suit with the conservative over-the-knee hemline and sensible black pumps, she certainly looked the part of successful
female CEO of a regional fast-food corporation. But how she felt
had more to do with motherhood than management.

She wasn't certain which emotion was strongest. There was
anger at the situation, annoyance at the extra work. And there was
a healthy dollop of worry. All of those feelings were overlaid with
a feeling of general disappointment.

She could remember the conversation with her son verbatim.

"Are you going to be there?" she'd asked him.

"Yes, I'll be there."

"If you're not, then tell me now. I can deal with it better if you
tell me now."

"Mother, I said that I'll be there and I'll be there."

But, of course, he was not going to be there. Not only was he
not going to be there, he'd given no warning, no excuse.

"My little Sean, he's a chip off the old block," Garrett, Gwen's
husband, always used to say.

But it hadn't turned out to be true. Garrett had worked himself to death by the age of forty-three. Sean, who was thirty, didn't
work hard enough to give himself a hangnail, much less a heart
attack.

Gwen assumed that it was probably her fault. Wasn't that the
verdict of pop psychology? If the kid is screwed up, it was the

mom's fault. She hadn't bonded with him properly. Or she'd over-indulged him. Or she hadn't made time for him. Or she'd made too much time for him. Not enough mothering, or too much smothering. Anyplace on the sliding scale—if the kid couldn't make it on his own, she was the one to blame.

Gwen took a sip of her coffee and wished she had a cigarette. She'd given up smoking when she got pregnant with Sean. Thirty years nicotine-free, yet there were still times when she longed for the calming effects of lighting up.

She looked down at her paperwork determinedly. Then with a sigh, allowed her gaze to drift out the magnificent windows of her eighteenth-floor corner office in the Edgecity Tower, which offered a beautiful but suburbanly distant view of the St. Louis sky-line. Spring had arrived, crisp and cool. The very newness of life just made her feel tired and old.

She'd come a long way in thirty years. Longer than thirty years, she reminded herself. She'd met Garrett when she was still in high school. She and her girlfriends giggled over French fries at the good-looking guy in his twenties who ran a hamburger stand out of a rusted bread truck up on blocks. Gwen was never sure what about her had captured his attention. There were always pretty girls around, but he focused on her. He flirted with her, of course. But more often, he just talked with her and fed her his crazy creations, like French-fried peppers or corn chips with chili and cheese.

"Try not to look at me as if I'm a grease-soaked hamburger flipper," he told her once. "I'm the owner of a business and I in-tend to make the most of it."

When she'd come home from college in the spring of her sophomore year, she immediately noticed the shiny new drive-in on the highway. Dodsonburger, its sign proclaimed in flashing neon.

That same company logo now adorned the Edgecity Tower along with the designation Corporate Headquarters. A lot had happened between then and now. And this morning it was a good thing that nobody had asked Gwen if it had all been worth it. Today she wasn't sure of her answer.

She got up from her desk and, grabbing her still mostly full coffee cup as a prop, she headed out of the office. Myra was on the phone. She gestured mutely at her cup, as if announcing her destination, and then headed in the direction of the break room. It was also the direction of her son's office.

She had given Sean a directorship three years ago. She had wanted to make him a vice president, or even more than that. But he was not ready. Gwen had begun to wonder if he ever would be.

It had been her hope that he would take over the reins of the company and that she, who'd never asked for the job and had never wanted it, would be able to finally hand it over. She had kept it operating, growing, adapting, through hard times and decades of hard work. Hundreds of fast-food companies had gone under, or had been bought out by big conglomerates. Gwen had gone regional with Dodsonburger and kept it a family run business in a climate that no longer tolerated the concept. She'd made money and earned respect. But she hadn't done it for that. She'd done it for Sean. It was her son's legacy from his father. That hope had faded significantly over time.

Gwen stepped into the break room. The place, thankfully, was empty. She set her cup on the counter next to the coffeepot and went back out the door and around the corner to her son's office. He, too, had a full-windowed corner office, an executive assistant and his name on the door. All the trappings of an important, successful executive. The only thing missing was a strong work ethic that was absolutely required.

Sitting at a desk out front, Khaki was giggling on the phone. Most people thought the cute little brunette had been hired by Sean for her good looks. In fact, Gwen had hired her specifically for her airheadedness. The girl wasn't smart enough to take advantage of Sean.

She was also not smart enough to get away with anything. When she caught sight of Gwen her eyes widened and she abruptly slammed the phone down without a word.

Gwen almost laughed out loud at her overreaction. Nothing could have made the girl look guiltier. It was not exactly a surprise that she was wasting company time on personal phone calls. In truth, Gwen could hardly blame the young woman. What else was she going to do? Her boss showed up only when he wanted to, and rarely bothered to actually accomplish anything while he was there. Probably the most strenuous work she did all week was fill out her own pay slip.

"I need to get something out of Sean's office," she lied.

It surely was an unspoken understanding that nobody should be allowed to rummage through someone else's office on their own. That's why they all had lockable doors and executive staff to oversee them when empty. But Khaki made no attempt to stop her.

Gwen knew that Myra would never be so compliant. She would have jumped to her feet with a generous smile and a firm attitude saying something like, "Tell me what are you looking for and I can help you find it." Fortunately Khaki was far too afraid of Gwen to do more than sit with deer-in-the-headlights wide eyes and nod mutely.

Gwen went into her son's office alone, with no idea what she was looking for. Was she trying to find a clue to his current whereabouts? It didn't really matter, if he didn't come into work he obviously was in no frame of mind to do so. Was she hoping for some kind of evidence that he was not the lazy ne'er-do-well that he seemed to be? Perhaps she thought there might be an answer in this room as to why her only son had turned out to be such a disappointment to her.

There! She'd thought the thought that had lingered at the edge of her consciousness for years now. It was almost a relief to finally look at it and examine it. She allowed the hurt of it to wash over her. Like biting down on a sore tooth, it was better somehow to just go with the pain.

His office, a masculine dark leather version of chic contemporary decorator perfection, offered no hints as to why. The place didn't even look like her son, who still seemed like a messy teenager in his blue jeans and T-shirts. Everything was neat and tidy. No papers unfiled on the long expanse of polished ebony desk, no yellow sticky notes stuck to the computer screen. The only clue that the office was occupied was the old-fashioned calendar with "Wise Words on Business" that she'd given him last Christmas. Today's quote was from John Maynard Keynes: *The difficulty lies, not in the new ideas, but in escaping the old ones.* The Carlisle meeting was written below it in Sean's own hand and circled twice with a red marker.

Clearly, her son had intended to be there. But good intentions had not brought Sean very far and didn't bode well for his future.

Gwen took a seat in the big, comfy leather chair and began opening the desk drawers. Like the outside, the inside was neat, impersonal, unused. She'd almost given up when she opened the bottom drawer. There she found a half-dozen letters, their envelopes handwritten. Neither the penmanship nor the return address were familiar to her, but she knew immediately and without question who they had to be from.

She picked up the one on top and looked inside. The missive contained only one line. "Our new address is on the envelope."

Gwen glanced again at the return address: 1 Fishhook Rd., Warbler Lake, Missouri 65481.

"I wonder what she's doing there," she mumbled aloud.

It didn't matter. Far away or next door, Sean had, thankfully, lost complete interest in the silly girl. Gwen was the one who ought to be thanked for the settlement. She'd set up a modest trust fund for the child's future education and made a one-time cash settlement with her. It was not nearly as much as she might have gotten in monthly child-support payments over the next twenty years, but Gwen knew human nature well enough to be sure that those big dollar signs would bring the whole foolish episode to a quick conclusion.

Katy Collins was, perhaps, not the worst mistake her son had made. But she was certainly one with long-term consequences.

After Sean had finished college, his degree in humanities totally inappropriate for the business world, she'd sent him out in the field to learn the daily operation of Dodsonburger firsthand by managing one of the store sites. At first she was very impressed with his ability and she was thrilled that he seemed to have found something he was good at.

That euphoria was unfortunately followed by the rumor that he was having an affair with one of his employees. She'd immediately called him into her office.

"Your personal life is your own," Gwen told him. "But in this day and age, you just can't get involved with an employee. No matter how consensual, it has the appearance of sexual harassment."

Sean had nodded dutifully. "You're right, Mother, I'll take care of it."

Two days later he'd married the girl in a quickie courthouse wedding.

Gwen had been horrified.

Thank God that's all over, she thought to herself. Though, in truth, such things were never over. The divorce had scarred Sean in a way that Gwen had not anticipated. He felt like a failure and turned that emotion into a template for everything he did.

She refolded the letter and tried to slip it back into the envelope.

It got stuck. She glanced down inside to see what, at first, just looked like a square piece of paper with writing on it. When she pulled it out, she saw that it was a photograph. On the back it read: Josh, age 5. She turned it over and her heart caught in her throat.

The child in the picture was her child. Well, of course, he wasn't *her* child. The clothes, the haircut, were all too new to be her Sean, but beyond that, the face, the smile, the intelligent eyes, it was her little boy, a preschooler once again.

Gwen's elation was suddenly deflated into a hard pit in her stomach that made her nauseous. The child of her son's undesirable union had never really been a child to her. She had thought of him only as a complication, an unfair bargaining chip that Katy had gone to court with. She'd even suggested to Sean that he insist upon DNA evidence of his paternity.

On that her son had shaken his head. "I know he's mine," Sean said.

Anyone who saw the boy would have agreed.

Gwen had wanted to argue with him, but he was already so beaten, so listless, so pained that she just didn't have the heart the push him further. She paid for the divorce, the education fund, the settlement, and then she'd marked the whole episode off of her to-do list. As if it were just another commercial transaction, bothersome and slightly unpleasant, but no more than that.

Now, as she looked into the eyes of this little Josh, the situation was suddenly and inexplicably much different.

Gwen started to put the photo in her pocket and then hesitated. Instead she clicked on the computer and carried the picture to the scanner. She made a copy that she sent to herself in an e-mail. Then she carefully put the image of Josh back into the letter his mother had sent and placed it back in the bottom drawer in what she thought was precisely the way it had been there before. She wasn't sure exactly why it was so important that nothing seem disturbed. Gwen wasn't sure if she was doing it so that Sean wouldn't know that she'd been rifling through his desk, or so she could continue to pretend the child didn't exist.

She wiped both the drawer and the top of the desk with a tissue, as if she were a criminal covering her fingerprints. Then she left the office, giving Khaki, who was still sitting nervously at her desk, a quick wave and a thank-you. Gwen stopped back in the break room, filled her cup and carried it back to her office. She smiled at Myra, and it wasn't completely fake. Her disappointment, sadness, loss, were now somehow seasoned with hope. A sweet, small hope.

Gwen sat down at her desk and pulled her e-mail up on the computer. She scrolled through quickly until she saw what she wanted. With the click of a button that sweet five-year-old smiled at her from the screen. For several long moments she just gazed at him. Then she smiled back.

She clicked open her address book window in the corner of the screen. She paged through it quickly until she found the entry she wanted. *Bradley, Hicks, Rodgers, Litham & Braun, Attorneys-at-Law.* She fired off a quick e-mail.

"Call me at my office to discuss current custody arrangements for the child Joshua Dodson."

Bitsy's Wisdom 5

Bitsy's Wisdom 5: They call it dabbling, dipping, flipping or a hundred other names. It just means dropping live bait into the water and waiting for something to happen.

It was a Saturday morning, less than two weeks after her arrival in the picturesque town of Warbler Lake. The horns began honking at 4:30 a.m. Emma rolled over on the narrow, lumpy cot and peeked out of the blinds. A half-dozen pickup trucks were parked around the building, their occupants, clad in various versions of fishing hats, stood around impatiently.

Field note: Pre-fishing ritual begins early, requires outlandish dressing, loud camaraderie and acquisition of live insects, leeches, crustaceans or feeder fish.

Someone apparently saw the movement at the window.

"Come on, lady," a voice called out. "It's nearly dawn and the fish won't wait."

The upper window was opened a healthy two inches. When she stood up she could speak directly through the space.

"I'll just be a minute," she assured them.

Staggering sleepily through the upstairs apartment, Emma

found the bathroom and turned on the one naked bulb above the mirror. The image she saw reflected there looked nothing like her. She was classic and fashionable without being trendy, attractive without excessive girlieness. She was neat, orderly and in control. She was exactly the person she had spent the last decade struggling to be. That person was not peering back at her through the scratchy, scarred mirror.

Emma splashed water on her face, hastily brushed her teeth and pulled a comb through the short brown hair now desperate for a trim.

"Only twelve miserable days and I'm already going native," she said, sighing.

The horns had begun to honk once more. Emma hurried to the doorway of the main bedroom.

"Katy! Katy!" Her tone was sharp but covered in a whisper. Her kid sister, the one woman in the world who could always find bad luck anytime, anyplace and upon any occasion, was sleeping the sound, undisturbed sleep of the innocent. "Katy, wake up," she tried again.

Beside the tousled blond hair of her sister, a smaller, darker, curlier head stirred.

"Auntie Em?"

"Go back to sleep, Josh," Emma whispered. "It's too early to get up."

The little boy complied and was dreaming once more before his head hit the pillow.

Alone, Emma made her way out the door and flipped on the porch light before heading down the dark stairs at the side of the building. The air was cool and crisp and the scent of springtime on the lake was one she'd begun to appreciate. But there wasn't even any gray yet on the horizon. For a city girl, this was still the middle of the night.

She needed coffee.

The men continued their haranguing and had begun banging on the door. Emma didn't hurry one bit faster. It wasn't that she didn't care, but she'd already figured out that even if she ignored them, these guys would never go away.

She came around the corner with the key in her hand. A spattering of applause accompanied her arrival.

"Excuse me," she said. Her voice had a cutting edge. "Excuse me."

The crowd of men stepped out of her way. She opened the door and switched on the light inside the little windowless room. It didn't offer much, but outside four feet of red neon loudly proclaimed Live Bait.

A cheer went up from those waiting outside. Without even expending the energy for a roll of her eyes, Emma went inside. The half-dozen men and two women who filed in, did so quietly. They were hushed, businesslike, respectful. It could have been because no one really knew Emma. She chose to believe their behavior had other origins.

Field note: Upon entering the storehouse of the creatures destined for sacrifice, members of the tribe show marked reverence, and verbal exchange is limited to only the necessary. They line up informally, but in some obvious order, gender notwithstanding and the old giving way to the younger and more impatient.

In the past two weeks she'd come to imagine the inhabitants of Warbler's Lake as a lost tribe, humans cut off from the real world, as curious and unfamiliar as Borneo headhunters. It was the one thing that had kept her from going stark raving mad in Warbler Lake. She approached the community not as a resident but as an anthropologist, observing local customs and rituals as if conducting a scientific pursuit.

"Give me a dozen fatheads and a small box of mealworms," the first customer requested.

"Shiners," the next wanted. "A couple of netsful, I guess."

"Two dozen night crawlers and a half batch of crickets."

"You got grub worms? I need a tubful."

Emma fulfilled each order betraying as little squeamishness as possible. The minnows were not bad. They swam around in tanks of fresh water and she simply netted them up and put them in the fisherman's bucket. The worms and insects were pre-sorted into foam containers of damp loamy soil. Splitting a dozen was unpleasant and far from a mathematical exercise. Emma could always make sure that the customers got half the dirt, but she was unwilling to count the worms themselves. Thankfully nobody complained. Night crawlers were especially tricky. When she grabbed them they would constrict the muscles in the neck and tail so she couldn't pull them out without snapping off their heads. She'd already learned to hold the slimy, icky bugs gently for a moment until they relaxed and she could pull them out easily.

The room was like a temple, cool and dark. The only artificial light in the place was directed into the minnow tanks. The old cement floor was cold and scarred by thousands of footsteps. Still, Emma could not like the place. It was too fishy, too fetid.

A gray-haired senior citizen in an ancient, sweat-stained fishing cap sidled up to her. He was the last one in line.

"Stink bait," he requested.

Emma reached for a carton from the cool box.

"No, not the liver flavor," he told her. "Give me the blood. Catfish just knock one another out of the way to get to that stuff."

She handed over the disgusting balls of muck and managed a slight, truly insincere smile.

He grinned back broadly, displaying a mouthful of empty spaces where teeth should have been.

"So tell me, babydoll," he said to her. "What's a nice gal like you doing in a place like this?"

"Oh, it's a long story," she answered.

That was the truth, she supposed, but in many ways it was an anthropological story of nomadic counterculture. Their mother, a free spirit and late-blooming flower child with only vague suggestions of heritage, managed to give birth to two daughters without acquiring any forwarding address for the father, or fathers, responsible for their existence.

They had never gone hungry, been naked or lacked shelter, but they'd never really managed to have a home. Their mother loved the wandering life, in the same way that Emma loved seeing new places and discovering new people.

Katy, however, was a homebody. Uncomfortable with every move, quick to try to set up a new life wherever they went.

When Emma was in high school, her mother fell in love. She met and married a happy carefree guy, equally as unfettered to earth as herself. They seemed a perfect match. And Emma, who'd worked hard in school after school, had managed excellent grades and a great SAT score, left for college with her scholarship and complete confidence that Mom and Larry would get along fine.

But the road Emma had expected to travel had turned out to have some very unexpected twists and an alternative destination. It had led her here, to the middle of Nowhere, Missouri, dead tired, dressed like a bum and smelling of fish bait.

"Have a nice day," she told the toothless old fisherman with her best ethnographical nonjudgmentalism.

The early morning rush accomplished, Emma checked the bell above the door to make sure it would warn her of the arrival of customers and walked across the front of the building to the restaurant doorway. The place did not officially open until eleven, but Emma had already learned that the natives of Warbler Lake did not allow themselves to be constrained by official notices like Open and Closed.

Two patrons were seated at the bar. One was Newt Barker, a deputy sheriff for the county who lived in Warbler Lake. He had probably unlocked the door. According to Spurl Westbrook he had keys for all the businesses in town. A third guy wearing a ball cap that advertised a septic tank service was pouring coffee. Emma was grateful that somebody had made some, but was still annoyed at finding the place occupied.

"Gentlemen," Emma said, privately noting to herself that she was using the term loosely. "I hate to break up the party, but this is Saturday. We don't start serving for five more hours."

Everyone nodded.

"We're just having some morning coffee," the guy pouring explained.

"But it'd be nice if you could scare up some toast," the deputy suggested.

"Yeah, and maybe a little oatmeal, that would sure be welcome."

The third fellow was younger than the other two, and answered to the name Pearly. He had been a customer every day Emma had been there. He wore a bandanna around his hair emblazoned with the logo from a smokeless tobacco product. That was covered by a hat promoting his favorite beer brand. Emma assumed these were meant to accessorize his T-shirt, a cigarette billboard in one-hundred-percent cotton. Definitely a man of many vices.

"We don't start serving until eleven o'clock," Emma repeated succinctly.

"Oh, I'm sure you can stir up something, ma'am," Pearly told her with a smile that, for a less cranky woman, might have been winning.

Emma was incredulous.

Field note, Emma wryly thought to herself. *Communication with natives particularly difficult, though there is no indication of actual hearing loss. Decision to humor them.*

Emma walked into the kitchen and, against her better judgment as well as her inclination, she found a metal pot, filled it with water and retrieved a huge can of oatmeal from the pantry. She lit a burner on the stove and measured out the oats.

This was crazy. Her life shouldn't be like this. She couldn't help but feel resentment. Katy was now, and had been for the last decade, her responsibility. And with Katy there was always cause for concern. But in truth, Emma wanted to get back to her own life to start pursuing her own goals. If this had been truly a little vacation bed-and-breakfast, she might have been able to do that. Bitsy's, however, was clearly no one-woman operation. Katy was going to need help. And Emma felt trapped by that need.

The swinging door between the kitchen and the public area was suddenly filled by Lattimer Meicklejohn, their bait supplier, looking and smelling as if he'd already put in a full day's work. Fish and licorice, never a pleasant combination.

"Pearly said you were making oatmeal back here," he said. "I thought I'd put in my order."

Emma looked up at him with deliberate disdain. "We don't open for five hours," she said.

He nodded. "Everybody knows that," he told her. "But we can't miss our breakfast. Oatmeal is about the only decent food that comes out of this kitchen."

He was grinning as he said it, but Emma resented his words while recognizing the truth of them. The barbecue thing had not gone well.

"We're getting better," she assured him. "Katy's practically memorized Bitsy's cooking tips, and now she's ordered a book and I'm sure that as we get used to the pit…"

He waved away her explanation. "Barbecuing is an art, not

something you can learn from a book," he said. "What you need to do is hire a good cook. And until you do, I'd suggest you stick to oatmeal."

The last word reminded her to stir the pot, whose contents were dangerously close to sticking.

"Where are you girls from, anyway? St. Louis?"

"We've been living there for several years," Emma answered.

"But you're not from there." It was a statement, not a question.

"Why do you say that?"

"'Cause they make some dang good barbecue in St. Louis," he said.

"They have barbecue in Chicago, too," she said.

He nodded. "So you're from the Windy City," he said.

"No, but we lived there several years," Emma said.

The man was thoughtful. "Several years in St. Louis, several years in Chicago. Where else did you live several years?"

"Davenport, Indianapolis, and I graduated from high school in Des Moines."

"Did you move a lot for your dad's job?"

"Do you always play twenty questions with people you hardly know?" she shot back.

He laughed. "How else am I going to get to find out anything about you? You're not a woman who offers much information."

"Maybe there's nothing to tell."

"Well, that's not what I hear from your sister," Lattimer said.

"What about Katy?"

"She told me all about wanting to find a nice place for herself and the boy. Somewhere that they could stay put and always call home."

"And this is the place she chose!"

Emma words were facetious and she regretted them the minute they were out of her mouth. It was one thing for her to shake her head at her sister's decisions. It was quite another to voice her criticism to strangers. That was just plain disloyal.

She spooned out the oatmeal into four bowls set on a tray.

"Look, Mr. Meicklejohn," Emma said. "It's nice of you to want to get to know us, but I'm not really the chummy type."

"Call me Latt," he said. "Everybody does. It's a very chummy community."

She added side plates with toast and four sets of flatware wrapped in napkins. She picked up the tray and handed the whole thing to Meicklejohn.

"Here, if you're going to hang around you might as well make yourself useful."

"My pleasure," he responded without the slightest suggestion of unwillingness.

Latt carried the food through the swinging door with all the dexterity of an experienced waiter.

Emma could only shake her head.

As Meicklejohn went out the mailman came in.

"Hi," Emma said.

"Curt," he reminded her.

"Hi, Curt," she repeated.

He was about thirty, tall, lean and blond. Friendly, as everyone was, and slightly flirty as well. Emma had already decided that she liked him.

"You're here pretty early," she said.

He nodded. "You're my first stop and I try to get everything delivered before noon on Saturday," he explained. "Hope I see you in church tomorrow?"

Emma's response was vague. Sunday-morning invitations were not that typical in any of the cities she'd lived so far.

"Maybe so," she answered.

He nodded and headed out.

Emma sifted through the pile of envelopes and flyers that he'd left on the corner of the prep table.

It was mostly junk. Then an envelope caught her eye. It had been sent to Katy, the return address was a five-name law firm in St. Louis, one only too familiar to Emma.

Without an instant of consideration of her sister's mail and her sister's privacy, Emma ripped open the letter and read it. It was only three paragraphs long, but that was enough to practically have steam spouting from Emma's ears.

She wasn't sure who made her most angry, Katy, who had obviously been keeping things from her, or her ex-brother-in-law, Sean. The former was going to get a piece of her mind. The latter…well, Emma had hopes of running his wimpy backside out of the state of Missouri.

Bitsy's Wisdom 6

Bitsy's Wisdom 6: The broader the surface of the meat, the more marinade soaks in. Flank steak will get more juiced up than a hillbilly at harvest time.

Something awakened Sean Dodson; he wasn't sure what. He rolled over. Every muscle in his body ached, his head was pounding and his mouth tasted as if a camel had crawled inside it and died.

He nudged against someone beside him and squinted one eye open. She was a blowsy, bleary-eyed brunette. She opened her eyes and smiled at him.

"Morning," she said.

Her breath was easily no better than his own.

Deliberately he smiled at her. She was nice. He remembered that. She was nice and funny and it had felt really good to be inside her. He couldn't recall her name, but what he did remember was all good.

"What time is it?" he asked her.

She turned the other direction to look at the clock on her bedside table.

"Eight-thirty," she said. "But it's Saturday, so no big deal."

"Yeah," Sean agreed. "No big deal."

The bedroom door opened, and a small head peeked inside. The sight of the little boy in Spider-man pajamas froze Sean in place.

"Mommy, I tried to make cereal but I spilled the milk."

"Jamie! Get out of here. You know you don't come into Mommy's bedroom when the door is closed."

"I can for emergency," he insisted. "I spilled the milk, Mommy, that's an emergency."

He didn't even look in Sean's direction.

The woman threw back the covers and hustled the little fellow out.

"Sorry," she said in Sean's direction. "Be right back."

The minute the door closed behind her Sean was on his feet. He hustled himself into his briefs, his pants, his shirt. He caught a glimpse of his reflection in the mirror on her closet door. It wasn't good. He looked as bad as he felt and he couldn't cover himself up quickly enough. A discarded condom had landed on one of his socks. He threw them both in the trash and put on his left shoe sockless.

He made it to the door at the exact minute that she returned. She was surprised to see him dressed.

"I've got to go," he said.

"Stay, I'll fix you breakfast."

"No, I can't. I gotta go."

"Coffee at least."

"No, no, I gotta get going."

In the living room, the little kid knelt watching *Digimon* on the television as he shoveled spoonfuls of cereal into his mouth. Across from him, Sean could see the outside door and began moving in that direction.

She was following him. Talking to him. Pleading with him to stay.

He opened the door and stepped out into the hallway of the apartment. She came with him.

"You don't like kids," she said.

He was surprised at the suggestion.

"I do," he insisted. "I do. I…I have a boy of my own."

She nodded.

They stood there together, silent for a long moment.

Sean was desperate to get away.

"I'll call you," he said, feigning lightness.

"No, you won't," she said.

"Of course I will," he insisted, pretending it was true.

"You don't have my phone number," she pointed out.

That stopped him momentarily.

"Oh, yeah, right," he said.

Sean looked at her. She looked at him. Finally she shook her head.

"Go!" she said.

She didn't have to tell him twice. He hurried down the hallway and took the stairs, two at a time.

Out in the parking lot he spotted his car, a respectably boring Volvo sedan, and headed in that direction. He paused at the driver's side door to pat his hip pocket, making sure that his wallet was there. It was full of cash and credit cards, of course. But he didn't really care about that.

His wallet was where he kept his photo of Josh.

It wasn't Josh as he was now. Katy sent him a new picture every month or so. His son was growing, changing. The one he carried in his wallet was of a curly-headed toddler, his arms upraised, smiling at Sean. That was how he remembered his son. That was how his son had looked the night he had walked out on him.

The memory on its own was enough to twist his gut painfully.

Sean unlocked his car, got behind the wheel and turned the ignition. He'd left his Blackberry on the console, never really a good idea, but it was still there and he checked it quickly for messages. He also clicked on his calendar. Since missing the Carlisle meeting a few days earlier, he was trying hard not to let his mother down. But these days letting people down seemed like what he did best.

He didn't know how that had happened. He'd come home from college full of optimism and confidence. Yes, he'd led a privileged life. He'd gone to an elite private school, got into the college of his choice and taken a course of study that interested him. He'd come home perfectly willing to find a place for himself in the family business. And he quickly discovered that he liked the everyday world in the fast-food trenches at Dodsonburger.

And then he'd met Katy.

Sean put the car in gear and made his way out of the parking lot and along the busy Saturday-morning streets. The city was filled with shoppers out early to get a jump on the weekend, moms and dads in minivans full of young soccer players, joggers and dog walkers getting a late start on the only day of the week that they could. He watched them like an alien observer. How did they manage to get their lives in order? Why did the normal and everyday come so easily to the rest of the universe?

He took the entrance ramp to the loop and merged into traffic. He drove until he caught sight of a Dodsonburger sign. This was not a part of town that he frequently visited, but he knew all the restaurants.

Sean pulled off the expressway, into the location, and found a parking spot in the back. He used his key card at the employees' entrance. To say they were surprised to see him was putting it mildly. The manager wasn't there and the assistant manager was stuttering nervously at the reality that someone from corporate headquarters had showed up on a Saturday morning.

"I'm just here to help out for a few hours," Sean assured her.

He had done this now so often, barged in so many places so many times, that he'd gotten good at settling down the jitters of the employees.

He visited the restroom to clean up and make himself present-able, then he donned an apron with the company logo and went to work. Nobody in management, certainly not his mother, had any idea that he snuck away two or three times a week to do ham-burger flipping and counterwork. It was a secret he kept to him-self. He doubted anyone would approve, and he was sure no one would understand. He wasn't sure he understood it himself. He did the work because he liked it. He enjoyed the camaraderie. He enjoyed the customers. He even enjoyed the hot, difficult opera-tion of the kitchen. It comforted him in a way that his office at headquarters never did. Sean liked the restaurant business. He just didn't care for the business of restaurants. He threw himself into the labor with enthusiasm.

As he did so he let his mind wander where it would, and as it so often did inside the walls of the fast-food franchise, it settled upon Katy.

The memory alone brought a smile to his lips. Vividly he re-called the first time he'd seen her. It had been in a burger joint identical to this one. He'd thought he already knew a lot about her. He'd read over her application quickly, and had been favorably impressed with her experience. She'd had lots of part-time jobs throughout high school and had been waitressing at a local pan-cake house since graduation. Her reason for leaving was because there were no openings on the day shift. At Dodsonburger, where most of the employees were students of some sort, a responsible person for day shift was always in demand. He had been predis-posed to like and appreciate her. But he'd never expected love.

Their eyes met across that narrow plastic table and something incredible happened. It wasn't a buoyant joy or exuberant happiness. It was as if all the props that held up his world had been knocked out from underneath him.

It was wrong. It was so wrong in so many ways.

She had been just an eighteen-year-old kid. He was a grown man of twenty-three. She was not exceptionally bright, barely educated and somewhat naive. He was academic by nature and not particularly trusting. She was his employee and he was the boss.

It should never have happened.

It had been inevitable.

From that first day across the table, his world tilted. He couldn't imagine being anywhere with anyone else.

In truth, the affair of which his mother had accused them had never happened. Sean had never even kissed her until the day she agreed to be his wife. Because he'd known, even then, that if he ever started he'd never be able to stop.

And he hadn't. It had been three years since he'd walked away, but he had never stopped loving her.

The morning shift went quickly. Customers placed their orders at the counter. They were entered into a computer with a readout observable from the grill and steam tables. The sandwiches were put together as they were ordered, and to the specifications requested. It was more time-consuming than having them premade in standardized form, but it was what made Dodsonburger different from its competitors. Sean took over sides and sacking, making sure that everything that was requested was actually packed together. Then he handed that off to the drink girl, who filled the paper cups with the appropriate liquid and passed the completed meal to the customer. It was hot, rushed, repetitive work. Sean reveled in it.

He enjoyed the morning so much, he decided to work through the noon rush, but by two o'clock he could hardly make up any excuse to linger. He thanked the staff, complimented the assistant

manager and made his way to the car. With each step away from
the building, his spirits went lower and lower.

Deflated, Sean got back on the interstate and drove across the
St. Louis metropolitan area into the Royal Oaks section of Ster-
ling township. It was the affluent neighborhood in the Ladue sub-
urb where he'd spent his teenage years. His mother had bought a
large house with a pool and substantial grounds when Sean was
just starting junior high. He knew his mother hoped and expected him to make friends among the finer families who lived
in the area. And he had, to some extent. He had buddies among
them, now doctors and lawyers and investment bankers. They
called him Dox.

Dox was short for Dachshund, which was a play on the name
they'd given to his family business. Dachshundburger. Sean had
laughed when the kids had said it. But it had never been that funny
to him. He'd spent far too much of his childhood sitting in a booth
with a coloring book and crayons while his mother, in a hairnet,
sweated and smiled and eked out a living for them through hard
work and smart management.

By high school he understood that it had to do with social class.
Just because they made enough money to live among the promi-
nent people of the city didn't make them equals. The ladies of
Royal Oaks and Brentwood and Palestine were quick to include
his mother on any fund-raising campaign, but no one ever invited
her for anything strictly social. His mother was so busy, Sean
doubted that she even noticed. But he did.

Sean steered the Volvo through the curved avenues of tall trees
and well-manicured lawns until he pulled into a bricked driveway
with a set of tall wrought-iron gates. He clicked the remote on
his sun visor and waited as they opened.

He remembered when he'd first brought Katy here.

"Wow, it's like some mansion or something!" she'd said.

He'd laughed. "It's just a big house with a big gate," he'd assured her. She'd looked at him with a little line of worry across her brow.

"I'm not sure I could be comfortable living in a place like this," she warned him.

Sean wasn't worried. "Our home is wherever we are together," he'd told her.

Now they weren't together.

As he headed up the driveway, he wondered if that was why he always felt the way that he did. Was the truth about him that he was homeless?

His mother's house was a long white-brick one-story that angled off into two wings. It had dozens of long narrow windows in front. At the back all the rooms had French doors that opened on to a grotto-scape pool with series waterfalls.

Behind all of that was a four-car garage with an attached garden house. Sean had moved in there temporarily the night he'd left Katy. Inertia being the mainstay of his life, he was still there, three years later.

He parked next to his mother's Mercedes and went inside the small, cluttered place where he lived.

The garden house was never meant to be more than an overnight residence for anyone. It was one large room with a sofa bed, an easy chair and a tiny kitchenette. Every surface was covered with clothes, papers, books, discarded junk mail and ancient greasy pizza boxes.

Sean didn't even notice as he headed straight for the bathroom. He turned on the water in the shower and then sloughed off his clothes into a pile on the floor before stepping under the pulsing spray.

The hot water was welcome, soothing. He scrubbed himself thoroughly, washed his hair and then he just stood there, leaning against the wall, allowing the water to wash over him. It felt good.

The cocoon of warmth, the isolation from everything outside. It was perfect. It was like the womb.

That thought momentarily jarred him.

He was a grown man, somebody's father. He couldn't just go back to being a helpless baby. And he shouldn't even want to.

Sean ruthlessly twisted the shower knob, turning the water to completely cold. The icy needles took his breath away, but not his memory.

"You've lived like a coddled child all your life," his mother had declared five years ago when they'd come to this house to announce their marriage. "You've had everything given to you and you've not appreciated any of it. Now you're off making stupid decisions, inappropriate choices and expecting that there are no consequences for that. Well, there are."

His mother was as angry as he'd ever seen her. But hers was no hot, boiling point. It was cold, calculated fury, as chilling as the water against his skin.

"You want to live your own life, make your own decisions? I say fine, do that. But there will be no more special favors from me. The condo you live in. The corporation owns that. I'll have the business manager contact you about vacating or taking a lease. I have to warn you, rents are high in that building. And that may be a problem for you. You, of course, can keep your job managing the Manchester Road site, as long as you continue to perform well. But that grade level in the company does not include an expense account and you'll be paid the same as every other manager with your experience. Oh, and that position doesn't include a company car. Leave your keys on the table in the foyer. You'll either have to take public transportation or walk."

Sean had left his mother that day with his head high.

It was bowed now.

He turned off the water and stepped out of the shower. He was drying off as he heard a knock on his door. He wrapped the towel around his waist and went to see who it was.

His mother was unexpected. She never came back to the garden house. If she wanted him, she called on the phone. He opened the door immediately.

"What's up?"

"Oh, good, you've already showered," she said. "You need to get dressed. We're meeting David Faneuf for a drink at the club."

Sean's brow furrowed. "David Faneuf? My divorce lawyer?"

"Yes," his mother said. "I've been talking to him and he agrees with me. It's time to get your son back."

Bitsy's Wisdom 7

Bitsy's Wisdom 7: Don't worry about what bait goes with which jig. Just observe the preferences of the fish in the water.

Katy Dodson was the kind of woman who could sleep until noon. Unfortunately, her life had never quite been in synchronization with her biorhythms. The minute Josh opened his eyes, she did, too.

His were big and blue and full of wonder, curiosity and occasionally mischief. Hers were soft and sleepy and brown, full of empathy and capable of total devotion.

"Good morning, Joshua," she said to the little guy beside her. "Did you sleep well?"

He smiled up at her. "I didn't sleep sick," he answered, and then giggled at his own joke.

Katy thought her son to be the cutest, smartest, most fascinating little guy on the planet. The rest of the human race might not have been quite as impressed, but he still caught admiring eyes from friends and strangers. His mahogany-brown hair was so thick it could never seem to lie down, and it billowed in a crown of curls on top of his head. He was slightly small for his age, but generally a very attractive boy. Probably anyone who knew Sean would say that Josh looked just like his daddy. These days no one knew Sean Dodson and it seemed as if no one would ever see him. For a father determined to get his child back, as his lawyer assured Katy that he was, Sean seemed amazingly absent.

"I just can't do it, Katy," her ex-husband had said the night he'd walked out. "It's just too hard."

"What's too hard, Sean?" she'd asked him. "Loving me? Loving the baby?"

"I'm not used to taking care of people," he answered. "I'm used to having people take care of me."

"I can take care of you," Katy insisted.

"You need to take care of yourself," he said. "And now you have Joshua, too. It's no good, Katy. I've tried. I've really tried. I thought I could make it. I thought that even without my mother helping us, we'd do all right. But it's not like I thought."

"So you made a mistake, things turns out different than you hoped they would," Katy said. "That sounds like a perfectly normal life."

"That may be the truth for you, Katy," he said. "But I prefer my world to be a whole lot easier. I'm happy that way. I want to see a few friends, have a few laughs, drink a few brews. I'm not cut out to be a paycheck slave and dependable dad. You're lucky that we found that out sooner rather than later."

Katy didn't feel lucky about that at all. Sean was Joshua's father. That alone made him a better man than he thought he was.

She wrapped her arms around her son and held him close.

"I love you," she whispered into his curls.

The little fellow had heard it so much, the words were taken for granted. He wiggled away. Katy would have loved to snuggle with him a little bit, maybe read a story, but she knew he couldn't. Only a half minute from dreamland, he was already scooting toward the edge of the bed. As soon as his feet hit the floor, he ran toward the window.

"The lake is still there," he announced.

"Any pirate ships in sight?" his mother asked.

The little boy's brow furrowed seriously as he scanned the length of lake visible on the horizon through an imaginary telescope of two curled fists. "Nope, we're safe."

She hoped it was true.

The minute she'd seen Warbler Lake, she'd loved the place. Actually, she was already won over before she'd ever arrived. Just the name conjured up an image that was far different from her own childhood, and was exactly what she wanted for Josh.

The restaurant had come as a considerable surprise.

Katy had never heard of a "bait and barbecue." She was pretty sure that most people didn't think that the initials B & B stood for that. Almost immediately she began to rethink her disappointment, rethink her initial reaction that she'd made a mistake. Maybe this place would be exactly what they needed.

Her sister, Emma, didn't agree. But something about Bitsy's had appealed to her on a level that was separated from reason. She was drawn to the place by some emotional attachment that didn't stand up to logic. Maybe it was something about that photograph. It was like an announcement that read: Bitsy McGrady, alone in the world, found happiness and a big fish in this place.

Katy thought of Bitsy coming here to make a life for herself after losing the man she loved. The community was just getting started then, better roads and leisure time in the post World War II era made fishing vacations an all-new and profitable thing. The heyday of the area had grown up around Bitsy and then faded as she did herself. The woman had lived the bulk of her life here, and that had counted for something. Something ordinary. Something stable.

That's what Katy needed to provide for Josh. Ordinary stability. Home. People took the word so for granted. But it was hard to come by and harder to keep. Katy felt like she had a chance at it here and she wasn't about to pass it up.

"I'm going to make a go of it," she'd told her sister.

Nothing or no one could make Katy feel as ditzy and incompetent as Emma. But this time she'd let her have her way. That was almost worse.

The two were closer than most sisters. And Katy was so beholden. Emma had given up so much for her. Katy had taken the divorce settlement with the express purpose of making herself independent of her sister. And finally allowing her sister to fly free.

"I wanna go downstairs and see the people," Josh stated as he began pulling open the drawers of the chest, looking for his clothes.

"There are no people downstairs today," Katy told him. "Saturday is our morning off."

Josh turned and gave her a lowered-eyebrow look, an exact replica of his father's frequent expression of skepticism.

"There sure are a lot of cars outside, Mommy."

Katy glanced out the window and then groaned aloud. A quick check of her sister's bedroom confirmed the worst. She'd messed up again and Emma was covering for her.

Katy had the two of them washed, dressed and downstairs in a record five minutes, but it didn't matter. She was late. The tables were full of customers and Emma had had to handle things by herself.

"Sorry," she said as she came breezing through the kitchen. "Let me get Josh set down with some cereal and I'm ready to help."

"He can have a bowl of oatmeal," Emma said, dishing the child a small scoop. "Do you want raisins and bananas on top?"

He nodded appreciatively. His aunt knew exactly what he liked.

Emma handed him the bowl. "Take this into the dining room and find yourself a place to sit," she said. "I need to talk to your mommy for a minute."

"Okay," he obeyed. The two sisters watched him maneuver his way through the swinging door.

Katy hesitated until he was out of earshot.

"I thought we'd agreed that we were closed this morning," she said. "If I'd known we were going to be serving, I would have been up."

"Apparently the bait shop never closes," Emma told her. "So, I guess the locals figure the restaurant has to stay open, too."

"I'm sorry, I—"

"I don't care about that," Emma said. "I want to know why you didn't tell me that Sean is taking you back to court."

For an instant, Katy didn't know what to say.

"I was going to tell you."

"When?"

"I don't know," Katy admitted. "How'd you find out?"

Emma held up the letter.

"You're reading my mail?"

Emma shrugged. "So call the postal authorities," she said. "Why didn't you tell me?"

"It's just threats," Katy assured her. "Sean would never take Josh from me."

"I don't know why you would say that," Emma told her.

"Because I know him," Katy said.

"Yes," Emma said. "And you know his mother as well. Once she decides on something there is no stopping her."

"This lawyer called me just a couple of days ago," Katy told her. "I'd let Sean know that I'd moved, but I was really surprised that he called the lawyer about it."

Emma's expression was stern. "I'm not surprised at all. "What did he say?"

"That Sean wants to 'revisit' the custody agreement," she answered. "I explained that I'd just bought this business and I really don't have the cash to go back to court right now."

Emma moaned aloud. "Katy, you didn't tell him that!"

"I thought honesty was supposed to be the best policy."

Her sister rolled her eyes. Katy felt defensive, but she wasn't sure how to defend herself.

"He suggested we could settle out of court," she told Emma. "I simply allow Josh go to St. Louis to live with his grandmother during the school year."

"What did you tell him?" Emma asked.

Katy was startled at the question. "I told him no, of course," she answered. "Like I would let that happen!"

"I just hope we can do something to prevent it," Emma said.

Katy could see the set of her sister's jaw. She would have been willing to warn anyone who didn't know better that it was never good to get Emma Collins angry.

"Don't get like this," Katy said.

"Like what?"

"Don't get all huffy and hateful," she said. "Sean won't take Josh from me. I don't know what his mother is after or what game she's playing, but I trust Sean."

"Yeah," Emma said facetiously. "He's a heck of a guy. That's why he left you high and dry with a baby to support while he ran home to Mama."

It was a mean thing for her sister to say. But, if Katy was going to purport that honesty was the best policy, then she couldn't really challenge the statement.

"I'd better get out there and see who needs what," Katy said, choosing to change the subject. Emma was like a mama bear when it came to protecting her kid sister. And she knew from experience that Emma could be very negative about Sean. Katy just didn't want to hear it.

She went through the swinging doors to find her son still standing uncertainly trying to decide which chair suited him best. Katy helped to make the choice for him.

"Josh, do you want to sit at the counter while I wait on people?" The little guy agreed and she helped him carry his oatmeal.

The place was half full and just the sight of her had empty coffee cups all over the room raised in her direction.

"Just one more minute," she responded rather generally to the customers.

"May Josh sit next to you?" she asked Waymon Riley, one of the morning regulars.

"I'd be honored to have the gentleman at my side," Waymon answered, and Josh giggled.

"I'm not a gentleman," the five-year-old told him. "I'm a little boy."

"Is that so? Well, any little boy who's eating my favorite Bitsy's oatmeal breakfast is a gentleman in my book."

Katy got Josh settled in with a booster chair.

Waymon winked at her. "I'll keep an eye on him, ma'am. You can go on about your business."

"Thanks," she said. She needed to do that. A coffeepot in each hand, she made her way from table to table, taking orders, collecting money, making small talk. Business was booming. Breakfast was fast becoming their busiest meal. Even with the Closed sign still showing in the window, people continued to come in. And they had nothing to serve beyond toast or oatmeal.

It was getting close to eleven before she found out the reason.

She brought the order of a young mother. The thin, wan, overworked woman was, Katy realized, close to her own age. She had three-inch-long bright blond hair, with an inch and a half of dark roots, sticking out in all directions around her head, the ends looking as if they were self-cut with a razor. None of her three children looked like her, or for that matter, like one another. A quiet boy about seven was reading a comic book. He had dark hair and dark eyes. The little girl, who was talking nonstop even when it was obvious no one was listening was about Josh's age. She was a redhead with milk-white skin and freckles. And the baby in a high chair, who was about eighteen months, had his mother's coloring but the snub nose and upward slanting eyes associated with Down syndrome.

The young mom got a cup of coffee for herself and one order of toast to share among the three hungry kids. Katy worried about that.

"The toast is really 'All you can eat,'" she said. "Just let me know when you need some more."

"Thanks," the woman said. "The kids already had cereal at home."

"You have breakfast before you came to breakfast?" Katy asked, smiling. She thought it must be a joke.

"Everybody wants to support you," she said. "The town really wants you to be able to make a go of this place."

Katy nodded as the realization dawned upon her. She'd been thinking of the B & B as only a chance for her and Josh. She knew her purchase of it had helped the local school. Now she understood that its success was a success for the community.

"So we're all trying to eat here as much as we can," the woman said. "But the word is, breakfast is your best meal. Everyone says stay away from the barbecue, it's inedible."

"Well, it's not inedible," Katy said, attempting lamely to defend the main menu item of the place. "My sister and I just haven't quite got the hang of it yet. It's better every day."

The young woman nodded, but her expression indicated a willingness to humor than agree. She changed the subject.

"I'm Nadine," she said, reaching across the table to offer her hand. "And this is Parker, Brianna and this little guy is Natty."

The two older children acknowledged her politely. The baby just smiled, displaying seven tiny white teeth.

"Hi, Nadine, I'm Katy," she responded. "My son, Josh, is about the same age as your daughter. Maybe we could set up a play date or something?"

"Something," she agreed with a dismissive nod. "Listen, I can make you some money in this place. Have you got, say, ten bucks you can loan me?"

Katy didn't even hesitate. She dug down into her apron pocket, pulled out her tips for the morning and counted out that amount. It was almost everything she'd made. She handed it over to Nadine.

"Aren't you even going to ask me why I need it?" the woman asked.

Katy shrugged. "You're going to make me some money," she said. "A businessperson is always looking for a good investment."

Nadine shook her head. "I think you must be new at this businessperson thing," she said.

Katy laughed. "This is my second week," she answered.

Bitsy's Wisdom 8

Bitsy's Wisdom 8: When it comes to hog parts, the closer you get to the bacon the better the meat is on the barbecue.

The quiet of afternoon had not yet been shattered by the school bell, and the dining room at Bitsy's was mostly empty. Emma poured tea and coffee for the few patrons and served up slices of pie. Her sister had procured the latter, from a local woman with three little kids. Katy paid the woman ten dollars per pie, then cut each into six slices charging two dollars a slice. That should have allowed a modest profit, but her sister kept giving slices away.

Which was why, during midafternoon, the big pie-eating part of the day, Emma had purposely taken charge of waitressing.

"Here you go," she said, setting a coconut meringue in front of the ancient toothless fisherman.

"Babydoll, I cain't decide who looks better, you or this pie."

Emma grinned with studied tolerance, Crank, as this old man was called, was an unflappable old flirt.

"You'd better stick with the pie," she told him. "It's a lot less complicated."

Field Note, she thought to herself. *The silverback continues to make advances at females long past the time when such actions might conceivably lead to future progeny.*

Her sister, Katy, was out back. The pit was fired up and she had a couple of slabs of nice ribs that she was hoping to successfully prepare. The cooking was not getting any better, and Emma had completely given up on it. It was a very expensive way to ruin good meat day after day. She'd suggested that they just give up on barbecue and become a hamburger joint. If you were the only restaurant in town, you could serve anything you wanted.

Katy wouldn't hear of it.

"This place is important," she said. "It's important that it's a real restaurant and serves a full menu."

"It's more important that we make enough money to pay the light bill," Emma pointed out.

"I'm going to learn how to do this barbecue thing if it kills me."

Emma was pretty sure that it wouldn't result in her sister's demise. But she was worried about their customers. Every day it was as if one local person had been designated the royal taster, or maybe the guinea pig. He or she'd come in early, order the barbecue. Then the rest of the night everyone else would stick to grilled cheese or BLTs.

Katy had agreed to add chicken salad to the lunch menu. But Emma was certain that the best they could hope for was to become a hamburger joint.

"Bitsy's is a Bait & BBQ," Katy insisted.

"Just because we've got a sign doesn't mean we can't change the name of the place," Emma told her. "Katy Dodson's Burgers has a nice ring to it.

"No, thank you," her sister answered. "I'm already facing a cus-

tody hearing, I don't want them suing me for trademark infringe-
ment."

"I don't think anyone could confuse Katy Dodson's Burgers
with those crappy Dachshundburgers."

"Sean would be livid if he heard you use that term," she
pointed out.

"Dachshundburger. Dachshundburger. Dachshundburger," she repeated in a tone that mimicked childish teasing. "If my ex-jerk-
in-law doesn't like it, let him come down here and shut me up."

Katy shook her head and laughed. But cautioned Emma as well.

"Don't say bad things about Sean. It's a bad habit to get into
and sooner or later Josh might overhear something."

Emma nodded. "You're right. My lips are sealed. But my
thoughts are running strongly against the man. I was hoping that
the guy was just going to be a bad memory that continues to fade."

Her sister didn't comment, but Emma knew that the custody
question was not far from Katy's thoughts. They had talked about
it several times, careful to keep Josh far away from the discussion.
But they hadn't come up with any answers.

They'd contacted Katy's divorce lawyer, whom they'd finally
managed to pay in full when the settlement was reached. He
wasn't interested in taking on the Dodsons again and suggested that
they find someone locally to represent them. The telephone di-
rectory had listed one attorney. He was forty miles of crooked road
away and when they called for an appointment they learned that
the man, in his mideighties, was recovering from a stroke.

Neither of the sisters had come up with a next move.

An old couple vacated their table and Emma cleared it, stacked
everything onto a tray and then wiped the tabletop with a wet cloth.

She glanced at her watch, then deliberately stopped and mentally took stock of her surroundings; who was still seated, what
they'd ordered, who had left since her last note-taking.

There were two sampling techniques used in anthropology that were proving helpful to Emma at Warbler Lake. First there was focal follow, where she tracked the movements of one person through an entire day. She learned a lot that way, but since most everyone at Bitsy's came and went, it wasn't a good method to work with. It proved better, she decided, to rely on scan sampling. Every half hour or so, she would stop, take a hasty census of every person she could observe and, if she had time, she'd make notations of what they were up to.

She was learning a lot about the locals and discovering patterns in their everyday behavior.

As she carried the dishes to the kitchen, one of those patterns came through the front door. Curt, still dressed in his postal uniform of navy shorts, blue shirt and a sun helmet, came by every afternoon at the completion of his mail route. He gave Emma a very broad smile and a friendly wave. He was much too friendly, she thought, for a mere acquaintance. It always caught her off guard and she momentarily juggled the tray. She was an observer, not a member of the group. Curt apparently had difficulty distinguishing that.

"Be right back," she assured him.

She carried the dishes to the dishwasher, hastily scraped and stacked them, washed her hands and headed back to the dining room.

By the time she got there, the place was completely empty except for Curt, seated at the counter, bright-eyed, smiling, eager to talk to her. It seemed very strange. One table had just been served a few moments before. And another had appeared comfortably ensconced for the afternoon.

"Where'd everyone go?" she asked.

He shrugged, appearing embarrassed and a bit guilty. She gave him some distance as she picked up the money left on two tables and added it into the cash register. Then she grabbed a rag and carefully wiped down the counter in front of him.

"You look very nice today, Emma," Curt said. "I missed you earlier when I came by with the mail."

"I must have been in the back," she told him.

"You know, the weather is nice this time of year," he said. "But a lovely face like yours could make the world seem like sunshine even on the rainiest day."

The sentiment was sweet, but the words seemed slightly rehearsed.

"Then I guess the guy from the fishing report shouldn't use me as a barometer," she countered.

"I'm sure…I'm sure you'd be excellent at it."

He was very obviously attempting to flirt with her. But he wasn't particularly good at it. Emma was not unaccustomed to the attention of men. He was clean-cut, blond and reasonably intelligent, she supposed. She was slightly flattered but completely uninterested.

"What can I get for you?" she asked him. "Coffee, tea, soda?"

"Soda. Just because I love it when you say 'soda' for soft drink," he said. "Around here we call it 'pop.' It makes you seem foreign, kind of exotic."

This guy was really trying too hard. It was all Emma could do not to roll her eyes. Instead, she made a joke.

"Yeah, I feel exotic," she said. "And I feel like dancing. Maybe that's what this town needs. I could guarantee success of the Bitsy's B & B by performing as an exotic dancer."

Curt smiled uneasily, clearly embarrassed, his cheeks flushed bright red. He was an attractive man, in a clean, GQ Boy Scout kind of way.

"I…well, we don't see a lot of that at Warbler Lake," he said.

"Pity, it could sure liven the place up," she teased.

He cleared his throat.

Emma put his drink in front of him and proceeded to leave him on his own as she bussed the other tables and carried the dishes to the kitchen. She got everything loaded up on the dish conveyer. It was mostly full and it was late in the day, so she started it up. It was best to begin the evening rush with everything clean. She glanced out the back door to see her sister anxiously watching the coals in the firebox of the barbecue pit. Sighing, she headed back to the dining room.

Curt was still there, nursing his drink. He still had the straw between his teeth as he smiled at her. Emma walked over to him and dragged up a stool to sit down. The man wanted to talk and talk was cheap. About the cheapest thing not on the menu.

"So what's up?" she asked, feigning a cheerfulness that wasn't completely sincere.

"We missed you and your sister in church on Sunday," he said.

Emma eyed the guy for a long minute and then shook her head.

"If that's your best pickup line, Curt, you really need to work on it."

He choked slightly on his soft drink and began blushing again.

"It's not exactly a pickup line," he said.

"I guess with no movies or concerts or even a bar with a dance floor, church may well be the only place to take a girl in this dinky town," Emma said. "But you've mentioned it to me twice now and it's a little off-putting."

He hesitated, looking momentarily confused, and then laughed, suddenly seeming a good deal more certain of himself.

"What?" she asked him.

"The thing about Warbler Lake," he told her. "The town is so small a lot of people have to take on more than one role. Old Man Crank isn't just an old ogling fisherman, he's also His Honor the

Mayor. Spurl Westbrook isn't just the school principal, he's also our local real estate agent. And me…"

"And you?"

"I'm pastor of the church."

"Oh, God, no!" Emma exclaimed in disbelief, and then immediately realized how bad that sounded. "I mean, gosh…uh…goodness, I'm very surprised. Aren't you supposed to wear a collar or something?"

"I could do that," he said, nodding. "Or maybe just a sign around my neck that says, 'Caution! Man Of The Cloth.'"

"I didn't mean it like that."

"I know and I understand, truly," he said. "I walk around here and everybody knows who I am. I need to get in the habit of introducing myself."

"I thought I already knew you," she said. "I knew you were the mailman."

"At least now I know that your reticence toward me is based on lack of chemistry and not an aversion to my profession."

"I've got a lot of things going on in my life right now," she attempted to explain. "Men in general, none specific, are just not on my radar now."

"I understand," he said. "Sometimes timing is everything."

"So," Emma said conversationally. "You're a minister and a mailman."

"That's me," he said. "I'm the postman/pastor."

"How did that come about?"

"The little church can't afford to support a full-time staff member. So, I have to have a second job to support myself. The U.S. Mail is about the only place around here where you never have to work on Sunday."

"I apologize for the exotic dancer comments," Emma said. "And it is very nice to meet you, Reverend."

"Just call me Curt, everyone does."

"That seems kind of informal."

He shrugged. "It can't be helped," he said. "Most of my parishioners are older than I am. And most have known me since I started spending summers here with my parents when I was six."

"Is that why you came here, because the place was a part of your childhood?"

"Yes, I guess that's a part of it," he said. "It just sort of happened. I'd finished seminary and had the summer off. Pricy Metcalf called me and said that old Pastor Harvey had died and would I be willing to come and fill in for the summer. I said yes and I've been here ever since. Nine years in June."

"So you must like it," Emma said. "And they must like you."

"They do," he agreed. "It's a strange mixture of pride in having a hand in raising me and respect for what I do here. So, it's great. But they do worry about me."

"They worry about you? Why?"

"Because I've never married," Curt answered. "A preacher is supposed to have a helpmate and a family. Here I am, past thirty and still not wed."

"Ahh."

"I've thought about hinting that I'm gay," he said. "That would stop all the matchmakers in their tracks. But I'm not gay and lying to the congregation, that's not really a gray area, it's one of those Ten Commandment things."

He was relaxing now, being himself and his self was funny. Emma found herself smiling at him.

"So everyone in town is trying to marry you off," she said.

He nodded and gestured to the empty dining room. "That's why everyone made themselves scarce," he said. "They wanted to leave us alone."

"Us?"

"Yep. If you haven't noticed, Warbler Lake is not exactly awash in single young women. You and your sister are the answer to a thousand prayers petitioned to heaven by the Women's Worship Auxiliary."

"Oh, no."

"Oh, yes," he said. "I thought you needed to know what's going on. I'm going to be hanging around here a lot and I didn't want you to think that you'd picked up some weird postal-packing preacher stalker."

Emma laughed. "Maybe I should try to convince your congregation that I'm gay."

"That Ten Commandments thing," he said. "It goes for you, too."

"Rats."

"So are you praying you'll find some gorgeous soul mate to make your life a heaven on earth?" she asked him.

Curt grinned. "I'm pretty careful about what I pray for," he said. "There's a story the old preachers tell about the guy who needed transportation. He saw a rusted, old, beat-up Volkswagen on a used-car lot and the price on it was five hundred dollars."

"Must not have been much of a car for that kind of money," Emma said.

Curt nodded. "Not much," he agreed. "But every night and every day the man prayed, 'Father, please give me that Volkswagen. Please, Father, let me have that Volkswagen.' So after a very, very long time and thousands of prayers, up in heaven, God called over one of his angels and said, 'Go down and see about getting that Volkswagen for the guy who keeps praying for it.' And the angel said he would and he thanked God for showing mercy on the guy and providing him with transportation. And God just shook his head very sadly and answered, 'I really had my eye on a brand-new Mercedes for him, but he seems to have his heart so set on that beat-up Volkswagen.'"

Emma chuckled.

"So," Curt said. "I let the ladies of the church pray. And I try to trust that God loves me and has a plan that's better than any that I could come up with."

"Hmm," Emma said. "You're worried I might be a rusted Volkswagen?"

He shook his head. "I'm thinking you might be a Mercedes and what would I do with a fancy car like that in this town?"

She laughed.

"That settled, would you please take a walk with me along the lake some evening?"

Emma hesitated. "I'm not really dating," she began.

Curt held up a hand. "Believe me, there is no dating in War-bler Lake. All that's available is talking, walking and fishing. I thought we could start with the first, move on to the second and hold the third out as a last resort."

"Okay, we can take a short stroll along the shore," Emma said. "But that's all I'm agreeing to do. I'm sure it's a slippery slope until a woman finds herself baiting her hook with a minnow. And it'll have to be a very slow night here."

"That seems fair," he said. "As long as I can hold out hope, I'll keep coming by to sip on 'soda.'"

"Don't limit yourself to that," Emma said. "We serve a full menu at Bitsy's B & B."

He shook his head, feigning unwillingness. "It's those Com-mandments again," he said. "I have to speak truth and the truth is, your barbecue is bad."

"Yes, I know," she said. "Everyone is being so honest to tell us so. We're trying to get better."

"Maybe I can get the church ladies to pray for that."

Bitsy's Wisdom 9

Bitsy's Wisdom 9: In the summer, when the weather gets changeable, bass go belly to the bottom, hiding in the weeds and snarls of the lake floor. The only thing that has a chance of bringing them out is live bait.

Day after day the barbecue continued to be a failure. The meat would be overcooked one day and rarer than rare the next. It was stringier than jerky, or so greasy it could slide down the throat without the bother of chewing. The sauce was simple enough to be easily replicated, but some days it was burned onto the side of the meat and others it smothered it like gravy. The locals continued to try it every day. But only the gang of stray dogs that hung around the garbage can had any appreciation for it.

"It can't be that hard!" Katy complained in frustration.

But it was.

As the flowers of spring began to bloom and the tourist season drew near, Katy became convinced that the only thing that

kept Bitsy's in business was the unflagging optimism of the community and the pies that Nadine baked.

So the morning that the pies failed to appear was bleak.

"What's happened?"

"My oven's not working right," Nadine told her. "The danged
thing is a million years old. I've been babying it along, but this
morning it just wouldn't heat up."

"Can't you get somebody to fix it?"

"I probably could," Nadine said. "If I knew who to call and
had some money to pay them. Right now, I've got the trunk of
the car full of unbaked pies. I was hoping I could put them in
the oven here."

"Sure," Katy said, with more hopefulness than confidence. The
kitchen area was cramped at the best of times. One more person
working around the oven was bad enough. But Nadine had three
kids with her as well.

"Can Parker watch Brianna and Natty outside? There's hardly
room for them in here and it's a dangerous area for kids," Katy said.
As if to prove her point, Brianna and Josh, who were chasing each
other in, out and around the prep table, accidentally knocked over
a glass measuring cup. Its handle broke off as it hit the floor.

As Katy picked up the mess she added, "I don't even like Josh
hanging around back here."

"Parker can watch Brianna until he has to go to school," Nadine said. "But I can't leave the baby with him."

"I wouldn't let anything happen to him," the boy chimed in.

"I know you'd be careful," Nadine told him gently. "But a baby
is too much for a seven-year-old. You're not allowed to have that
much responsibility."

"No, of course not," Katy agreed. "Wait! We have an oven upstairs in the apartment."

"Does it work?"

"When we moved in Mr. Westbrook said it was like brand-new."

The two women, accompanied by all the children, carried the boxes of pies upstairs.

"This is great," Nadine said, inspecting the oven. "The first one or two may not be perfect, but I'll get the hang of it very quickly, I'm sure."

"And you and the kids can just hang out up here," Katy said. "It'll be just as good as home."

"It's a lot better than our home," Parker said.

Nadine blushed. "Our place is pretty small," she said. "It was meant to be a weekend cabin, not a family home year-round. But it's ours and we're happy to have it."

She said the last with a very pointed glance toward her son.

Katy piped in, "Well, this kitchen wasn't meant to be a pie bakery," she said. "But I think it will work."

"This will be just fine," Nadine assured her. "Now, let me get this baking started."

Katy turned to go downstairs. "Come on, Josh," she said.

"Can't I stay here and play with Brianna?"

"No, Brianna's mom is busy."

"Pleeease," he whined. "I want to show her my toys. Please, please."

"It's okay," Nadine said. "They'll keep each other occupied."

"You sure? It might be too much."

She shook her head. "No, it's fine. Parker will be off to school in a half hour. These two will entertain each other and Natty and I will bake some pies."

Katy went down the stairs to work with a lightness on her shoulders that was inexplicable for the small thing that had happened. Not dividing her attention between her business and her little boy was a luxury unfamiliar to her since before Sean walked out.

She wasn't naive. She knew that plenty of women in her position would have put the squeeze on the ex-husband and set themselves up for life. A wealthy guy callously walks out on a wife and child. A lot of women would have insisted on the kind of monthly support that would have kept them living high forever.

For Katy, it had never been about the money. That had been true before the wedding, during the marriage and afterward. Cash hadn't been her motive and it couldn't be the cure for her heartache.

"Of course you would have abandonment issues," the marriage counselor had told her. "You're fatherless and your mother deserted you. It would be extraordinary if you didn't cling to the man who is your husband and the father of your child."

The marriage counselor had been some help. It's always good to have someone to talk to. Unfortunately, she couldn't save their marriage. Sean refused to even show up for the sessions. When he was done with the marriage, he was done. He saw no reason to try to sort anything out so they could try again.

"The one thing you must come to grips with," the counselor said, "is that none of this was a failure of yours. Your mother went on with her life and didn't see the need to drag you along. Your husband decided he didn't want to be married. But that was about him, it was not about you."

Katy tried to hold on to that, to understand it. Intellectually, she knew that was right. Nothing she'd done had driven her husband away. But he'd still gone. And that still hurt.

She thought about the letters from the lawyer. What was that about? After all this time, after Sean's complete indifference to the son he'd walked away from, why was he now wanting custody? And how could he, a virtual stranger, even imagine that he could take care of a child he didn't even know?

Katy's feelings about it were all so jumbled. She was frightened of the idea of losing Josh. She was angered that after all this time Sean thought he deserved input into his son's life. Yet there was a part of her that wanted very much for Josh to know his father, to know the wonderful Sean that Katy had married. The man who was capable of such tenderness and such care.

And the possibility that she might see Sean again made her heart race and filled her stomach with butterflies.

Back inside the restaurant, the regulars were fending for themselves. Emma was still over in the bait shop. Katy washed her hands, grabbed the coffeepot and began making her rounds. She was beginning to know people. Not just their names but their stories as well.

The Dempseys showed up early every day. They'd been married forever, both professors at the university in Rolla. They'd bought their little weekend lake cottage when their children were little and had retired to it twenty years ago. Now, with failing eyesight, Mrs. Dempsey could no longer see to cook much. They relied on Bitsy's for a meal or two every day.

Waymon Riley was a truck driver who'd never been able to stick to a marriage. When he wasn't on the road, he wanted to be on the lake. He'd kept his life simple. If he wasn't driving or fishing, then he was seated at Bitsy's counter. Often next to Hiram Gouswhelter, local carpenter, and his father, Gus.

The Gouswhelter family had farmed the area on the east and south sides of the lake for generations. When Gus returned from World War II service, too shot up to do that kind of labor, he'd got the idea of making the lake, already a prime fishing spot, into a resort area like those he'd seen in other parts of the country. He'd built a marina and a circle of little cabins. He got some developers interested and from there the whole town had come together. For almost ten years it had been on the cusp of being a dynamic success. But the completion of the White River Dam that created

Table Rock Lake and a bright future for the southwestern part of the state spelled failure for the locals. The area around Warbler Lake could never compete with the wonder of Marvel Cave, the thrills of Silver Dollar City or the music and shows in Branson.

Katy poured the old man a fresh cup of coffee. He was a bit of a grumpy old soul, but he liked Katy. Probably because she was always willing to listen to his complaints.

"How are you doing this morning?" she asked.

"I'm living like a boarder in my own house," he told her. "I raised that roof myself with timber I cut down on my own land. I hammered every nail into every joist and crossbeam and that mean-mouthed Birdie thinks she can tell me 'come here or sic 'em'! I wouldn't have a woman like that."

The woman, otherwise known as mean-mouthed Birdie, was his son, Hiram's, wife of thirty-four years. That the old man and his daughter-in-law didn't get along was one of the most widely known facts in the county.

Hiram, who was seated next to his father, kept the peace in his house by refusing to hear the complaints of spouse or parent. Voluntary deafness was his only protection from the fray.

"Anytime you're feeling unwelcome, you know we love to have you around here," Katy told him.

The old man was pleased.

She spotted Harriet Welborn and, without having to ask, brought her a little pot of hot water, tea bag and cream.

"Good morning, ma'am," Katy said, and she served the woman her preferred beverage.

"Morning, dear," the woman responded.

Her age was indeterminable, because she was straight and strong and lean. The result, she was quick to inform, of a daily "constitutional" around the lake. Miss Welborn had come to Warbler Lake when the ink was still wet on her teaching certificate. She'd been

employed at the school when it had only one teacher, in one class-
room with twelve grades. Now the school had twelve classrooms,
eight teachers and six grades. Miss Welborn had been retired so
long that an entire generation had passed through Warbler Lake
Elementary without being taught by her. Still, she continued to
have an interest in each and every one of them.

"Where is Joshua this morning?" she asked Katy.

"He's upstairs," Katy answered. "Nadine's oven went out and
she's up in my apartment baking the pies."

Miss Welborn nodded. "Nadine bakes very well," she said. "People gossip about her, I'm sure you know. But Parker is an excellent young man. Bright, inquisitive and thoughtful as well. So she
must be doing something very right."

"She's a good mom," Katy assured.

"How is her baby?" she asked. "He has Down syndrome, I
believe."

"Yes, I think that's it," she replied. "Though Nadine doesn't talk
about it. He seems like a very happy little guy."

"Is he receiving any therapy?"

"It's like a genetic thing," Katy told her. "There's not any cure
for it."

Miss Welborn choked slightly, disguising a chuckle. "Yes, I
know," she said. "But I believe that regimens are available to help
him make the best of his abilities."

"Really?" Katy was surprised. "I'll tell Nadine. I bet she doesn't
even know."

"Perhaps not," Miss Welborn agreed. "Even if she did, there are
no therapists around here. She'd have to drive him into Tedburg.
That's a long way for her old car."

Katy nodded in agreement.

Katy moved on to wait on a very impatient Pearly Ross. The
man, younger than most in Warbler Lake, owned his own rusty

tow truck and claimed to be a fishing guide, but was mostly a ne'er-do-well.

"Where's the pie?" he asked. "I don't see one damn slice of pie up there."

"The pies aren't ready yet," Katy told him. "How about eggs," Katy said. "Or oatmeal. Both are better for you than a bunch of sugar for breakfast."

He cursed. "I had my mouth all set on pie."

"Nadine's oven is broke," Katy told him.

"Oh, yeah?" Pearly smiled. It wasn't the pleasant, friendly smile Katy was accustomed to, but a nasty grin. "Well, maybe that's a good thing. Maybe she's had one stray bun too many in her oven."

Pearly's voice had risen until it could be plainly heard anywhere in the restaurant. He obviously thought his joke was very funny.

"That last one of hers didn't turn out so well." He laughed in a way that was mean, humorless.

Every other voice in the dining room was stilled. Katy was shocked. She stared at the young man she thought she knew, speechless. She wasn't sure who she should defend first, her new friend or the innocent baby. The moment went on interminably.

"Katy!" Latt Meicklejohn called out to her, breaking the silence. "Honey, you'd better check the kitchen, I think something's burning."

"Oh!" She hurried quickly across the room and through the swinging doors. It wasn't until she got there that she realized that she wasn't even cooking anything.

She did start cooking then. She put on a big pan of oatmeal and laid out a pound of bacon in strips across the griddle. By the time she made it back to the dining room, the world there seemed back to normal. People were chatting amicably, or reading the paper, or minding their own business.

Pearly had gone without even finishing his coffee.

The memory of his unkindness lingered in her mind. She wouldn't mention it to Nadine, but she wondered about it nonetheless.

After the noon rush and most of the cleanup, Emma agreed to handle things in the dining room and Katy went out to face the barbecue. She was not willing to give up Bitsy's namesake, but daily she faced her fire with more and more trepidation.

The pit was basically a brick trough with a firebox on one end and a chimney at the other. Inside it was thoroughly blackened from the thousands of fires that had been laid there. The interior brickwork had been constructed so that every fifth layer of brick was turned lengthwise, creating notches along the sides about a foot apart. The grate, which was actually more like a tray of criss-crossed metal bars that could be set at several different heights, was closed off to bathe the meat inside in the smoke as it made its way from fire to flume.

It all looked incredibly uncomplicated, but Katy had found that looks were deceiving.

The information on how to actually cook meat on one of these ancient outdoor cookers was not readily available. All the barbecue books she'd consulted and the tips that Bitsy had written down assumed a basic knowledge that she simply didn't possess. They made it sound as if you simply threw some meat on and it all turned out wonderfully.

On some days Katy's barbecue had been better than others, but it had not once been even close to wonderful.

With a determined sigh, she began cleaning out the ashes, disposing them in the big metal container designed for that purpose. There were always a number of hot coals on the bottom. Katy was very careful with those. She already realized how quickly they could cause a fire and how long they could remain hot under the ash.

Once the pit was clean and tidy, she rolled the wheelbarrow to the woodpile. She'd bought a load of firewood from a farmer down the road who was clearing a brushy area in his pasture. He and his son had delivered it very promptly and had stacked it very professionally.

Katy pushed the load of wood back to the pit where she neatly laid it out in the firebox and squirted it liberally with lighter fluid. Katy tossed in a match.

With an audible whoosh and a plume of black smoke, the blaze flamed up nicely. She walked into the restaurant kitchen, took the tray of carefully rubbed spareribs from the refrigerator and carried them out and laid them atop the metal grate of the smoker and closed it up securely.

Please God, she silently implored the heavens, *if you want me to make a go of this place, the barbecue has just got to get better.*

Bitsy's Wisdom 10

Bitsy's Wisdom 10: When you carry raw meat to the smoker on a plate, don't ever put cooked meat on it to bring back.

The world was spinning out of Sean's control. That was one thing that he and his mother agreed upon. But she seemed to think it had something to do with privilege, immaturity and his personal lack of discipline. Sean thought it was mostly about Gwendolyn Dodson's unwavering certainty in knowing what was best for him. Perhaps most mothers felt that way. Maybe it was just a mothering thing. But most moms didn't have the resources, tenacity and determination to follow up the thought.

His mother did.

The very fact that he was awake, appropriately dressed and seated in the offices of Bradley, Hicks, Rodgers, Litham & Braun, Attorneys-at-Law was evidence of that.

She was sitting beside him, festooned for battle in a St. John knit and sensible pumps. No middle-aged female warrior had ever looked more fearsome.

Even his tough-as-nails, mean-as-the-devil lawyer, David Faneuf, kept tugging at his tie. Most people would have interpreted that as nervousness. Sean saw it as proof that his mother was a pain in the neck.

"The problem, as I see it, Mrs. Dodson," the lawyer told her, "is that we virtually wrote the agreement that's in place. We stalled, we contested, we delayed until we got every concession that we wanted. Then we sat on it for as long as the law would allow. Now the agreement is finally in force. If we go before a judge right now, it will look as if we're doing it for spite."

"We are," Sean said under his breath.

"We are not!" his mother insisted.

Faneuf looked at them uneasily. He was in a difficult spot. He was supposed to be representing Sean. But it was Sean's mother who hired him and paid his fees. The ninth-floor corner office at Walnut and Memorial Drive had a dead-on view of the Gateway Arch and the Mississippi River beyond. A guy, no matter how smart he was, didn't get to park his desk in that kind of real estate by ignoring the person with the checkbook.

"Perhaps if we had some substantive change in the former wife's suitability for sole custody," he suggested. "Maybe she's getting depressed or you suspect she's using drugs or she's been neglectful."

Sean wanted to speak up for Katy. Fortunately he didn't have to.

"It's nothing like that, David," she said softly. "In the previous agreement we focused almost entirely on the monetary aspects of the divorce. Because the child was a mere baby when we started, it was correct and completely natural to allow the mother full custody. But the *baby* is now a *boy* and will be off to kindergarten in just a few months."

The lawyer nodded. "A change in the child's age does frequently call for an adjustment in the agreement."

"An adjustment in the agreement," she repeated. "Yes, that's exactly the way it should be presented. An adjustment that allows Josh to come live with us in Ladue."

Faneuf tapped his Milano leather desk pad with his Mont Blanc pen. Softly he said, "That may be a bit more of an alteration than the current custody holder is able to tolerate."

"Well, we've certainly had to tolerate some unexpected changes from her," his mother said.

"How so?"

"The woman has taken Josh, without consulting us, to the wilds of the Ozarks, far away from the excellent private school that we planned for him to attend."

Faneuf was taking notes.

"School choice is not usually sufficient for a change of custody," he pointed out.

"Well, if it's not it should be," Gwendolyn Dodson stated firmly. "Nothing is more important to a child's ultimate success in the world."

Sean thought to point out that in his opinion a stable family life without parents involved in constant legal wrangling trumped even the best education, but decided not to say so.

"Where has the ex-wife relocated?"

"Warbler Lake," his mother answered.

Sean wasn't sure how his mother had come by that information. She hadn't asked him. And he hadn't told anybody.

"Where exactly is that?" the lawyer asked.

"It's south," Gwen said. "Somewhere in that empty part of the state between Poplar Bluff and nowhere."

Faneuf chuckled politely at Sean's mother's unkind joke.

"And the school there is…"

"Nothing special," she told him. "It's a public elementary with barely a midlist rating."

"Perhaps we can find an acceptable alternative school that is near enough to still allow him to live with his mother."

"No, that won't be possible," she told the lawyer.

His eyebrows went up, but he didn't say a word as he allowed her to continue.

"We want Josh to be raised and educated in his family's faith," she said piously. "We want to enroll him at Principia."

Sean was so shocked at that statement, he nearly fell off his chair. He managed to disguise his gasp with a cough, but just barely.

Ostensibly his father had been a Christian Scientist, though Sean had no memory of him ever talking about his religion or even attending church. His mother had raised Sean early on as a Presbyterian. Once they moved to the affluent suburbs they'd become Episcopalians. Sean was certain that his mother had never even suggested Principia, a unique institution in the city run by Christian Scientists, as an educational option for him.

"You have to agree," his mother continued, "that the Principia experience could not be duplicated anywhere else. And yet it is here, so convenient to our home."

The lawyer instantly seemed more enthusiastic. "The religious issue is good," he said. "Comparing schools can always run into snarls, but freedom of religion is hardwired in the constitution and even family court judges don't like to get crosswise on the record."

Gwen was smiling, pleased. She was a very smart lady and she knew that it was a smart idea.

"Mother, no." Sean spoke up finally; he felt as if he had no choice.

She turned to look at him, surprised.

Sean directed his next words to the lawyer. "I have no intention of sending my son to Principia and I'm not a Christian Scientist."

"Oh." The lawyer looked surprised and deflated. "But you are interested in pursing a change in custody?"

Sean opened his mouth to reply before realizing that he had no answer. *Did he want his son? Yes, he realized he did. Did he deserve to have him? No, he knew that he did not.*

"I'd…I'd like to find some middle ground," he said.

"That's what we're here for, Sean," his mother said, her voice conciliatory. She patted his hand. "We just want to divide up his time. He'll spend the school year with us and then perhaps have a little vacation with his mother in Warblerville."

"Warbler Lake."

"Wherever."

Sean just stared at his mother, trying to take it all in. From the moment he'd come crawling home, his mother had encouraged him to forget that Josh and Katy had ever existed. Her reversal on this issue was inexplicable. She had been extremely annoyed at his "unfortunate marriage." She'd described his wife variously as a "brainless blonde" and an "unprincipled gold digger." When he'd told her she was to be a grandmother, she didn't believe it.

During the nearly three years that he was married, he and his mother had had minimal contact. Except for the days when he'd come back begging.

"The basic health insurance plan the company offers doesn't cover any maternity expenses," Sean had told his mother shortly before Katy gave birth to Josh.

She'd nodded. "It was a negotiated agreement with the provider," she said. "It's how we've kept our premiums so low."

"Without health insurance, the hospital wants us to put up a deposit before the baby's delivery," he told her.

"That seems very reasonable of them," she said. "They're providing a service and they want to make sure that they get paid for it."

"I don't have that kind of money," Sean said.

She had given him a brightly fake smile. "Why don't you take it out of your savings account?"

"Mother, my savings account has about fifty bucks in it," he said. "It takes everything I make just to get from one paycheck to the next."

"And whose fault is that?" she asked him.

He knew that she thought the answer was Katy. But that was not the truth. Katy was accustomed to not having money. She'd gone back to waitressing. She kept all her tips in a coffee can and used that money to buy furniture and baby equipment at Goodwill and Salvation Army stores. She had the gift of doing much with very little and appreciating all that she had. It was Sean himself who continued to blow money on beers with his buddies. And who succumbed to the pressure of looking successful among those former classmates who'd never respected him, anyway.

"The reality is that with both of us working full-time, our income just barely gets us by," he told her. "When Katy has to stay home with the baby, it will be hard to even be able to manage that."

"It is very imprudent of you to be bringing a child into the world, then, isn't it?"

"It wasn't like I planned this, Mother."

She gave a huff of disgust. "Wake up, Sean," she said sharply. "This is the twenty-first century. There is no such thing as an unplanned pregnancy, just a scheming woman. Do you even know that this child is yours? At the very least you should insist on a paternity test."

"You're talking about my wife. And I don't need a paternity test."

"Well, that's certainly up to you," she said. "But what I do with my money is up to me. And I'm not investing one dime in aiding this little tramp in the ruination of your life."

She had kept her word. Sean had put the entire hospital expense on a new credit card, the old one already having been maxed out. And when he'd called her with the news that Josh was born safe and healthy, she hadn't so much as offered congratulations, let alone come by to the see the baby.

"I understand that you've already missed three days of work," she said.

"I got it covered," Sean said. "Emilio and Greta both agreed to rearrange their schedules. So everything is getting done and nobody is getting overtime pay."

"Nevertheless," she said sternly. "It is not the policy of Dodsonburger to offer paternity leave. And you haven't accrued any vacation time. So I've instructed the payroll department to dock you for the time you've missed."

Sean was too angry to even respond. He simply hung up the phone and walked away.

"What's wrong?" Katy had asked him.

"Nothing," he replied. "What could be wrong when I'm here with the most beautiful woman in the world, who is busy feeding the most handsome baby ever born?"

She had been beautiful. Still plump and pretty, her breasts were nearly as big as cantaloupes. The tiny dark-haired baby sucked greedily on the nipple. Sean knelt on the floor next to the couch and stroked the newborn's cheek with one long finger.

"This is everything I ever wanted," Katy told him. "A man I love and a baby of my own. Our life is like a dream come true."

For Sean it had turned into a nightmare.

"I do want to have more contact with my son," Sean now told the lawyer as his mother smiled at him approvingly. "I...don't want to hurt Katy, but I do want to see him."

"And that is the best course of action," David told them. "Right now, if we go before a judge, it may appear as if Sean has little or no relationship with the child. We have to change that."

His mother was nodding.

"I'll send a letter, informing Josh's mother of Sean's intent to visit his son," the lawyer said. "That's a win-win. If she says yes, then we establish a relationship between the two. If she says no, we can take that to court as evidence against her."

"That sounds good."

"So, Sean, clear some time on your calendar for a trip down to Warbler Lake," he said.

"We'll do better than that," his mother said. "We'll rent a place there for the summer."

"The whole summer?" Faneuf was obviously pleased, but skeptical of the possibility. "Can you be away from the business that long?"

His mother's gesture was dismissive. "This is a new millennium. With technology I can run the company from any spot on the globe."

The lawyer nodded. "And perhaps, while you're there and Sean is busy with the boy, you can make some observations about the circumstances. Any information about his living conditions, his safety and welfare, or his mother's fitness as a parent can carry significant weight with a judge."

Gwen smiled and gave him a nod of understanding.

"Josh is a Dodson," she said. "Getting to know him, gaining his confidence and affection, is our top priority. It's for our own good as well as the good of the corporation."

Faneuf seemed to understand that.

Sean wasn't sure that he did. His heart was in his throat. He didn't know what frightened him more. Renting a house with his mother for the summer or seeing Katy and Josh again.

Bitsy's Wisdom *11*

Bitsy's Wisdom 11: Horneyhead minnows are often confused with creek chubs. Maybe you can't tell the difference,
but the fish can.

"Are you sure you don't want to go to church with us?"

Katy stood in the doorway of Emma's bedroom, looking young
and happy and full of optimism. Emma raised her head just enough
to puff up her pillow before settling back down into its comfort.

"Come on," Katy said. "If you hurry we can still make it and
not be late."

Emma wanted to throw something at her.

"This is the only morning all week that we get to sleep in," she
answered. "I can't believe you don't want to do that."

"And waste our only morning off?" Katy shook her head. "Besides, Josh needs to go, so I'm going."

"Okay, bye."

"Everybody in town is going to be there."

"Okay, bye."

"Curt will miss seeing you and you'll miss seeing him."

"Okay, bye."

"Why's Auntie Em not coming with us?" she heard Josh ask from the living room.

"'Cause she's a sleepyhead," Katy answered.

Josh giggled. "Auntie Em's a sleepyhead. Auntie Em's a sleepy-head."

Emma was glad to hear the door shut behind them. But alone in the silence of the apartment, she couldn't go back to sleep. There were too many thoughts on her mind. Too many worries that she just couldn't ignore.

She threw back the covers and rolled to a sitting position, her feet planted firmly on the floor. For several moments she just sat there, gazing at the multitude of faded faces gazing back at her. There were ancient old couples staring into the camera stone-faced. There were several fat, happy little babies. A set of twin girls in identical dresses with wide ribbon sashes. There was a World War II airman in a leather bomber jacket smoking a pipe. Was that the man that Bitsy had loved? The husband she'd lost in the war? Had she cherished this picture? Had she cherished all of them? She probably never imagined that some stranger would spend a Sunday morning staring at her family gallery.

And if she had any nesting instinct, they wouldn't still be on her wall.

Katy had, in her clever lemonade-from-lemons way, made the apartment very much their own. Without much time or money or even fresh paint, she'd cleaned and de-cluttered to the point of real livability. She'd left Emma's room, however, to Emma. And so far, all Emma had done was wipe off a few layers of dust and change the sheets on the bed.

She knew she should pack all this stuff away and make this her own place. But she didn't want it to be her own place.

Field note: The tendency for nomadic hunter-gatherers to continue to migrate is not necessarily negated by the opportunity to sustain themselves in a settled environment.

Emma got to her feet and padded into the kitchen. Katy had left her a half pot of coffee and she poured herself a cup. She opened the doors to the roof terrace and walked out there. The morning was beautiful. The air was crisp and fresh without being cold. The sun was just high enough to peek through the top of the trees on the eastern slope. It slashed across the water making it glimmer in a way that was too magical to be earthly. The water lapped along the shore in lazy regularity. And the scent from the lake breeze was more spring flowers than fish.

It was nice here. Nice in a lot of ways. Nice for a lot of reasons.

Emma sighed, wishing she'd never laid eyes on the place. The activity of her mind wouldn't allow her to sit and bask in the beauty of the morning. She went back into her room, pulled on jeans and a sweatshirt and headed out to walk it off.

Down the stairs and across the vacant parking lot, the world seemed almost empty. There were no cars circling the giant fishhook statue. On the far side of the park she could see the clunky clapboard tower that passed for a church steeple; she could also hear the sound of organ music coming from that direction. That appeared to be the only place in town with any activity. The beach was completely deserted and the hiking trail around the lake's edge looked very solitary.

That appealed to Emma just fine and she began jogging in that direction.

Treating worry with exercise was something she'd been doing for a very long time. The hiking path was hilly and in places quite steep. She'd learned that if she pushed herself, if she kept moving, all the fears and anxieties that plagued her would never be able to keep up.

The entrance to the path was marked by a wooden railing, and she had just reached it when she heard her name called. Emma stopped and glanced around, surprised. She'd felt so alone out here, she didn't immediately see anyone, then she noticed an upraised hand from inside a boat moored to one of the nearby docks that extended out into the water.

"Morning," she called out dismissively, expecting to limit the encounter to a greeting.

Unfortunately, the man stood up and waved her over. It was Lattimer Meicklejohn, the licorice-smelling bait supplier. With resignation, she walked down the dock, determined to make the encounter short and sweet.

As she approached she could see him more clearly. His small boat rocked with the movement in the water, he stood legs apart, confidently oblivious to the sway. He was dressed, as always, in faded, dirty blue jeans and a long-sleeved shirt. His aging orange Windbreaker had a logo on one side that pictured a set of scales, beneath which was written *Poverty Encounter 1976*.

Emma thought, unkindly, that he may have *encountered* poverty then, but it had obviously stuck with him through three decades.

"How are you today, Mr. Meicklejohn," she said politely.

"Call me Latt, girl," he answered. "Everybody does. It's good to see that I'm not the only heathen in this village."

"Heathen?"

"Maybe that's too strong a word for non-churchgoer," he said, chuckling. "But I'm especially surprised that you're not perched in a pew this morning."

"'Especially surprised?'" she questioned.

He shook his head. "Never mind," he answered. "I guess I misjudged you. You out in the morning air to exercise?"

"No," she answered. "Just to get out. The B & B is a bit limiting. Sometimes it's like the whole world has narrowed down to a barbecue pit and a minnow tank."

He smiled. "Hop aboard, then," he said. "You can't really see the bigness of this place anywhere but out on the lake."

"Oh, no, I—"

"Get in," he insisted. "It'll do you good. And you don't have to worry. I'm not old Mayor Crank. I don't see a young woman like you and say, 'Hey that could be my sweetheart,' I think, 'Hey, that could've been my daughter.'"

Emma hesitated. The daughter image momentarily stopped her. Emma had thought of herself as independent, the head of her family, since girlhood. Even her stepfather, Larry, had never, in any way, indicated any paternal feeling toward her. She wasn't sure how to respond to it.

Latt held his hand out to her and, surprising herself, she took it.

The boat wobbled dangerously as she stepped in it. She quickly seated herself on the seat bench closest to the bow. Latt untied the rope that secured them to the dock and then pushed off with a small paddle.

Seated in the back, he lowered the motor into the water and turned it on.

Emma glanced at it and frowned. "That looks like a kitchen mixer," she said.

He grinned. "Oh, it was once," he told her. "A very good, reliable kitchen mixer. So I reworked it to run on a battery charge, attached a propeller to it and mounted it here on this homemade rudder."

He seemed so proud of his accomplishment. Emma wondered if she'd just stepped into a Rick Moranis movie. Nervously she swallowed and glanced at the distance back to shore.

"It's very dependable," he assured her. "It'll run ten full hours on a charge and it's simple enough not to have a big risk of breakdown."

She nodded, hoping it was true.

"I prefer running on electric," he told her. "Most of the fellows around here run on gasoline, but I hate the noise. Besides," he said, nodding toward the church that was now much more visible than it had been from the beach, "If I were to start up an engine down here on Sunday morning, everybody from Preacher Curt to the old deacon Ambrose asleep on his pew would know it."

He laughed at his own little joke. Emma managed a tight smile.

Field note: Native transportation may be primitive. While it is imprudent to criticize or indicate a lack of confidence, unobtrusively seeing to one's own protection is wise.

"Does this boat have life jackets or something?" she asked.

"Lord, yes!" he said.

He pulled a couple out from under his seat. He looked them both over quickly and then tossed the cleaner-looking one in her direction.

Emma slipped her arms into it and securely fastened the Velcro closures. Latt put his on as well.

"I don't know what I was thinking," he said. "I always wear these out on the water. Senior brain, they call it. I'd read it suggested that if we older folks stood on our heads we'd get more blood flow and would not be as forgetful. Of course, for most of us attempting a headstand would probably be more dangerous than drowning. Can you picture old Mr. Dempsey?"

Emma smiled. "Maybe not him, but Miss Welborn could do it."

Latt nodded. "Probably, but *she* doesn't really need it."

"Maybe not," Emma said. "But I'd like to get Crank to try it or Gus Gouswhelter."

"Perhaps you could open a stand-on-your-head therapy clinic," Latt said. "People are always talking about how much this community needs some kind of health care."

Emma smiled. Deliberately, she tried to calm her jitters. As they headed out into the lake, the sounds of the water against the hull of the boat was rhythmic but failed to lull her into tranquillity. Edgy, she kept glancing back toward the shore.

"This doesn't seem to be relaxing you," Latt noted.

"I've never really been out on the water much," Emma admitted. "I've taken a few ferry rides. But this boat seems very small and the lake seems very big."

"It's all perspective," he said.

"Yes, I'm sure it is," Emma agreed. "It's just that I'm not accustomed to being in the boat, I'm usually watching the boats."

Latt smiled. "That's been my impression of you," he said. "Even in the thick of the action, you're always the observer."

She was surprised that he had any opinion of her at all.

"Am I wrong?" he asked.

She shook her head. "No, not really."

"Ever wonder, as the observer you are, why you've turned out that way?"

She shrugged. "I suppose it's the result of years of meeting new people and passing through communities where I knew we'd never stay long," she said. "I've met lots of people, but I've never really needed a lot of friends."

"I see," Latt said. "So you find people interesting more in the laboratory sense than the personal one."

Emma had never really thought of it that way, but his estimation seemed very close to truth.

"It's been my dream, really since I was a young teenager, to become an anthropologist," she told him. "Observation is a big part of that."

He nodded. "So it's science to you," he said.

"Yes."

"It's not just an excuse for being nosy."

She knew he was joking with her and laughed.

"You'd said that you moved around a lot," he reminded her.

"Constantly," Emma admitted. "All through my childhood my mother was flittering from place to place, never really able to settle anywhere for very long."

"You hated that."

She shook her head. "On the contrary," she told him. "I think it suited me just fine."

"Really?"

"Yes, well except for worrying," she admitted honestly. "With all the changing work schedules and uncertain paychecks and just the financial costs of family uprooting, I became a habitual worrier at a young age."

"What did your mother have to say about that?"

"Oh, mostly she'd just let me do it," Emma answered. "She's very laid-back about everything. I knew that worrying was probably her job. But I guess I didn't think she was very good at it."

Latt raised an eyebrow at that.

They had reached a section of the lake that was sheltered somewhat by a point, though it was perhaps fifty yards from shore. He cut the engine and threw the anchor, which was actually an age-darkened flatiron, over the side.

"This spot is called the Snake Shallows," he told her. "It's a submerged island, the area is not very deep and it's surrounded by an abrupt drop-off. Every January we tote all the discarded Christmas trees out here and sink them around the edges. The fish just love that."

Latt pulled his minnow bucket closer to him. He retrieved a fishing pole from along the inside of the boat.

"So, have you thought about a twelve-step worrier program or some such?"

Emma laughed.

"When my mom married my stepfather, I had been so hopeful that things would change," she said. "But those two are true soul mates. Free spirits, untamed by responsibilities. They both love bumping around place to place. Finally, I was out on my own and could make my own decisions, control my own life. That felt wonderful."

"So what happened?"

Emma hesitated. It wasn't typical of her to reveal so much to a near stranger, but somehow this man, this father-figure, generated trust.

"One day they moved away from my sister, Katy," Emma said. "I've been responsible for her ever since."

Latt looked thoughtful for a moment and then began nodding slowly. "This Katy, your sister, she's the perfectly functional grown woman that I've met, the mother of the little boy, the one who owns the Bait & BBQ?"

His tone was so facetious with such feigned incredulity, that Emma couldn't help but squirm a little.

"My sister is a lovely, bright, sunny person," she said. "But she's naive and sees the best in people, even when it's not always in her best interest to do so. She doesn't always watch out for herself and I'm the only one available to do that for her."

"What happened to her husband?"

"He's more interested in watching out for himself."

"Ah." Latt's comment was noncommittal and offered with a sagacious nod. To the end of the fishing line he'd attached a two-prong hook.

"This is different than the one on the pedestal."

"Huh?"

Emma pointed in the direction of the town. "Our big fish-hook," she said. "It's not like this."

"Oh, you mean Abby?" he said.

"Abby? It has a name?"

He nodded. "It's an Aberdeen hook," Latt told her. "The simplest and most popular type used around her. I'm not a local, so I'm a little out of the ordinary."

"You're not a local?" Emma was surprised.

He chuckled. "Well, I guess I'm getting too old to be insulted," he said. "I take comfort in the idea that I'm fitting in."

He explained the various components of the rod and reel. The obvious parts, the pole, line and the mechanism for cranking one along the other. But there were other things, too.

"These little metal weights are called sinkers," he said. "And the little bright plastic bobs are called floaters. The sinkers keep the hook down in the swimming range of the fish," he said. "The floater keeps it from dropping all the way to the bottom."

From the minnow bucket he pulled out what Emma recognized from her recent weeks in the bait business as a golden shiner. The deep-bodied little fish was covered in loosely spaced golden scales that shimmered in the sunshine.

He handed her a fishing pole. "I don't suppose you know how to bait your hook, do you?"

Emma shook her head. "I just sell the stuff, I try never to touch it."

"You don't sell anything this good," he told her. "I have a reputation for being one of the best fisherman on this lake. I'm going to share my secret—I keep all the best bait for my own use."

"What makes you think I won't out you to the Warbler Lake fish folk?"

"You're an observer," he pointed out. "You're not interested in altering the balance, you're just passing through."

He grasped the fishhook on the end of her line.

"I'm going to do this for you once," he said. "The next time, I'll want you to do it for yourself."

Emma nodded and kept her silence, secretly hoping that next time would never come.

"You grasp this little fellow by the body," Latt said. "You put the hook into his mouth and pull it out through his gill. This way, he stays alive, but he can't get free of the hook."

She watched the procedure uncomfortably.

"Does it hurt him?" she asked.

Latt eyed her over the top of his sunglasses, his bushy gray eyebrows raised in question.

"We're putting him in this water to get eaten by a bigger fish," Latt explained with exaggerated patience. "Then we'll take the bigger fish home and eat it ourselves. That's the way this fishing thing works. The happiness and well-being of the fish doesn't enter into the equation."

She nodded. "Yeah, I guess the steer is not all that thrilled about heading for the barbecue pit, either," she said.

"Especially as bad as you girls serve it," Latt replied. "Now, hold the reel out to your side and give it a pretty good flick forward, sort of like lobbing a tennis ball."

"I don't play tennis, either," she told him, but managed to send the little hooked minnow flying about a dozen feet from the boat.

"Oh! that's good, you're a natural."

Emma felt genuinely pleased with herself.

Latt handed her a stained and weathered dark green bucket hat. "Put this on to keep the sun off. You really need something wide-brimmed with straw, but this is all I've got for you today."

Emma pulled it down on her head.

Latt grinned at her. "Perfect," he said. "Makes you look like you were born to the fishing life."

Emma scoffed at the suggestion. But as the morning wore on, she found it more to her liking. The two of them sat there, companionably quiet, in the beauty of the day.

It seemed to Emma that the sport of fishing mostly involved watching the plastic floater for evidence of action below the water. Sometimes the fish would toy with the minnow, or manage to get it off the hook without getting snared. This meant re-baiting, which after a couple of tries, Emma found wasn't really that distasteful at all. The best part, of course, was when the floater disappeared when the line jerked and the fish was hooked. Adrenaline surged through Emma's veins and Latt would talk her through it, like some made-for-TV drama where the spunky heroine lands the big passenger plane by listening to the instructions from the airport tower.

"Give him some line, give him some line…no, pull him up easy. Keep it taut, don't give him any wiggle room. Steady, steady, reel him in and don't jerk the line."

Slowly, patiently, she got the fish pulled in close to the boat. Then Latt scooped it up in the net and set it down on the floor of the boat to remove the hook.

Emma caught three before Latt had even gotten a bite.

"That's the unfair thing about this sport," he told her. "A rank amateur will come out and pull in the best fish of the day, every dang time."

The third fish she caught, however, he made her throw back. He showed her how to bend the fin down to take its measurement.

"It's not legal if it's under fifteen inches," he told her. "You have to throw him back in the water and catch him again when he gets bigger."

"Okay," Emma agreed, and followed Latt's direction on release. "What about this other one, it looks even smaller."

"It's a spotty," Latt said. "A different type of bass. It's full grown at twelve inches."

They only had a half-dozen fish on the stringer when Latt told her that it was time to start back. She was surprised at how many hours had passed and how relaxed she felt. Latt started up the lit-tle homemade motor and they headed back to the dock.

"Now, I'm going to clean these fish for you," he said. "Then I want you to put some butter and salt and pepper and a little piece of onion on them, wrap them up in foil, and set the packet in the oven for about fifteen minutes. Can you do that for me?"

"Seems easy enough," Emma said.

"I'm trying to come up with something you can cook that a human being might actually want to eat," he teased.

"You look like you're getting your share of meals," she teased him right back.

He laughed as if he were delighted at her pointed humor.

The sun was warm, the breeze was cool and Emma decided that she loved just being out on the water.

"Uh-oh." She glanced over at Latt to see him staring ahead. She turned to see someone standing at the end of the dock as if wait-ing for them.

"You're in trouble now, girl," he said.

"Who is it?"

"It's your preacher," he answered.

"My what?" Emma didn't immediately know what he meant. As they got closer she recognized him. "Oh, it's Curt," she said. "Why do you call him *my* preacher?"

"That's what the whole blame town is praying for," Latt an-swered. "The two of you living happily ever after."

Bitsy's Wisdom 12

Bitsy's Wisdom 12: Throw a couple of onions in the smoker now and again. It smells good and makes folks think that you really know what you're doing.

The little white clapboard church was sparse and sweet and quaint. Inside the steeple-tapered front doors was a small foyer. On either side of the wall were two rows of pegs. Near the top the gentlemen hung their hats, below hung coats of every size and description, from Mrs. Dempsey's ancient fox fur to a small child's Blue's Clues jacket. The people there were open and friendly as they made their way down the wide center aisle. The strip of floral carpet had been worn into soft hues by a million footsteps. Pews on either side were bare, wooden and devoid of fancy decoration, but they were sturdy, polished to a shiny gloss and were somehow welcome.

Mrs. Bullock waved Katy into the pew beside her. The older lady was one of the few people in the building who didn't come to the B & B. At ninety-two she rarely ventured from her front porch. But Katy had talked to her there. She was the woman who lived in the big house next door with the wraparound porches. The house that Katy had thought she was buying. That seemed so silly to her now. How boring a bed-and-breakfast would be! Bitsy's was a much better business venture, except, of course, for the bad barbecue.

"You sit right here with me, sweetie," Mrs. Bullock told her. "We single ladies must stick together." Then with a wink and mischievous smile she added, "That way we can talk about how all the married ladies have let themselves go."

Katy couldn't help but giggle. One thing that no one would ever say about Mrs. Bullock was that she had let herself go. Slender and petite, she was dressed in a bright pink suit cut in a classic style. Her hair was pure white, but it was still long and pulled back into a sleek French twist at the back of her head. Her wrist and hands were adorned with a tasteful but expensive array of fine jewelry, and her nails were polished with the exact shade of her outfit.

"As my dear Carlton used to say," she quoted, "'Just because we're living in the sticks doesn't mean we have to look like we belong here.'"

Mrs. Bullock's philosophy must have been generally agreed upon, because from Katy's perspective, the ladies of Warbler Lake Community Church were very fashionably arrayed.

A notable exception was Flora Krebs, one of the regulars at the bait shop. Katy had seen her only in ragged coveralls, sweatsuits or jeans. For Sunday, she was dressed in Dockers and a man's white shirt. She came across the room to speak to Katy.

"Are you going to be opening the Bait Shop later?"

"No, we're closed all day today."

"Damn!" the woman swore under her breath. "When I was walking to church I saw a whole row of birds sitting on the line. That means the barometer is dropping and rain is on the way. There's nothing like crickets to make fish bite during a rain."

Katy was just about to suggest that Flora could come by after church and she would unlock and let her get some crickets. That seemed to be the neighborly thing to do. A timely interruption from Mrs. Bullock stopped her.

"Flora, you are not to be out on the water in a thunderstorm," she told the woman firmly, as if instructing a child, not a woman in her forties.

She shrugged. "I do it all the time," she said.

"Well, you must stop," Mrs. Bullock told her. "You may think it doesn't matter if you're struck by lightning, killed doing something that you love. But think of the young man or woman who might see it from the shore and risk their own life trying to rescue you."

Flora rolled her eyes, but she did walk away.

Mrs. Bullock directed her next comment to Katy. "We've had several drowning tragedies here at Warbler Lake."

Katy nodded sympathetically.

A minute later a group of children overcame their initial shyness to hurry over and sweep Josh up in their group. He was so excited and eager. But Katy was a little hesitant to let him go with them. She had met a few of them at the B & B but most of these future schoolmates were strangers. A familiar young face reassured her.

"Don't worry," Parker said, apparently sensing her concern as Josh rushed away without even a backward glance. "I'll keep an eye on him."

Allowing a seven-year-old to take responsibility for her child was not something Katy would normally do, but they were within the confines of the building and Parker, quiet, thoughtful, Parker, was accustomed to being responsible. He'd apparently come to church on his own with five-year-old Brianna in tow.

"I wonder where Nadine is," she'd asked Mrs. Bullock.

"Nadine Graves? Oh, she doesn't come," the woman told her,

lowering her voice to a whisper. "I suppose she thinks she might not be welcome."

"Why would she think that?" Katy asked, surprised.

Mrs. Bullock sighed and shook her head. "Maybe because she's right."

Katy was taken aback by that suggestion but didn't have time to ponder it. She was far too busy. Person after person came over to greet her. Of course they told her how glad they were to have her in church, but many also mentioned how happy they were to have the Bait & BBQ open once more.

Curt came in, looking not at all like himself. He wore a very well-cut gray suit with white shirt and tie, his hair neat and tidy; even his stance and his step appeared different from what she was accustomed to seeing. Smiling, he extended his hand.

"Good morning, Katy," he said. "It's so good to see you here." He greeted Mrs. Bullock with equal enthusiasm and much deference before returning his attention to Katy. "Where is Emma?" he asked.

"She didn't come with us," Katy answered.

His brow furrowed. "Surely she's not working today?"

"No, oh no, she…" Katy hated to tell him that her sister preferred sleeping over sermons. "She had something else she had to do this morning."

She knew her answer was vague and Curt's brow furrowed in response, but Katy made no attempt to elaborate.

The service was a surprising mix of Protestant traditions, reflecting, Katy supposed, the range of the community. In his sermon, Curt, as pastor, seemed sufficiently wiser than he did as postman.

With the benediction, the rounds of handshakes and small talk began again. Katy enjoyed it. She already felt like she knew these people. She knew this community and she was a part of it. That's what she'd always wanted and now she had it.

By the time she'd gathered up Josh and was walking through the park toward Bitsy's she was lighthearted and humming the postlude to herself. Josh was ahead of her, skipping.

It was her son who spotted Nadine at a picnic table and went running over to her. She met him with open arms. Josh hugged Nadine and then dropped to his knees on the little blanket that she laid out for Natty. Josh kissed the baby on the top of the head.

"Hey there, little guy, do you want to play with me? Huh? Do you?"

The baby only grinned, soaking up the attention.

Katy called out a greeting as she approached.

"I've got fried chicken," Nadine said, indicating the plastic-covered containers she was laying out on the table. "Why don't you two stay and have lunch with us?"

"Oh, no, we don't want to intrude," Katy said. "I'm sure you're tired of seeing us every day."

Nadine shook her head. "You're the closest thing I've got to a friend in this town," she said. "And the kids play well together. Brianna doesn't pester Parker as much when she's got Josh to hang around with."

"Where are the kids?"

"I sent them over to the pop box at the gas station to get cold drinks," Nadine said. "Sit down. We've got plenty and I could use the company."

"Well, at least let me help you," Katy said.

Nadine shook her head. "No," she answered her. "You wait on people all week long. On Sunday, let somebody wait on you."

Katy felt decidedly spoiled as she seated herself on the bench. She watched her son trying to teach the baby to play pattycake. Nadine was grinning at them, pleased.

"May I take Natty to meet Brianna and Parker?" he asked.

"Sure," Nadine said. "Do you know how to strap him?"

"Yes, ma'am," Josh answered. "And we won't cross the street, we'll just wait for them on this side of the road."

"Great," Nadine said.

Katy watched her son, very gently and efficiently, get Natty strapped into the stroller, explaining every move to the baby.

When they were out of earshot Katy said, "Josh must have learned to do that from your kids. He's never been around babies before."

"That guy is a natural," Nadine told her. "It's time for you to be thinking about getting him a little brother or sister."

Katy laughed and shook her head. "I don't even have a boy-friend. I can't see how that's going to happen."

"Not having a boyfriend has never stopped me," Nadine replied. "I moved out here when Parker was born to get away from boy-friends. I guess sperm is in the air around here, that's how I ended up with three fatherless kids instead of one."

Katy was so taken aback by her words, she didn't know what to say. She stumbled and mumbled inarticulately for a moment. Nadine laughed.

"It's a joke," she told Katy. "Don't take it seriously. Have the old biddies been gossiping to you about me?"

"No."

"Well, they'll get around to it," Nadine said. "I'd just tell you that if there's anything you want to know about me or my kids, don't bother with the rumors, just ask me direct."

Katy nodded. "Okay," she said. "Did you love him?"

"Him who?"

"The children's father," she clarified.

"They all have different fathers," Nadine said. "And I guess I love that they gave me such great kids."

Katy nodded but didn't say anything more.

Nadine shrugged, as if throwing off her guard. "I certainly

loved Parker's father," she said. "I loved him like crazy. But then, crazy is how you love guys when you're sixteen." She shook her head. "He was on his way to the door the minute I said I was pregnant. When I said I was keeping the baby that was all the excuse he needed. The court collects child support from him. He's never seen Parker or shown the slightest interest in him."

"It's his loss," Katy said.

Nadine agreed. "I moved out here and met Brianna's dad. He was an older man, a perfect family man, I thought. He would be wonderful for Parker. His only problem was that he was slightly married."

"Slightly married?" Katy repeated. "How can somebody be only slightly married?"

"See, that's how smart you are, Katy," Nadine said. "You ask that question right off the bat. I didn't even think to ask it. I thought he was leaving his wife. He kept saying he was going to, and I thought he would. I finally decided that all he needed was the slightest little push and he'd leave her and marry me." Nadine shook her head ruefully. "Brianna was my little push. It pushed him back into the arms of his wife. They sold out and left town. That's what most people in Warbler Lake blame me for—having an affair with him."

"Oh, gosh, Nadine, I'm sorry."

"No, it's okay," she said. "He's actually been a good guy. He and his wife have been to see Brianna several times. He sends me a check the first of every month and he never forgets her birthday. He's even putting money away for her in a college fund. So, it's hard to feel sorry about that."

Katy nodded. She glanced up and saw the kids headed in their direction, but taking the long route, distracted every few steps. They were loud, laughing, happy.

"What about Natty's father?" she asked.

"I didn't love him. He didn't love me. He doesn't love Natty."

The words were cold and final. Katy glanced up, surprised.

"He was bragging all over town about 'knocking me up,'" Nadine said. "But when Natty was diagnosed with Downs, he took it as some kind of slap in the face. Hurt his ego, I guess. He calls my baby a freak and a retard. And now he claims he's not the baby's father."

"You could prove it," Katy said. "With blood tests or DNA."

Nadine nodded. "I decided that if he felt that way, we were better off without him."

"You're right," Katy said.

"What about you?" Nadine asked, turning the tables. "Did you love Josh's dad?"

Katy turned to watch her young son approaching. "Did. Do. Always will," she answered. She sighed. "There's nothing much else to say about that."

Her friend raised an eyebrow in speculation and then nodded. "Lucky you," she said.

"Lucky?" Katy asked. "I'm divorced, remember."

"You still love him and you have his child, that's a lot when you think about it."

"Yeah, I guess so."

Nadine urged the kids to take their places at the table. They were all happy and exuberant, though having filled up on soda pop on the way back from the machine, they weren't all that hungry.

Katy and Josh, however, after weeks of bad barbecue, savored the fried chicken, Josh declaring it was "the best chicken ever!"

Nadine enjoyed her children and Katy found herself laughing with them as well. They were lively and curious. But they were also polite and well behaved. Somehow this tattooed single mom with a checkered past had achieved the fine balance of encouraging independence and insisting upon obedience.

The kids were finished and back to the playground equipment

in just a few short minutes. Katy and Nadine lingered over their plates. Natty had fallen asleep in Katy's lap, his little mouth open and his tongue peaking out on one side.

"There's something I've been wanting to talk to you about," Nadine said.

"Okay, spill it."

"Well, the last day of school will be Wednesday," she said. "So I'll have Parker at home alone with the kids."

"That'll be nice for you."

She nodded. "Good for me, not so good for Parker."

"What do you mean?" Katy asked.

"Parker is a solitary kid," Nadine said. "On his best day he likes being alone. He's comfortable with his own company and very slow to make friends."

"Maybe because he's so much more mature than the kids around him," Katy suggested.

Nadine shrugged. "Maybe so," she said. "But he's just beginning to come out of his shell and have some buddies at school. If I keep him up at the cabin all summer, I'm afraid he'll lose that. We can't go with him all the time because of the baby's schedule and the other kids. And I won't just wave goodbye and send him off to fend for himself."

Katy nodded.

"The past week when we've been baking at your house, well, it's just been perfect. Brianna has Josh to play with, so Parker can pursue his own friends and we're close to everything and all the other kids are around. He's loved it."

"That's great."

"It's been good for me, too. Trapped up in that little house day after day, I think inside I'm beginning to turn bitter. Being around you and Emma, laughing, talking, it helps me feel okay about my life."

"You've just been too isolated," Katy said. "I've loved having you there, too. I can work without being anxious about Josh. And I like having a friend. Emma and I are close, but sisters are always sisters, and sometimes it's a friend that you really need."

"Thank you for that," Nadine said. "I'm...I'm honored to be a friend of yours." She blushed as if the sentiment embarrassed her. "So, anyway, here's my plan. I bring my kids to your place every morning this summer. I do the baking in your apartment and spend the rest of the day hanging around and watching Josh as well as my own. That frees you up to keep your eye on your job knowing that he has plenty of things to occupy him."

"That sounds really good, Nadine," Katy said. "But I don't really have any money to pay for a babysitter."

"You don't have to pay me," she said. "I'll do it for free, just for the summer."

"No, I can't let you do it for free," Katy said. "I...I'll split my tips with you. That's what they do in a lot of restaurants to compensate the people who work behind the scenes. I'll split my tips. You'll never know how much you're going to make, but you'll always make something."

"Fair enough."

They shook hands across the table, laughing.

Nadine glanced up and startled before Katy realized someone had walked up behind them. She turned to see Curt.

"Oh, hi," she said with a whisper, and then pointed to the sleeping baby in her arms.

"Hi, Katy," he said, and then nodded across the table. "Nadine."

"Curt," she responded.

"I'm looking for Emma," he said. "I saw you out here and thought she might be with you."

"No," Katy said. "I haven't seen her since I left for church."

"She's out on the lake," Nadine said.

"What?" The question came in unison from both Curt and Katy.

"Yeah, I saw her go over to the dock to meet Latt Meicklejohn." She turned toward the lake. "They went out around Snake Shallows, I think."

Katy followed Nadine's direction to see a small boat visible on the lake horizon.

Katy was incredulous. "She went fishing?"

"Fishing instead of church?" Curt sounded as dumbfounded as Katy felt.

"Yeah, well, it's a great day to be out there," Nadine said.

"I guess so," Katy said.

She was pretty sure that her sister could do anything she set her mind to do. But fishing was not the kind of activity that typically sparked her interest.

"Well," Curt said. "They're bound to be back soon. I'll go to the dock and wait for them to get in."

"Don't be silly," Nadine said. "Sit down. You'll be able to watch and see when they start coming in and you'll have plenty of time to get to the dock before they do."

"Oh, I…I don't want to impose…."

"This is a small town," Nadine pointed. "Imposing is one of our most prized virtues."

Curt chuckled and shook his head, but he did scoot in beside Katy.

"Here, have a chicken leg," Nadine said. "I'd bet dollars to doughnuts that you've not had a thing to eat all day."

His expression registered surprise.

"How did you know that?" he asked.

Nadine shrugged. "You've got to speak first thing, your stomach is probably all full of flutters, so you don't eat any breakfast. Now you've hurried out here to find Emma and you haven't had a chance for lunch."

"Very insightful," he told her.

She smiled brightly as she handed him a heaping plate of picnic lunch.

"That's the safest way to live in Warbler Lake," she told him. "Keep all your adversaries in sight."

He hesitated and then glanced toward Katy, embarrassed. "Surely you don't think of me as an adversary."

"Isn't that your job?" she challenged. "To root out the forces of evil in this town?"

Curt chuckled and shook his head. "No, that's not my job," he said. "And imagining yourself as the 'forces of evil'? That's a bit over the top, don't you think? Besides," he added with a teasing grin, "I don't want to run you out of town. You're about the only person making a genuine effort to keep the school population growing."

There was a moment of hesitation; Katy sat in openmouthed silence.

He took a bite of his chicken. "This is really good."

Then Nadine laughed. "I didn't realize you had a sense of humor," she said.

"Because you don't come listen to my sermons," he responded. "I'm not a stand-up comic but I manage a funny story or two every Sunday."

"I suppose you're the best entertainment in town," she said.

"I'm the only entertainment in town."

The atmosphere was relaxed, easy, as if they were all old friends. Katy liked that.

Parker ran over and stood at the end of the table beside Curt. He gazed at the man, appearing both eager and anxious.

"Hey, Parker," Curt said. "How are you today?"

"Good, real good," the child answered. "Pastor Curt, I...I've been thinking about what you said."

Curt raised an eyebrow. "What I said about what?"

"About the people from Thessalonika," he answered.

"From where?" Nadine asked.

"It's in Greece, Mom," Parker said.

"And in the Bible," Curt added. "First and second Thessalonians."

"Oh."

"I liked the part about being an encourager," Parker said. "How being an encourager of great things is as important as actually doing great things. That's what I want to do. To be an encourager of great things."

Curt smiled up at the boy. "That's a good start," he told him. "It's something you can do even today. But I'm pretty sure, Parker, that as time goes on you're going to be a man with some pretty impressive deeds of your own as well."

Parker beamed.

"Thanks," he said softly, suddenly shy.

"You know, your mom is really proud of you, how you take care of your sister and brother and watch out for them," Curt said. "It's a big help to her and very important."

Parker blushed and turned to look at Nadine. His obvious surprise at the words spoke volumes.

"Aw, Mom," he said.

Nadine smiled at him and shrugged. "I can't help myself. I've been bragging on you again."

"I'd better go, before Brianna and Josh get into trouble," he said, hurrying away with a lightness to his step.

"How do you know I'm so proud of that boy?" Nadine asked Curt.

He grinned. "You're not the only one in town who's keeping other people in sight."

Bitsy's Wisdom *13*

Bitsy's Wisdom 13: Crawdads make good bait only if they are of sufficient size to look natural away from the shallows. The little ones live their life hanging on to the underbelly of their mama.

The state-of-the-art GPS navigation system brilliantly directed turn after turn on the narrow, two-lane Missouri roads, making it impossible to get lost or stranded. Yet, Gwen Dodson was atypically nervous.

It was not a particularly convenient opportunity for her to take a vacation. But, she reminded herself, in the restaurant business there was no downtime. She just had to bite the bullet and leave the best people in charge. It wasn't as if she was off to Kathmandu. She had her laptop and her PDA so she was able to be in constant contact both by phone and e-mail. Her assistant was just a speed dial away and could conference her in on anything and everything. So company-wise, everything was in order. There was absolutely no cause for her concern. A fact which she continued to remind herself of as the shiny midnight-blue Mercedes whizzed along just slightly above the speed limit for the last few miles of her journey.

Still, she was nervous. Maybe it was the whole uncertainty of their destination. Myra had tried, unsuccessfully, to find nice, recommended accommodation for them at Warbler Lake. There was nothing on the Internet. And several travel agents consulted weren't even certain that the resort was still open. Finally, they'd been forced to the Yellow Pages and reserved two lake cabins, sight unseen. Myra had not been optimistic. She described the woman she'd talked to as "difficult." But Gwen was not the type of person to be intimidated by anyone's bad behavior.

What was worrying her, and she hated to admit it even to herself, was seeing little Josh.

It was one thing to sit among the splendor of her own success in St. Louis and believe she could orchestrate the world to her liking. That she could make everyone behave as she thought they should. And ultimately have everything work out to suit her. It was another thing entirely to step out of that comfort zone and take action.

She glanced over at the young man in the passenger seat. Even in sleep he looked older than he was, tired, strained, disappointed. Gwen knew honestly that she was disappointed as well. She'd struggled and sacrificed to make a good life for Sean. He seemed destined not to make anything of it.

She'd seen very little of her son since the decision to fight for Josh. In what was becoming a dismally typical manner, he stayed inside the garden house all day with the shades drawn. Then late at night when the rest of the world was going to sleep, she'd hear him leaving, not to return until nearly dawn.

She would have been thrilled if she thought he was seeing someone, or even out in the singles world, looking. But she knew he wasn't up to that. He was lying around depressed all day and then sitting in noisy places in the evening hoping that life might rub off on him.

Gwen was a realist. That was why she suffered no illusions about her son's future. He was a failure, a ne'er-do-well, a miss. His type, unfortunately, was not all that rare among the executive elite. Sons and daughters who didn't live up to the success of their parents were almost typical. As his mother, she was luckier than most. He didn't do drugs, drink to excess, gamble or live dangerously. But he wasn't happy. And he wasn't living up to his potential. And there wasn't anything she could do to change that. She tried to force him, coerce him, shame him. Nothing had really worked. She'd always support him. But she wanted another chance.

Josh would be her chance.

But she couldn't get him without Sean's help.

Gwen saw the Welcome To Warbler Lake sign just before the car's route guide announced their arrival.

"Your destination is ahead on the left," the vaguely robotic female voice told her.

Sean sat up immediately, alert and on edge, indicating that either he had not really been sleeping, or that he was in a fight-or-flight adrenaline response.

The little town was unimpressive, slightly seedy. A fifties-era resort that was run-down and rotting. As they approached a circular drive around a monument that appeared to be a giant fishhook, Sean spoke up for the first time.

"There it is," he said.

Gwen glanced over in the direction he indicated to see a paint-deprived, falling-down building on the corner. She slowed the car as she crept around the circle and then barely coasted as they drove past the barbecue and bait shop that was her former daughter-in-law's new business.

"Good God! What a dump!"

Gwen thought of the generous amount of the cash settlement. The young woman could have easily made the down payment on a Dodsonburger franchise with a reasonably good location. Instead, she'd apparently bought this horror show of a run-down restaurant. "I never thought the girl was particularly bright. But here we have vivid evidence that she's plainly stupid."

Sean didn't say a word, but the look he gave her was angry. Gwen didn't apologize. Why should she? She was right.

She continued back up the street to the next corner where she pulled into a gas station. A ragged-looking man with a rusty old van was parked in the next bay.

"Get out and asked directions to this place," Gwen said, attempting to hand her son the handwritten memo that Myra had given her.

Sean turned away from her as if pretending that he was going back to sleep. "Ask him yourself," he suggested.

Gwen thought about calling him down for his rudeness, but decided it wasn't worth the argument. She unhitched her seat belt and got out of the car.

"This place is closed on Sunday," the raggedy man informed her immediately. "I'm just airing up a tire."

"I'm just looking for directions," she told him.

As she got closer, he courteously rose to his feet. The behavior, so natural, was that of a gentleman. She realized that he was neither as old nor as unkempt as she'd initially thought. He carried himself with the kind of unselfconscious pride of a man accustomed to much finer clothes and polite company.

"Are you from around here?" she asked him.

"These days I am," he answered. "Who are you looking for?"

"Not who," Gwen answered. "What. Gouswhelter Lake Cabins. Do you know where I can find them?"

"Oh, sure," he said. "You take this next road to the right and…"
He hesitated. "If you'll wait a minute, why don't you just follow
me. I'm headed home and I go right past there. That way you don't
get turned around on all these twisty roads and approaches."

"Oh, fine," she said. "That would be very nice, thank you."

He squatted down again to pump more air into his van's left
front tire.

"What brings you to Warbler Lake?" he asked.

"Summer vacation," she answered, smiling.

He ran a long slow look from her Kate Spade shoes, up her Ann
Taylor slacks and across her Ferre blouse. By the time he locked
eyes with her behind her Bvlgari sunglasses, his gaze was openly
skeptical.

Gwen supposed that she didn't look much like the area's typical tourist, but he didn't ask for further explanation and she didn't
bother to enlighten him. It wasn't really any of his business.

He finished his task and checked the tire pressure with his own
gauge, carried in his shirt pocket. The number apparently suited
him and he stood.

"I'm Lattimer Meicklejohn," he told her. "I won't offer my hand
because I don't want to get grease on you."

Gwen acknowledged his reasoning over protocol with a nod.
Normally she wouldn't have introduced herself to a stranger, but
she knew that rural ways were less formal.

"I'm Gwendolyn Dodson," she told him.

For an instant she thought she saw some kind of recognition
in his eyes, but it was gone so quickly that she decided that she
had imagined it.

He nodded to her companionably. "It's nice to meet you, Gwendolyn," he said. "Now, if you'll just follow me, it's not far and I'll
wave you off when we go by Gouswhelter's."

"Thank you."

She walked over to her car and got inside. Sean was sitting up, no longer pretending laziness.

"We're going to follow this fellow," she told him.

His only response was a grunt.

Gwen pulled out behind the ancient rusting van and made the first right turn in his wake. There were a couple of more rights and a left before the man's arm was visible out of the driver's side window as he indicated with his thumb the turnoff beside the road.

She spotted the wooden sign with the peeling paint that indicated this was, sadly, the right place. Gwen drove the Mercedes up the poorly maintained gravel roadway, only to find the road dropped off suddenly and steeply into a wooded area. Her foot firmly on the brake, she maneuvered around the trees on either side of the track, praying fervently that no one would come barreling up in the opposite direction. The trail wound its way through the cool shade for what seemed like a very long distance. Then finally, surprisingly, they came out of the woods and into the sunlight with the bright vision of the lake before them.

The drive led to the front of a modest two-story house. A sign hanging from the porch railing declared it to be the office.

"This must be it," Gwen said brightly as she parked the car.

Sean's response was negligible, but Gwen was grateful that at least he got out of the car without her having to urge him.

There was an old man sitting in a rocking chair on the front porch. He had a small knife in one hand and a large chunk of wood in the other. His lap and the floor around him covered with tiny slivered shavings.

He appeared very pleased to see them, eagerly waving them up on the porch.

"Well, hello there, ma'am, mister," he said to them. "It's pretty weather that's brought you out here this afternoon, I'm thinking."

"It is a lovely day," Gwen agreed. "We have reservations for two of the cabins—"

"I'm Gus," he said, setting his work on the porch railing and managing with some difficulty to rise to his feet. "I guess I've been sitting too long. My bones have stiffened up on me." He held out his hand. "Gus Gouswhelter. I built this house myself and all the cabins as well. My boy helps me now. He's a good'un.

"I'm sure he is," Gwen said politely. "I was hoping that—"

"Do you like to fish?" The question was directed at Sean.

"No, not particularly."

The old man's eyebrows shot up in surprise. "Well, there ain't that much else to do around here," Gus said. "Oh, we got a nice beach for swimming, but that's mostly for the kids. It's not a good lake for waterskiing or fast boating of any kind. There are lots of shallow shoals and hazards under the surface."

"We aren't here for boating, either," Gwen assured him.

The old man looked puzzled. "Then what are you doing here?" he asked.

Fortunately, the front door burst open and Gwen wasn't pressed to come up with an answer.

"What's going on here?" A middle-aged woman with a teased bowling-ball hairdo and a neat white apron stepped out on the porch. Her question was directed at Gus rather than her guests and it was full of anger and suspicion.

"I'm just greeting our new visitors," Gus said.

"You got no right to do that," she snarled at him. "This is my business, I bought it and it don't concern you one iota. You just keep to yourself and keep your mouth shut!"

The harshness of the woman's tone was so off-putting and over the top, Gwen was completely taken aback. She hardly had time to take it in, before the woman turned to her all smiles, like Mr. Hyde transforming back into Dr. Jekyll.

"Welcome to Gouswhelter Lake Cabins," she said. "I'm Birdie Gouswhelter and we're so tickled to have you staying with us. You're the people from St. Louis, right? Two single cabins with a view for the whole summer?"

The woman was holding out her hand, her open, pleasant demeanor such a contrast that it took some determination on Gwen's part to make the transition.

"Uh…yes," Gwen admitted. "I'm Gwendolyn Dodson, and this is my son, Sean."

"Dodson?" The question came from Gus. "Ain't that the name of the new gal at the B & B? Are you folks kin?"

Gwen hesitated. In a small community like this it was certain that everyone would find out everything about everyone else. She also knew that it was possible that local gossip might ultimately help her in some way, but she hated to wade into that immediately.

Her choice in the matter was taken away before she had a chance to decide.

"Didn't I tell you to keep your mouth shut!" the woman said, turning to rail at Gus.

"Katy Dodson is my ex-wife," Sean volunteered.

"Is that so," Gus said, completely tuning out Birdie. "Is that young'un your boy?"

"Yes, he is."

"Oh, he's a good'un," Gus told him, smiling. "Smart as a whip, he is, and got proper manners already. You and that gal are surely raising him right."

"Katy gets most of the credit for that," Sean said.

"Nonsense," Gwen countered. "Sean is too modest. The child comes from a fine family. Good genetics is very important."

Gus nodded. "I can see that the boy favors you."

Sean was beaming from the faint praise.

"So you're down here to spend the summer with the little fellow," Gus said.

"Why are you playing twenty questions with my guests?" Birdie asked furiously. "Go back to your make-work nonsense and let me show these people to their cabins before they get it in their mind to go somewhere else."

"There ain't no place else, Birdie," Gus said. Dutifully, he went back to his rocking chair, his face as dark as a thundercloud.

"If you'll just point us in the right direction and give us our keys," Gwen suggested.

"We don't have keys, around here you don't need them. We don't have crime or such as that."

Gwen opened the car's trunk and Sean took her hanging clothes bag and mounted his small duffel atop her rolling portmanteau. She carried her computer and briefcase as they followed Birdie along the path toward the lake.

"I gave you two of the remotest cabins," she said. "Way up here you won't hear a thing from us or anyone else. But it's a quick walk down the lakeshore to town, the park, the beach and the dock."

Looking around, Gwen wondered if this is what it felt to step through a time warp. If she squinted she could almost see the vacations of her 1950s childhood. The cabins were nestled among the trees a respectful distance from one another. Each had a front porch that faced the lake and a fireplace chimney. There were no actual windows, but she could see on the cabin that Birdie was directing her to that top-hinged shutter doors on three sides of the little building were propped open, revealing a layer of wire mesh screening to keep the bugs at bay.

"This one over there is yours," she said to Sean. "We'll get your mama settled first and I'll take you over there."

Sean nodded. Gwen glanced in the direction that Birdie had

indicated. The other cabin appeared to be identical and was about fifty yards away.

"Close enough to call for help," Birdie said. "And far enough away not to be a bother."

A well-placed chunk of limestone served as the step onto the narrow porch. Two aged cane-bottom chairs were leaned against the wall. Birdie opened the screen door and allowed Gwen and Sean to go in first.

The place was, Gwen thought gratefully, neat as a pin and very clean, although the furniture was sparse. The double bed in one corner took up most of the room. Next to it was a built-in chest with two drawers and a small mirror on top. There was one armchair next to the fireplace and a small drop-leaf table where one could sit for meals. The kitchen consisted of a narrow sink, two-burner hot plate and an under-the-cabinet refrigerator.

"The bathroom is in here," Birdie said, indicating a small room at the back about the size of a standard closet. "There's no tub, but you can take a nice shower. Don't let the water run too long before you get in. The hot water tank is only five gallons and when that's gone you get cold in a hurry."

Gwen was nodding politely as she mentally rearranged the room into a workable office. The kitchen table would not be a particularly comfortable setup, but it was manageable.

"I don't suppose you have high-speed access," Gwen stated.

Birdie stared at her mutely, befuddled, as if she'd just addressed her in Japanese.

"Where's the phone jack? The place where the phone plugs in."

"Oh, I've got a pay phone up in the office at the house," Birdie said. "It costs fifty cents now to make a local call."

"There's no phone in the cabin?"

"No, ma'am," Birdie answered defensively. "You didn't ask me about a phone. If you'd asked me, I would have told you, but you didn't ask me."

Gwen was sure that she hadn't. It wouldn't have occurred to her that you could rent a room without one.

"It's fine," Gwen said as she calculated the extra trouble in downloading and uploading from her PDA. "I'll just use my cell."

Birdie opened her mouth as if to make a comment and then apparently thought the better of it.

"I'll let you get settled in here and show the young man his place," she said instead. "Towels and essentials are in the bathroom cabinet."

"Fine, thank you," Gwen said.

The woman suddenly seemed to be in a hurry. Gwen was grateful to be left alone.

She dragged her portmanteau up on the bed and opened it up. She took her makeup bag and toiletries to the bathroom, discovering that the only place to put them was on the floor under the sink. She filled the chest of drawers up quickly. When she ran out of space, she decided that the rest would just have to stay packed, and stored the suitcase under the bed. Sean had draped her hanging bag over the footboard, and she picked it up with the intent on storing it in the closet. It was then that she discovered there was no closet, no hangers nor any section set aside for that purpose. She'd brought a suit and several nice blouses. She had no idea what she might need to do or where she might have to go and it was a part of her professional strategy to have plenty of clothes for any possible situation. Gwen felt that if she looked the part, she could always muddle through despite the difficulties.

She surveyed the room for several minutes before deciding that her only closet possibility was hanging her clothes from the fire-place mantel.

She was satisfied she'd made the best of a less-than-optimal situation. This small rustic cabin was to be her living space and the headquarters of her business for the next few months. It was important to make the place as functional as possible.

The distance from her assistant and lack of a land line was an annoyance, but by utilizing technology a competent executive could take care of business from anywhere. Gwen was not unaccustomed to adversity and reminded herself that challenges always invigorated her.

She opened the drop leaves on the little table and began setting up her office. She plugged in her laptop and laid out her papers in a usable system. She needed to get in contact with Myra and check her e-mail. After a couple of minutes familiarizing herself with the Internet-uploading option on her computer, she retrieved her PDA from her purse. Quickly she punched in the correct codes. It didn't work. She tried again. Still it didn't work. She glanced down at the PDA, wondering what the problem might be. The screen had a bright message all in capitals. THIS AREA NO SERVICE.

Bitsy's Wisdom 14

Bitsy's Wisdom 14: Rub down your clean cooking grate with a smidgeon of oil. It will cut down on cursing when you're taking the meat off.

Emma was surprised that Curt met her at the dock. He greeted Latt politely and inquired about the day's catch.

"Emma did better than me," the older guy told him. "I swear that girl is a natural. I'm going to try to talk her into being my regular Sunday morning fishing buddy."

He put the suggestion out there like a direct challenge. Curt didn't rise to it but merely laughed it off.

"Nadine gave me a sack lunch to go," he said. "I figured you'd be starving after a morning out on the water."

Emma was hungry.

"Nadine's serving takeout now?" Latt asked. "I tell you, if I turn my back on this town for a minute, I never know what I'll come back to."

The joking comment was so far from the truth, it wasn't even funny. Emma offered a groan instead of a laugh and allowed Curt to help her out of the boat.

"I caught four fish," she announced. "I've never been out on a boat in my life and I caught four fish."

Curt nodded solemnly. "You had a good time?" he asked.

"Oh, yes."

He feigned a serious glance toward Latt. "So, I guess you can signal that scuba diver who's been putting the fish on the end of her line to come out of the water now."

Emma playfully slugged him in the ribs.

"Come on up the trail," he said, indicating the path that she'd spotted that morning. "There's a great high spot, just perfect for a Sunday lunch."

She was being led away when she turned abruptly.

"Oh, my fish," she said.

Latt waved her off. "I'll drop them by the B & B," he said. "You've got enough here to invite the preacher for dinner."

Emma didn't even know if she *wanted* to invite Curt for dinner, but he accepted immediately.

"Go on, kids," Latt said. "Have some fun."

They walked down the dock, across the small stretch of beach, past the entrance railing and on to the privacy of the mountain path. Emma could still hear the lap of the water, but it seemed far away beneath the shady canopy of green leaves. The sunlight pierced through at intervals creating a dappled walkway of light and shadow.

Curt took her hand, which to Emma felt a bit more friendly than they actually were. The idea that his congregation was praying they'd be a couple and even Latt, apparently, thought that they were, was more disconcerting than she liked to admit. She didn't want Curt to start believing that the two of them were going to get together, because it just wasn't going to happen. And she needed to tell him that.

"I'm sorry about blowing off church this morning," she said instead.

She was surprised at the lie emerging from her own lips. She rarely went to a Sunday service and she felt no guilt whatsoever about missing this morning.

"A lot of people feel that they can be as close to God on the lake or in the woods," he said. "I don't personally ascribe to that view, but I can understand it."

"I wasn't communing with God," she confessed. "I was catching fish."

He smiled. "Our Lord was a great admirer of fishermen, you know," he told her. "They were the men he chose to be around him."

"Yeah, I guess so."

"When I imagine St. Peter," Curt said, "in my mind I find he often looks and sounds a lot like Lattimer Meicklejohn."

Emma's jaw dropped open in shock and then she laughed out loud.

"You're kidding, right?"

"No, I think those two would have a lot in common."

"Except Latt is not religious," she said.

Curt nodded. "He's lost his faith. But it's the kind of thing that sometimes happens to people who've been dealt a blow that is inexplicable. But they often find belief again, when they allow themselves to."

Emma wasn't sure she agreed, but refrained from saying so.

"I am sorry that you didn't hear my sermon," he said. "A lot of what I came up with occurred to me when I was thinking about you."

"About me? You're kidding?"

"I was thinking how you've come to our town to help your

sister," he said. "The B & B isn't yours, you're at the lake for only a few months and you've made it clear that this is not the place that you really want to be. Still, you're here, helping, encouraging. Only good can come from that."

"Are you sure?" Emma asked him. "'Cause it seems to me that if I had been firmer with Katy, she might be sitting in a nice, snug apartment in St. Louis with cash in the bank."

"You had to let her make her own choices," Curt said. "And I'm convinced that when you take action with positive intent, eventually things turn out that way."

"How long is 'eventually'?"

Curt shrugged. "Well, I admit it could be a very, very long time."

"But ultimately it works out," Emma said.

He nodded.

"Is that biblical, Pastor Curt, or just a personal philosophy?"

"Maybe a little of both," he answered. "But I can always quote 'all things work together for good.'"

"Ministers use that one a lot, huh?"

"It does come in handy," he admitted with a grin.

The discussion drifted off as the path became steeper, with occasional jutting corners of limestone acting as steps. She was grateful for Curt's hand as he went ahead of her adding pull to her climb. It went up and up. They came to a fork in the trail. The well-worn direction paralleled and headed downward. The less-traveled path was rough and more overgrown. It continued straight up. Curt headed that way. Emma followed, sometimes holding his hand, sometimes requiring both of hers to navigate the ascent.

She was nearly out of breath when she reached the top, but it was worth it. As she stepped out of the tree cover and into full sunshine, the lake stretched out before her, beautiful, glistening, like a giant blue sapphire nestled down within dark green mountains.

"Oh, wow."

Curt was smiling. "It's the best view of the lake," he said. "It's pretty from almost any perspective, but up here it is magnificent."

He was right. It was easy to lose oneself in the beauty of it, the vivid color, the sparkling freshness, the sense of magic about the place. Emma stood there, awed for several minutes. It was only when she realized that Curt's hand was on her shoulder that she moved.

"It's very nice," she told him. "Thank you for bringing me up here."

"Oh, you would have found the place on your own eventually," he said. "I just wanted you to associate it with me."

Emma glanced over at him to see if he was kidding. She couldn't tell.

"Come sit here," he said, indicating a sun-warmed boulder.

Emma scooted up onto it and made herself comfortable. Curt handed her the paper bag; its contents included a plastic container with a snap-on lid. Inside the baked beans, potato salad and coleslaw had invaded one another's territory on the edges and coated the underside of the crispy chicken on the bottom, but it was the kind of taste mixing that always made picnic food so special.

Emma picked up the chicken in her fingers and took a bite. She made sounds of positive appreciation as she chewed.

Curt smiled at her.

"I guess I forgot to bring you a napkin," he said. "You're welcome to use the tail of my shirt."

She shook her head and wiped her mouth with her hand. "No thanks, my own clothes make a perfect, if slightly fishy-smelling, tablecloth. This chicken is very good. Did you fix this?"

"Me? I'm the guy who eats two or three meals a day at your place," he said. "Nadine fixed it. She brings lunch every Sunday for her kids."

"Really?"

He nodded. "Yeah, she sends Parker and Brianna to church by themselves and then waits for them in the park with the baby."

"I wonder why she doesn't come to church herself," Emma mused. "Is she another one who's lost her faith?"

Curt shrugged. "I think she's just lost generally," he said, and then quickly clarified his words. "Not lost in the religious sense. She just seems like a person who got off on a sideroad on life's highway and can't figure out where to get back onto the main traffic flow."

"I guess that's how she ended up here," Emma said. "Warbler Lake may not be the ends of the earth, but I think you can see it from here."

Curt tutted reprovingly at her. "You capture our fish, you enjoy our view and you still have disparaging comments to make about the place."

She smiled at him. "It's a nice place," Emma admitted. "But it's not the place for me. I think when you find your place, you want to stay. I've been trying to get out of here since the day I showed up."

"You haven't left yet," he pointed out.

"Katy needs me," she answered. "As long as she needs me, I'll be here."

"And when she doesn't need you?"

Emma grinned. "Then I've got things to do and people to see," she told him. "I want to study anthropology. I want to travel to distant places and study native people. That's my plan."

"Oh." Curt sounded slightly deflated. Emma thought that was undoubtedly for the better. She thought he might be taking the community's matchmaking plans a little more seriously than he should.

"Now, Katy, she's a homebody," Emma said. "She loves this place and she fits right in here."

"She seems like a very nice person," he said.

It was at that minute that the idea came to her. Curt was a nice guy, with two responsible jobs and a need to find a wife. Her sister, Katy, was a wonderful homebody. She'd loved being married. She was a wonderful mother to Josh and wanted, maybe even needed, to have more kids.

Emma suddenly realized that this, more than a stable business, was what could make her sister's life. As she listened to Curt talk about the people of Warbler Lake as neighbors, friends and family, Emma imagined for the first time in a long time what it might really be like for Katy to be out on her own.

She visualized her sister, safe, secure, happy and content in this little community for long decades to come. Emma, herself, would be jetting in and out. After finishing school, she'd be traveling all over the world learning everything that she could learn. And then returning to this place from time to time, to rest and relax and see Katy and Josh. It could be a solution, a very good solution. The best thing for everyone.

"What?" Curt said, catching her attention.

"What? What?"

"Your expression completely changed," he said. "You suddenly look entirely different than I've ever seen you before. What happened? Was it something I said?"

"No, no," she assured him. "I was just thinking about Warbler Lake and about my sister."

"It's a great place, Emma," he told her. "But there is one thing that you're right about. There is nothing for couples to do."

"No, there's not," she said. "But there are not a lot of couples here, either."

He disagreed. "There are tons of couples. Most of them are older and married, but they're still couples."

"Yeah, I guess so."

"The only time anything goes on here of an entertainment na-

ture is during fishing tournaments. And that's always for the tourists. There ought to be something we can do to entertain couples,
our couples, on a regular basis."

"That's a great idea," Emma said. "And you know, Katy is really good at this sort of thing. I know if you'd approach her about
this, she'd come up with a fabulous idea."

"Do you think so?"

"I know so. She's very social and people love her. Anything that
she plans, everyone will show up to."

"Okay then," he said. "I'll talk to her. Maybe tomorrow."

"No, let's go talk to her right now."

"Now?"

"Yes, you're not working, she's not working, it's the perfect time
to talk to her."

"But what about the beautiful day?" he asked. "Our walk around
the lake?"

"Look at those clouds coming in," she said, pointing off into
the distance. "I bet it's going to rain, anyway."

She knew he was disappointed, but she ran roughshod over
those feelings and he was a good-enough sport not to whine
about it. They made it down the steep sloping path at least twice
as quickly as the climb up and through the wooded trail with none
of the dawdling expected of a Sunday-afternoon stroll. Emma just
kept walking and with every step she subtly praised her sister's virtues and temperament.

Curt kept up with her the whole way allowing Emma to do
most of the talking.

When they reached the B & B and Katy was nowhere in sight,
she suggested they check upstairs. She found her sister in the
kitchen scrubbing away.

"Don't you get enough of this during the week?" Emma asked
her facetiously.

Katy chuckled. "I can't have Nadine coming in here to bake in the morning and finding the place a mess."

Her sister looked a little bit of a mess herself, but fortunately Katy was so attractive that she could even pull that off.

"I see you found her," she said to Curt. "I thought you were going on a hike."

"It looks like it's going to rain," Curt answered.

"That's what Latt told me," Katy said, and then turned to Emma. "He cleaned your fish, brought them here, along with cooking directions. I put them in the refrigerator."

"Oh, great," Emma answered. "Where's Josh?"

"He played so hard at the park that we decided he could take a little afternoon nap."

Perfect, Emma thought to herself.

"Curt's got an idea he wants you to help him with," Emma said. "You two go out and sit on the roof garden. I'll bring us all a glass of tea."

She hurried them through the kitchen doors and took her time brewing tea, getting glasses and filling them with ice. She lingered in the kitchen as long as she could, feeling more excited and hopeful than she'd been since the day they'd moved to this place.

When it seemed as if her absence would appear too noticeable, she put the glasses on a tray and carried them out to the comfortable little rooftop space.

"You're right about your sister," Curt said immediately. "I'm thinking we could have some kind of weekly church social and she's come up with a spectacular idea."

"What?" Emma asked.

"We're going to start having music on Saturday nights," Katy said.

Emma frowned. "But we have to work Saturday nights," she said.

Katy's smile was so full of life it almost glittered. "That's the best part," she said. "Bitsy's used to have music. Remember Spurl's story of his first date with his wife? We're going to revive that old tradition."

"Katy, how will we afford musicians?" she asked.

"We won't have musicians, we'll have volunteers," she answered. "And we'll have a jar for people to put money in."

"Do you think people will perform for tips?"

"Sure they will," Curt said. "You'll be surprised at how many secret talents there are just hanging around waiting for this kind of invitation."

"We've already got that old piano," Katy said. "Curt's going to get Deacon Ambrose to tune it up."

"I thought that old fellow was deaf," Emma said.

"Well, he is very hard of hearing," Curt admitted. "But he once made a living as a piano tuner, so we'll see what he's still got."

"I can hardly wait for our first big show," Katy said. "Once we get it started, there'll be no stopping us."

Their enthusiasm was contagious. Emma wasn't sure if the plan would be successful, but she could see Curt and Katy working together on it. That couldn't be anything but good news.

Their excitement was abruptly interrupted by a tap on the kitchen door. They all looked over to see Lattimer Meicklejohn standing there.

"Sorry just to walk into your house," he said. "I knocked at the front, but I thought Josh might still be sleeping and I didn't want to make a noisy entrance."

"Come on out here," Katy said. "We're hatching up a plan for big Saturday-night entertainment downstairs."

Excited, they filled Latt in on the details.

"Sounds great," he said. "Sounds really great."

Emma could see that he was trying to be enthusiastic, but that something was not quite right. She got to her feet.

"I'm going to get some more tea," Emma said. "Latt, come help me."

Faking a big smile for Curt and Katy, she grabbed Latt's arm and led him into the semi-privacy of the kitchen.

"What's going on?" she asked immediately.

"Nothing…well, maybe nothing," he said. "I don't know, I just got a weird feeling and I thought I ought to say something about it. You girls aren't hiding out here from anybody, are you?"

"Hiding out? No, of course not."

"Good, because they've found you."

"Huh?"

"Two strangers just blew into town," he said. "A woman about my age and a man about yours. They've got the same last name as your sister, Katy."

Uncharacteristically Emma swore.

Bitsy's Wisdom *15*

Bitsy's Wisdom 15: If the water is murky and dim, a juicy bait like a wadded night crawler or catalpa worm can get a fish's attention.

The rain started late in the afternoon. It woke Gwen up. With no way to contact her office, no phone, no fax, no e-mail, she'd found herself with time on her hands and nothing to do. Napping had not been a deliberate choice. She simply lay down for lack of a comfortable place to sit and had fallen fast asleep. She awakened with a crick in her neck and a growling stomach. She wandered drowsily, aimlessly, around the narrow confines of the cabin for a couple of minutes, doing things that were not undone and straightening things that weren't unstraight. She checked the fridge to discover the truth she'd learned from Old Mother Hubbard decades ago, if you don't buy food, then the cupboard remains bare.

She stood by the front door for several minutes just staring out into the wet, gray solitude. There was a loneliness about it that was almost palpable. Perhaps it was the sense of being closed off from the rest of the world. A person thought that her life was full of people and then a rainy day could unexpectedly emphasize the fact that she was really all by herself. Thoughts of Garrett came to her, of course. Mostly out of habit than from genuine longing. She'd been widowed now longer than she'd ever been married. Normally, she was too busy to notice. But in the absence of purpose, longing raised its inexorable head.

Determinedly, she went to the minuscule bathroom, and in the dim light of the overhead bulb she brushed her hair and refreshed her makeup. She and Sean would go find a nice restaurant and have a lovely dinner together. She'd call him and tell him to meet her at the car. She picked up the phone before remembering that it didn't work.

With a growl of dissatisfaction she located her small, convenient purse umbrella. It was tiny and hardly covered her head and shoulders, but on a typical day it was perfectly sufficient to get from her office door to her Mercedes. It was not, she quickly discovered, all that useful in dealing with a downpour in the woods.

Gwen made her way along the path to Sean's cabin, head down, dodging puddles. She was grateful to step up on his porch.

"Sean!" she called out. "Sean?"

There was no answer. Was this the right cabin? She tried the screen door. It opened easily, and once inside, she turned on the light. Her son's duffel was sitting just inside the doorway. No attempt had been made to unpack. Like herself, he'd obviously taken a nap. His bed was a mess of balled-up sheets tossed to one side.

"Sean," she called again, although she knew he wasn't there. *Okay, I'll just eat by myself,* she thought.

But before she left, she straightened up the bed, smoothing the sheets, carefully tucking the corners, fluffing the pillows. Gwen didn't examine her action or her motives. Doing things for Sean, things that she knew were obviously his own responsibility, had become a habit. If questioned she might have answered that she was simply doing something nice for her son, grateful that he was going along with her in her pursuit of her grandson.

But there was also a message, less altruistic, which was to remind Sean that the *right* thing to do when one got out of a bed was to immediately put it back in order. He failed to live up to her standards and she thought he needed to know that.

Outside the rain continued to fall. She held the small umbrella over her head and splashed her way up the trail to the parked car. By the time she'd fumbled with the lock and gotten inside, she could add wet and cold to the problem of hungry.

Gwen had imagined that Sean might be at the office, but the Gouswhelter business/residence was dark and empty. She started up the car and fiddled with the GPS navigation for a few minutes. Usually it would give her information on nearby restaurants. But for some reason the only thing that was showing up was Bitsy's Bait & BBQ. She decided that she'd just drive until she found something.

She backed out of the parking lot and headed for the entrance of Gouswhelter Lake Cabins. She remembered vaguely that there really had not been anything on the road they drove in on. So it made the most sense to go in the opposite direction. Gwen turned right onto the blacktop road just as it began to rain harder. A little soggy weather was never a serious deterrent. The road, however, was slippery and dark. It was bad enough that there were no streetlights, but the overhang of the trees and the lack of even painted white lines on the road surface made it difficult for her to even see where she was headed. Gamely she continued on, though she was beginning to wish she'd stayed in her cabin. The road curved around and around and fishtailed back in the other direction. She crept along it mile after mile with the expectation that around the next curve was a brightly lit motel with an all-night

restaurant attached. As the distance passed, she was willing to settle for a gas station with a bag of stale potato chips and a cup of
coffee. But nothing.

Finally, she decided that she would have to turn around. Even
that was easier said than done. The road was narrow, the shoulder
nonexistent and the bends in the road were so frequent and so
steep that traffic coming in either direction would be blindsided
by a car making a turnabout. Eventually, she came to a wider spot
where she was able to make a U-turn. As she headed back the way
she came, she relaxed, realizing for the first time how tense she'd
been. She was still hungry, the road was still dark and the rain was
falling harder, but somehow retreating seemed safer. The primitive cabin she'd left behind so casually had been transformed in
her mind to a warm, comfortable haven from the storm.

Gwen became more accustomed to the winding mountain
blacktop, and as she made her way through the night, she gradu-
ally went a bit faster and faster.

She began thinking about Josh, imagining him in her life and
what that would mean. There would, of course, be a lot more
working from home. But she could do that, especially when she
got back to the world of the cell phone tower and the PDA. He
would probably be traumatized from being estranged from his
mother, but her love and the advantages that she could give him
would overcome that, she was sure.

Sean would have to play it very carefully. If he pushed too hard,
there was no telling how Katy might react. And if he didn't push
at all, then she'd continue to make the rules and have all the advantages on her side. Gwen knew that she would win. She had no
doubts about that. But she wanted to win with the least damage
to Sean and without Josh being poisoned against her by Katy.

She tried to imagine Josh living in her house. She would re-
decorate a bedroom, of course. And maybe change the family

room to make it more cool and up-to-date with the latest tech toys. She imagined him taking piano lessons, going to soccer practice, laughing with her over joke books. Hers was a warm, happy image, a Kodak moment of family life. It was then that she realized she was no longer imagining a future, she was remembering a past and the boy she saw in her mind was her own.

The smile on her face faded and the joy in her heart turned to lead.

"Oh, Sean," she moaned aloud. "What happened to you?"

Lost as she was in that thought, it was a half minute before she realized that she was hydroplaning. She'd come around the corner too fast and her big, heavy Mercedes was now skimming across the top of the wet pavement. She tried to adjust, steering away from the skid, only to find that she'd overcorrected and was now careering toward the other side of the roadway. Again she tried to veer away from the trees that were racing into her path and then there was an open space, a break in the sentinels of post oak and pine. With the instinct of self-preservation, Gwen headed for it and managed to bring the car to a halt, straddling a drainage ditch at the front of a property entrance.

She sat there for a moment, stunned and shaking. Then she realized that she was all right. Mentally she scolded herself for not keeping her attention on the road. But she still wanted to go home. The engine continued to run, but when she tried to pull away from her position, terrible scraping sounds were heard. She tried putting the car in Reverse. She couldn't even move. Back to Drive she tried again, and more loud, scraping sounds, as if the whole underside of her car was being ripped off. She stopped. This was not good. It was not good at all.

She grabbed her purse from the passenger seat and sifted through it until she found her PDA. She was trying to think of who to call, when she realized she still didn't have any towers. She couldn't call anyone.

What do you do when you can't call for help? she wondered to herself. You walk.

With her tiny inefficient umbrella, she got out of the car. Although she was completely out of the roadway, she was blocking a property entrance, so she left the emergency flashers on. She wondered how far she was from the Gouswhelters'. It could be just around the corner. Or it could be five miles. Fear of the latter had her peering down the well-kept approach to a house with a light on. When she saw it, she didn't think twice about heading off the public roadside onto a private lane in a part of the world with which she was completely unfamiliar.

Gwen was wet and cold and miserable before she'd even gone ten yards. She would have thought that the canopy of trees would have provided some protection, but it didn't feel that way. She trudged on. In the complete blackness of the night, she stepped into puddle after puddle. Her shoes were not just soaked but sloshing. The distance to the house was quite a bit farther than it had seemed from the road. When she got close enough to see the porch, she picked up the pace until she was almost running.

That's when she heard the dog.

He came racing out toward her, growling ominously. Gwen stopped stock-still. That's what she'd always heard she was supposed to do. If an animal comes after you, don't move. That's what she did.

The dog stopped a few feet away from her, snarling and growling and barking. She didn't move. The water continued to drip down from her undersize umbrella and she didn't move. Her shoes sunk deeper and deeper into the muddy ground and she didn't move. The dog barked and barked and she still didn't move.

Finally the door to the house opened. Relief was immediately swallowed up by fear as a man stepped out on the porch carrying a shotgun.

"What've you got out here, Sparky, a possum?" the armed resident called out.

"Don't shoot!" Gwen pleaded.

"Good grief! Sparky! Get back here."

Immediately, the dog relaxed his posture, and tail wagging, the animal sauntered back toward the dry shelter of the porch overhang.

"Sorry, ma'am," the gunman said to her. "Sparky wouldn't hurt a flea."

Perhaps the fleas were safe, but Gwen was not certain about herself.

"I've run my car off the road. Can I borrow your phone to call a towing service?"

"Sure," he said. "You can call, though I doubt you'll get Pearly to come out in this weather."

"But—"

"Come on in," he told her. "You're not going to get any drier standing out in it."

She was hesitant to follow the suggestion, but there was nothing else to do.

Gwen slogged her way through the yard; the ground beneath her feet had the consistency of peanut butter.

"Sorry about the mud," he said. "I keep thinking every year that the grass will grow, but Sparky keeps the lawn dug up all the time."

It wasn't until she stepped up onto the porch that she recognized him.

"You're the man from the gas station," she said.

He nodded. "Latt," he reminded her. "And you're Mrs. Dodson."

"Yes."

"Come on in, but maybe you'd better leave those shoes out

here," he suggested. "And don't worry, Sparky's a barker but he doesn't chew."

Gwen slipped off her muddy shoes, thinking to herself that the dog might as well chew them, they were completely ruined, anyway. In stocking feet, she stepped over the threshold into the little house. A strange feeling came over her. The place was very masculine, floor to ceiling with crowded bookcases, strange pieces of primitive pottery, and canvases, both large and small were tucked into every spare nook of the room, all featuring bright brilliant sunsets in vivid oils.

The sense of welcome was so strong that she almost felt as if she'd been there before.

"Got ya."

"I beg your pardon?"

"The house," he said. "It got you, right? It did the same thing to me the first day I walked in. It must have like killer feng shui or something." He gestured toward the wall of glass at the far end of the room. "Wait until you see it with the lake view. It's just perfect."

Gwen had no intention of seeing it with the lake view. It was a very comfortable house, but she was eager to get her car out of the ditch and get to her uncomfortable cabin down the road.

"What were you doing out driving in the rain?" he asked her.

She felt like answering that it was none of his business, but instead she found herself relating the facts.

"I took a nap and woke up hungry," she said. "I went out looking for a restaurant, but I couldn't find one."

"The only thing around here is Bitsy's B & B," he said. "And it's closed on Sunday, though I guess you wouldn't want to go there. I've got fish I was going to fix for dinner. I just hadn't quite got around to it. Give me a half hour and I can serve you a very nice meal."

"Oh, no," she insisted. "I'll just borrow your phone to call the tow truck."

"I'm telling you, Pearly won't come in this rain," he said. "And even if by some miracle he does, you'll still be hungry. Come on."

He walked into the little kitchen off the side of the main room. It, too, was brightly lit with a small table in a corner full of windows.

"Really it's not necessary, I—"

At the exact instant that she made her denial, her stomach growled. Gwen put her hand on her abdomen as if to quiet her hunger, but Latt heard it and laughed in her face.

"You're hungry, I've got food. We don't have to be in a brain trust to figure this one out."

It did sound reasonable.

"All right, maybe I'll have a quick bite," she said.

"Good, good," he said. "It'll just take me a second to get something together. The bathroom is through that door across the living room. Go dry off, get a towel, whatever."

Suddenly, that sounded like an excellent idea. Gwen went through the doorway that he'd indicated. A small bedroom, with window views, was neat and no-nonsense. The bathroom was clean and well lit. That was not exactly the good news. Gwen caught sight of herself in the mirror and nearly screamed in fright. The umbrella had kept her hair mostly dry, but the moisture had it lying like a limp rug atop her head. Her makeup, what was left of it, had dribbled down in unpleasant furrows along her cheekbones. Her slacks were damp and clingy. Her blouse was apparently not designed for inclement weather. She peeled it off her body and shook it out. It was sodden and dripping. She hung it on the doorknob. The slacks she removed as well and was able to actually wring water out of the pant legs. She dried off as best she could.

There was a fluffy bathrobe hanging from a hook and she

longed to wrap herself in it. But that was not a good idea. The whole situation put her in mind of some ancient Doris Day movie, where the heroine stupidly surrenders her clothes only to discover that the hero has designs upon her.

It wasn't so bad, just wrapping the towel around herself and waiting in the bathroom. It felt so warm and so safe, but as the fish began cooking and the smell wafted its way through the walls, her stomach had begun to growl once more. She washed her face and combed her hair. Totally free of makeup, she looked every day of her fifty-three years. She turned to don her wet clothing once more. And she just couldn't do it.

"You're not Doris Day, you're somebody's grandmother," she reminded herself aloud.

With that thought, she pulled on the robe and it was just as soft and warm and comfortable as she'd imagined. And it smelled, surprisingly, like licorice. She pulled it together tightly and it almost wrapped around her double. She tied the sash securely and, gathering up her clothes, went out to see what was for dinner.

The food smelled great. She stepped into the kitchen to see him busy at the stove sautéeing vegetables.

"May I put these in your clothes dryer?" she asked.

He glanced up. If he was surprised to see her in his bathrobe, he didn't say so.

"Sure," he answered. He turned and took the wet things from her. "Keep stirring the veggies, will you."

Gwen stepped up to the stove, taking his place as she used a wooden spoon to keep the brightly colored assortment of squash, sweet potatoes and peppers from sticking to the bottom of the pan.

Latt started up the dryer and then returned to take over the cooking.

"Have a seat," he told her. "I'd say real food is less than two minutes away."

She turned to the table to see that it was already set, rather nicely, with a linen tablecloth and napkins. A bottle of wine sat uncorked and waiting next to two long-stemmed glasses. Gwen raised a skeptical eyebrow, as visions of Dear Doris returned once more. She tugged slightly at the bathrobe and sat down.

She allowed her gaze to take in the entire room. There was a homey aspect to the kitchen, but it also felt chic and professional. She wasn't sure how it managed those two things simultaneously, but she was certain that if this man could bottle it, designers would spend a fortune to purchase the feeling.

"Do you cook a lot?" she asked him.

"Not so much," he answered. "Cooking for one is my least favorite thing about my single status. I'm sure it's the same for you."

"Hmm," Gwen commented without admitting agreement.

Latt opened the oven and took out the glass baking dish that was inside. The sounds of the kitchen, the pop of hot oil, the whistle of steam, the clanging of pans was a music that was nostalgic to her. Garrett had loved to cook, of course. And in the early days of their marriage, before he became so successful and busy, he often cooked for her in their little kitchen, not so different from this one. The pleasantness of the present and the memory of the past coalesced into a very deep contentedness that tasted as smooth and lingering as the wine she sipped.

"Here we are," he said, bringing the plates over to the table. He set hers directly in front of her. "This may not be St. Louis, but I think I cook up a nice piece of bass."

It did look fabulous. The deboned fish filet was topped with tomato and onion and the vegetable medley appeared just cooked enough to bring out the flavor and to absorb the seasoning. And it was presented in a fashion as appealing as a fine restaurant.

Gwen was aware that she was in the presence of a stranger and wanted to be reserved and reticent. But her hunger trumped her civility and she dug into the meal. It was as tasty as she'd thought it would be. She had several bites of the wonderful fish as well as the vegetables, before she managed any polite small talk. She allowed him to carry the conversation, which he did surprisingly well. He was funny and intelligent. Clever with words and easy to listen to. She had become accustomed, maybe too accustomed, to being the center of her own conversations. But then her typical conversations never covered subjects like weather patterns, insect life or organic herbs. Latt was very succinct and knowledgeable about things she'd never bothered to think about.

"So you grew all of this, including the spices, in your own garden?" she asked.

Latt nodded. "Everything but the fish," he answered. "And I caught him in the lake this afternoon."

"Well, it's all very good," she said.

"Thank you."

"You're going to have to confess," Gwen said. "You do more of this cooking than you admit."

He smiled at her. "They say confession is good for the soul, but I think it's bad for the digestion. More wine?"

He filled her glass.

"Not too much of that," Gwen cautioned. "I may still have to get my car out of the ditch and drive home."

He shook his head. "I called Pearly while you were drying off," he told her. "He said he'd be out here as soon as the rain lets up. Between him and myself, we can get your car back on the road."

"How soon will the rain let up?" Gwen asked, surveying the windows. The water was still coming down steadily.

"Later on tonight, maybe early morning," Latt answered.

"I have to get back to my cabin."

"I'll walk you around there," he said. "It's a half mile on the road, but walking on the lakeshore is maybe half that distance."

"Oh." Gwen felt suddenly foolish. She could have walked to her own cabin. She could be there in her own space, not here in this man's house, dressed in his bathrobe and eating his food.

"You should have said something immediately," she told him. "I'd have gone back to Gouswhelters' and wouldn't have put you to this trouble."

"Now, why would I have done something like that?" he asked her. "So that you could go back to your food-free rental and I could get by on a bowl of cereal all alone. I haven't had a lovely woman for dinner in a very long time."

The compliment soothed her more than she should have let it.

"You're divorced?"

Latt nodded. "Ten years."

"What happened?"

He shrugged. "Nothing dramatic," he said. "We wanted different things. She wanted money and I wanted my time."

"Ahh."

"It was a perfect division of the assets," he said. "She got all my worldly goods. I got my body and soul."

Gwen glanced around. "You seemed to have a few things here and there."

He nodded. "Stuff piles up. I try to live simply, but I still manage to accumulate."

"You have a weakness for sunset art," she said, referring to the numerous canvases he had sitting around.

"Sunrises," he corrected. "Not sunsets, sunrises. I paint them myself. Some of them are pretty nice, but most are ordinary."

She took another sip of her wine.

"Like real life," she said.

He angled his head slightly and raised an eyebrow. "Very astute, Mrs. Dodson," he said. "I can see why you're such a clever businesswoman."

Gwen smiled and was about to thank him for the compliment when the origin of it caught her attention.

"Now, wait a minute," she said. "I've spoken, in total, maybe three dozen sentences to you. Including several why, when and wheres and a 'don't shoot.' But you seem to know who I am, where I live and what I do. How is that possible?"

"See, that's how perceptive you are," Latt said. "You've only been here a few hours and you've already discovered the secret of small-town life. It took me years to understand how personal information can just float along on the breeze so that everybody knows everything about everyone. Even strangers just passing through."

"I don't think I believe you," Gwen said.

"There you go again, hitting the nail on the head. I used to lie for a living."

She knew the statement was facetious. "I don't think they pay people for that," she said.

"You're mistaken," he told her. "They actually pay very well."

She shook her head and picked up her wineglass. "I think perhaps you should explain yourself on that one," she said.

"I prefer not to talk about what I did with my yesterdays," he said. "That's the thing about the sunrises, a whole new start every twenty-four hours."

The concept caught her attention, a whole new start. That was why she was here. Somewhere, somehow, when she was busy keeping a roof over their heads and food on the table, she'd come up short in some way in raising her son to be the man she wanted him to be. She'd tried to fix that, but she was no longer sure that it could be fixed. She hated failure. She pitied it in other people and found it intolerable for herself. Now she had an opportunity to mold success from the ashes of her disappointment. Sean had not turned out to be the man she needed to carry on his father's legacy. But her grandson, Josh, was going to give her another chance.

Bitsy's Wisdom 16

Bitsy's Wisdom: 16: Use unsalted butter. You don't want somebody else deciding how much seasoning is right for you.

The drive had been interminable. Every mile made him more anxious and jumpy. Sean had pretended that he was asleep. That way he didn't have to talk to his mother, he didn't have to go over the plan again. He didn't have to examine his feelings. That was the worst part, actually thinking about what he was doing. It all reminded him very much of the night he'd walked out on Katy. He'd felt exactly the same way. He knew what he was doing was wrong, but he just felt pulled along on the tide of his mother's will.

No, that was not fair, he admonished himself as he stood in the middle of his lonely primitive lake cabin. He had not left Katy just because his mother wanted him to. And he'd not come here just because it was a part of his mother's plan.

His mother was pushy, opinionated and accustomed to having her own way. But she couldn't make him do anything against his will. He had no one to blame for his choices but himself.

He'd walked out on Katy of his own free will.

And now he'd apparently come down here to steal her child away with an equal amount of selfish callousness.

The truth was more complicated than that. He'd come to Warbler Lake for completely different reasons. Most of which he couldn't quite put into words.

And he didn't want to.

Sean ran a worried hand through his thick dark hair. He tried to nap, but only tossed and turned until he got up in disgust. He began pacing back and forth across the narrow stretch of floor, too wound up to sit down.

He wanted to see Josh. He wanted to see Katy. He wasn't sure that he could wait. He was sure he couldn't just hang around in the cabin.

Sean headed out the front door. Without a single glance toward his mother's cabin, he went trudging down the path in the opposite direction from the way in which he'd come. The day was not really hot, but the air was humid and heavy, and even in the shade of the trees, he was sweating.

He was reminded of the summer that Katy was pregnant. They'd just moved into their small third-floor apartment with no elevator and no air-conditioning. They were both working all day. He was putting in especially long hours as much for escape as for extra money. When he'd finally return to the apartment, Katy would be so pleased to see him. She never scolded about the time he was gone. She always pretended that he'd been hard at work, even when he wasn't. She'd fix him a glass of iced tea and chat about her day. Not her real day, of course. She never talked about the heat or her aching back. She never mentioned the long walk to and from the bus stop or the hours on her feet carrying plates full of pancakes for a pittance in tips. Katy always made her life sound fun. She'd see silly things that nobody else noticed. She'd report on the wrens that nested in the top of the bus shelter. She'd talk about the interesting people that she'd shared words with at her tables. And the ongoing soap opera of the restaurant dishwasher's unrequited love for the seating hostess.

She'd always have him relaxed and laughing as they lay awake late into the nights that were too hot for sleeping.

He'd loved being around her. She'd made his life happy.

He'd made her life miserable.

Sean stepped out of the shelter of the trees to stand on the sandy lakeshore. He gazed out over the water. It was pretty, pristine. And the wooded green hills that surrounded it made it seem as cozy and secluded as it was. He'd been to lovely lake resorts all over the country, he'd even been to some famous ones in Europe and New Zealand. This place was tiny in comparison, hidden from development, but in terms of natural beauty it ranked with the best of them.

Sean had done a fair amount of fishing as a teenager and a single man. It had seemed to him to be the perfect father/son sport. So as a fatherless boy he'd been drawn to it, hoping to capture some of those things that his friends with dads took for granted. He'd never be a fishing fanatic, but he'd enjoyed himself. And was aware of the huge numbers of people attracted to the activity and the amount of money this type of recreation could generate.

His mother thought Katy was an idiot to buy a restaurant way out here in the middle of nowhere. She'd made that very clear. But Sean thought maybe his ex-wife was onto something.

Thinking of Katy caused him to begin walking again, this time along the edge of the lake in the direction of the town. His footsteps were muffled, the gentle lap of the water and the call of the birds were the only sounds that intruded on his thoughts. But those thoughts themselves were noisy.

Was he headed in this direction specifically to speak with Katy?

Was he planning to warn her of his mother's plans or threaten her with them? Were his motivations ulterior or just vengeful? He'd decided long ago that his child was better off without him. Had he changed his mind? And if he now wanted to see Josh, did he want to wrench his child away from the only security he'd ever known?

The questions swirled through Sean's mind. The answers eluded him.

He came around a bend in the trail to see the little hamlet ahead of him in the distance. A string of houses, big and small, lined the near side of the road with a solid-looking brick schoolhouse just on the rise above them. And the curvy tree-lined streets had no discernable definition or grid. The far end of town was balanced by the marina with its lines of docks and a wide stretch of open area. The center was pinpointed by the giant fishhook, though the white clapboard church with its tower steeple dominated the scene. He could see Bitsy's. From this long perspective, it didn't look so rustic and run-down. It just looked old-fashioned. A throwback to another era, long gone.

At that moment, despite all the thoughts and feelings about important issues of which he was uncertain, he decided that he liked the little place. He tried to imagine Josh growing up here. It could be an idyllic childhood close to nature and full of small-town friendliness.

Of course, his mother was probably right about the advantages of St. Louis. He was the heir to Dodsonburger and probably should, like Sean, grow up around the business.

Sean, himself, had always been interested in the restaurants. He still loved the work, the atmosphere, the routine. But any proprietary feelings he'd had for Dodsonburger disappeared after his marriage to Katy. If there was one thing that his mother had made crystal clear to him during that time, it was that the business belonged to her. She'd always said that it was his father's legacy to him. But that wasn't how it was. At the time it had hurt him, angered him. But not anymore. Now he just felt estranged from it. Like when he saw a Firebird like the one he drove in high school. He remembered clearly how great it had felt to own it, but now he didn't and the loss was negligible.

As he neared the village, he slowed his pace. He hadn't decided whether to see Katy. He didn't know yet what he wanted to say. In the distance he saw people out on the beach. He thought about joining them, getting lost in the crowd. But he wasn't ready to make small talk with strangers.

He noticed the tire swing in the yard of the restaurant and moved away from the lakeshore deciding to get just close enough to look things over. Obviously Katy and Josh weren't there, but he wanted to see the place where they lived, see the things that they saw.

Sean moved closer, taking it all in, the picnic tables, the huge brick barbecue pit, the toys in the yard. He wondered how much time Josh spent out here. Was he a rough-and-tumble, active guy, eager for baseball and Capture the Flag? Or maybe he was someone sensitive who watched bugs moving along in the grass and tried to put baby birds back into their nests.

Sean leaned against the post of the fence next door watching the empty yard, lost in his imagining.

"Are you a stalker?"

Sean was startled at the question called out to him. He turned toward the house he was standing in front of to see an old lady sitting on her porch.

"If you're looking to buy the place you're too late," she informed him loudly. "Somebody's already got it."

He glanced anxiously at the B & B as adrenaline surged through his veins. The woman's loud voice carried. Someone might hear.

Someone might look out the window and see him. Here. Standing, staring at his ex-wife's house, uninvited. That someone might be Katy.

Sean's first impulse was to simply turn and run. But he knew that kind of stupid reaction would only cause more speculation. Instead, he found the gate to the front walk and headed up to the old woman's porch. At least if he was closer, she wouldn't have to holler.

"Good afternoon," he said as he came up her steps. "I'm Sean and I'm not stalking."

"Then are you selling?" she asked.

"No, ma'am, not stalking or selling, just passing the afternoon."

"Well, have a seat, then," she told him. "There's no better place to pass an afternoon than on this porch. I should know, I do it every day."

Sean considered refusing but decided to sit with her. She was smiling, she appeared to be a friendly, charming old lady. He could spare a few moments to pass the time of day with her. And he could keep an eye on the yard next door while having a quiet conversation. His experience with elderly people being that they were usually content to talk if someone was willing to listen.

"I'm Luella Bullock," she told him.

"Very happy to make your acquaintance," Sean responded, deliberately putting on the best manners his mother had taught him. "Have you lived here long?"

"Oh, yes, indeed! My father-in-law built this old house and I moved in as a new bride," she said. "The Bullocks had a little grocery store down the road. My husband began running it in 1939. That was before there was anything else built up around here. Back then it was just farms and a few fishermen coming and going."

Sean glanced around, thinking that it didn't seem so different from that right now, but decided not to say so.

"So you must have seen plenty from this porch."

"I should say so," Mrs. Bullock agreed. "Everything that needed to be seen and more than a few things I would have been happy to have never known about."

Sean laughed. "I suppose so."

"When I moved out here some of my girlfriends from Springfield were very worried about me," she said. "They thought that without parties and such, I might just expire from boredom."

"But that didn't happen."

"Places aren't boring, the people in them might be boring, but places are not."

"And the people here?" Sean asked.

"Oh, definitely not."

Sean sat across from her, smiling and nodding.

"I bet this old barbecue place has a lot of stories to tell," he said, leading.

"Bitsy's? I knew that woman for forty years," Mrs. Bullock said. "She was a fine, hardworking old gal. And her business was the hub of this community. There were buckets of tears shed at her funeral, that's for sure. And more than a few of those were for the loss of a place to idle away the long hours."

Sean smiled.

"When my husband, Carlton, was alive, we went over there at least one night a week," she said. "Usually on the weekends when they had live music and dancing. We could sure cut up a rug. It was great fun and such good food, oh my mouth waters, just remembering it."

"It's been around for a long time," Sean said.

"Just opened back up," she told him. "A couple of nice girls from the city came down here and paid cash money for the place."

"Really," Sean answered, pretending ignorance.

"They seem real sweet and eager to make a go of the place."

"That's good."

"Everyone wants them to stay and tries to throw as much business their way as humanly possible, but the truth is, their barbecue is just awful," she said.

Sean was momentarily caught off guard by the revelation. Mrs. Bullock must have read his disbelief in his expression.

"I'm not just carrying tales," she said. "Pricy Metcalf brought me a plate over. Pitiful, just pitiful. I swear, I've eaten stewed possum that was better."

Sean laughed.

He sat there on her porch listening to her stories as his eyes and his thoughts explored the building next door. He caught a glimpse of Katy from what must have been a second-floor patio. His heart caught in his throat. It was just a moment, just a fleeting figure at a distance, but his pulse was pounding. Katy and Josh were just next door. A hundred yards away they were living their lives.

"Where are you staying, young man?" Mrs. Bullock asked, rousing him from his daydreams.

"At Gouswhelter Lake Cabins," he answered.

"Well, you'd better be heading on your way," she said. "There's a storm coming up."

He glanced around to notice that indeed the late afternoon had darkened into early evening and there was the smell of ozone in the air.

"Yeah, I guess so," he said, standing up, surprised that he'd stayed so long.

Mrs. Bullock rattled out her cane from beneath the arm of her chair and used it to rise to her feet as well.

Sean realized that her concern for him might be partially based on her own need to go inside. He held the door for her.

"Thank you, Sean," she said to him. "I need to rustle me up some dinner and I suspect you ought to be doing the same. Next time you come by to see me, maybe I'll have some cake or cookies."

"Okay, Mrs. Bullock," he told her as he shut the screen. She was a nice old lady. And he'd be happy to sit on her porch, as long as he could watch his wife and child next door.

That was crazy. He would be a stalker if he continued. But there was no chance that he would. Tomorrow he would have to face Katy and Josh. The thought of that simultaneously thrilled him and scared him to death.

Shaking his head, he walked across the porch and down the steps. As he walked along the path to the front gate, the wind picked up and the first drops of rain arrived on the breeze.

Sean didn't even hurry. He knew he'd be drenched by the time he made it back to Gouswhelter's. So be it. Spring rain could wash away dust in the air, maybe it could clear up some of the cobwebs in his brain. When he reached the lake path he turned to glance back at the restaurant roof, where he'd briefly caught a glimpse of her.

Of course, she wouldn't be there now, he reminded himself. It was raining. Still, he turned back to look.

The empty patio roof was exactly what he'd expected. Then suddenly she was there. His breath caught in his throat as he saw her walk to the edge, press her body against the railing and raise her arms out to the sky, as if welcoming the wind and water. Her head was thrown back, and though he couldn't hear the sound of her laughter, it echoed through him.

She was a goddess. Not a vision of beauty like Venus or a warrior for love like Athena, she was Mother Earth herself and she was everything that he'd ever wanted in the world.

Suddenly, as if his thought had been screamed in her direction, she lowered her chin, her gaze searching the shore, then she saw him. Across the rainswept night, their eyes met and held.

Sean didn't know how long they stared at each other. But when she turned and hurried away, he was more lost and lonely than he'd ever felt in his life.

Bitsy's Wisdom 17

Bitsy's Wisdom 17: The layer of pink just under the surface of the meat is called a smoke ring. It runs from the outside in and the deeper the better.

At first she thought she must be dreaming. Katy had been drawn out into the storm by the dark billowing clouds on the horizon. It was the waning moments before the sun, now hidden behind clouds, disappeared beneath the world completely. She walked out into the rain, just because it felt good. It had been a perfect day, she thought, or as near perfect as an ordinary Sunday could be. A wonderful, welcoming church service, a tasty picnic lunch in the park and the excitement of the music nights they were planning, to give the new Bitsy's some of the fun from the old days.

Katy felt grateful. Blessed, protected, grateful. She walked out to the railing, admiring the beauty of the storm and the gift of the rain. She held her arms out to it, receiving it. She wasn't an overtly religious person, but she knew how fortunate she was to have her life, her son, her sister and this place to live full of kind friends and relative security. The loss and grief of her divorce still stung her, but she wouldn't give in to disappointment and fear. Her heart was full of gratitude. She closed her eyes and laughed aloud, hoping that her thankfulness and the joy she felt would be transmitted to all angels in heaven watching over her.

It was then that she felt it. That primeval sense that had saved her ancestors from predators, the sense that she was being watched. The hairs on the back of her neck stood and her eyes, slitted, focused, searched the open ground along the lakeshore.

Then she saw him.

He was as familiar as her own body. And the sight of him was so unexpected, she was sure it must be an illusion. She drank in the vision eagerly, expecting any moment to be awakened to another morning without him. Then she felt cold, sharp prickles of the rain against her skin, and was assured that it was really happening. Sean was really there and he was looking straight at her.

Katy turned and fled. It wasn't enough to get out of sight or into the kitchen, she raced all the way to the living room where Josh and Emma were sitting together on the rug playing Uno Junior. They were both startled by her abrupt entry.

"Are you all right?"

"What's wrong, Mom?"

Katy opened her mouth to speak but hesitated, glancing first at her son and then at Emma.

"Ah…nothing, nothing," she answered him, managing a smile that was so faked it nearly strained her face muscles. "Josh, isn't it about time for you to be in bed?"

The child looked momentarily puzzled and then glanced at the digital clock on the radio and laughed.

"Mom, it's only six o'clock," he told her. "I'm not a baby that goes to bed at six o'clock."

"Oh, right," Katy said, flustered. "I guess it just seems later, because it's turned so dark."

Emma was looking at her, apparently trying to pick up signals.

"But you know," Emma said to Josh. "It's not too early for a shower and to get your pajamas on."

"Aw, Auntie Em, we're in the middle of a game," he complained.

"We'll set our cards down and we'll come right back to it as soon as you're clean and dressed for bed."

"Oh, man," Josh whined. But he did put his cards down and rose to his feet, reluctantly complying with her demand.

"I'll start the water for you," Emma said, and hurried into the bathroom.

Katy paced the floor. She heard her son and her sister joking and laughing, she heard the water running, and a couple of minutes later, Emma returned to the room.

"I saw…I think I saw, no, I saw Sean outside. He was watching this place."

Emma nodded. "I knew he was here."

"You knew he was here," she repeated. "Why didn't you tell me?"

"I was going to, after Josh went to bed. But I didn't see any reason to ruin the afternoon. I didn't expect them to come by until tomorrow."

"Them?"

"Mrs. Dodson is here, too," Emma said. "She and Sean are staying at the Gouswhelters' cabins."

"How'd you find this out?"

"She asked Latt for directions and he picked up on the name immediately. And when he got a look at Sean, he knew that he had to be related to Josh. So he came back by here to give us the heads-up."

"Thank God for that, but you should have told me immediately."

"Why? So you could spend the rest of the afternoon worrying?"

Emma was probably right, she was most usually right, but Katy felt threatened.

"I don't want you keeping secrets from me," she said. "I'm not just your kid sister, somebody you're in charge of. I'm a grown woman with a grown-up life. I don't want you trying to protect me from it."

"Sorry," Emma said. "I… I know you're an adult. It's just hard for me to stop doing what I've always done. I'm sorry. I'll try harder."

Katy could hardly start an argument after an apology. She plopped down in a big armchair, but after only a half minute was nervously back up on her feet again.

"Why are they here?" she wondered aloud.

"They have visitation rights," Emma answered. "They said they are going to exercise them."

"They can't do that."

"Of course they can," her sister said. "That's what all those letters from the lawyer were about. There's no way a judge would give Sean custody of Josh without him having even seen the little guy for years."

"Sean would never take Josh," Katy said firmly. "I know Sean and he knows how much I love Josh. He'd never try to take him away."

"Wake up, Katy," Emma said. "It's happening. He's a jerk now, he's always been a jerk and he's the kind of jerk who will steal your son from you. You're going to fool around in that stupid, Pollyanna place of yours and let him get away with it."

"No, no I'm not," Katy insisted.

"We should have hired another lawyer," Emma said.

"We don't have money for a lawyer right now."

"We'll use my college money."

Katy looked up at her sister and her eyes welled with tears. "No, Emma," she said. "You've been saving up that money long enough.

You're going back to school this fall. I've messed up your life over and over again. But I'm not messing it up again this time."

"We don't have any choice."

"I do," Katy insisted. "I'll sell the B & B before I let you use one penny of your college money."

The water in the shower stopped running. Katy lowered her voice to a whisper.

"We'll talk about this later. But I mean what I say."

Emma nodded, as if she were willing to comply.

There was no more discussion about Sean or custody or lawyers, but that didn't mean that Katy's mind could just let it go. She busied herself around the apartment as Josh finished his game with Emma. Then she settled into a chair with her son to read. She tried to make it just a typical evening. Her mind continued racing. And her emotions rode a roller coaster.

The fear of losing custody, the anxiety of a confrontation, those were things that she should be expected to feel. Those were the things that she could discuss with Emma.

The other part of it she had to keep private. The exhilaration that swept through her at the sight of her ex-husband. The eager anticipation of seeing him close up again tomorrow, of talking to him, just being near his side. That had her jittery as well. And she couldn't talk to anyone about that. She tried not to even acknowledge it to herself. The last thing that she needed was to carry a torch for her ex-husband. Yes, she could love him. He was Josh's father and for that reason alone it was okay to have tender feelings for him. But she couldn't allow herself to be that love-struck teenager again. She couldn't afford to dream of them being together again. For her own heart, she might have been willing to take the risk. But not now, now that Josh was old enough to have his heart broken as well.

Her night was mostly sleepless. She went to bed but tossed and turned so much, she worried about Josh's rest. So she spent much of the night pacing the living room. When she finally fell asleep on the couch, she couldn't say. But the next thing she knew, Josh was waking her up.

"Mama," Josh prodded her.

Katy opened her eyes to see her sweet little son peering down at her.

"Hi," Katy said sleepily, stretching.

"Hi," he replied. "Mama, Miss Nadine's at the door. You told me never to open it for strangers, but she's not a stranger, is she?"

"Nadine?"

It was then that Katy noticed the morning light streaming in through the kitchen. It was late.

"Where's your Auntie Em?"

"Downstairs, I guess."

"Oh…drat!" Katy said, wishing she had the freedom to curse, as this was definitely a cursing situation. "Let Nadine in."

The little guy hurried to the door as Katy got to her feet. The entire Graves family came barreling into the room.

"I overslept," Katy announced.

Nadine shrugged. "Well, you're up now. Do you want me to go help Emma while you get dressed?"

"Could you?"

"Sure. Parker, keep your eyes on the kids until it's time for you to go to school," she said. "Then come by and let me know before you leave."

"Okay," he said.

"I'll just be a few minutes," Katy assured the seven-year-old. "Then I'll get your mom back up here."

Katy took a two-minute shower and raced to dress, grabbing the first clothes in sight. She barely ran a brush through her hair before pulling it into a ponytail. Makeup, she decided, would take way too long. She dabbed a little blush on her cheeks and smeared on a line of lipstick.

In the kitchen the kids were all sitting around the table. Parker had helped Josh get some breakfast cereal. Baby Natty was munching on the same.

"I'll go down and send your mom back up here," Katy said.

It wasn't until she was heading down the stairs that she remembered why she hadn't slept all night. She was going to see Sean today and she wanted, she needed, to look her best. Glancing out at the full parking lot, she knew that wasn't going to happen.

The restaurant was incredibly hectic. Apparently spring fishing after a rain was irresistible and every angler in the area was eager to get out on the water. With Emma forced to spend most of her time in the bait shop, Katy was frantically trying to cook, wait tables and clear by herself. She was already growing accustomed to these multitask mornings, but today was especially tough. She was tired, and when she started out late, she always felt as if she were running behind.

Fortunately, most of the patrons were patient. Katy figured that the waiting was as ordinary for them as the pace was for her. She knew her job was as much to greet them with a smile as it was to get them fed. She made a point not to let the pressure show.

That resolve was tested when Sean and his mother walked through the door.

She looked straight at him, just as she had the night before. Again, she felt that inexplicable jarring of emotions. She was so glad to see him and so scared about his purpose for being there. Abruptly she turned her back on them, gathering her composure.

There was a part of her that wanted to storm over to them and order them off the premises. This was her place, hers and Josh's, and she'd defend both from anyone who threatened. A wiser, more rational instinct warned her against rashness.

"Sean would never take Josh from me," she whispered to herself. The truth of that statement, despite all evidence to the contrary, gave her strength. She picked up the coffeepot and a couple of mugs, raised her chin and turned back to head in their direction. They were seating themselves at the only empty table. Katy put on her biggest, brightest, cheeriest smile.

"Good morning, welcome to Bitsy's B & B," she said to them as if they were strangers. "Coffee?"

She was looking at Sean, but it was his mother who answered.

"Yes, please," she said. "We didn't mean to just drop in on you like this. My PDA isn't working."

Katy observed the older woman, who was fashionably dressed, perfectly made-up and had every hair in place.

"The nearest cell phone tower is quite a ways away," she told her. "About the only place you can get a signal is on top of Cemetery Hill."

Katy deliberately turned her attention to Sean, defying him to allow his mother to take the lead.

"What brings you to my neighborhood?" she asked.

"Sean wants to see his son," Gwen answered. "Where is he?"

"Josh is upstairs," she answered, never taking her eyes off Sean. "Do you want to see him?"

Her ex-husband hesitated.

"Of course he does," Gwen butted in.

"Josh doesn't even know that you exist," Katy said.

"Well, that's your fault. You certainly should have told him about his father," the woman said.

Katy turned to give her former mother-in-law a long look. "I thought about it," she told her. "I thought about telling him Sean's name and where he lived and showing some photos. But then, how would I explain why he doesn't come around, why he never sends a birthday card or a Christmas present? I didn't know how I would explain that, so I've just been waiting until Josh got around to asking."

That shut them both up.

"Excuse me, I've got to wait on some other customers. I'll be back to your table in a few minutes."

Katy walked away. Deliberately smiling at the other patrons. She knew there were no secrets at Warbler Lake and having a public discussion with one's former spouse was not likely to pass unnoticed. But she would just as soon that everything appear amiable.

She continued to do everything she normally did. She took orders, did the cooking, served and cleaned up. All the time being uncomfortably aware that Sean was just across the room. And that he was watching her. Although it seemed as if an inordinate number of patrons lingered over coffee, eventually the place began to clear out. Still it was a while before she made it back to their table.

"Have you decided on something?" she asked them.

"You do realize that the service here is abysmal," Mrs. Dodson told her.

"Sorry," Katy responded with a very professional smile.

"Why do you keep going back in the kitchen?" the woman asked. "Is your cook incompetent?"

"I keep going back there," Katy said, "because I'm doing the cooking."

Mrs. Dodson did seem surprised by that answer, but she didn't comment on it. She handed Katy her menu.

"So what do you recommend?" she asked. "What's your culinary specialty?"

"Toast," Katy answered.

Sean sniggered.

She glanced over at him and an instant of sweet remembrance passed between them. For a second they were transported back to the time when they stood as a united, if sarcastic, front against the displeasure of his mother. Then as quickly as it came, it was gone. Gwen shot her son a look of displeasure and the sparkle in his eyes disappeared.

"I'll have toast," Mrs. Dodson said.

"Sean?"

"That's fine," he said.

Katy was turning to go when Emma walked through the door. From her tired expression, Katy knew her sister had had enough of mealworms and wax moths. Unfortunately, things in the res-taurant were equally as fishy.

Emma spotted Sean and his mother immediately and her vis-age immediately changed from worn and weary to battle ready. Katy felt, for the protection from mutual annihilation, she'd have to keep her sister and her former mother-in-law separate.

"You remember my sister, Emma," she said in the most pleas-ant and genial tone that she could manage.

Her sister's thundercloud expression did not change.

"Could you handle the tables for me for a few minutes while I talk with them?"

Emma could hardly refuse the request. And Katy thought it would be better if she did the talking, at least for now.

"Two orders of toast," Katy said. "And I'll take a cup of coffee."

With visible reluctance, Emma left the table. Katy pulled out a chair and sat down. She tried to appear confident and comfort-able. But that's not how she felt. Sean's leg was only inches from her own. And it felt as if some kind of electrical circuit was run-ning between the two of them. An electrical circuit that had the disconcerting effect of making her suddenly extremely aware of a region of her body ignored and neglected for several years now. Mentally she admonished herself. The most important thing in her life was in jeopardy and she was in danger of being sidelined by sexuality.

Deliberately, she readjusted her seat and turned her chair slightly so that she was looking more directly at Gwen. She crossed her legs.

"I'm not giving up Josh," Katy stated flatly to the woman. "He's my son and he's going to live with me."

"We're not here to talk about that," Mrs. Dodson said. "That involves a change in the custody order. Our lawyers will be the ones to discuss that. We're simply here to exercise our rights within the order already in place."

Emma came up to the table and sat Katy's coffee down with more force than was necessary, sloshing some on to the side.

"Hey, if I'm remembering correctly, Mrs. Dodson," Emma said too snidely for civil conversation. "Your name is not mentioned anywhere in that document. Although I suppose a good case could be made that you were the co-respondent, responsible for alienation of the spineless worm's affection."

"Emma!" Katy snapped at her sister. "You're not helping."

"Indeed not," Mrs. Dodson added very loftily. "And I don't believe *your* name was on the divorce decree anywhere, either."

Katy could almost see steam coming out of her sister's ears. She had to keep these two from engaging in any dangerous escalation of warring words, but she wasn't sure how. She needed help and it came from an unexpected source.

"That's settled, then," Sean said from beside her.

Everyone turned to look at him in surprise.

"We've definitely concluded that none of this is Emma's business or yours, Mother. It's between me and Katy."

He rose to his feet and offered his hand.

"Let's leave these two to their toast and coffee," he said.

Almost unbelievably, Katy found herself being led out the front door of Bitsy's by her ex-husband. There was one instant when she thought about looking back. But she knew that if Emma thought she was unsure, she'd never let Katy go. So she kept her eyes on what was ahead of her and just kept walking.

Outside the air was clean and cool after the rain and the sun was sparkling on the lake. The fishhook, like a giant sundial, sent a shaft of dark shade across the parking lot. There were boats out on the water and kids playing on the beach.

"I love this place," Katy whispered, realizing that she'd voiced the sentiment only after she'd said it aloud.

"It's okay," Sean agreed. "More than okay, it's nice."

She nodded.

"I didn't mean to scare you last night," he said. "I just wanted to see where you live. I wasn't spying on you or anything like that. I just wanted to see."

"I suppose it didn't come up to your high standards," she said, a bit defensive.

"It's all right," Sean answered. "It's what it is. I like it."

"It'll be a really nice place for Josh to grow up," Katy said. "He's already getting to know some of the other kids. He'll be able to walk to school until sixth grade. Then he can catch the school bus to Tedburg right here in Bitsy's parking lot. He'll be safe here, he'll be known here and he'll always know where home is."

Sean nodded, but he was noncommittal.

She knew she was talking too fast, explaining too much. She sounded defensive, maybe even a little desperate, but she couldn't help herself. Standing next to Sean, walking beside him, talking to him. It was all just too familiar, too natural. She felt like his wife. She knew that if he turned and took her into his arms, she'd never resist.

Fortunately, he did not.

"I'd like to see him, Katy," he said. "I've missed him. I've missed you both."

Katy raised her chin and turned to look at him directly. He

looked like the same handsome guy that she'd fallen in love with. His hair was longer, there were more lines on his face and no smile in evidence. Still, he was the man that set her heart pounding that first day in the Dodsonburger. And he was the man who broke it in a million pieces less than three years later.

"I don't think he remembers you," Katy warned him.

"I'm sure he doesn't," Sean said. "In fact, I hope he doesn't. I'd hate it if he remembers me walking out on the two of you."

"But you did that, didn't you," she said. "I remember it."

"Yes," he answered quietly. "I did. And I'm sorry."

"Sorry you hurt me?" she asked. "Or sorry you left?"

"Both."

There was a moment of hesitation between them. It hung there transitory and fragile.

"Me, too," she said.

Sean stopped in his tracks and turned to look at her, his expression both bewildered and searching.

"I don't know if I can explain myself," he said. "I wanted what was best for you and the baby. Somehow, it seemed like having me drop out of the picture was the right thing."

"But now you're dropping back in," Katy pointed out.

He nodded. "I was wrong back then," he said. "Totally wrong. I should have tried harder. I should have gone to counseling. I should have…been a better man than I am. I can't change any of that."

"No," she said quietly.

"I want to do the right thing now," Sean told her.

"And you think taking Josh from me is the right thing?"

"I don't know," he admitted. "There's no question in my mind that you love him and take good care of him."

"And that's not enough?"

"I don't know," Sean repeated. "There are things that we can offer him—my mother can offer him—that he just could never get here."

"Like what?"

"Lots of things," Sean insisted. "Private school and violin lessons, museums, the ballet…even Cardinals baseball."

"You think those things are more important than his mother?"

"No," Sean answered. "I don't think that. But a father is important, too."

"You didn't think so three years ago."

"And I was wrong," he said. "I've apologized. And I'll continue to apologize. Back then, I chose to do what was easiest. Now I just want to make sure that I do what's best, even if it's hard."

They'd reached the lakeshore and Katy turned and began walking along the water. He had just caught up with her and they walked side by side in silence.

"I'm not here to hurt you, Katy, or to cause you trouble," Sean said finally. "I'm just trying to think about Josh more than I think about myself."

Katy didn't know how to respond to that statement. It fell on her ears like a criticism. She couldn't let her son go. She wouldn't let her son go. Was she thinking more about herself than her son? She let the question hang there in her mind unanswered until the sound of laughing children reached her ears.

Josh and Brianna were playing in the backyard. Nadine was out there with them. With baby Natty at her side, she was blowing bubbles from a small plastic ring and the two five-year-olds were racing around laughing and shouting and jumping as they tried to catch them.

"That's him?" Sean asked, his voice shaky and anxious beside her.

"Yes."

They stood there together watching the children. The tension emanating from Sean was obvious without even looking in his direction. It was like electricity in the air.

"Could I meet him?" he asked finally, his voice nearly cracking like an adolescent's.

"Come on," Katy said.

She began walking away from the shoreline toward the grassy yard behind the restaurant. Sean was at her side. She caught a telling glimpse of his expression; he was as pale and ominous as if facing a firing squad.

Katy was anxious herself, but not for the same reason.

She knew Sean feared that Josh would reject him. For Katy it was more complicated. She wanted her son to have a father. But she couldn't help feeling a certain amount of loss at relinquishing her status as only parent and most important person in her little boy's life. She thought about what Sean had said. That he was trying to do what was best, not just what was easiest. Determinedly she reminded herself that she didn't want to deny her son any good thing that she could provide. A relationship with his dad would be Josh's gain.

The little boy caught sight of her and waved excitedly. As he came rushing toward them, she was strongly reminded of how much he was like Sean, not just in his looks, but in the way he thought and how smart and curious he was. It couldn't be right for Josh not to know that.

"Mama, we're catching bubbles and I caught more than Brianna 'cause I can run faster and Natty didn't catch any 'cause he's a baby except one landed on his nose and it popped and he kind of smiled or something."

"That's great," Katy told him. "Listen, I have somebody I want you to meet."

Josh turned to the man beside her. By now, in a new place with all new people, he'd become very accustomed to introductions. Like a young man twice his age, the five-year-old held out his hand.

"Hi, I'm Josh."

Sean grasped the child's palm in his own. "Hi Josh, I'm…I'm Sean."

Josh's face split into a wide grin. "That's my name, too," he said. "Joshua Sean Dodson."

"I know," he said.

"Sean is your father," Katy said.

Josh looked shocked and was speechless. Beside him, Brianna was not. She turned to her mother and yelled.

"It's Josh's daddy," she called out loudly enough so that people a block away might have heard.

Nadine was frantically waving to her daughter, motioning her back into the yard and away from the small family drama in which she was intruding. Brianna ignored her, wanting to stay in the thick of the action.

But Katy was watching Josh. She had expected surprise, perhaps confusion. She knew there would be a lot of questions. But as she stood there, watched her son's face, his lip began to tremble.

Katy's heart caught in her throat. She had made a terrible mistake. She should have warned Josh. She should have prepared him for this moment. What had she been thinking to just spring something like this on him out of nowhere?

Desperately she tried to think of something to say, something to do, some way to soften the blow. Then she watched the little boy run to his father and throw his arms around him. Josh looked up into Sean's eyes, his face shining with adoration.

"Daddy," he said. "You're home."

Bitsy's Wisdom 18

Bitsy's Wisdom 18: No need to restock leeches, once you've got them, they are easy to keep alive for months.

Emma couldn't believe it when her sister just got up and walked out with Sean. She was left standing beside the table with Mrs. Dodson. The woman seemed as surprised as she was. Emma was uncertain about her sister's ability to manage her ex-husband, but she wasn't about to give Gwen Dodson the satisfaction of knowing that. With an unpleasant humph, she headed into the kitchen.

She put a couple of slices of bread in the toaster and then hurried back into the dining room to check on her other customers. She cleared dishes and wiped down tables with a rag. She hurried back to the kitchen to put the toast on a plate with a dollop of butter and a serving of jam.

When she returned to the dining room, Mrs. Dodson was completely engaged in typing something out on her PDA, if typing could be the term employed for using your thumbs on a tiny telephone keyboard.

When Emma set the plate in front of her, she looked up.

"If you're here and Katy is with Sean, who is watching my grandson?"

My grandson. Emma mentally repeated the phrase to herself and bristled at the possessive description.

Field note: The matriarch, despite any active intervention in the care of tribal offspring, openly expresses ownership as if her exalted position entitles her to possession. Being accustomed to wielding power in other spheres, she assumes that she can do likewise in every sphere.

"The whereabouts of my nephew, Katy's son, a child you wouldn't recognize if you saw him on the street, is not really any of your business, is it?" Emma answered. "He happens to be with the babysitter."

Mrs. Dodson nodded with a smugness that was unjustified.

Emma turned her back on the woman, deliberately busying herself with getting the morning rush completely settled and setting up for the arrival of the lunch crowd. The woman made her angry. She hadn't wanted her sister, who was too young and too naive, to marry Sean Dodson. She would have cautioned against it if she'd been given a chance. But once the two were married, Emma would never have tried to break them up. She wasn't about to forgive Gwendolyn Dodson for that.

She put the last of the breakfast dishes in the dishwasher and started the machine up. When she went back into the dining room Mrs. Dodson was gone. Emma's thought was that if the woman had walked out without paying, she was calling the sheriff on her. Unfortunately, there was a crisp ten dollar bill left on the table. Far more than enough to cover the price of a cup of coffee and two pieces of toast.

She hoped that the woman hadn't followed Katy and Sean. Her sister had a hard-enough time defending herself without being ganged up on by the entire Dodson family.

Emma's fears proved groundless. As she wiped down the table and righted the metal caddy that held the salt and pepper shakers and the sugar packets, Katy came through the door, Sean following in her wake.

Katy didn't say anything, but she didn't look teary or frightened.

"I guess my mother left. The car is gone."

Emma nodded. "I was in the back. She didn't say where she was going. If she hadn't left *you* here, I'd be rooting for St. Louis as her destination."

Sean flashed a bright grin. It caught Emma momentarily off guard. She couldn't remember seeing him smile like that since the early days of his marriage to Katy.

"You always say what you think, Emma," he said. "It's one of the things I like about you."

"And you try to get by on your charm," Emma answered. "It's one of the things I've never liked about you."

He nodded. "Fair enough," he said. "If it makes you feel any better, I'm not as charming these days. And I'm not getting by so well."

Emma was a little surprised at his candor, but refrained from giving him any points for it.

He followed her back into the kitchen. She glanced up to see him surveying it critically.

"So you really don't have any help back in the kitchen," he said. "I was hoping that was an exaggeration."

"Just Katy and me," Emma answered. "We manage fine."

He nodded slowly. "What happened to college? Did you give up on that?"

You are what happened to my college plan, she wanted to tell him. Helping to support Katy and Josh had to come first. And now, if they were going to have to go to court again, they would have to use her savings to pay for it.

"I'm starting back this fall," she lied. "I'm just here helping Katy get the place off and running."

"Okay," he said. His tone suggested that he didn't quite believe her.

"Are you setting up for lunch?"

"Just starting," Emma said.

"I'll help."

"That's not necessary."

"What's not necessary?" Katy asked as she came through the back door.

"I asked to help with lunch," Sean told her. "I've got nothing else to do. And you know I'm good at this."

"Okay, you can help," Katy said.

Emma shot her a look. Katy shrugged. "We can always use an extra pair of hands."

That might be true, but Sean's hands were not ones that Emma wanted touching anything that belonged to Katy.

With a sigh, she decided not to argue. "Okay, lay out the sandwich stuff on the steam table, we don't use it at lunch."

"You don't use the steam table?"

"That's what I said," Emma snapped. "We fix cold sandwiches and cook hamburgers on the grill. No steam table at lunch."

"You don't serve barbecue?"

"Not for lunch," Emma said. "We barbecue in the afternoon and serve it at dinner."

"Of course, but don't you take your leftovers from the night before and heat it up for barbecue sandwiches?"

"No, we don't."

Sean's expression bordered on dumbfounded. Emma wasn't about to enlighten him. Unfortunately, Katy had no such compunction.

"Our barbecue is awful," she admitted flatly. "We can hardly get anyone to eat it in the evening and its reputation would certainly follow it into the next day."

His puzzlement turned to incredulity. "What's wrong with it?" he asked.

Katy shrugged. "It just doesn't taste good. It's burned, or it's raw or it's both. It's always more scorched than wood-smoked. It's just bad."

Sean laughed and shook his head. "Sweetheart," he said, "you can't have a good barbecue place without good barbecue."

"Listen, just butt out," Emma said nastily. "And don't call her sweetheart! Two minutes after offering to help out, you're already trying to give advice. This is not one of your 'Dachshundburger' palaces. This restaurant belongs to Katy. And she can make a go of it without any advice from you."

"Emma!" Katy scolded her with one word.

"No, she's right," Sean said. "My lips are sealed. But I'm happy to help. From now on I take orders, I don't offer suggestions."

Katy seemed pleased enough to have the harsh words smoothed over. Emma wished they'd been harsh enough to send the ex on his way. Over the next couple of hours, however, he did make himself useful.

That made sense, of course. He'd grown up in restaurants. He'd worked in them since he was old enough to bus tables. He fit into the flow of the lunch crowd easily. He knew what to do and efficiently got it done. His competency made the meal go much easier. For the most part, he stayed in the kitchen, getting the orders put together. But he did come into the dining room to clear after the first group, and a new face at Warbler Lake always attracted attention.

"I don't believe we've met," Waymon Riley said to him, offering a hand.

"Sean Dodson," he introduced himself. And Emma heard him add. "I'm Katy's husband."

When they passed each other going into the kitchen she corrected him under her breath. "You're her ex-husband," she reminded him.

Emma knew it was too late to stop the gossip. It wouldn't be a half an hour before everyone in town had heard. If they were going to be talking about it, and they were, Emma wanted to make sure they had the whole story.

"They're divorced," she told the Dempseys.

"He walked out on her, left her alone and penniless with a baby to support," Emma explained to Pricy Metcalf.

"He's here with his rich mother trying to steal custody of Josh," she said to Miss Welborn.

The news went through the place like a wildfire.

"He seemed like such a nice fellow," toothless Old Man Crank said, shaking his head. "You just never know."

Sometimes you did know. And Emma wanted to make sure that this was one of those times. It was especially critical, considering her hopes for Katy and Curt, that the people of Warbler Lake weren't taken in.

By the time Spurl Westbrook stopped in for his regular "after the bell last lunch of the day," the news had already made it to him.

"Now, this ex-husband of Katy's, he's here throwing around his money and power trying to take that little boy away."

Emma nodded. "That's exactly right. You know Dodsonburger?"

"The fast-food place?" Spurl was stunned. "Good Lord, You mean that's him?"

"It's his mother," Emma said. "She owns the whole company and he's the spoiled rich boy who's had the whole world handed to him on a plate."

"Oh, my God, Katy's got her work cut out for her."

"That's why we need a good lawyer," Emma told him. "The Dodsons, they probably have a whole army of slick, greasy attorneys from the city on their side. We've got to find somebody to represent us."

Spurl nodded. "Well, you won't find any lawyer army here," he said. "We've only got one member of the Missouri Bar Association in the whole area. And he doesn't exactly have his shingle out. He takes on a client every year or so, just cases he's particularly interested in."

"What's his name? I'll have to contact him, beg him to help us."

"It's Latt," Westbrook said.

"Huh?"

"Lattimer Meicklejohn," he answered.

"He's a bait supplier."

Westbrook nodded. "Yeah, that's who he is now, but he used to be some fancy lawyer up in Jeff City."

"If that's true, what's he doing down here?" Emma asked.

Westbrook shook his head. "He's just living like the rest of us," he answered. "Trying to do some things that matter."

After the lunch mess was cleared, Emma waited for a few moments of privacy. That wasn't so hard to find; Katy and Sean appeared to be working as a team on getting the barbecue going. Emma sat down on the cool box behind the counter and dialed the telephone. He answered on the third ring.

"Latt, this is Emma."

"Hey, fishing partner," he responded. "What can I do for you? Have you run out of crickets and leeches?"

"No, my leech population is fine," she answered. "What I need is a lawyer."

There was a long silence on the other end.

"I take it that the *whatever* has hit the fan over there," he said.

"They showed up here for breakfast," Emma said. "Sean's been hanging around her all day."

"There's no need to panic," Latt said. "Katy's a good mom providing a good home. It's hard to fight that."

"Even with all the money in the world?"

"The Dodsons don't have all the money in the world," he pointed out.

"They might as well have," Emma said. "I need you to represent us. We've got to have a lawyer. I think it's best to have somebody local. Somebody we can trust."

"I can recommend someone out of Rolla maybe," he said. "I still have a few contacts."

"We don't want 'someone,' we want you."

"Aw, Emma, this is not really the kind of thing I do. I'm sure you can find somebody else who would—"

"There is nobody else, certainly nobody else we know," she said. "Now, we don't have a lot of money, but I've got several thousand dollars I can give you up front. And I'll pay off the rest over time."

"I thought Katy sunk everything she had into Bitsy's."

"This isn't Katy's money," Emma said. "It's mine. And it's probably best if you don't mention that I'm paying it to you. That's another reason why you have to take the case. You're the only lawyer in the state that Katy might believe would help her for free."

"It probably won't even go to court," he said. "Any judge in his right mind would insist on mediation."

"See, so it would be a snap for you," she said. "You'd hardly miss a day of fishing."

He gave a long sigh, vacillating.

From the front window, Emma could see Curt headed in the direction of the B & B.

"Think about it," Emma said into the phone. "I'll talk to you later."

He agreed.

Curt was smiling as he came in through the door. Apparently,

Emma thought, he hadn't been privy to today's gossip. He was so much nicer than Sean. He was going to be just perfect for Katy.

"You're looking very pretty today," he told her as he sat down at the counter.

Emma glanced down at the T-shirt and jeans she was wearing and shook her head skeptically.

"Thanks," she said.

She set a big glass of soda in front of him and headed toward the kitchen. "Be right back," she told him, lying.

Katy and Sean were standing outside at the barbecue pit, ostensibly watching the meat cook, though it appeared that they were mostly talking.

"Katy," Emma said, interrupting. "I'll do that. You're needed in the dining room."

"Now?"

Emma nodded. "Curt's here," she said. "You two need to discuss your plans. I'll take care of this. Sean can help me."

"Oh, okay."

As her sister went into the building, Emma stepped up to the barbecue pit, standing across from Sean. She slipped on the asbestos gloves and he watched her in silence as she used the tongs to turn the meat. When she picked up the bowl of sauce and used the brush to spread it on top, he made a slight sound. Not exactly clearing his throat, but something similar.

Emma looked over at him. "I suppose now you're going to try to tell me how to barbecue."

"No," Sean answered. "I'm not. But I'm pretty much convinced that somebody should."

Bitsy's Wisdom 19

Bitsy's Wisdom 19: To gauge how much smoke flavor is getting into your food, just look at the chimney. If nothing much is coming out, add more wood.

Sitting astride a bench that read Beloved Rest Here in Memory of Carlton Bullock, Gwen spread out her notes on the space in front of her, carefully holding down each piece of paper with one of her fingers. The intermittent breeze on the high flat-topped hill could easily blow something away. She wanted to get every scrap of information relayed to the lawyer.

"David, if you need to hire an investigator or do some background research, you have my permission and encouragement," she told him. "I'm not concerned with the expense."

She'd spent the morning surreptitiously gathering gossip. The residents of Warbler Lake, she'd found, were chatty and eager to pass on interesting details. Though as the day moved on and the rumors began to spread through town, she was less and less able to coax any facts out of anyone. She wasn't too bothered by that, she'd already found out quite a lot.

Gwen drove around Warbler Lake as if she were doing a site survey for a new franchise location. She checked out the neighborhood, which was clearly unplanned and unzoned, but surprisingly free of overbuilding. There was some flimsy construction, but that might be expected for seasonal cabins. There were a few mobile homes scattered among frame construction dwellings. The only apartments available appeared to be the ones above the businesses. Both the traffic patterns and the pedestrian walkways were significantly impacted by the lake. It was the center of the community and everything was constructed with it in sight.

Even the long, one-story school building, its aged red brick and casement windows attesting to its age, had lake views all along the front side. Gwen parked in the visitors' lot for a long time, imagining her grandson inside. It was picturesque. A nostalgic reminder of her own childhood. But she didn't allow herself to soften. She could afford to provide her grandson with the very best of everything, including education. Despite its folksy charm, she was certain this was not it.

She wrote copious notes on everything she saw, including quotes from the locals on specific topics. And then took that information to the only place in town that could handle it: Lake Hill Cemetery.

It said something about Warbler Lake that the only group of people in town who had updated access to global communications were the dead ones. It was only atop this hill that little towers showed up in the corner of her PDA, and she'd walked through the tombstones to find the best signal. The Bullock bench wasn't the very best, but it was close. And it offered a place to spread out her papers, something she couldn't do among the tall thin slabs above the bodies of the ancient Gouswhelters of the Civil War era.

"I really want you to press on this babysitter," Gwen told her lawyer, David Faneuf. "The guy who towed my car had terrible things to say about her. Her reputation is trash. There are rumors about her concerning everything from home-wrecking to drug addiction. And my ex-daughter-in-law is trusting my grandson to her, a woman she didn't even bother to investigate. That shows a very dangerous lack of judgment, I believe."

He said he would find out everything there was to know about the woman.

"And it needs to be noted that the child plays in an unfenced yard that has both an open flame in the barbecue pit and a quick run to a dangerous body of water," Gwen said. "She's putting the boy at risk for both burning and drowning on a daily basis."

He agreed with everything she'd said. And she thought she'd prodded him enough to make sure that he kept things happening. She finished her conversation and hung up.

She gathered up her papers and slipped them carefully in their folder. Then, verifying that she still had plenty of battery, she checked her e-mail. It was a typical morning. Two or three small crises, a couple of larger ones, and a number of people who simply tried to take advantage of not having the CEO in place at the helm.

She wrote a long e-mail to Myra. Then another to Pete. Randy had handled a difficult situation with the produce supplier. He'd gotten the right results, but it was politick that Gwen make a call to smooth the ruffled feathers of the loser. She was good at that and she didn't mind. She'd spent a lot of her life playing good cop to give cover so somebody else could lower the boom on them.

It wasn't until the warmth of the sun began to be unpleasant that she realized how much time she'd spent at the cemetery and how hungry she was getting. She checked her watch to discover that lunchtime had come and gone. It was midafternoon already and a couple of pieces of toast for breakfast was not sufficient to keep her stomach from rumbling. She gathered up her things and began walking toward the car.

It was the flowers she noticed first. They were not fancy, florist-bought blooms, but a big armful of buttercups, puccoon, phlox and Johnny-jump-ups. They had been tied together with a length of blue ribbon. Gwen smiled to herself, imagining a widow or widower and an undying love. She glanced at the name on the tombstone and her brow furrowed.

Barbara Jane "Bitsy" Wilson McGrady—1924-2005.

This must be the woman responsible for the restaurant, Gwen thought. From what Gwen had heard, she was a single woman who'd outlived all her family and left her property to the school.

Gwen shrugged to herself. It was surprising to think that a woman who'd narrowed her entire life to a less-than-stellar hill-billy eatery could apparently be remembered and cared for enough to have a few wildflowers on her grave.

At the car, Gwen reorganized her files and made sure that there wasn't anything else that needed to be taken care of. If there were going to be more calls to make today, she wanted to make them now, not drive back up here later. It was amazing how little she found absolutely necessary to say when the difficulty of communication became more challenging. It made her wonder if she normally wasted words that really need never have been said.

After assuring herself that her work was done, she headed down the hill, wishing that there was someplace else to have lunch in this place besides the Bait & BBQ. Unfortunately, unless she was willing to try to cook on her hotplate in the cabin, Bitsy's was the place.

She pulled up to the restaurant, just as the big yellow school bus was dropping off a rowdy group of exuberant young people, whose backpacks were bigger than they were.

The kids were dispersing in all directions, talking to one another, yelling across the distance and generally horsing around, oblivious to Gwen's car, assured that they, as precious pedestrians, surely had the right of way. Gwen tapped her fingers on the steering wheel as she waited. Finally she pulled into a parking spot, and carefully locking her car, though no one else on the street seemed to bother, she walked into Bitsy's. The place was noisy. The young kids were crowded into and around the corner booth. She sat at a table near the other end of the room putting as much distance between herself and the loud, boisterous teenagers as possible.

Katy, who had looked up in dismay when Gwen entered, was waiting tables. Or rather, she wasn't. She was talking to a mailman as she served up soft drinks on the counter. One of the kids carried them to the booth for her.

Gwen raised a disapproving eyebrow.

"She wouldn't last a week in *my* place of business," Gwen muttered to herself.

She knew the charge was unfair. Katy had worked for Dodson-burger for several months, and according to everything her subordinates could dig up, she was a competent, hardworking employee. But Sean deserved more than that. He deserved a woman who was his intellectual equal. A wife who could elevate his social status in the community. A person who brought out the best in him, not the most mediocre.

Gwen had been that person for Garrett. Of course she wanted no less for her son.

But Sean had fallen for this insignificant nobody, Katy Collins, and even with all of Gwen's help, he couldn't seem to get back on his feet again.

The future of her business, her husband's legacy, now depended upon young Josh. Gwen didn't crave twenty more years of managing things, but she knew she could do it and she would do it.

And she'd see that her grandson lived up to his potential, even if his father did not.

Katy had just begun to walk in her direction when the kitchen door opened and Sean walked through. Gwen was surprised to see her son clad in an apron. She was even more surprised when he waved Katy off and came toward her.

Something about him seemed strange, she thought. She was taken aback when she realized what it was. Sean was smiling. She hadn't seen him do that in a long time.

"Hi, Mom," he said.

She was momentarily speechless. He never called her the diminutive name from his childhood. He'd been referring to her as Mother for a decade.

"What are you doing?" she asked him, finally.

Sean shrugged. "Just helping out a little," he answered. "I talked to Josh. I actually talked to him. He's like a real little person who can carry on a conversation."

"Well, of course he can, he's five."

"I knew that in my head, but it's so different to actually talk to him, and he's so happy to see me." Sean was glowing. "We're going to spend some time together this evening."

"When do I get to meet him?" Gwen asked. "May I join the two of you this evening?"

Sean's grin faltered. "Uh, well, I don't know," he said. "Maybe tomorrow. I'll talk to Katy about it. Maybe tomorrow."

Gwen was disappointed, but she managed to disguise it. Perhaps it was good to allow Sean to break the ice with the boy. She'd have plenty of time to get to know him after they brought him back to St. Louis.

Sean visibly relaxed when she chose not to pursue it.

"Can I get you something to drink?" Sean asked, changing the subject. "Tea? Coffee?"

"Just some ice water will be fine. I was actually hoping for some lunch," she told him. "I seemed to have lost track of the time. Is there anything to be had here or will I have to wait until dinner?"

"Oh, I'm sure I can come up with something," her son assured her. "Let me see what's in the kitchen."

Sean brought her a drink in a blue plastic glass before leaving the dining room.

Gwen silently surveyed the place. She was not one of those women who hated to eat alone. Perhaps it was simply that she'd done it for years. But more likely it was that restaurants were her business. She never ate in one when she wasn't mentally on-the-job. Seeing what worked, how it worked and why it worked. As well as what wasn't working at all.

She'd reserved judgment on Bitsy's. It was one of those places that relied on regulars whose patronage was seasonally augmented by tourists. The site was as good as it could be in this community. The facilities were passable. But the key to success here would be the quality of the food. She couldn't speculate on that. So far, Gwen had only been served toast.

The front door opened and there was her rainy-night rescuer. He was dressed in faded overalls and there was a distinct odor of fish that lingered around him like a cloud.

They greeted each other with a polite nod.

"I need to wash my hands," he announced as he headed in the direction of the restrooms. "Katy, tell your sister I unloaded some stock. I left the bill on the counter."

Katy acknowledged his words with a smile before returning to her very animated discussion with the mailman. Gwen wondered what the two could possibly have to converse about with such excitement.

When Latt returned to the dining room, he made himself right at home, pouring himself a cup of coffee. Then he walked over and seated himself across the table from Gwen. The fish smell was gone, replaced by the faint odor of licorice. He took a sip of his coffee and then smiled at her.

It was a great smile. She couldn't help but be reminded of the warmth of his bathrobe and the homey welcome feeling of his kitchen.

"So, things going better today?" he asked.

"Yes," she answered. "At least it's not raining."

"Rain is what the weather does in springtime," he told her. "Being unhappy about it is just a waste of energy and effort."

Gwen made a noncommittal response.

"What do you think of our little hamlet?" he asked.

"It's fine," she answered. "At least what I've seen of it."

"The way people are talking," he said, "it seems as if you've been nosing around pretty thoroughly."

"I'm a tourist," she said. "Like the rain in spring, looking around is what tourists do."

She was smiling at him. He was smiling back.

"If you're trying to dig up dirt on the girls, it's way too early," he said. "They just got here and have been too busy getting this business going to give the local yokels even the time of day."

Gwen feigned shock. "What would make you think that I'd be seeking gossip about the Collins sisters?"

His grin broadened. "Because you're getting ready to have a low-down, fight-to-the-finish, battle royal for child custody," he answered. "And rumor-mongering is the fastest way to a judge's heart."

Gwen shrugged. "Apparently you aren't immune to them, either. Sounds like you've been doing your share of listening to neighborhood gossip."

"Not exactly," he answered.

"How else would you have heard the news?"

Latt was saved from answering by the arrival of Gwen's meal. Sean brought it in and set it down on the table in front of her.

"Hi," he said, nodding to Latt.

Gwen quickly introduced the two.

"Can I get you something?" he asked. "I'm helping out Katy today."

"I had lunch three hours ago," he answered. "But what you brought your mother sure smells pretty good."

Gwen looked down at her plate. It did smell good. And it looked good, too. The hearty chicken breast sandwich was served on diagonally cut wheat bread, with crusts removed. The vivid contrast of lettuce and tomato peeked out on all sides and a small twist of sliced dill pickles was used for a garnish. It was a very nice presentation.

"I couldn't find any marinade," Sean told her. "So I dipped it in some lemonade. See what you think."

Gwen picked up half the sandwich and scooted the plate over toward Latt. "If I have to be a guinea pig, you have to, too."

He didn't argue.

They bit into the sandwich only seconds apart and their reactions were almost identical.

"Umm!"

"Mmm!"

"This is really wonderful," Gwen heard Latt tell him, while he was still trying to chew.

She nodded in agreement. She swallowed before she spoke.

"I don't know if I'm starving or you're a culinary genius," she said. "But this really tastes great."

"Thanks, Mother," he said.

As Sean walked away, Gwen followed his retreat with her eyes. There was more enthusiasm in his step than she'd seen in a long time. Getting Josh was going to be so good for him. It was going to be a true win/win situation. Josh would get a privileged up-bringing, all the advantages and his rightful place in the world, not to mention the ultimate control of a fabulous business. Sean would perhaps discover some purpose in fatherhood that he had been unable to connect with otherwise. And Gwen would have hope again. She would have an heir for Garrett's business, a reason to keep doing all the things she was doing.

Yes, Gwen thought proudly to herself, the change in custody was going to be the best thing for everybody.

Suddenly the door to the kitchen burst open and a small, big-eyed, dark-haired little dynamo came charging into the dining room.

"Mama! Mama! Look what I found!" he said. "Parker says it's a real arrowhead, real like from Indians, and I found it. I found it myself in my own backyard."

Gwen's heart clutched and her breath caught in her throat at the sight of the boy, so much like her own not that many years ago.

His mother squatted down to be on his level. Gwen watched as Katy oohed and aahed over his discovered treasure.

Josh was talking a mile a minute and she listened with attention, too rapt to be feigned.

"Those two are quite a pair," Latt said across the table.

She turned her attention to him. She detected something judgmental, perhaps even superior in his attitude, and she didn't like it.

"You shouldn't be so hasty to take sides," Gwen told him. "You don't know as much about the situation as you think."

He nodded. "You may be right," he said. "But I know more about it than you give me credit for."

"Just what you've heard from gossip."

"No," he said. "Mostly what's been shared with me in confidence. I'm representing Katy."

"Representing?"

From inside the front of his overalls pocket he retrieved a card and handed it to her.

"I dug one of these out of the storage shed just to hand to you," he said.

Curious, Gwen turned the card over and read what was written there. Lattimer P. Meicklejohn, Attorney-at-Law.

Bitsy's Wisdom 20

Bitsy's Wisdom 20: If you want to sweeten a rub, use raw
sugar. It flavors like molasses and is not as likely to scorch.

Katy was more jittery than the situation warranted. She knew
that. Mentally she lectured herself, over and over again.

He's your ex-husband, you have to remember the "ex" part.

He's only here to see Josh, to try to steal him away, don't make it easy
for him.

He walked out on you when things got tough. Don't let his charm today
affect your memory of yesterday.

She knew, without a doubt, that all those things were true. Her
brain was right on target. But her heart kept dancing in her chest.
It was so good to see him. It was so good to talk with him, just to
be with him.

And she couldn't admit those facts to anyone.

Sean was a threat, a very dangerous threat. With his mother's
help, he could ruin Katy's life. She should be afraid. And intellec-

tually she was. But that didn't seem able to dampen the soaring lightness of her heart when Sean was around, or the cheery tune on her lips morning and night.

She hadn't known what she'd expected from Sean or from Josh. But the relationship the two had established almost from the moment that they met seemed idyllic. The little guy never questioned where his father had been, or why he hadn't come to see him before. He was completely willing to just accept his good fortune at finding his father at last.

And Sean was surprisingly attuned to him. He didn't seem uncomfortable with Josh or unaccustomed to children in general, which, in fact, he was. Instead, he treated the active five-year-old with a basic respect for his opinions and ideas that made the child open up to him. Yet, he didn't try to be his best friend or just one of the kids. Somehow he had instinctively mastered the balancing act between attentiveness and authority. He and Josh had lots of fun together, but Katy could trust that Sean would be in charge and thinking like a responsible adult.

And Josh wasn't the only one being helped by Sean. From the very first day, he'd made himself useful. Emma suggested, in turns, that he was either spying or trying to sabotage them. Katy didn't believe it was either. She told herself, quite firmly, that her ex-husband enjoyed the restaurant business, that he knew what he was doing, and in a town with nothing much else to do, it was natural for him to fill endless idle hours hanging around Bitsy's. If only to be close to his son.

Katy also secretly hoped that he wanted to be close to her as well. She knew that he had loved her once. She hoped the recollection of that would be enough to keep him from hurting her again. She was almost counting on it.

But even if that didn't figure in with his reasoning, she was grateful that he was there. His contribution was far more valuable than just an extra pair of hands. He was teaching Katy how to barbecue.

The second day after he arrived, Sean had followed her out to the brick pit in the backyard. That day, like every day previously, her first chore was to clean. She picked up the scoop and began shoveling the coals and ashes out of the firebox.

He stopped her effort with a hand on her arm.

"What are you doing?" he asked her with a puzzled frown.

"Cleaning," she replied. "It's the first rule of restaurant management. Nothing is good if everything isn't clean."

It was a philosophy that Katy had learned her first day working, and she knew it was one he agreed with wholeheartedly, but his reaction was strange.

"What?" she asked.

He shrugged, hesitant. "I don't want to tell you how to run your business."

"Tell me," she said.

"I guess I ought to ask you instead," Sean responded. "Who taught you how to barbecue?"

"Nobody," Katy answered. "Bitsy left a collection of notes and tips but it assumes a knowledge that I don't really have. That's one of my biggest challenges. I don't really know what I'm doing, and so far the outcome hasn't been all that good."

"Did you think about consulting with somebody? Maybe spending a day working in somebody else's kitchen?"

"Would they let me do that?" she asked.

"They would if you paid them," Sean answered. "If they're far enough away that they're not competitors, you can find someone to allow you to observe their process. They won't sell recipes or anything like that—"

"Oh, I don't need recipes," Katy answered. "I got a huge metal box of them when I bought the place. But so far, nothing has really tasted right."

"Well, cleaning out the pit every day probably doesn't help that," he said.

"What do you mean?"

"This isn't a charbroiler or a deep-fat fryer," he explained. "The coals and residue are the essentials of fire-pit cooking. There's no substitute for it. And believe me, the folks who sell umpteen gallons of liquid smoke products every year have tried."

"Oh."

"If you're cleaning the pit out every day, then you might as well be microwaving the meat, for all the flavor you're going to give it," he said.

"I didn't know."

He showed her how to stir the fire.

"We just lay some fresh wood on this and it ought to spring to life pretty easily."

"This is great," Katy said. "Doing it this way, I won't even need starter fluid."

"Yeah, I wouldn't think that petroleum products would be doing the meat a lot of good, either."

They rolled the wheelbarrow to the woodpile and Katy began loading it. Sean held up a piece, eying it unpleasantly.

"Katy, this is pine," he said.

"Pine's not good?"

"It's good for floors and coffins and…and Pine-Sol, but it's not good for cooking. You need hickory or pecan."

"Oh, gosh, I thought I was saving so much money buying this off of a guy who was clearing his pasture."

Sean was digging down along the edges of the woodpile.

"We've got something else down here," he said.

Katy nodded. "That was here when I came. I had him put the pine on top of it."

They dug out enough of the old wood, which Sean thought was alder, to fill the wheelbarrow.

That night's barbecue was improved so much that they sold out and got compliments from every customer served.

With all the other feelings stirring up in Katy's heart, a tremendous sense of gratitude to Sean and a dependence on him grew as well. That was not a good thing. It made Katy introspective and kept her awake at night.

Sean was right about he and his mother being able to offer things to Josh that she couldn't. A boy needed his father. Nobody would question that statement. And with Josh and Sean it was more than that. They were good together. They had a lot in common. More than a similar intellect and interest. The two were alike in temperament as well. They could sit in solitude together, just enjoying each other's presence, or they would be completely engaged in a serious game of chess. Katy could rarely be still without chatting. And she found board games of all types boring, and chess, in particular, completely inexplicable. She could never give Josh those things, but that wasn't all that worried her.

What she wanted for her son was security and stability. That was why she'd bought her own business. That was why she'd worked to make a place for them in the Warbler Lake community. But who better could offer her son those things than his well-heeled grandmother—things like the comforts of wealth and privilege in St. Louis. Was Katy denying Josh that advantage, that shelter from her own selfishness? She loved her son and wanted him with her. Was that always, automatically, the best thing? Katy had always thought so, but as she watched father and son together, she began to wonder.

Emma didn't like it. And she didn't hesitate to make her feelings known. Katy deliberately tuned her sister out. It was not that she didn't trust Emma's judgment or believe that she had Katy's best interests at heart. It was just that she had to work it out for herself in her own time. She had to see the truth fully to recognize it. And until she could see it, she had to give Sean a chance.

Which was why Emma called for reinforcements. She had asked Latt to have a talk with her.

Katy had been so grateful he'd offered to take her case. She'd promised him that she would pay him, she'd even offered a partnership in Bitsy's.

"We'll worry about that later," he told her. "Right now we've just got to worry about you and Josh."

They were seated together in one of the front booths on a slow midmorning.

"The Dodsons will be taking notes and taking names," Latt warned her. "That's the way these things are done. Of course, Sean and his mother are here to see Josh, but they're also here to see you and use anything you say or do against you if they can."

Katy glanced toward the door of the kitchen, behind which she knew Sean was busy getting ready for the lunch rush.

"I don't think Sean is trying to trap me or spy on me or anything like that," she assured Latt. "He's only trying to help me. He likes the business and wants to see it succeed."

Across the table Katy could see Latt frown.

"Sometimes people think they are helping you even when they are working against your best interests."

Katy hoped that wasn't the case with Sean. But she thought it might very likely be true about Sean's mother.

The woman obviously cared a lot about Josh. From the moment the two had met, the hard-bitten, all-business Gwen Dodson appeared completely smitten.

"I'm your grandmother, your father's mother," Gwen had told him. "And you must call me Grandmother."

Josh had nodded, but instead referred to her persistently as GramMarr. The very well-spoken and particular Mrs. Dodson never once corrected him.

Josh took the appearance of a never-before-mentioned grand-mother with the same pleasure and acceptance that he'd shown upon meeting his father. But the two members of the Dodson family approached their relationship to him very differently.

Sean took him fishing, swimming, hiking, they played board games and card games and guessing games. He'd come by early in the morning, before Nadine and her kids arrived, to take Josh down to a quiet glade by the lake where they'd sit in silence listening to the birds wake up.

Gwen's approach, to Katy's way of thinking, was far less positive. After five years of ignoring her grandson completely, she'd now apparently decided that every day was Christmas.

Presents of clothes, toys and electronics began arriving at rapid-fire intervals. When Gwen thought of anything, she went up to the cemetery, clicked on to the Internet and had it shipped to Josh.

The little guy was stunned and overwhelmed.

Katy was annoyed at the deluge.

The Game Boy was stored away until he was older.

But the eight-foot trampoline with the mesh enclosure went up in the backyard and was the excitement of the summer for Parker and the older kids in the neighborhood.

The new books and puzzles crowded out some of his former favorites from the shelves.

The expensive designer clothes clogged their meager closet space, and seemed too good to wear for everyday play.

The action figures were often characters with which he was not familiar. And the sports equipment was meant for teams he wasn't old enough to be on.

Josh always thanked her, but it was clear that some gifts were way off the mark for him. Gwen tried to get a better average by simply asking him what he wanted.

Josh shrugged and refused to ask for anything.

Katy was pleased, both because he was too polite to be greedy, and because he saw himself as a happily satisfied kid.

"I've got mostly everything, GramMarr," he told Sean's mother. The woman could never take no for an answer.

"What do you watch on TV?" Gwen asked him. "Do you like *Pokémon? Blue's Clues?*"

Josh's brow furrowed and he glanced over at his mother. "Do I like them, Mama?"

Gwen gave Katy a withering glance, not appreciating having her drawn into the discussion at all.

"No, I don't think he really does," she said.

"Surely, he has a favorite program."

The answer was directed at Katy, but the smile was all for Josh.

"I can't think of one," he admitted.

"Josh doesn't watch much TV," Katy explained to her. "We have a TV, but we can only get one station and it's pretty fuzzy so we don't watch it."

"You don't get cable?" Gwen said.

"There isn't any cable."

The older woman gave a huffy sigh. "That doesn't surprise me a bit."

Two days later a truck showed up at her door. Apparently Gwen had purchased a new television with integrated technology and a satellite dish to be installed on Bitsy's rooftop.

Gwen arrived just after the truck. To avoid an argument inside the restaurant, the two sisters and Sean confronted her as she got out of her car.

"Are you out of your mind?" Emma asked the woman, absolutely livid. "You don't go off and buy something like that without consulting Katy."

"It's my gift to my grandson," Gwen insisted. "And I can give him anything that I choose."

"Mother," Sean cautioned. "You can't behave this way."

"Of course I can," she said, waving away her son's concern. "It has nothing to do with you."

"Anything that has to do with Josh has to do with me," Sean told her. "But Katy gets the final say on anything that comes into her house."

"Parents don't get to discriminate on what gifts their children accept," Gwen said.

"They sure do," Emma insisted. "It doesn't matter who you are, you can't buy a child a car or an assault rifle. You're not buying him a TV."

"You would deny this bright little boy one of the basics of comfortable American life just because his mother can't afford to provide it for him."

That statement stung, but Emma took up for her.

"Katy is perfectly able to give Josh everything that he *needs,*" her sister replied.

Sean agreed. "Watching a lot of television is not one of the essentials."

"I suppose he won't be able to have a computer, either," Gwen complained. "You'll stunt him technologically and he'll never achieve his potential."

"Josh will do just fine," Emma snarled. "It's none of your business, anyway."

"Oh, I believe it is," Gwen said. "And I'm sure my lawyer

will, too. Does your *lawyer* know you're making these arbitrary decisions?"

The word *lawyer* put both Sean and Emma on high alert. They both tried to answer her at once, but Gwen couldn't hear either of them because she was talking herself. The sound of voices grew louder and louder. Finally Katy was forced to cut through the conversation.

"No!" Katy's refusal was adamant.

All three of them turned to look at her, eyes wide in surprise. She was a little surprised herself. Normally Mrs. Dodson intimidated her completely and usually she allowed Emma or Sean to do any necessary talking for her. But not now, not this time. She felt surprisingly certain and confident.

"No TV," she repeated. "That's my decision and that's the end of it. I'll go tell the driver to put it all back on the truck."

Bitsy's Wisdom 21

Bitsy's Wisdom 21: Keeping bait alive and in the best condition goes a long way toward providing a full stringer of fish at the end of the day.

The cool dark morning in the confines of the bait shop was becoming a way of life for Emma. Maybe not so much a way of life as a life sentence.

Field note: Coded communications among inhabitants are best translated by both interpreting the nuances of the local language and mastering the hunter-gatherer rituals peculiar to the tribe.

"What am I carrying?" an early morning fisherman asked her, meaning what type of bait was currently most popular.

"Depends on what are you're hooking?" Emma replied, hoping to determine his target fish.

"Whatever's biting," he answered.

"Well, bream and sunfish are going for crickets," Emma told him. "Crappie on grubs. And catfish are hitting night crawlers and chicken livers."

"What about bass?"

"We've got minnows," she told him. "But everything I hear is about spinners and lures."

The guy took a couple of dozen chubs, just to be polite.

With the end of the school year, summer visitors were beginning to arrive at Warbler Lake. The population of barely a thousand locals was swelling to almost twice that size as every day more and more boats dotted the lake and Emma's mornings trapped inside the bait shop were getting longer and longer.

She found that she didn't mind it. Observing her customers as if they were an alien culture piqued her interest and made the days go quicker. Also, her summer assistants were a help as well. Josh and Brianna loved to hang around the bait shop. It might have been more accurate to say that Josh loved the bait shop and Brianna refused to let the guy out of her sight.

The two would kneel beside the huge troughs of galvanized steel that were filled with different kinds of tiny fish moving like synchronized swimmers in their clear water.

"Look at these, Bri," he said to the little girl. "They're goldfish. I got a goldfish like this one in the plastic bag at the fair. Those are shiners, not as pretty as the goldfish, but close. The ugly ones are called fatheads."

When he wasn't watching the minnows, Josh investigated the crawfish, crickets and even the disgusting leeches and worms. And he took genuine delight in showing Brianna everything.

"You can herd a night crawler better than a sheep or cow," he explained to her. "If you touch him on his head, he walks backward. If you touch him on his tail, he walks forward. To make him go left you touch right or to go right you touch him on the left."

"I don't want to touch him at all," Brianna admitted.

They moved on to another box.

"These are crawdads," he told her. "They're like cousins to lobsters."

"What are lobsters?" Brianna asked.

Josh shrugged. "Just crawdads that live in the ocean."

Emma was impressed at how much information the little guy was accumulating. He listened and asked questions of every old fisherman who walked into the place. He soaked up their answers like a sponge.

Field note: No formal instruction is utilized in the passing of knowledge from one generation to the next. Watching and listening are the only tools. Sorting the truth from lore is accomplished by expanding the number of sources for inquiry.

Latt was Josh's most consistent source of information and the boy always tried to be in the shop when he made a delivery. The two managed long animated conversations about harvesting catalpa worms or bee moth larvae.

"You know, Auntie Em," he confided to her one morning. "When I grow up, I want to have my own bait store."

Emma smiled at him. "I'm sure you'll be good at whatever you decide to do," she told him.

Secretly she hoped that he would repeat his desire to his grandmother; Emma would love to see the old gal's face.

The spring fishing eased into summer and in some ways the days were moving too fast. Emma found the arrival of Sean Dodson and his mother in Warbler Lake to be a real complication to her matchmaking efforts between Katy and Curt. Emma had thought that just throwing the two together would be enough. Surely, even Katy could see what a kinder, more hardworking, dependable guy the pastor/mailman was compared to her spoiled mama's boy of an ex-husband.

And Katy obviously did like Curt. They got along great and

were both excited with their upcoming music night plans. But her sister's real attentions seemed increasingly focused on Sean.

Of course, Curt could have competed for Katy's attention. But he appeared unmotivated to do so. He was becoming entirely too chummy with Sean. The two seemed to have hit it off immediately. And Emma got the distinct feeling that Curt was rooting for Sean and Katy as a couple again.

That was definitely not a plan that Emma could endorse. Though she did have to admit the barbecue was getting better, and just in time. The summer visitors filled the restaurant and kept them hopping until late into the night. Emma had never worked such long hours or done such strenuous labor. She was exhausted by the time she climbed into bed.

Her sister, in contrast, seemed to draw energy from the long, busy days and the never-ending trickle of hungry diners.

She enjoyed the people and they enjoyed her. She moved throughout Bitsy's with grace and confidence. She got things done very quickly, but never appeared to be in a hurry.

Emma found herself admiring her sister and being astonished at her as well. The way she'd backed Gwen down on that television was something. Emma had been trying to reason, shame, demand. Katy just said "No!" and it worked perfectly.

She was thinking about that as she glanced at her watch and decided the bait shop could take care of itself. She went out the door and turned over the Come On In sign to the side that read Ask Next Door and walked around the side of the building to the backyard and the kitchen door.

She saw Parker sitting on the bottom steps of the stairs, posed liked *The Thinker* and staring off into space. He startled slightly when she came up behind him.

"Sorry," Emma said. "Didn't mean to steal you out of your castles in Spain."

"Huh?" the boy responded. He had obviously never heard the expression. "I...I was waiting on you," he said.

Emma stopped and looked at him, surprised. "Me?"

"Yeah, I wanted to talk to you."

Emma liked Nadine and Nadine's children just fine. It seemed like a good idea to keep Josh right here at home and still have somebody to watch him. Nadine was willing to do that for very little cash money. And her pies were a consistent seller. But, unlike Katy, Emma had really never gotten to know the young woman and barely noticed her kids at all, except when they were too loud or in the way. She couldn't imagine what this dreamy seven-year-old could possibly have to say to her.

She shrugged. "I've got a couple of minutes," she said, managing a smile for the kid. "What's up?"

Parker hesitated.

Emma wanted to just take off, hurry into the restaurant and get on with her day. But, she knew what it was like to be the oldest, to feel like you have a lot on your shoulders and to wish that there was somebody to talk to.

Deliberately, she took a seat on the steps beside him. She just sat there, in the cool shade of the building, feeling just a hint of the lake breeze in her hair, willing herself into calmness and waiting for him to talk.

After a couple of minutes, he did.

"I need you to talk to the preacher for me," Parker said.

"Curt?" Emma was surprised.

"Yeah, I know he's a friend of yours. He'll listen to you."

"Yes, we're friends," Emma said. "But I think Curt is friends with everybody. I'm sure he'd listen to you, too."

Parker shook his head. His dark, unruly brown hair was badly in need of a summer haircut and his big dark eyes were as serious as an old man's.

"I've already tried to talk to Pastor Curt," he said. "He won't do what I want."

"What do you want?" Emma asked him.

Again, Parker was reticent.

Emma was urging. "I can't talk to him if you don't tell me what to talk about," she said.

"He knows," Parker said.

"Yeah, but I don't know. Tell me."

"You can't tell anyone else," he said. "Not anyone, not your sister or nobody."

Emma held up her hand. "Girl Scout's honor," she said.

He looked skeptical. "Were you a Girl Scout?"

"No, but I still have honor," she said. "Tell me, I won't breathe a word to anyone but Curt."

He sighed heavily. "I want to get baptized," he said.

Emma had no idea what she had expected the boy to say, but she didn't expect him to say that.

"Well…well, that's great, Parker," she said.

"I know it's the right thing for me to do," he said. "I know it's what I want to do. I'm almost eight and a guy can know a lot about what he thinks and feels, and what he feels about God even when he's a kid."

"Yes, I'm sure a guy can," Emma said. "And you're a very bright guy. I think you're very sincere and if this is what you want, then that's a very good thing."

Parker was nodding.

"So you've talked to Curt about this," Emma said.

"Yeah," he answered. "I told him that it's what I want to do. And I want to do it now, this summer. It's really important to me. And he said he's very proud of me and all that."

"Okay then, so what's the problem?"

"The problem is, he won't baptize me unless I get permission from my mom," Parker said. "He said that I can't make a public profession of faith behind the back of the most important person in my life."

"Well, that makes sense," Emma said.

"No, it doesn't," Parker insisted. "It's about me and my life. Mom's life is…it's different from mine and she'll never see things the way I do."

Emma thought of all the hundreds of important decisions she'd made for herself and her sister without any input from her flaky and absent mother. She did believe that everyone, including kids, could oftentimes be the best judge of what was best for them. But Nadine did not appear to be disconnected from the needs of her children. She definitely wasn't June Cleaver, but she wasn't *Mommie Dearest,* either.

"Maybe your mom won't see it the way you do," Emma admitted. "But you've got to give her a chance. She's your mother and she loves you."

"I love her, too," Parker said. "That's why I don't want her to know. You don't understand."

The last phrase, uttered hourly by kids who came into Bitsy's, was apparently the "whatever" of the new generation. But Emma sensed that for Parker it wasn't just a throwaway line.

"If I don't understand, then help me understand," Emma said. "Explain it to me."

The boy's brow furrowed. "I don't know if I can exactly," he said. "Mom doesn't like church."

"She's an atheist? Agnostic?"

Parker's expression was blank; he obviously didn't recognize the words.

"Your mom doesn't believe in God?"

"Oh, yeah, of course she does," Parker said. "I talked to her about Natty once and she told me that he was a special gift to us from heaven. So she must believe if she thinks we get stuff from there."

"I guess so," Emma agreed.

"It's not God that's the problem," Parker said. "It's the people in the church. They think Mom is a bad person. She didn't marry any of our dads, so she's a sinner. But my dad didn't want to marry her and Brianna's dad was already married and Natty's dad is a big jerk of a loser. So she didn't really do anything wrong really."

Emma didn't feel qualified to get into the fine points of Nadine's personal life. She just listened.

"Mom says the church is full of hypocrites," he said. "That they act like *her* mistakes, which everybody knows about, are bad, bad. But the stuff that *they* do wrong, which nobody finds out about, is not so bad at all."

"What do you think?" Emma asked him.

Parker shrugged. "Well, she's kinda right," she said. "But she's kinda wrong, too. Some people do whisper about her. And some do act like she's too dirty for them to talk to. But Pastor Curt doesn't. And my Sunday School teacher doesn't and…and God doesn't."

Emma nodded solemnly. "I'm sure God doesn't," she agreed.

"So I feel like I just really want to be part of the church," Parker said. "But I don't want Mom to think that I'm taking their side over hers."

"No, of course not."

"It would just hurt Mom and I can't do that."

Emma was nodding.

"So, could you talk to the preacher and make him understand that I need to be able to do this without letting my mom know about it?"

"I'll talk to him," Emma promised. "But I can't guarantee that it will be any help."

"Oh, he'll listen to you," Parker said with confidence. "Everybody at the church thinks he's going to marry you. And they're all really happy about it. They like you a lot, even if you never show up for service and always go fishing instead."

Bitsy's Wisdom 22

Bitsy's Wisdom 22: When fishing with leeches go to the lightest weight and work the line making it drop and flutter. Bass will usually bite on the drop.

Gwen was seated in her usual spot on Carlton Bullock's cemetery bench. Managing the Dodsonburger franchise corporation through e-mail and phone calls was not easy. She wondered if she was going to end up being the test case for a new work-related repetitive injury syndrome—Blackberry thumb. Typing long instructions with her two opposable digits was an exhausting challenge. But Gwen was not accustomed to an easy life and she was getting used to the struggle of living in a near-camping situation and having restricted access to the world outside.

Her frustrations were not as abject as they might have been, because she felt certain she was winning. David Faneuf was accumulating evidence in her favor.

Gwen had been right about the babysitter, Nadine Graves. The girl had been arrested for possession of marijuana and public intoxication when she was sixteen. It was a first offense, but she was remanded to the state reformatory for girls as her parents had declared her incorrigible. After eight months she was released to her elderly grandmother. She lived there until the old lady's death, when her parents, aunts and uncles had her evicted. Somehow they'd ended up giving her the small cottage at Warbler Lake.

"With that in her past, and three illegitimate children from different fathers, she's pretty much disqualified from being an appropriate caregiver to your grandson," David said.

He was sounding very optimistic and assured her that he'd be requesting a court date very soon. Once that was set, Gwen and Sean could go back to their lives. And wait for Josh to join them.

Gwen was not unaware of the changes in Sean. Since they'd arrived in Warbler Lake there were no late nights, followed by all-day sleeping. Sean had stopped looking unkempt. He stopped disappearing. And he seemed to be genuinely interested in the barbecue restaurant. If Sean could show enthusiasm for that place, how much more interested could he be in the real food-service industry?

She was hopeful.

The only fly in the ointment, really, was Sean's ex-wife. The woman was definitely on the pudgy side of curvaceous and a walking fashion faux pas, but Sean had been attracted to her once. And he was spending a lot of time with her now.

"I hope that you're not allowing that woman to snare you into another romantic attachment," she'd said to Sean just that morning. "I'm sure she'd do anything to try to make you look bad at the court hearing."

Sean had turned beet red at the suggestion. Gwen couldn't tell if he was angry or embarrassed or both.

"Mother," he said in a very calm whisper. "Please keep your voice down. Bitsy's is already the biggest source of gossip in town."

"Well then, you should make a real effort not to add to it," she said. "She was all wrong for you once. And as far as I can tell, she hasn't changed one bit."

Sean didn't answer, but Gwen was certain that she'd gotten her point across.

She heard a sound to her left and glanced up. She expected to see old Gus Gouswhelter, who was often seen walking across the bone-yard, tending the graves of those long gone. The two had established a nodding acquaintance up in the quiet solitude of this place.

But it wasn't the old man at all. It was Latt Meicklejohn. He spotted her and waved.

"Are you out here spying on me?" she called out to him.

He grinned. "If I thought you were sunbathing nude instead of just working, I might be guilty of that."

It was then that Gwen noticed he was carrying a little handful of wildflowers, tied with a ribbon. In the weeks since she'd been coming here, she'd seen those little impromptu bouquets many times. She was surprised to discover that he was the one who put the flowers on Bitsy's grave.

"I don't suppose those are for me," she said, indicating the flowers.

Latt chuckled. He looked at the brightly colored bunch and then at her and shook his head.

"I would never peg you for the wildflower type," he said. "You're much too elegant and far more expensive."

"Why does a compliment like that from you somehow sound like a criticism?"

He grinned at her as he scooted her papers across her make-shift desk and took a seat on the bench beside her. "Not because it is," he said. "I think it's more that you're seeing me as the enemy."

"And you're not?"

"Not at all," he said, clearly feigning magnanimity. "We're all just thinking of Josh and what might be best for him. Should he have a caring childhood with a hardworking mother who loves him? Or an expensive upbringing with the cold, wealthy stranger who managed to rear the unfeeling father who callously deserted him?"

Gwen rolled her eyes. "Save it for the judge, Counselor. I'm not about to argue our case with you in the middle of a cemetery."

"I like that word," he said.

"Cemetery?"

"No, argue," he said. "For years in my life as a lawyer, argument was a specific segment of a case. Not any more important really than petition or interrogation. But in my new life as a bait man, I find that argument is what makes the world go round."

Gwen was skeptical. "You mean quarreling, don't you," she said. "I would imagine that there's a lot more of that going on around here than argument."

"Well, you'd be wrong," Latt told her. "Not that we don't have that, we do. Gouswhelter and his daughter-in-law pick at each other every day, I'd guess. And more than one big fish tale has nearly led to blows, but I think for the most part argument is a good thing."

Gwen shrugged with half acceptance. "I suppose it does clear the air," she said. "And it certainly does release a great deal of pent-up tension. But it creates as much stress as it relieves. And solves nothing."

"I disagree about that," Latt said. "I think that sometimes argument solves everything."

"Oh, really?" Her question was dubious.

"Yeah," he answered. "You think you know something, you think you know all about it and you've looked at every angle and you see it just like it is. You're that way. I'm that way. It's just human."

Gwen nodded agreement.

"Then someone comes along who sees it differently," he continued. "And it forces you to look at whatever it is from a new perspective. You get an opportunity to state what you think. They get a chance to explain what they think. Sometimes neither of you change your mind, but sometimes you do."

"And that solves things?"

"If people hadn't learned to sort out their disagreements, we'd still be hunter-gatherers living on a flat earth," he said.

"And your point for me is, keep an open mind, try to see what a happy boy Josh is here in the land that time forgot but poverty didn't."

Latt chuckled. "No, actually my point is, there's no reason to avoid me. The worst that can happen is that we get into an argument. And that always has the possibility of working out for the best."

"I'm not avoiding you," Gwen assured him.

"You're not? Well, I haven't seen you for a week or more and it's a mighty small town."

Gwen started to make excuses and then decided not to bother. She had been avoiding him. Maybe not for the reasons he thought. Yes, he was now the legal representative of her daughter-in-law, which would rightfully evoke wariness. But more than that, Gwen found herself inexplicably disappointed in having him on opposite sides in this. She'd enjoyed their little impromptu dinner. And it had been wonderfully pleasant talking to an attractive, intelligent man who had nothing to do with her job. She hadn't really had much time for that kind of luxury. And once Josh came to live with her, she'd be busier than ever.

"All right," she said. "I promise not to avoid you in the future. Though if you want to run into me, most days, this is the place."

"As far as offices go," he said, "this one is not so bad. Did you hear the one about the hillbilly gal who went to town?"

Gwen raised an eyebrow and sighed.

"No, I don't think so."

"She was sitting in a coffee shop with two city women," he said. "Suddenly there was a beeping sound and one of the city women touched her forearm. The hillbilly gal asked her about it. 'That's my pager,' the woman told her. 'I have a microchip imbedded under the skin of my arm.' The hillbilly gal was pretty impressed. Then a couple of minutes later the other woman lifted her palm to her ear and began talking. When she finished she told the hillbilly gal, 'That's my digital phone. The entire integrated system has been surgically implanted in my hand.' Well, the hillbilly gal was almost overwhelmed with the idea of that."

"I'm sure," Gwen said.

"So she was feeling very backwoods and low-tech and she just had to think of something to impress these city women. Suddenly she got up and went to the bathroom. When she came back she had a long trail of toilet paper hanging down from the back of her dress. 'Well, will you look at that,' she told the city women. 'I'm getting a fax.'"

Gwen closed her eyes and shook her head.

"You can't even manage a little chuckle?" Latt asked her.

"That's a terrible joke," she said.

"Hey, consider the source," he said. "Spurl Westbrook told it to me."

"You need to get out more," Gwen teased him.

"That's what I was thinking," he said. "In fact, it was my exact purpose for coming up here today."

"Oh?"

"I wanted to ask you if you'd accompany me to the musical night at Bitsy's," he said. "I know it's short notice, but I've planned it as a pretty low-key evening. A walk along the lake, a little bit of barbecue, a little bit of music and a walk back home."

She shook her head. "Oh, I don't think—"

"Gwen," he said, interrupting her. "Are you listening? I said that it's no big deal."

"I'm not really dating," she told him.

"Dating?" He sat back and eyed her, incredulously. "Gwen, if I were going to ask you on a date, believe me, I could come up with a better evening than pork ribs and amateur fiddlers. You know that you're going to go. Everybody in town is going to go, there's nothing else to do. So go with me. We'll observe."

"Observe what?"

"The local culture," he said. "That's what Emma does. She's a wannabee anthropologist. I think the only thing that keeps her from pulling out her hair and running for the hills is observing and analyzing the natives."

Gwen shrugged. "I suppose it's better than watching soap operas. Which is probably what she'd be doing if she wasn't here."

Latt turned to look at her, surprised. "Emma? Watching soap operas? Not hardly. That's a young woman who so wants and needs a college education it just seems criminal that she goes without it."

"Then why doesn't she go?" Gwen asked.

"She's tried. The first time her mother dropped a teenage sister on her to raise. Then, when she'd finally gotten started back again, your son dropped his wife and baby on her."

Gwen winced.

"She was planning to re-enroll this fall, once she got Katy settled in here, but that may not happen, either."

"Why not?"

"Because she's given me her college money to represent Katy in court," he said.

"Tough break," Gwen agreed. "The world can be a very difficult place without a family and some financial cushion to back you up."

He nodded.

"More reason," she went on, "to make sure that Josh Dodson has those family and money connections."

"Hmm," Latt said thoughtfully, and then added, "a lot of grandmothers would make sure the child had those things without insisting upon custody."

"Touché," she responded.

"See, we can argue without quarreling."

"Yes, I suppose so."

They walked across the cemetery. He stopped to lay the flowers on Bitsy's grave. He patted the headstone.

"She was a good friend?"

"The best," he said.

Gwen nodded.

Latt said nothing more until they reached the passenger side of her car.

"So, I'll pick you up about seven," he said.

Gwen still wasn't sure if she *should* go, but she *wanted* to, so she agreed.

That evening, she was regretting the impulse. She'd changed her clothes three times and she still felt overdressed. He said it wasn't a date and she didn't want to look as if she thought it was. But dressing down in a place as lowly as this style-deficient corner of the Ozarks was difficult to do. She finally settled on a pair of denim look-alike designer slacks with a knit top and a teal linen jacket. Gwen was thinking that she appeared sufficiently dowdy.

When Latt showed up on her front porch, he was profuse with compliments, but she assumed that he was merely being polite.

He looked pretty good himself, in khaki slacks and a neatly pressed sport shirt. They walked together along the lakeshore, mostly in silence, enjoying their shared solitude and the sun setting over the edge of the mountains.

"You should paint that one," she said.

"You remember my paintings?"

"Of course," she said. "I thought they were actually quite good."

"Thank you," he said. "Coming from you, I know it's an honest opinion. And that is an incredible sky. But I only paint sun*rises.*"

Gwen nodded. "That's right, I remember," she said. "Though you have to admit they basically look the same."

"They may look the same, but they aren't the same," he said. "One is full of possibilities, the other of no more importance than turning out the light."

They arrived at Bitsy's to see the place already abuzz. Virtually every person who lived in town was in attendance. And squeezed among them were knots of tourists and weekenders. The front parking lot was roped off from cars, and tables from the church recreation hall had been borrowed for the overflow. The bad-news babysitter, Nadine, had been drafted into waitress duty. And her seven-year-old son was bussing tables.

Sean was wearing a white apron and looking, Gwen thought, disturbingly like an employee. It was good to see his enthusiasm again. It was good to see him working. But there was something unsettling about the amount of time and effort he was expending in a business that belonged to his ex-wife.

"Hello, Mother," he said, surprising her by laying a kiss on her cheek just like used to when he was younger. "We're so glad you came. And you look wonderful."

His compliments had her frowning. The "we" was the most disturbing part.

"The place is filling up fast," Sean said. "Let's see, where's the best spot to seat you…? Why don't you two share a booth with the Dempseys?"

Gwen was not keen on sitting with strangers and would have said so, if Latt had not acquiesced immediately. She found herself greeting the old couple. Another woman was already sitting with them. Mr. Dempsey moved to sit in a chair at one end of the booth and Gwen had no polite choice but to scoot across the upholstered seat and allow Latt to sit beside her.

"We're so excited," Mrs. Dempsey told her. "Armon and I don't go out at night at all anymore because he can't see a thing after dark. But that sweet little Katy came and got us. She said she'd make sure we got home safe and sound. Such a precious girl."

"Yes, absolutely precious," Latt said, and sent a little side wink to Gwen.

"I don't believe we've met," Gwen said to the other woman with them. The sight of whom put to rest any fears Gwen might have had of being overdressed. She was slim and chic in an aging but elegant Oleg Cassini cocktail dress. "I'm Gwendolyn Dodson."

"Luella Bullock," the woman answered, accepting Gwen's hand. The older woman's wrist was dripping with a diamond-and-sapphire bracelet.

"Gwen knows your husband," Latt said.

The old woman's face lit up with surprise. Gwen turned to glance at her companion, completely dumbfounded.

"She sits every day on that wonderful bench you put up for him in the cemetery," Latt explained.

Gwen was momentarily horrified that Latt should make such a casual mention of something so sad. To her surprise, Luella laughed.

"Trying to make cell phone calls, I'd wager," she said. "I swear, I should have had them design it like a phone booth, that's what everybody uses it for."

"I…uh…" Gwen felt that she should apologize, but she wasn't quite sure how or why.

"I'm sure Carlton enjoys the company," Luella said. "But I'd be careful, an attractive young woman like you sitting above him, that old coot will be trying to get a look up your skirt."

Mrs. Dempsey put her hand over her mouth and giggled like a little girl.

"Maybe all us roosters should just take a strut around the pen and let these young chicks have their laughs at our expense," Mr. Dempsey said to Latt.

"I can take it if you can," he said to the man. He then turned his attention to Luella. "It's good to see you here tonight."

"Sean came to get me," she said. "He said I just couldn't miss it. I told him I'd been missing things here at Bitsy's for years, but he wouldn't hear of it."

Emma showed up with a tray of iced teas and took their orders. The regular menu was suspended for the evening for a choice of two specials, pork butt on a bun or short ribs. Gwen chose the latter.

The conversation was divided by gender, the men discussing the current fishing season and the ladies speculating on the entertainment of the evening. Gwen was half listening to both confabs when suddenly there was a surprising interruption.

"Hi, GramMarr," Josh said.

"Oh, hello," she said to the little smiling face that showed up at the end of the table.

"Pastor Curt is going to play the piano and Mr. Riley has brought his fiddle. They're going to make music right here," he said.

"Yes, won't that be fun," Gwen said, smiling. She could hardly look at the little dark-eyed, dark-haired child without smiling.

Suddenly his mother was beside him. She had smiles for everybody, but she was clearly cautious around Gwen.

"I hope this guy is not bothering you," she said. "Come on, Josh, I'll set you up at the counter."

"Can I eat here?" he asked. "I want to sit with GramMarr."

Katy hesitated as if she was thinking it through. Latt plunged into the breach.

"Sure you can, partner," he said. "We've got just the spot in here between your grandma and me."

He grabbed the boy under his armpits and lifted him up and over to the space beside Gwen.

"I don't want him to be any trouble," Katy said.

"He'll be fine," Latt said. "We'll keep an eye on him."

"Are you sure?" She directed the question at the table in general.

"Yes, of course," Mrs. Dempsey said.

"Leave him here," her husband concurred.

"Don't give another thought about him, he's all settled in."

Katy looked directly at Gwen.

"I'll take care of him," she told her simply. "Go, do your job, take care of your business. He'll be with me."

If there was a reluctance, she covered it well and with a big smile for Josh and an admonishment to be on his best behavior, she left.

The conversation at the table resumed. At first it was centered on the five-year-old, but by the time the food came, they were focused on more grown-up topics.

The food was surprisingly good, causing the discussion to be more sporadic, except for Josh, who had some trouble remembering the rule about not talking with your mouth full.

Curt, Waymon Riley and a guitar player who was described by Armon Dempsey as "Stymie Wilham's stepnephew" began tuning up.

Sean bussed their table, talking both the men into having a piece of coconut cream pie. Josh claimed to want one as well, but Latt assured him that he could share.

The tiny stage area was lit with some utilitarian lighting stands that provided as least as much heat as light. They didn't bother with microphones, but when they were ready, Curt stood up in front and raised his arms to get everyone's attention.

"Welcome, everybody, to the first, but hopefully not the last, of the New Musical Evenings at Bitsy's Bait & BBQ," he said. "I've got some good news and some bad news."

A small chuckle rumbled through the room in anticipation.

"I woke up this morning with a tickle in my throat and I don't think I'll be able to do much singing."

"Is that the good news or the bad?" Spurl Westbrook called out.

Curt laughed. "I think it's both," he answered.

The crowd loved that and offered some lighthearted applause.

"So," Curt continued, "we're going to warm up with a couple of instrumentals. Those are the songs you don't sing to. I found that out just recently. Before I learned better, I used to sing a lot of my instrumentals."

There was a fluttering of groans and chuckles in the audience. Latt glanced over at Gwen, his expression wry. "He'd better keep his day jobs, I don't think he'd make it on Comedy Central."

"What's Comedy Central?" Josh asked.

"It's a television network," Gwen said. "You know television, that blank-looking black box in the corner of your living room."

Josh giggled. "Of course I know television, GramMarr," he said. "I'm not a baby."

"It's a sore subject with your grandmother," Latt said, and he winked at her.

The amateur musicians played tune after tune. Skipping across genre lines with the ease of a flat stone on the surface of the lake. They'd perform a knee-slapping bluegrass picking, followed by an aging rock anthem and then on to a smooth piece of forties jazz. And Gwen thought that it was not really too bad. Or maybe she'd been there long enough to be as desperate for entertainment as the locals.

There was a tiny dance floor in front of the makeshift stage area, but it was so closely surrounded by tables that there was hardly room for two couples. One of the first to take the floor were Spurl and Vivy Westbrook. Gwen had met the school principal and his wife, who taught fifth grade. They were both significantly sizable. Spurl's gut hung over his belt so far that his belt buckle was completely hidden. His wife was dressed in a brightly colored muumuu, not simply because she liked the island fashion, but also because she had so much trouble finding colorful clothes that fit. However, when the two began to sway together to the music, they were very light on their feet.

"Do you want to dance?"

The question came from Latt and caught Gwen off guard.

"Oh, no," she said. "I haven't danced in years."

"I'm sure you still remember," he said.

She shook her head. "No, I think taking to the floor here would be a bit more public than I'm ready for. Besides—" With a nod she gestured to the child beside her. He'd pulled his little sneaker-clad feet up onto the seat and had snuggled up next to her. He was watching the stage, but his eyes had that distinctly unfocused far-away look and his lids were closing for longer and longer intervals.

Gwen surreptitiously put a finger to her lips. Latt signaled understanding. They turned their attention back to the music at hand. By the time the final note was played and the applause began, Josh was sound asleep, his warm young body pressed against her, his little mouth slightly agape.

He was wonderful.

The thought came to her mind, not for the first time. It was almost like a theme that replayed over and over like a loop in her brain whenever the boy was near her. It was amazing, really. This young child whom she'd spent almost no time with, whom she hardly knew, pulled on her heartstrings with the same intensity that she'd felt for her own son. But somehow there was more pleasure in it. As a young parent she had been so responsible, so serious, so busy. And during most of Sean's young life she'd spent endless hours worrying. Now older and wiser, she let none of those anxieties slip in. Her moments with her grandson were raw joy, with nothing mixed in.

She wondered if that would change once he was hers to keep. She vowed that she wouldn't let it.

"Do you want me to take him?"

The music was playing again and Sean had to speak loudly over the sound of it to be heard.

"Take him where?" she asked.

"I can carry him upstairs and put him to bed," Sean said. "He'll be fine."

"I'll take him," Latt said. "You mind your customers."

"Thanks," Sean said, and patted him on the back.

Latt turned to Gwen. "What do you think? Can we move him upstairs without waking him up?"

She shrugged. "If he can sleep through this music, I can't imagine anything would wake him up."

Latt stood up and gathered the boy against his shoulder. Gwen followed him as they made their way through the crowd and out the front door. As they walked around the building, they came upon a group of men standing around a cooler at the corner near the door of the bait store. Gwen thought they were just standing around smoking cigarettes. Latt apparently detected something else and hesitated long enough to give them a warning.

"The deputy sheriff is inside," he said. "If you boys have any sense at all, you'll get that stuff off the premises."

"That's our problem, we got no sense," one smart aleck answered.

"Mind your own business, Meicklejohn," another said.

Gwen recognized the second voice as Pearly Ross, the guy from the tow truck. She ignored them and continued around the corner to the stairs.

"You go up first," Latt said, "so you can open the door."

Gwen nodded and scurried up ahead of him.

She got the door open and the lights on. She held the screen for Latt as he carried the boy inside.

The larger of the two bedrooms was now crowded with the addition of the new junior bed that Gwen had bought for Josh. She had very much disapproved of a five-year-old sleeping with his mother. Rather than waste time discussing it, Gwen had simply ordered the red race-car-style bed for Josh. Of course, the little guy couldn't resist it. It was very cool. Now all it needed was its own room, preferably in Gwen's own lovely home in Ladue.

The little boy stood, a sleepwalker with eyes closed, as they got him into his pajamas. Gwen raked back the covers on the bed while Latt took him to the bathroom to brush his teeth and use the toilet.

Josh was moving on his own power by the time he got back to the bedroom, but went immediately to the race car and settled in with hardly a murmur.

"Good night, GramMarr," he whispered.

"Sleep tight," she answered.

"I love you."

"I love you, too," she said, and planted a kiss on his forehead.

When she stood up, Latt was leaning against the doorjamb watching her.

She turned on the Bert and Ernie night-light and they left the room.

"He's a great kid," Latt said.

Gwen nodded. "I can't believe that I just ignored his existence for five years."

"Why'd you do that?" he asked.

Gwen didn't know exactly how to answer. "I'm not sure entirely," she said. "I didn't think of him as belonging to Sean. He was Katy's baby and I knew Katy was all wrong for my son."

"Why?"

Gwen scanned her memory for the answer. She was low class, without family or connections. She was undereducated and short of social graces. All of those things had been very important to her at the time. But measured against that child in bed in the next room, they seemed paltry.

"I don't think I need to bare my soul to the legal counsel of the opposition," Gwen said. "I'm neither naive nor stupid."

Latt gave her a lazy smile. "I wasn't asking as anyone's lawyer. It was just a curious question for my date."

"Date?" Gwen asked. "I thought you said this wasn't a date."

He raised an eyebrow. "It's gender inequality if you think only women have the prerogative to change their mind."

From below they could hear the music playing.

"Come here," he said, taking her arm. He led her into the kitchen and out into the darkness of the open-air patio. Then he turned and took her in his arms.

"You said you weren't ready for a public dance," he explained. "I thought we might have a more private one."

One hand at her waist, the other clasping her palm, he led her along the floor to the rhythm playing below their feet.

Bitsy's Wisdom 23

Bitsy's Wisdom 23: Although not likely to make your hands render the aroma of roses, red worms, a manure species, so closely resemble a common lake worm that the fish almost always bite on it.

The musical evening was a fabulous success. Katy was very grateful that Curt and Emma had come up with the idea to do it. And the timing was perfect. The locals, after the long quiet days of the off-season, were ready to kick up their heels. The summer visitors were not yet settled into the slow pace of Warbler Lake and still eager for vacation fun. And most important for their future, the barbecue was finally edible, thanks to Sean. With this crowd they had a great opportunity to display the new culinary improvements at Bitsy's.

And if those pluses were not enough, the cash register was stuffed with money. By nine-thirty there was virtually nothing left to sell in the kitchen. They'd simplified the menu to be able to handle the crowd and they'd sold out completely, serving almost three hundred meals. That fact would have been unbelievable, except for the ache in Katy's back and the exhaustion in her feet.

But as the evening ran on and there was nothing left to do but pour iced tea and soda pop, Katy found herself getting into the music and enjoying herself.

Sean dragged a prep stool out of the kitchen for her and she sat in the doorway. He stood behind her, leaning against the wall, his hands resting upon her tired shoulders as the musicians played an achingly slow and sweet version of Willie Nelson's "Crazy."

Katy leaned her head back upon her ex-husband's chest and closed her eyes, trying to hold the moment in time, to hang on to it for as long as it lasted, seeing it for what it was, one of the sweetest in her life.

Too soon it was over and she was applauding with everybody else. She and Sean jumped up for a quick foray through the crowd, filling glasses. Emma was picking up checks and making change.

Curt had gotten up from the piano. Their little group had taken a couple of fifteen-minute breaks already. Katy thought that he was going to announce another one right now. But he didn't.

"We'd like to welcome all the tourists that have shown up tonight for our little musical evening," he said. "We really appreciate you being here and want you to make yourself at home. If you need anything, please just ask any of the local folks. We love to help out. If you don't know who's a tourist and who's from around here, I'll give you a hint. We Ozarkers are the ones with the scars on our face from learning to eat with a knife and fork."

The crowd chuckled at his new use of the very old self-disparaging hillbilly joke.

"The guys and I have just about played everything we know twice," he joked. "The next tunes will be déjà vu all over again if we don't get some help up here. Now, I know that we've got some good singers in this group. Could we have somebody volunteer to step up here and take on vocals?"

There were some murmurs through the crowd, but nobody jumped at the chance.

"Come on now," Curt urged. "I'm not asking for a professional to perform at the Opera Theater of St. Louis. If you can carry a tune and project across this room, you're good enough to sing with this band."

Those words evoked good-natured chuckles.

"My mom can sing."

The words came from Parker, seated near the stage. They were followed by an instant of shocked silence before everyone turned to look at Nadine. She was sitting at the back booth, blocked from the sight of the stage by the counter. Brianna was stretched out asleep on the seat, leaving Nadine perched on a few inches on the outside, holding little Natty, who was wide-awake and watching the action.

"Oh, no," she said, shaking her head. "No, no, I can't."

Curt had turned to look in her direction. "Now, Parker says that you can," he pointed out. "And I know, as his pastor, that the boy wouldn't lie."

"No, I've got the baby."

"Here, let me take him," Mrs. Welborn said, getting up from her seat a few feet away. "He'll sit with me. You go up there and sing a song."

Natty went to the older woman without hesitation.

Nadine was still showing reluctance as the crowd began to offer encouragement. Katy set down her pitcher and walked over to her.

"Take off your apron and get up there," she said.

"I can't, not in front of all these people," Nadine said.

"Of course you can," she said. "You'll be fine."

The murmurs of encouragement had escalated into applause

and Nadine made her way across the room. She spoke to the musicians for a moment, and as Curt turned to take his seat at the piano, she spoke to the crowd, still blushing.

"I hope you all aren't going to be sorry," she said.

The boys began playing the intro to a catchy Nashville favorite. She stood nervously in front of them, trying to figure out what to do with her hands. But when her note came, she had no hesitation.

Hers was not a trained musical voice and initially the pitch was far from perfect, but the quality of her sound was clear and elegant, well suited to the song she'd chosen.

Katy listened with the same enthusiasm as everyone else in the room. Genuinely astounded as the unexpected voice came out of the mouth of her friend.

"She is pretty good," Sean said to her as they met back at their spot.

Katy agreed.

When the number was over, the appreciation was adamant. Nadine appeared quite surprised by the adulation. With thank-yous and bows, she tried to get away. The crowd was not about to let her go.

Curt suggested another song. She agreed and handled that one as well as the last.

The audience began making requests. If the musicians were willing to try to play it, Nadine sang. And her voice got better as her confidence improved.

Katy was very pleased about the accomplishments of her friend. Nadine had never, in any way, alluded to the talent that now entertained them all. She caught sight of Parker sitting cross-legged at the edge of the dance floor. His young face was beaming as he watched his mother.

Katy leaned back to whisper in Sean's ear. "Look at Parker."

Sean nodded. "The little guy couldn't be prouder."

"She needs that," Katy said.

"He does, too," Sean replied. "When your mom is the only parent you have, a kid can put a lot of pressure on himself to believe that she's perfect. She's twice as good as other kids' parents. The moments when she lives up to that are pure heaven."

Katy realized that Sean wasn't just talking about Parker, he was talking about himself. But what weighed on her mind was Josh. Had her son spent these past five years of childhood expecting her to be more than other moms? She was sure she hadn't lived up to that and was afraid that she never could.

She was distracted from her thoughts by some kind of disruption at the front door. People were being jostled and there were words, angry-sounding words coming from that direction. Pearly Ross emerged and staggered onto the dance floor.

Even from across the room, Katy could feel the anger emanating from him. Behind her she felt Sean stiffen.

"What's up with him?" he asked.

Katy shook her head.

They didn't have to wait long for the answer. Pearly pushed his way to the front of the dance floor and pointed an accusing finger at Nadine.

"Stupid slut!" he screamed at her, and cursed vividly. "Standing up in front of everyone. You're a whore and everyone knows it."

He was close enough to hit her and he pulled his arm back as if that was exactly what he was going to do. Sean moved immediately. Katy saw Curt jump up from the piano bench. But it was Old Man Crank who had been dancing with Flora Krebs that got there first. He grabbed Pearly's clenched fist as it swung forward.

Furious at the interference Pearly lashed out at the person who stopped him, easily flinging the old man to the ground. There was a communal gasp, followed by a stunned silence.

"Crank? Crank, are you okay?" Pearly asked.

"Damn, I think I broke my leg," the old man answered.

Quickly people gathered around him. Pearly stood back gazing at the scene as he allowed the rage to build once more. He picked up a glass of water from a nearby table and turned to Nadine.

"Look what you made me do!" he yelled, and threw the glass at her.

Curt stepped in front of her and took the glass on the chin, the water soaking the front of his shirt.

"Get out of here and sober up, Pearly," he said.

Newt Barker, the deputy sheriff, stepped up behind him, grabbing his wrist and encasing them in handcuffs.

"The county jail is a good place for this one to get a better outlook," he said. "I'll radio for an ambulance to get Old Crank to the hospital."

Katy hurried to the old man. Emma was already there, on her knees beside him.

"Just lie still," Emma said to him. "Don't try to move, you might hurt yourself more."

"Babydoll," Crank responded. "I swear a few busted bones are well worth it to get you this close to me."

"You'd better watch it, buster, or I'll break your other leg," she teased him.

Crank laughed and then regretted it as he winced in pain from the very slight movement.

Katy could see that the man's left leg was at an unnatural angle. He was pale as a sheet.

"I'm so sorry this happened," Katy told him. "I'm just so sorry."

"It ain't your fault, sweetie pie," Crank told her. "It's that damn knothead, Pearly. What was that boy thinking coming in here drunk as a skunk? And what kind of fight was he itching for? He goes after a woman and settles for a brittle old man."

"You were very brave to go after him," Katy said.

"Brave and foolish often go hand in hand," he told her. "My biggest regret is that my last dance was with Flora instead of your pretty sister."

"You can dance with Emma another time," Katy assured him.

He shook his head. "My dancing days are over," he said. "When you get a leg break at my age, a fellow will be dad-gummed lucky to ever walk again."

By the time the ambulance arrived, nearly twenty minutes later, his leg was swollen so badly that his pant leg fit tight as a glove. Two hefty EMS guys lifted him onto the gurney and into the back of the ambulance.

A lot of people were still milling around outside, apparently waiting to see Crank off. Encouragement was called out to him. Also promises to see him back here soon.

"Does he have family?" Katy asked Mrs. Welborn. "Is there somebody we should contact?"

"He has a son in Kansas City," she answered. "And another one out in California. I'll see if I can't get in touch with somebody when I get home."

"Oh, thanks, Mrs. Welborn," she said. "I'd really appreciate that."

As the ambulance disappeared up the road, Katy turned to find Nadine standing behind her. She was quiet and appeared shaken.

"I'm so sorry," she said to Katy.

"Sorry for what?" Katy asked her.

"Sorry for everything," she answered. "I shouldn't have been here. I shouldn't have gotten up to sing. I should have known it would make him mad."

Katy frowned at her and shook her head. "How could you have

known that?" she asked. "The guy was acting completely crazy. Who can see that kind of thing coming?"

"I know…but—"

"But nothing," Katy said. "It wasn't your fault. Nobody blames you."

"Oh, I'm sure people do," Nadine said. "I'm sure people will."

"Well, if they do, then they're stupid and wrong."

The words were not Katy's but Curt's. He'd stepped up beside her, Parker standing next to him and a sleepy Brianna clinging to his shoulder.

"You sang beautifully," Curt said. "It was a gift to this community. And if it threw some idiot into a jealous rage, nobody in their right mind would blame you for that."

Katy agreed with him, but she could tell from Nadine's expression that she wasn't as certain.

"Curt's right," she said. "The singing was fabulous and I am so grateful to you for that. I'm not only glad you did it, but I want you to promise me that you'll sing next time as well."

"Next time? You're going to want to do this again?"

"Of course we'll do it again," Katy said. "And now we know that some people with bad tempers and grudges will not be invited."

She hugged Nadine and little Natty tightly. "Thank you for singing," Katy said. "And for helping out with serving. And for being my friend."

"Okay," she said in a tiny voice, so small in comparison to the one she'd wowed them with.

"I'm going to walk Nadine and the kids home," Curt said. "Just to make sure they get there okay."

Katy nodded.

As she watched them walk away, she felt an arm slip around her waist. She glanced up to see Sean.

"I got Mrs. Bullock and the Dempseys home," he said.

"As least they weren't injured," Katy said with self-scoffing irony.

"These things happen," he said. "I'm sorry for Crank and I'm sorry for your musical night. It was great. You know that, don't you? It was a smashing success."

"It was good," Katy agreed. "I was just telling Nadine that I want her to sing at the next one, too."

Sean smiled broadly at her. "That's what's so amazing about you, Katy," he said. "I recognized it almost the very first minute that I met you. You have this optimism, this belief in the possibilities for the future that has no basis in all your past experience."

Katy shrugged off his compliment. "Except for Pearly's stupidity and poor Crank's injury, tonight's experience couldn't be described as anything but successful. I'm eager to go through the receipts. We made a boatload of money on this thing."

"It was a great idea," Sean said. "The limited menu, the music, the celebration atmosphere is exactly the kind of thing that can put a little restaurant like this on the map."

She loved how he was smiling at her.

"I couldn't have done it without you," she told him.

His brow furrowed. He hesitated, as if her words had caught him up short.

"You most certainly could and did," he said.

His change in tone caught Katy's attention immediately.

"What do you mean?

"You've done all this by yourself," he said. "You've managed to create a good home for Josh and a viable business to support yourself without any help from me at all."

She shook her head. "That's not true. I would never have been able to buy this place without the divorce settlement. That was *your* money. And I was about to give up on the barbecue as a lost cause before you came and rescued the place from becoming Bitsy's Bait and Chicken Salad Sandwich."

"The divorce settlement was my mother's money, not mine," he said. "And I haven't any doubt that you could have gotten a lot more of it if you'd chosen to play hardball instead of trying to be fair. As for the barbecue, you would have figured it out by yourself." Sean was shaking his head with certainty. "You didn't need me."

Katy felt all the joy at his nearness drain out of her.

"That's what you've never understood," she told him. "I do need you. I've always needed you. You're a good man."

Sean shook his head. "No, Katy, don't," he said. "I don't want you to start believing in me again. You always want to see the best in me, even after I've shown you the worst. You've got to stop doing that."

"Why?" Katy asked him. "Why should I hold a grudge against you, hold myself away from you, when all you've shown me since you've been here is helpfulness and caring? You love Josh. And I think you still love me."

"Is that what you think?"

"Yes, it is," Katy answered.

"And I suppose it's that love for you that's pushing us back to court to demand a custody agreement that's more to my liking."

The hurtful words momentarily caught her up short, but Katy deliberately pushed away all the fear and anxiety that swirled within her.

"You want to have more contact with Josh," she said. "That's good. He needs you and he loves you. He deserves to have a father. There are things that you can offer him. Things that I could never provide. I'm happy for him to have that chance. I'm not threatened by having you more involved in his life. Because I know in my heart, as much as I know anything in the world, that you would never take my son away from me."

Sean shook his head.

"My mother may be right about you," he said. "You're naive to the point of stupidity. Don't put your trust in me, Katy. It's just a matter of time until I let you down."

Bitsy's Wisdom 24

Bitsy's Wisdom 24: When barbecuing a fish, the object is to absorb the maximum amount of smoke before it's cooked through. Trout and catfish can take more smoke than most, making them really good for laying on the pit.

In the aftermath of the big musical night, Emma felt that somehow the world had altered, but she wasn't sure who was involved or what or how it had happened.

Field note: In all primate societies an act of aggression or dominance can trigger repercussions far beyond the principals involved. A change in everyday existence can jolt individuals out of roles they have maintained over time.

Also, she couldn't decide if it was good or bad.

The restaurant had brought in a lot of money that night, getting them caught up on all the money they'd spent on groceries. It had also spurred new interest in the place, and business picked up at both lunch and dinner.

That should have made everyone extremely happy. But instead, Katy seemed quiet. And while Sean was putting as many hours in as the day was long, the two of them no longer had their heads together giggling. In fact, it was almost as if they were keeping their distance from each other.

That was okay with Emma, of course. She had not liked the two of them spending so much time together. But it felt even stranger when they were being so quiet, so careful, so reserved. Emma wanted to ask Katy what had happened. They used to talk about everything. These days, however, her sister kept pretty much to herself.

Nadine was still baking pies and babysitting, and whatever she felt about the events of the musical night she kept to herself. According to the gossip, and Emma had no reason not to believe it, Pearly Ross pleaded guilty to public drunkenness and disturbing the peace. He'd paid a stiff fine and was released. He showed up every morning as if nothing had ever happened. Which was especially galling since Old Man Crank was still in the hospital. He'd needed a metal plate and seven screws to put his leg back together, and the prognosis was for a long, slow recovery.

It was difficult, even for a student of human behavior, to reconcile the angry, violent man that Pearly had been that night, with the casual, carefree fellow who hung around Bitsy's. Emma didn't even try. She made a point of keeping her distance. And noticed that Nadine did the same.

Unexpectedly, however, Nadine was being drawn out of her self-imposed shell and into the community. Part of that was her increasingly visible presence at Bitsy's. But after the musical evening Miss Welborn had, completely out of the blue, volunteered to spend some time each morning playing with Natty.

She approached Nadine as if the opportunity to spend several hours a day with the toddler was the pinnacle of Miss Welborn's esoteric retirement ambitions.

"I've been reading, doing some research on early learning and

Down syndrome, and I desperately want to try out some of the techniques. Unfortunately, the only child with the syndrome locally is your little Natty. I do know how busy you are, but could you spare the time for me to work with him?"

So gracefully had the older woman proposed her involvement in the child's care that Nadine, who was fiercely independent and suspicious of everyone, didn't even realize what had happened. She spent her mornings up in the apartment kitchen turning out pies, while Miss Welborn and Natty played together on a blanket in the backyard, the other children running around like banshees. After decades as a teacher, the older woman had fully mastered the ability to allow the children free rein while keeping complete control.

"Your babysitter has acquired a babysitter," Emma said to Katy.

Her sister nodded. "Just don't tell her, okay?"

"Not me," Emma pledged. "I'm just an observer."

"I'm hoping that once school starts and Brianna and Josh are in kindergarten, we can get Miss Welborn to watch Natty in the mornings and Nadine can work here in the restaurant."

"That would be good," Emma said. "It's a lot for you to take on by yourself."

"Especially since I'll be in the bait shop," Katy said.

Emma was startled by her words. "I thought bait was my job," she said.

"Silly, in the fall you're leaving for the university."

"Oh, yeah, right," Emma said.

She worried that her tone was a little too emphatic. She wasn't ready yet to tell Katy that she'd put up her savings as Latt's retainer. There would be no college for her again this year. She refused to just give up on the dream. That was what any reasonable woman would do, she realized. A reasonable woman would reevaluate her goals to something she was a bit more likely to achieve. She would continue to read everything she could get her hands on. She would fantasize about a life among native tribesmen. She would pore through the course selections at the University of Missouri, licking her lips as if starving for her bite of education.

And she would continue to do what she had to do to help her sister. All they had was each other. Katy and Josh were more important than all else. But sometimes it was hard to remember that.

Her hopes to leave her sister in the competent hands of pastor/mailman Curt Crisswall seemed to be going nowhere. She figured that he was not willing to take the initiative because of Sean. Emma decided that perhaps he needed a clearer understanding of what the situation was between those two.

One afternoon as she sat alone with him at the counter, she took the opportunity to, as the old men in Warbler Lake might say, "wise him up."

"Katy and Sean are divorced for a reason."

The abrupt entry into the conversation obviously startled Curt, who jerked his head up from his soda straw and gazed at her with raised eyebrows.

"I mean, if you were thinking they were just too young or just couldn't get along or something like that, you're wrong."

Curt hesitated as if choosing his words carefully. "I don't spend a lot of time speculating about how people manage to get into the situations they are in," he said. "It's more my calling to try to support them where they are and, if they need it, help them get out."

"Oh, I know, I know," Emma said. "I wasn't telling you that as a pastor, more as a friend. I just didn't want you to be rooting for them to get back together."

Slowly he nodded. "Because you're not?"

"Well, no," Emma said. "I'm not. I didn't think they were right for each other in the first place. And nothing that has happened between them has changed my opinion."

"Okay," he said.

"They come from entirely different worlds," Emma told him. "Sean grew up with money and privilege. He's got a great education and a family-business empire. I'm sure that's what was planned for him. To be a wealthy executive in St. Louis."

"Things don't always go according to plans," Curt said.

"No, they don't," Emma agreed. "He met Katy and I guess fell for her."

Curt smiled. "You can see how he would," he said. "She's a very sweet and likable young woman."

Emma agreed. "But Katy's not from his world," she said. "He fell for her, I don't doubt that. But he also left her. She was totally dependent on him, with a brand-new baby, and he just went home to Mama. When the going got tough, he got up and walked out the door."

"That was a very bad thing," Curt said.

"It certainly was," Emma said. "It was more than bad, it was unforgivable."

"I don't believe that anything is unforgivable," he said.

Emma shrugged. "Well, maybe that's true. I guess it might be possible to forgive him. But you can't let a man treat you like that and then allow him to walk back into your life."

"*You* can't," he said.

She was puzzled by the emphasis on the world. "What do you mean?"

"Just that," Curt said. "You wouldn't let a man walk back into your life. Katy may feel differently."

"Well, of course, he's Josh's father and she has to be nice to him," Emma said. "Especially with the custody arrangement at stake, and all the money he has to contest it. She's going to treat him carefully. But when somebody really messes up their life, they just have to live with the consequences. It's okay to forgive them and feel sorry for them. But that's as far as it goes. The consequences for Sean are that he's not going to ever get his wife or his son back. That's what he deserves."

Curt nodded. "Yes, it probably is what he deserves," he said. "Fortunately, most of us never get what we deserve."

"Huh?"

"All of us, you, me, everybody, we've all messed things up a time or two," he said. "Some people's messes seem a lot bigger than others, but maybe that's just perspective. For example, you and Katy buying this place sight unseen, believing it to be an entirely different business than it is—that was a pretty bad mistake. It could have meant financial disaster for Katy. And if she'd reneged on the deal, it would have been a hardship on our whole community. But if we had been a bit more specific in trying to sell it, she might never have made that mistake. If we all got what we deserved she would be broke and we'd have no place for the summer tourists to spend their money."

"I agree, we were stupid," Emma said. "But walking out on your wife and child, that's not just some stupid mistake."

"No, it's not," he agreed. "I'm not saying, oh forget it, no big deal. What I'm saying is that as long as we're here on this earth, humans can come back from very bad choices and make their lives better because of the experience they had."

"But there should be consequences," Emma said.

Curt nodded. "It's a hard thing to balance justice and mercy. Do we punish people to change them, or just to exact some revenge? These are hard questions, Emma. I don't have a list of answers. I just try to make the right decision every day, recognizing that people are who they are, which is not necessarily the same as what they do."

Emma wasn't sure what she might have replied for that, but she didn't get a chance. Nadine came through the kitchen door carrying a pie box. She caught sight of Curt and blushed.

"Oh, sorry, I didn't mean to interrupt."

Emma nearly rolled her eyes. She was getting sick to death of people trying to allow her time alone with Curt. They would not now, nor ever, be a couple. She wished she could take an ad in the paper saying so.

"You're not interrupting," Emma said. "Curt's just taking his daily celebratory, I've-delivered-every-piece-of-mail-in-town soda. What's up?"

"The kids are all down for naps," she said. "Even Parker. He lay down with Natty to get him to sleep and crashed himself."

"A full day of play on a hot summer day will do that," Emma said.

Nadine nodded.

"He's a good kid," Curt said.

"Yes, thank you," Nadine answered. "Anyway, I baked this pie for Miss Welborn. It's a kind of a thank-you for all the time she's spent with Natty, and I thought that if you could keep an ear on the upstairs for me..." She held up the receiver for the baby monitor.

Emma took it from her hand and set it on the counter. "I've got you covered," she said.

"Thanks."

"But wait," Emma said. "There's something that I wanted to talk to you two about."

"What?"

Nadine's question seemed defensively guilty and her complexion had turned beet red.

She glanced over at Curt to see that he appeared almost equally uncomfortable.

"I promised Parker I would talk to Curt about this," Emma said. "But I really think I need to talk to both of you."

"Parker?" She sounded relieved. "What about Parker?"

"I'm not eager to break a confidence here," Emma said. "But it just seems to me that the two of you have to talk about him. He wants to be baptized."

"Baptized?" Nadine eyed her curiously and then glanced over at Curt. "Did you know about this?"

Curt shrugged and then nodded affirmatively. "He asked me about it well over a month ago," he said. "I let him know how proud and pleased I was about it, and told him to get permission from you."

"Oh."

"That seems to be the sticking point for Parker," Emma said. "He asked me to talk Curt out of needing your permission."

Nadine looked momentarily stunned. "He thinks I wouldn't let him do it? Parker is a very thoughtful, spiritual kind of boy. Of course I'd want him to follow his heart on something like that. I can't believe he'd think I'd want to stop him."

"No, I'm pretty sure he's not worrying that you'd disapprove. I believe he's worried about taking sides."

"Taking sides?" Nadine looked puzzled. "I don't know what you mean," Nadine said.

"Me, neither," Curt piped in.

"Well," Emma explained. "From what he told me, Nadine, you and the church are on two different sides. And that if he chooses to be baptized, it might look to you as if he's taking the side of the church over his mom."

"Where'd he get some kind of crazy idea like that?" Curt said.

Nadine looked at him and sighed. "Well, probably from me," she said. "Though I didn't mean it exactly that way."

"What way did you mean it?" he asked.

She struggled to come up with the words. "I…well, those people," she began. "Those people in your congregation, Curt. They don't like me. They gossip about me and they'd all keel over in horror if I was to darken the church door."

He shook his head. "You're selling them short," he said.

"I'm not selling them at all," Nadine said. "And I'm not buying, either. They talk about love for their fellow man and doing good works, but the truth is most of those people wouldn't walk across the street to spit on me if I was on fire."

"If that's true," Curt said, "then I wouldn't want to be a part of them, either."

"Don't be silly, Curt," Nadine said. "You aren't a part of them, you *are* them."

"Then that hatefulness that you see in them, you believe it about me, too?"

"Oh, no, I didn't mean that."

"Then what did you mean?" he asked. "You think the people in church hate you, but I am the people of that church. And so is Old Man Crank, who got his leg broken standing up for you. And so is Miss Welborn, who's taken such an interest in your kids. And Katy, who's given you a job."

"Not everybody is bad," Nadine countered. "I didn't say everyone was against me. Just most of them."

"Most of them don't even know you," he said. "And they probably never will because you won't give them a chance."

"Give them a chance to put me down?" Nadine shook her head. "I don't make apologies to anyone about the things I've done."

"No," he snapped. "You expect other people to apologize to you for some slight that hasn't actually happened, but you're convinced it's going to happen, anyway."

"Everybody knows about those holier-than-thou church people," Nadine countered. "It's not like I'm paranoid. They really do think they're better than me."

"You accuse them of judging you," Curt said. "So you judge them first. Maybe if you gave them a chance, they'd give you a chance."

"Why should I take a risk like that?" she asked him.

"Oh, I don't know," he answered, his tone sarcastic. "Maybe just so you can move on from the whining, self-imposed isolation that you've become so comfortable in."

Curt was angry. Very angry. Emma didn't think she'd ever seen him mad before. He got up and stormed across the dining room, actually slamming the door as he left.

The two women stared after him for a moment, stunned.

"Whoa," Nadine said finally.

"I'm sorry," Emma told her.

"Are you apologizing for Curt?"

"No, no, I'm apologizing for breaking Parker's confidence and for not speaking to each of you separately. I just thought, I don't know, I thought we were all friends."

"We were," Nadine said.

"I just don't know how this happened."

"Oh, it's for the best," Nadine said. "I think Curt was…I don't know, I think he was getting a thing for me."

"What?"

"Nothing happened," Nadine assured her quickly. "I mean, I know you two are almost a couple. But the other night, I don't know, he was, like, really open with me. We sat for hours on the front porch just talking. It was a connection or something."

Emma just stared at her mutely, and when she realized her jaw was hanging open like a rusty gate she shut her mouth.

Nadine laughed. "See, even you were shocked," she said. "And you're the only other woman in town who doesn't race to that church door every time it's open. Nothing good could ever come of anything between Curt and me. I've just got too much mileage for that kind of relationship. It's much better if we nip that in the bud right away. So it's nipped, it's done. I'm on my way to Miss Welborn's and you're listening for the kids."

Emma nodded, but she didn't speak. Suddenly everything that Curt had said about Sean took on an entirely different meaning.

Bitsy's Wisdom 25

Bitsy's Wisdom 25: If you're in a lot of bottom debris or rocks, use a slip bobber to suspend the bait above the clutter.

Sean was nervous. Someone who didn't know him might have credited that to driving his mother's very flashy and expensive Mercedes through the run-down and ragged streets of East St. Louis, Illinois. But car thieves and chop shops were the last thing on his mind. All his thoughts were about Katy sitting in the passenger seat beside him. Their long drive from Warbler Lake had passed mostly in silence—not at all how he'd imagined it.

Sean had called Chickadee Ogden and gotten the thumbs-up for a visit more than a week before the musical night at Bitsy's. He had planned it as a surprise for Katy. As it turned out, it was a surprise, but not a particularly welcome one.

"I asked them if we could come and work a night for them, see how they run their place, pick up some pointers," he told Katy. "They agreed to let us come this week."

Chick's Pig-n-Blues was not just a barbecue restaurant. It was *the* barbecue restaurant. A tiny music eatery in East St. Louis believed by its patrons to have the best barbecue available on the planet.

"It's a long way," she said.

Sean nodded. "Yeah, but the food is fabulous and the place is about the same size you've got here. It seems like a good match. We…you could learn a lot."

"What will we do with Josh? Do you think Emma can run the B & B by herself?"

"It's just one night," Sean said. "I'm sure she can get help from Nadine and just keep it simple. Maybe my mother can watch Josh. We could leave early in the morning and be back by noon the next day."

She'd agreed to come, but there was none of the excitement and sense of adventure that he'd hoped for.

Their marriage had been that way, as well, he realized. It had seemed like such a brilliant idea, such fun, the two of them playing house and having sex. But it had quickly turned to all work and no play. He'd felt like a failure as a husband. He felt like a failure now.

"Here it is," he said, turning off Collinsville to a rough-looking side street.

The club was in the middle of the block, but most of the buildings around it were falling down or long gone. It stood alone, a reminder of a once-vibrant old city now gone rusted and shabby.

"Oh! Look at the sign," Katy said. "It's darling."

It was the first truly positive remark she'd made all day. And Sean supposed that she was right. The fat little pig was clad in a navy uniform and sailor's cap. Seated atop of the piano he played was a very svelte and sexy songbird. The whole image was outlined in different colors of neon tubes that probably shone brilliantly after dark. In the light of day, it just seemed a little silly and dated, but

Katy liked old stuff. It appealed to her in some kind of homey, family way, like that photograph that still hung in Bitsy's. Any other owner would have tried to spruce up the place and put their own stamp on it. A framed snapshot of the previous owner would have been the first thing to go. But Katy liked to keep ties to the past. Maybe she valued other people's ties because she lacked her own.

Just to the south side of Chick's Pig-n-Blues was a two-story red brick house with a wide corner porch. It was well kept up, though the trim was in need of a paint job. The small front yard was surrounded by an ancient chain-link fence. Within its boundaries were numerous lawn ornaments, gnomes and outdoor knickknacks strategically placed among brightly vibrant flower beds.

Sean parked at the curb and they got out.

"This place has been here for decades," Sean told her, hoping that she wasn't put off by the unassuming appearance. "All the great blues men played here. Louis Armstrong, Cab Calloway, Bessie Smith, B.B. King."

Katy smiled at him. "Is Bessie Smith one of the great blues *men?*"

"Ah," he replied, nodding. "I misspoke, it should have been blues persons."

"All right, then."

It was the first real crack in her polite demeanor and Sean was grateful for it.

They were just going through the gate when Chick appeared at the front door, opening the screen and holding it at arm's length.

"I bet you are my temp help," she called out to them. "Get in this house and get something in your stomach. Odom and I, we're fixing to sit at the table."

Chick was reed-thin, with short-cropped hair that was pure white. Her pink dress bespoke springtime and the apron that covered it was a testament to both her chief pleasure and her vocation.

They walked up the narrow sidewalk.

"It's wonderful to meet you in person, Mrs. Ogden. This is my wife, Katy."

As soon as it was out of his mouth, Sean realized that he should have said ex-wife, but he had no opportunity to correct his words.

"Well, look at you, young Mr. Dodson," Chick said. "I swear, you got your mama's good looks and your daddy's winning ways. And married to such a pretty girl. Honey, you just call me Chick, everybody does. Come on in and meet my husband. The poor man is probably dying for the sight of a pretty young gal like you."

They were ushered into the dining room of the house, where Chick's husband and her grandson, Theon, were already seated. Introductions were hastily made and within minutes Sean and Katy were eating lunch.

Odom Ogden, known to his friends and customers as O.O., was not in the best of health and needed a cane to get around, but he still worked in the club six nights a week and supervised all the barbecue served.

"I saw Chick one night in 1945, just after I come home from the war. She was the finest-looking gal I'd ever seen and I set my sights on messing around with her," he confided across the table. "She said there had to be a wedding first, so we tied the knot on a Tuesday afternoon. I figured the marriage might last through the weekend. But it's been more than sixty years and the woman has still got her claws in me."

Chick snorted and shook her head. "I couldn't chase that man out of here with a stick," she said.

O.O. laughed. "We've had some fun times," he said. "We've raised some fine kids and cooked some great barbecue. You'll be a lucky young couple to do as well."

Sean felt compelled to confess.

"We're not really a couple anymore," he said. "Katy and I are divorced. The barbecue place is hers. I'm just…I'm just helping her make contacts."

He couldn't quite interpret the look that Katy gave him, but it wasn't happy.

"Well, I was wondering if you was giving up those Dodson-burgers," Chick said. "Our kind of place doesn't much lend itself to chain business."

"No," Sean assured her. "Katy bought Bitsy's Bait & BBQ in Warbler Lake. She runs it with her sister. I…I still work for Dodsonburger."

O.O. gave Sean a long look, followed by an equal perusal of Katy.

"You must be a pretty sharp gal to be so young and own your own restaurant."

"I bought it with my divorce settlement," Katy said. "So Sean paid for it. I wanted a family business. A place for my son to grow up in."

"So, you have a boy," Chick said.

"Yes," Katy said. "His name is Josh and he's five."

"I have four boys," Chick told her. "And three girls. You can imagine how full to bursting this house was when they were underfoot. But it's kind of good, I think, to have your work and your family all mixed up together. I surely got to spend more time with them than if I was hurrying off to a job every day."

Katy agreed.

After lunch, Sean followed O.O. and his grandsons out the back door to a bricked area where the barbecue was located. O.O.'s gait was slow and when he made it to his metal lawn chair, he seated himself with a huff of exhaustion.

The barbecue wasn't completely cold and a haunch of brisket was smoking on the last of yesterday's fire, wrapped in foil and covered by an upended metal pot. With elbow-length asbestos gloves,

Theon retrieved it and carried it in through the back door of the business.

"We got a nice little prep area in there," O.O. said. "Though Chick does most of the sides in our place. She says there are better ways to heat up the dance floor than cooking beans."

Sean laughed appreciatively.

"I bricked this whole area," he said, drawing Sean's attention to the ground around the pit. "We had a grassfire about fifteen years ago and I got scared about having an open flame out here. The last thing Chick needs is for me to burn her house down."

Sean nodded. "That's a good idea," he said. "I'm not much of a handyman, but surely I can do something like that."

"Oh, there isn't nothing to it," O.O. assured him. "Just level up the ground the best you can. Lay them offset and sweep a bit of sand in between as a mortar."

Theon returned and Sean began helping to stoke the coals and to lay the fire. The grandson was about ten years Sean's senior, a quiet man, respectful and deferential to O.O., though very competent in his own right.

"It's pretty early to get the fire going," Katy pointed out. "I always wait until later in the afternoon."

O.O. looked concerned. "You can't cook straight off," he told her. "When the fire's young, it's still burning off that tough bark around the edge and boiling out all the sap. That's a bitter smoke and you don't want it in your food."

Once the fire was going well, the younger man took Sean inside the Pig-n-Blues to show him around. The place was not much bigger than Bitsy's, though it had more tables and no booths. The hardwood dance floor took up the space in front of a true stage, elevated, complete with lights, soundboard and microphones.

"This is a lot more music than we've got," Katy said, coming up beside him.

Sean agreed.

Theon smiled. "Music brings them in," he said. "Barbecue brings them back."

The afternoon was busy as they set up for business. Once the fire was right, Sean and Katy both watched and helped as Theon cooked.

"I don't know anything, so nothing is too unimportant not to tell me," she told O.O.

The old man laughed. "Folks that don't know nothing about it think that you just set some meat on a fire and slather it down good with some sauce and call it barbecue. That's just a waste of meat and a fire."

Katy nodded thoughtfully.

"And the men that barbecue, they are such liars, Honey, don't you listen to a word they tell you," he went on. "They talk about their fancy rubs and their mysterious sauces, but the main ingredient for good barbecue is your pit and how well you use it."

"Our pit looks a lot like this one," Katy told him. "Maybe it's bigger, what do you think, Sean?"

"It might be a little wider, but it's about the same height."

"The Africans in the Caribbean, where barbecue came from, they used to cook from a pit in the ground," Theon said. "But getting up this high keeps you from breaking your back."

They all chuckled.

"So you don't use rubs or marinade?" Sean asked.

"I do. Depending on the meat, I'll use a rub sometimes. But this is my secret," O.O. told them, indicating a spray bottle. "I tell everybody who watches me cook that it's the formula that makes my meat better than any other you've ever eat."

Both Sean and Katy looked at the spray bottle questioningly, but it was Katy who spoke up.

"What's in it?" she asked.

O.O. smiled. "You know, most people don't have the guts to ask me that," he said. "Should I tell her, Theon?"

He chuckled. "Only if you make her promise to keep it to herself."

"I won't breathe a word," she assured him. "I won't even tell Sean if you don't want him to know."

Both men laughed at that.

"It's plain old water," Theon said.

"Water?"

O.O. nodded. "With a slice of lemon. It cools the meat and slows the cooking," he said. "And smoke can't penetrate water, so you don't get it so fumed that you lose the natural savor."

"It also helps the sauce to stay on the meat without scorching," Theon added.

"But you got to be careful with it," O.O. added. "You're cooking with smoke, that's what gives the taste to the meat. If you get to putting too much water, then you'll be steaming and wasting your flavor."

Both Sean and Katy tried their hand at cooking. Theon and O.O. were generous with praise and eager with advice.

"The cooking has got to be slow," Theon told them. "You should keep the temperature of the pit about the same as the temperature you're aiming for when the meat is done. If you're cooking pork, it needs to be cooked to 160 degrees, so your pit temperature ought to be between 180 and 220."

"Keep it covered as much as you can," O.O. said. "It's hard to resist taking a peek, but keeping the heat steady, that's what works."

"If the temp gets too low," Theon said, "open the intake on the firebox a bit and let some air inside. It'll stoke the flame enough to raise the heat."

As the barbecue cooked, they asked questions.

"Is there a reason you didn't bring the meat straight from the cooler?"

"Room temperature makes it cook more evenly," O.O. said.

"But you can't leave it out very long," Theon added. "They say an hour is safe, so I go with a half hour, just to be safer."

Katy nodded.

"Some places have steak on the menu, too," she said. "Can you cook a steak on this fire?"

Theon nodded. "Some folks think steak is barbecue, but not how we think of it. You want steaks seared on a hot grill, it's a whole different cooking."

O.O. chuckled. "Steak is a fine piece of meat," he said. "Much too good for the pit. Barbecue was invented for meat as tough as shoe leather that needed to be turned into something fit for folks to eat. It is what it is, and there's no cause in trying to fancy it up beyond that."

Sean liked O.O.'s attitude. The man was proud of what he did, but there was no puffed-up superiority in his accomplishments. And he and Chick, they had something that he could see immediately was precious and rare.

"Do you just add the sauce to the cooking or just top it on when you're serving?" Sean asked.

"Both," Theon said. "We mop a little on just before it's done and then drip a quarter cup or more across it when we're setting it on the plate."

"Don't put the sauce on too early," O.O. warned. "It'll burn the surface of the food and it won't be fit to eat."

"I've already discovered that on my own," Katy told him, with a self-effacing grin.

O.O. chuckled and smiled at her. "It's always better to confess your sin and keep marching forward trying to do better."

She laughed.

The band arrived just as they were getting the barbecued meat transferred to the kitchen. They were older guys, mostly gray-haired and with more collective club experience than you'd find in Las Vegas. They played tunes that were decades old more often than ones heard on the radio last week. But they did so with a zest and vitality that made it fresh and immediate.

"Most of our customers are older these days," Chick told them. "So we're not signing up a lot of youngsters to play."

"We have lots of seniors at our place, too," Katy said.

By six-thirty, Sean and Katy were wearing aprons. A nephew and two other family members showed up to help. The music started promptly at seven-thirty.

It was busy, but nobody seemed to get into too big of a hurry.

"If they want fast food," O.O. said, "there's plenty of that out on St. Louis Avenue."

Sean liked the pace and the patrons. In his mind he contrasted it with the corporate life that his mother had created. Dodsonburger was a restaurant business, but it seemed far removed from the personal human-to-human contact of Pig-N-Blues. Sean was enjoying himself. And as he caught sight of Katy, interacting with the customers and laughing with Chick, he knew she was having a great time, too.

It was after ten and the band was taking its second break of the evening when Katy distributed another round of bottled beer. Sean was behind the bar, washing glasses. O.O. was seated in a chair nearby wiping them dry.

"What happened between you and your wife?" he asked, catching Sean by surprise. "I know it ain't none of my business, but you two seem way too fond of each other to be living apart. Did you have another woman on the side?"

Sean shook his head. "No, nothing like that. Not when we were married," he said.

"That's good."

"Not that I'm so faithful," Sean continued, unwilling to give himself any credit for his fidelity. "I was so busy, trying to make a living, I didn't have time to cheat."

O.O. chuckled at that. "I hear ya," he said.

"And I guess I loved her too much."

"You guess?"

"I did," Sean admitted.

"You do," O.O. corrected.

Sean sighed and then just nodded, unwilling to reveal more.

"So what happened?" O.O. prodded. "Just couldn't get along?"

He thought about simply shrugging. But the truth was, he didn't want to sugarcoat his failings. He liked O.O. He respected him. The only possible response was the truth.

"I walked out on her," Sean said. "Things got tough and I got going."

"Dumb," O.O. said simply.

Sean nodded in agreement.

A long silence settled between them.

"So," the old man asked finally. "Are you dumb enough to let a mistake like that ruin the whole rest of your life?"

Bitsy's Wisdom 26

Bitsy's Wisdom 26: Always consider the weather. A hot sun raises the temperature inside the smoker and a cold, cloudy day will keep it down. A blustery wind will play havoc with your vents and drafts. If it's raining, no need to add water to anything.

Gwen was so angry, she thought she might explode. She burst into the Bait & BBQ, opening the door so sharply that it banged against the wall, jolting the framed photography of Bitsy nearly off its wall hook, and causing every eye in the building to turn in her direction.

"Where is Latt Meicklejohn?" she demanded.

The customers just looked at her blankly.

"His van is parked here!" Her announcement sounded more like an accusation.

"He's not in here," Gus Gouswhelter said, volunteering the obvious.

"He came by with some bait a half hour ago," Emma told her. "He's probably out on the lake."

"He was still getting his boat ready five minutes ago," Waymon Riley told her. "If you hurry down to the dock, you might still catch him."

"Oh, that's just great," Gwen sneered sarcastically, and went back out the door, slamming it again for good measure.

She marched across the parking lot and jaywalked across the road in front of the fishhook statue. At the dock in the distance she could see somebody. She wasn't sure that it was Latt, but she decided that she had to assume it was. He was leaving. If her phone worked in this forgotten corner of the world, she would have called to stop him. If she hadn't been in her canvas slingbacks, she might have run to the dock and caught up with him. But with neither of those options available, she was forced to fall back onto the lady's least desirable method of getting a man's attention. She hurried down along the beach, clumsily trotting, waving her arms over her head and screaming his name. In this way, she managed to get the kids playing in the park to stop and watch. And the Dempseys, out for their morning constitutional, waved back as if she were simply greeting them on their morning stroll. The stupid fisherman on the lake didn't notice. As she reached the dock, the boat began to pull away, and she hurried to the end of the cross-tie lumber screaming, jumping up and down and flailing her arms to no avail.

"Damn it!" she cursed aloud.

"You need Flora for something?"

Gwen turned abruptly to find Latt sitting in a boat two moorings over.

"I thought that was you," she said.

"Really?" he chuckled as if he were delighted. "Well, I've had some women chase me in my younger days, but never quite like that."

Gwen was in no mood for humor.

"Stay right where you are," she commanded.

Angrily she marched back toward the shore and then across to the other mooring and back out to where Latt and his boat awaited.

He was standing, smiling.

"So glad that you could join me," he said.

"Don't you dare try to be nice to me," Gwen said. "Like we're friends and we're both just trying to do the best for Josh."

"We are."

"I am," she said. "You're trying…you're trying to undermine me. You've stabbed me in the back and I'm not likely to forget it."

"Okay," he said. "Fair enough."

As far as he was concerned, that was the end of the conversation. That was infuriating.

"This child's whole life and future is at stake and you're playing some kind of legalistic games."

He smiled. "Just doing my job for my client."

"Neither you nor your client are going to get away with it."

"Maybe not," he agreed.

He started untying the line that held the boat to the dock.

"What are you doing?" she asked.

"I'm going out on the lake."

"I'm talking to you," she said.

"And I'm listening," he answered. "But only for about fifteen more seconds, then I'm gone fishing."

He threw the rope into the bottom of the boat and pushed off from the timber. If Gwen had been thinking clearly, she undoubtedly would not have behaved as she did. But she wasn't thinking clearly, she was still steaming mad. And he was just walking away, or rather boating away, from her as if she didn't matter. Gwen Dodson was not accustomed to being treated that way and she wasn't going to stand for it.

So she didn't stand, she jumped.

The distance between dock and boat was perhaps four feet, growing wider by the second. Gwen secured her straw handbag on her shoulder, raised her chin defiantly and took a giant leap. She landed in the boat, but fell forward on her knees, grasping the side to keep from continuing headfirst into the lake. Latt cursed and the little craft teetered ominously, threatening at first to flip over. In the end it only took on a bit of water and then righted itself.

"Woman! If you wanted to go fishing you should have said so."

"When I'm having a conversation, it's not over until I say it's over," she said.

"Fine," he said. "Talk yourself blue in the face. But put on a life jacket."

She looked askance at the smelly thing.

"I have no interest in going out on the lake," she said.

"You want to talk to me, that's where I'm headed."

He started up the motor and began put-putting away from the shore. Short of throwing herself over the side, there was not a lot Gwen could do about it. That really annoyed her.

"I don't see what the big hurry is about," she said.

"The bass are schooling," Latt told her. "If I want to catch the big ones, this is the time to do it."

"What I have to say is a lot more important than fishing."

"Not to the fish it's not," he said.

Gwen ignored that statement. She felt like Latt's bass, trapped on the end of a hook and getting jerked around against her will. It was not a feeling she liked.

She'd talked to David Faneuf that morning. And the news had not been good. Meicklejohn had filed for a venue change: from the court in St. Louis to the local jurisdiction.

"That will hurt our argument," Gwen told him, understanding

immediately that speaking unflatteringly of local schools to the people who support them might not be a winning strategy.

"It's even worse than that," David had said. "It's very likely in a small town like that for a local lawyer to have undue influence. Ozarkers are notoriously suspicious of outsiders. And we were really counting on getting a sympathetic judge."

That was not all he'd been counting on. The Dodson name was very well known in St. Louis. And at one time or another Gwen had rubbed shoulders with most of the seated judges or their wives at charity functions or civic meetings. It wasn't truly power brokering, but her standing in the community gave her standing in court. If Gwen said the child would be better off with her, there would be some compelling reasons to believe her.

Stubbornly she glared at Latt across the length of the boat. "You may consider yourself a clever lawyer," she said, "but you really should utilize you powers of persuasion in getting Katy to cooperate."

He raised an eyebrow. "I don't see that as being in her best interest," he said.

"Maybe not, if you're just looking at the next day in court," Gwen countered. "Long term, however, it definitely is. Even if she wins this time, we'll refile, and then refile, and then refile. You may have sloughed off materialism, but you know as well as I do that, in court, money talks, and it's the side that can afford to talk longest that wins."

She knew it was a direct hit, but he hardly flinched.

"All those filings take time," he said. "Six months here, eight months there. Years pass. Money may be on your side, but time is on ours."

"How so?"

"Every day that passes, Josh's opinion gets more credence," he said. "They may not ask him his preference at five. But they will at seven or eight. By ten or twelve it will be almost completely his choice."

"And you're so sure he'll choose to stay here? With no TV, no movies, no…no nothing?"

Latt nodded. "I'd take more than even money on it," he said. "I think he loves you. I think he loves Sean. But he and his mother are a team. I doubt he'd be willing to split that up for a flat screen."

Gwen knew he was probably right. But she wasn't about to admit it.

"You hardly know the boy," she said. "And you forget, I've raised a child. Unlike you, I know what they're like growing up."

Latt shut the motor off and threw the anchor overboard.

"In court, Mrs. Dodson," he said. "We'd call that 'assuming facts not in evidence.'"

Gwen's brow furrowed.

"I was sure that you told me you didn't have any children," she said.

"Not now," he answered. "My daughter, Cassandra, was a freshman in college when she was killed in a freak accident. One of those things that never happen until they happen to you. She was funny and pretty and brilliant, and then she was gone."

Gwen was so surprised that she was momentarily at a loss for words.

"I'm sorry," she managed finally.

Latt nodded. He held out a pole to her; she eyed it curiously.

"If you're going to be out here," he said, "you might as well fish."

She might have argued if she hadn't been caught off guard by his story. As it was she accepted the reel and held it uncertainly as he opened up a container with something inside that smelled terrible.

"What in the world is that?" she asked.

"It's pork rind with some fat on it," he answered. "We're going to fish here near the shallows of the point and what we're going to need to catch bass is a jig-and-pig."

"What in the world is jig-and-pig?" she asked.

From his tackle box, Latt pulled out what appeared to be a small bundle of different colored rubber bands. "This weighted hook with the fancy skirt is the jig," he said, and then pointed to the smelly container. "We just need to add the pig."

"That's disgusting," Gwen said.

Latt shrugged. "The fish seem to like it."

"I will not touch that," she said adamantly.

"Okay, I'll bait your hook for you," he said.

"Gee, thanks," she answered sarcastically.

The pork pieces were cut into V-shapes. He attached one to trail after the skirted jig and then held it up for her inspection.

"There is nothing those bass like better than these," he said. "They'll follow that pork as if it were the Pied Piper. And once they grab hold and get that salty taste, they'll hang in there long enough to get hooked solid."

"Yuk," she said. "Drop it in the water and let's be done with it."

Latt shook his head. "That's not the way this works," he told her. "You're going to have to stand up."

"I don't think so."

"Come on," he insisted.

Gwen rose to her feet uncertainly. Standing up in a boat didn't seem like a very smart idea. She was nervous as it rocked slightly back and forth. But she was determined not to let him know it.

"The way you do this," he said, "I like to think of it as the sport of fishing as if done by method actors."

"What do you mean?"

"You don't just send down bait, you become one with it," he said. "You cast out and let the jig fall to the bottom. Then you immediately hop it up slightly and let it drop again. Lift and drop.

That's what it's about. You make your bait come alive down there. Try it."

Gwen flicked the reel and the bait went high into the air and then landed in a semi-swan dive not three feet from the back of the boat.

"That close you're only going to get one hop," he said. "Pull it up and try again, see if you can cast out a little farther."

Gwen mastered getting the reel in with more ease than the casting. But eventually she got the hang of it. She would drop the jig-and-pig out about fifty feet from the boat and then sort of hop and bounce it along the bottom until it was close enough to have to reel in. After about the third time, she was just getting a bit of confidence about doing it properly when suddenly all hell broke loose. The reel was nearly jerked out of her hand, and the rod bowed dangerously, nearly knocking her off balance. She squealed like a little girl. The boat rocked and she had to spread her legs wide to keep her footing. For an instant she considered just letting go. But Gwen was too much of a fighter for that.

"Easy, easy does it, don't get panicked."

He was reeling in his own line so that it didn't get tangled with hers. "Don't yank him," he advised. "But don't give him enough line to get away."

The fish pulled and jerked on the end of her line, fighting for his life. Gwen felt oddly powerful and out of control at the same time. She had been doing what she was supposed to, but she'd snagged something unexpected and now she was uncertain how to handle it.

Latt was there, standing right behind her. He wrapped his arms around her, but he didn't try to grab the reel, he was merely stabilizing her in place.

"You've got him hooked, honey," Latt said. "Just stay calm and take your time."

"Okay, okay." She sounded more in control than she felt.

"Pull up and reel in," he said. "Just find yourself a rhythm, pull up…reel in. Pull up…reel in."

"Pull up…reel in," she repeated, bringing the rod up high and cranking in the line.

"It's just like dancing," he said. "Or making love. Just find the pace that works and keep doing it."

"Okay, okay."

"It's a big one," he said. "It's a really big one."

"Oh my gosh, oh my gosh,"

"Steady, keep up the pace, but keep it steady."

She could see the fish splashing nearer and nearer the boat.

Latt was down on his knees with the net. "Guide it toward the net," he said.

Gwen wasn't certain that she was in enough control to guide anything, but amazingly the fish swam in that direction and Latt scooped it up.

"Oh, my God, it's huge!"

"It's a bigmouth," he told her. "We weren't even baiting for bigmouth and it's a miracle your line held."

"Oh, my God, it's wonderful," she said. "Just wonderful."

The excitement, the accomplishment, the adrenaline raced through her veins. To her own surprise, she reached over and hugged the man. He hugged her back, laughing.

"That's a good way to lose a fish," he warned.

"We don't want to lose the fish," she agreed.

Latt held it up while she removed the hook from inside his mouth. Amazingly, her squeamishness had vanished completely.

"It's beautiful," she said.

Latt agreed, smiling. "There's not that many bigmouths in this lake," he said. "Catching one any day is special. Catching one your first day out is downright miraculous."

It felt like a miracle. Gwen was astounded at the change in her attitude. Nothing in the world was different, but this fish had somehow made her feel one hundred percent better.

"I'm acting like an idiot," she admitted.

Latt waved away her concern. "We have a saying, 'What happens on the lake, stays on the lake.'"

"You made that up, huh?" she asked skeptically.

"Something like that," he answered.

They stayed out on the water for hours. They caught a few more, a couple of nice-sized white bass and a perch that was small enough to throw back. As the day warmed up, they quit biting and Gwen and Latt quit casting.

"I've got some lunch," he said. "I'd be willing to share."

She knew she ought to suggest that they go to shore, but she wasn't ready to get back there.

"Okay," she said.

Latt dug through his pack and passed her a tube of sunblock. She slathered it on her face and arms. He opened a soap tin and washed his hands over the side.

"That's the licorice smell," she said.

He glanced up. "It's anise soap," he said. "It's great for getting off the bait stink and the fish actually like it."

"I like it, too," she told him.

Once his hands were clean and dry, he opened his lunch box and shared the contents with her, a salami and cheese sandwich, a handful of potato chips and a cookie.

"And for liquid refreshment," he said, "you may take your choice of either a plastic cup of warm coffee from the thermos, or a half bottle of nearly tepid water from the cooler. Oh, wait, I have two bottles in here, so we can each have our own."

"What luxury!"

They ate and talked and laughed.

"Tell me about your daughter," Gwen said.

"Cassandra."

"Yes, tell me about Cassandra."

He did. Hesitant at first, as he began talking he warmed to the subject. The stories he told were funny. As a toddler, she didn't call him Latt or Daddy, she combined the two and he went by Laddie for a year or more. Her first day of school he'd walked her to the door and she'd patted his hand and told him not to worry. At age seven she'd portrayed the character of Granny Smith in a play about Johnny Appleseed. Gymnastics class. Cheerleading tryouts. Debate team. Moving her into her dorm room at college. Gwen watched as the memories made him smile and made him sad.

"One pretty spring day she was walking down the street with a girlfriend and passed by a building just at the instant when the second-floor balcony collapsed. She was killed outright. Her girlfriend and two people on the balcony were seriously injured."

"I'm so sorry," Gwen said.

He nodded. "That's when I started coming here," he told her. "I'd fished on this lake a few times. And I brought Cassandra out here for one long weekend when she was about thirteen. She wasn't that fond of fishing, but Bitsy made a big deal over her and made her feel better. When I showed up, broken to pieces by losing her, Bitsy made me feel better, too."

Gwen nodded with sympathy. She thought of all those little flowers on Bitsy's grave. She wondered if he put them there as much for his daughter as his old friend.

The water lapped lazily at the side of the boat. The comfortable quiet between them lingered.

"So now it's your turn," he said.

"My turn? For what?"

"To tell me about your son," Latt said.

"You know my son."

"But I don't know about him," he clarified. "Seems like a good kid, I'm sure you're proud."

Gwen raised an eyebrow and chuckled unkindly.

"I love my son," she said. "But if I'm honest with myself, and I try to be from time to time, I have to admit he's a disappointment to me."

"Really?" Latt seemed genuinely surprised. "You're disappointed?"

"Wouldn't you be?" she said.

"I don't know, from what I hear, his biggest lapse of judgment was walking out on his wife. But you approved of that. What else has he done?"

"It's what he hasn't done," Gwen said. "I spent my life bringing up that boy. I put in fourteen-hour days, 365 days a year for decades making sure that he had everything, even more than everything, that he had every advantage, every opportunity. I sent him to a good college. I took him into the business as soon as he graduated. And I'm willing, eager to hand the whole corporation over to him. Everything I've worked for, just his for the taking."

"He a fortunate young man," Latt said.

"He certainly is," Gwen agreed. "And I had high hopes for him. But do you know what the first decision he made on his own turned out to be? To marry a nobody from nowhere, a minimum-wage employee from the company."

"Oh."

"There were attractive, well-educated girls from excellent families all over St. Louis who were interested in him," Gwen said.

"But he wasn't interested in them."

"Sean didn't give them a chance," she told him.

"Is he giving them a chance now?" Latt asked.

"No," Gwen admitted. "I thought that after he finally saw the light and left Katy things would be better. But, the truth is, they got worse. At least when he was married he was enthusiastic and hardworking and responsible."

"He seems that way to me," Latt said. "He's at Bitsy's first thing every morning and he's the last one to leave at night. Except for the time he spends with Josh, working seems like his only pursuit."

That was true, but Gwen shrugged it off. "This is just temporary," she said. "He's playing at a job. It's not even his business. He's just doing it to get in good with her."

"Ah," Latt said. "I like Katy. She's a nice girl."

"Oh, I suppose she's all right," Gwen admitted. "If she hadn't been my daughter-in-law, I'd probably like her just fine."

"You just think Sean could do better," Latt said.

She nodded. "You want the whole truth?" she asked.

"And nothing but," he answered.

"I'm insulted by her," Gwen said.

"Insulted? She's said something to you? Done something to you?"

"No, nothing like that. I'm insulted by Sean falling in love with her," she said. "It's not easy being a single mother with a full-time business to run and creditors at your door every moment. I worked hard to make Sean's childhood happy and his future secure. And after all I've done, how hard I've tried, how much I loved and cared for him, when it comes time to choose a woman to spend his life with, he picks someone who is the complete opposite of me. Some trashy blond bimbo. It just felt like a slap in the face."

"I guess it still does," he said.

"Yes," she agreed. "It still does."

Bitsy's Wisdom 27

Bitsy's Wisdom 27: Once captured, mayflies will swim themselves to death. Don't give them enough water to do so. To
keep them alive you've got to make them crawl.

It was after three in the morning when Katy and Sean gave their
final hugs to Chick, O.O. and Theon. Katy was so exhausted she
could hardly stand. She couldn't imagine how the older couple did
this job, night after night for years on in. She said as much to Sean.

"I guess they must really love it," he answered.

She agreed. It was a great business, a fun place; they were very
fortunate. She thought she was pretty fortunate herself, but she was
willing to wait until she'd slept about a week to answer for sure.

She settled into the leather seat of the big, fancy Mercedes. It
was more comfortable than the sofa in her living room.

"Are you awake enough to drive?" she asked him.

"If I'm not, I'll pull over," he assured her.

As Sean merged onto the interstate, she leaned her seat back
and settled in.

"I should have called Josh," she murmured sleepily, realizing that she hadn't given him even a thought for hours.

"He's fine," Sean said. "And you can tell him all about it when we get home."

It was the last thought she had before drifting into a deep, restful sleep.

She awakened in what could have been minutes or hours. Sean opened the car door beside her.

"Katy, come on," he said, leaning forward to help her to her feet. "We'll sleep here for a while and then go home in the morning."

"Where are we?" she asked.

"My place," he answered.

Groggily, she followed him to the doorway of a little house. He unlocked the door and led her inside. She glanced around the room. It was surprisingly neat. She remembered Sean as being messy, dropping his clothes wherever he took them off and expecting them to miraculously find their own way to the laundry and ultimately get cleaned, pressed and arrive back on hangers in his closet.

The little apartment was only one large room with four pieces of furniture and a tiny kitchenette. He pulled open the sofa bed, revealing the sleeping arrangements.

"The sheets are clean," he told her. "Go ahead and make yourself comfortable."

Katy walked over and sat down. The bed seemed far too comfortable to be avoided. She slipped off her shoes and lay down. It felt good. A few moments later in another room she heard the shower running.

A shower would be really great, she thought to herself. It had been a long day with lots of hard work. Her muscles ached. A shower would ease all that. It was exactly what she needed.

With that goal firmly in mind, Katy stripped down to her bra and panties, draping her clothes across the back of the couch. She wrapped the sheet around her and waited for her turn under the hot, steaming water. While she waited, she lay back down.

As soon as her head hit the pillow she was back in dreamland. Laughing and walking in a warm, flower-strewn countryside full of Josh's laughter and Sean beside her.

It was the morning sun in her eyes that awakened her next. Momentarily disoriented, she relaxed when she caught sight of Sean. He was asleep in the nearby chair, his long, lean body all folded up into some version of a fetal position. She smiled at the sight. He looked so young. This was what her Josh would look like just a few years from now. Young and handsome, drawing lovelorn sighs from young girls everywhere.

Katy stretched languidly, taking in her surroundings.

She'd assumed that he was living somewhere on his own, but she recognized the back of the main house as belonging to his mother. She remembered the garden house as his mother had called it. The way she'd said the name always sounded pretentious. Katy had never been inside before. It had been for guests. She was in here now, she thought. And she honestly wasn't that impressed. It was a nice efficiency apartment. Not the dreamy dollhouse that she'd imagined from the outside.

She untangled herself from the sheet draped around her and stood up. She toyed with the idea of making coffee. But the grotto-scape pool outside the long wall of glass beckoned her.

Noiselessly, she opened one of the French doors and let herself outside. She padded over to the edge and gazed into the water. A series of small fake rock falls circulated the water, giving both the sense of a refreshing stream and the white noise of privacy. She'd missed her shower last night. It would feel good. It would feel very good.

She walked around to the side with the steps. She gave one self-conscious glance toward the garden house. There didn't seem to be anyone stirring there.

Katy reached behind her and unhooked her bra, dropping it on the deck. She peeled down her panties and stepped out of them. Then she walked down into the water.

It was colder than she expected. Cold enough to make her breath catch in her throat and to make her nipples pucker. But slow was more difficult to bear than quick. When she reached the end of the steps, she immersed herself completely. The shock passed and she casually swam the length of the pool. In truth, she was sensual enough to love being naked in the water. It was strange how the tiniest scrap of bikini could make one feel confined; and without it there was a sense of oneness and freedom that was hard to duplicate on dry land. It was as if the water inside the body and the water outside the body merged, and the person that was Katy was no longer restricted to the confinement of her muscles and bone and skin.

She felt like a mermaid, cavorting about in a world much different from the one in which she'd lived her life. Diving deep, she explored the bottom of the pool. The dark liner was printed with images of irregular stone. Up close it was obviously only vinyl, but through the water it appeared to be the clearest and most natural forest-glade pool. She thought of Sean and Josh, sitting quietly on the lakeside grass listening for the birds to wake up. She was smiling as she allowed herself to float to the surface.

Before her face broke through the water, she had already spotted him.

Sean lay along the edge of the deep end of the pool. He was bare-chested and bare-footed, but the longest length of him was covered by blue jeans.

"Good morning," he said. His words were very casual, but his tone was not.

"Good morning."

Katy smoothed the water out of her face with both palms. Sean was holding something in his hands, examining it. She swam in his direction. When she got closer, she realized that he had her panties.

"Those are mine," she blurted out.

He looked directly at her then, his eyes brightened with humor. "I thought so," he said. "I knew immediately that they weren't mine and I really had my doubts about Mother."

Katy shook her head, embarrassed.

"I never realized that when you blush, you blush all over."

She refused to allow herself to slip into bashfulness. "You've seen it all before," she said, feigning a sophisticated lack of reticence.

"Yes, I have," Sean agreed, nodding. "But that doesn't mean that I don't enjoy seeing it all again."

Katy moved back a few feet from the edge, treading water. Her instinctive reaction was to put some distance between them. It was only after she'd moved that she realized she was more exposed at a distance than clinging closely to the side of the pool. Sean was looking at her in a way that was overtly sexual. Katy had not felt sexual in a very long time.

"So what about you?" he asked.

She frowned. "Me? What?"

"Would you enjoy seeing all of me again?"

He didn't wait for an answer. Katy couldn't quite muster the capacity to give one. Danger warnings were going off in her brain like Roman candles on the Fourth of July, but she made a deliberate effort to ignore them. She was not naive. She knew where this was headed. And she knew that she should resist. Having sex with your ex was tacky at best and often devastating. Katy was certain that this would be the latter. She wouldn't be able to have just a casual coupling with him, based on desire and opportunity.

If she made love with him, she'd be in love with him. Of course, the truth was, Katy pointed out to herself, she was in love with him already.

Emma said that she always made bad, impulsive choices that got her into trouble. This was absolutely, without question, another one of those.

His hand moved down to his jeans. He undid the button and drew the zipper downward. Her whole body tingled. Imagination and memory danced together inside her, filling her stomach with butterflies and creating an empty ache between her legs.

"Katy?"

She should say no, she knew she should say no. Surely, she had learned by now not to trust her instincts. But when it came to Sean, all her instincts pushed her in his direction. He was her love, her soul mate, her husband.

She swam to the side and held up her hand to him. The expression in his eyes was not triumph or even delight. It was a look of solemn determination, almost reverence. He leaped to his feet and pulled her out of the water in one motion. She stood beside him, naked, as the morning air cooled her skin. She sought his warmth, wrapping her arms around him. He drew her as close as he could be without climbing inside his skin.

Their mouths met and it was hot and sweet. Katy wanted to take her time, to savor the taste that she had missed so much, but she was too greedy. She buried her hands in his hair and moved her mouth upon his own.

She felt his hands on her breasts, caressing and exploring. His mouth drifted away from her own to plant kisses on her neck and throat and shoulder. He was talking to her as he did this, mumbling words of love that she could not hear; the pulse pounding in her brain obliterated all sound.

He slipped an arm behind her knees and lifted her off the

ground. He carried her across the deck, through the doors of the garden house and to his bed.

She looked up at him, the sunlight streaming in upon his head.

"I remembered how much I love you," she said. "But I'd forgotten how beautiful you are."

That made him smile.

"I hadn't forgotten how beautiful you are," he told her. "It haunts me. Even now I'm worried that you might not be real."

"I'm real, Sean. I am very real."

He apparently had to prove that to himself, which he did by running his hands, his mouth, all over her body. She tugged off his jeans, eager to couple with him, but he resisted. Instead he buried his face between her legs, teasing and tasting her until she was screaming. She entwined his hair around her fingers. One minute she was trying to push him away, the next she was pulling him closer. All her efforts at control were futile. It was as if he had waited to feast at this banquet forever and he was not stopping until he was sated, until she was sated.

She lay on the bed, relaxed, smiling.

"That was so good," she told him. "I'd almost convinced myself that sex was something that I could mostly live without. But I've missed it, a lot."

"Evidence that you need me," he said. His attempt at making a joke about their recent fight didn't entirely succeed.

Katy's response was thoughtful. "You know, my sister thinks that I can't manage without her and that taking care of me comes before pursuing her own life. She's wrong about that. You seem to think that I'm better off on my own than with your help. You're wrong, too. The two people in my life who are supposed to know me the best really don't know me at all."

Sean rose up on one elbow. He looked down into her face, caressing her cheek. "I want to know you, Katy," he said. "I want to understand you. But I don't even understand myself. I felt so pressured, so trapped when we were married. So breaking up should have felt better. It didn't. It was like I'd lost all my bearings, all my purpose. Now my mother has given me a great job with plenty of perks and status and only as much work as I'm willing to do. I can hardly show up there. I despise the place. I feel happier flipping burgers and wiping down tables at one of the sites. I see myself turning into exactly the guy I would never want to be, and I feel helpless to stop it. It's like I'm being batted back and forth between two strong women whom I love. I don't want to hurt either of you, but I've got to stand on my own, so I end up hurting both of you. What's that about?"

"I guess it's about how complicated everything is," she said. "I try my best to make my world simple, but every time I turn around it's all knotted up in tangles again."

He smiled a little sadly. "I'm another tangle, aren't I, Katy?" he said. "*This* is another tangle"

"No," she answered. "This is right. You and me together, trying to do the best for our son, that's right."

He sighed and nodded. "I do want what's best for our son," Sean said.

"I do, too," Katy told him. "I've been thinking a lot about what you've said. And even more about the time you and Josh have been spending together. Every boy needs a dad. And my Josh really needs you. I'm willing…I'm willing to work out some kind of custody arrangement that makes that possible. I can't even imagine letting him go live somewhere else. Just thinking about that makes it hard for me to breathe. But I want to do what's best for Josh. I guess the hard part, really, is figuring out what that is."

"I already know," Sean said. "What's best for Josh is the one thing that I've made it impossible for us to give him. A mother and father who are married to each other, raising him together."

The words hung out in the empty space between them for a long moment. Then Katy grabbed at them as if they were the brass ring.

"It's not *impossible* that we could give him that," she said quietly. "All you have to do is ask."

A line of worry creased Sean's brow. "I walked out on you, Katy, remember that?"

"Yes, it still hurts me every time I think about it," she said.

"I don't want to hurt you. I don't want to hurt Josh," he said. "How can I know that it won't happen again? I've already proved that when things get tough, I'm capable of just bailing. How can you know that I won't do it again?"

"I don't," Katy said. "Life doesn't come with guarantees. But there are promises. You probably didn't think much about it the first time you promised 'for better or worse.' I know that before you make that vow again, you'd take it more seriously."

"I would," he agreed. "Since I left you, I haven't been able to commit to anything, not to my job, not to my own goals, certainly not to a woman. Though I think you ought to know that I've... I've been with other women."

Katy laid her fingers across his mouth, halting his confession.

"I don't want to know that," she said. "I just want to know that you're here now with me."

"Take me back, Katy," he said. "Give me another chance and I'll live the rest of my life trying to keep my promises. Be my wife again."

She gazed up into his eyes. "I will," she answered.

They kissed, not with pent-up passion or waves of desire, but as if they were sealing a pact.

Still holding her in his arms, Sean issued a warning. "We've both got to understand that our marriage is like a precious piece of glass," he said. "I dropped it and broke it. We can mend it, but it will never be what it was. The evidence of what happened will always be there. We've both got to know that and accept it."

Katy thought about his words, but had an analogy of her own.

"I think our marriage is like the barbecue fire," she told him.

He looked at her questioningly.

"It was all hot and bright at the beginning and we just plunged right into it. But while we burned off those outer layers and the baggage we brought with it, the smoke was bitter. But it doesn't have to stay that way. If we just keep stoking it, Sean, giving it time, it will make our lives taste so good."

This time when their lips met, it was with eagerness and desire.

Afterward Katy ran her hand along his chest and down his stomach to his penis, which was completely erect.

"It'll come down in a minute," he assured her.

She eyed him with speculation. "Now, Mr. Dodson, why on earth would we want it to come down?" she asked.

"You're sure?"

"I'm sure, Sean," she said. "I want you inside me."

He pulled her tightly into his arms and looked down into her face. "That's what I want, too, Katy. I want you so bad, I'm not even thinking about how stupid it probably is for us to do this here and now."

"Here and now is our whole world, Sean," she said. "Let's take it."

"I can't resist," he admitted. But as if to put a lie to his words, he rolled out of bed and jumped to his feet. He began rifling through the drawers of the bathroom counter.

"What are you doing?" Katy asked him.

"I'm trying to find a condom," he answered.

"We don't need one," she told him.

Bitsy's Wisdom 28

Bitsy's Wisdom 28: After dark, emerald shiners will rise close to the surface to feed. Thin and delicate with green color along their silver backs, they are almost too pretty to use as fish bait.

The Sunday of Parker's baptism was a perfect one to be out in the water. The summer had arrived full tilt. At nine o'clock in the morning the thermometer was already inching up near eighty degrees. And the humidity made it seem even hotter.

Emma stood alongside Nadine as the latter nervously made bad jokes.

"The church people thought it would be a cold day in hell before I showed up on Sunday. Turns out, it's the only hellish hot on earth."

Neither Emma nor her sister Katy managed a laugh.

"Of course, they must have believed that the church would fall to ashes if I went inside, otherwise why would they have moved the service out here?"

That wasn't funny, either.

The little church didn't have a baptistry and utilized the waters of the nearby lake instead. Perhaps because of the unwalled nature of the event the crowd was three times its normal size. Apparently knowing this would happen, the churchwomen planned a luncheon in the park—fried chicken and biscuits for everyone. And everyone in town showed up.

Some, undoubtedly, came just for the food. Some for the novelty of having church outside. Emma, who had never before observed this kind of evangelical baptism ritual, was curious. She assumed that there were others, like her, just there for the show.

Field note: The natives gather around the water. Those most spiritually bent form a body up close. Those less so hang back among the shrubs and trees, alert and observant. The shaman of the tribe adorns himself with flowing white robes that cover more-utilitarian hip-wader boots. He walks down to the shore and is surrounded by the most ardent of the followers, dressed in costume most respectful for the occasion. He turns to the mass of people and in a loud voice reads from an ancient text that describes the rite and explains its meaning. When finished, he holds the book up high above his head.

"This is the word of the Lord."

"Thanks be to God," *the followers mumble.*

With hands clasped and eyes closed, he commences a supplication to the deity. He offers thanks for the fine weather and plentiful fishing and praise for the miracle of creation. He asks forgiveness for the failings of all mankind. And he calls down blessings upon all those gathered.

The followers lower their heads respectfully. The onlookers lower their heads as well, making it difficult to differentiate followers from onlookers.

"Amen."

After the pronouncement, he hands the book to a deacon nearby and, turning, he wades into the lake. A small line of postulants trail after him. They are arraigned in ordinary attire, each carrying a folded white handkerchief.

When they are about thigh-high in the water, the shaman turns and stays the line with his hand. He steps back a few feet farther until he is waist-high in the water. Then he holds out his hand and the first person in the line, a woman, comes forward.

He asks for a declaration. She gives it.

He takes the folded cloth from her hand and places it over her mouth and nose. He proclaims the meaning of the ritual and his part in it. Then he places his hand over the handkerchief and tips her backward, completely immersing her in the water until she disappears from the sight of all those on shore. Then she emerges from the water, drenched and changed. The shaman sets her back upon her feet, urging her to keep this commitment and she makes her way to the water's edge.

He calls the next supplicant to him and does likewise.

And the next. And the next.

Then he calls the last to him, the boy.

Parker, standing alone in the lake, wades in Pastor Curt's direction. Curt comes closer to shore so that the water is not so deep for the young guy to stand in.

Emma is momentarily startled by a hand that clasps her own. She glances beside her to see Nadine. Looking on nervously, her eyes well with tears.

"Parker Graves, confess your faith," Curt says to him.

Across the distance of the water the shaky answer in a boy's soprano voice rings clear. "Jesus is Lord."

"As John did for Jesus at the River Jordan, I baptize you, my brother, in the name of the Father and the Son and the Holy Ghost. Buried with Him in baptism and raised to walk in the newness of life."

The actions in the lake mirrored the words as they were spoken. He buried Parker from sight beneath the water and then lifted him out as a resurrection.

Everybody applauded. Parker wiped the water out of his eyes

and cast a shy glance through the crowd until he caught sight of his mother and smiled. Emma turned to glance at her, too. She was smiling through tears.

"He's a great kid," Emma told her. "You're a good mom."

"Thanks," Nadine said.

Parker waded out of the lake and through the crowd. Everybody he passed patted him on the back or shook his hand. When he got to his mother, she went down on her knees and hugged him.

"Mom, you'll get all wet," Parker said.

"I don't mind," she assured him. "Besides, look at me, I'm soaked, already bawling like a baby."

"Did I make you cry?"

"I'm just so proud of you," Nadine assured him. "You've grown up so fast and I'm so proud."

"I'm not all the way grown-up, Mom, I promise."

Nadine laughed. "Good, I want you to take your time on that," she said.

Almost spontaneously the people began to sing. It was not just the congregation that raised their voices. It seemed nearly everyone knew the song—even Nadine, whose throaty mezzo-soprano was a joy to hear.

"Shall we gather at the river, where God's angels' feet have trod…"

Emma, unfamiliar with the song and not a singer by nature, listened and eventually began humming just a bit.

As the last chorus faded, her attention was drawn back to Curt. He had moved closer into the shallows, but he was still standing out in the water where everyone could see him. The deacon handed him his Bible again and he opened it to a marked passage and read it aloud. It was an interesting choice of scripture. Not one of the parables or a letter from Paul, but an obscure little argument among the disciples. Emma couldn't imagine that its importance was anything except an observation that even very religious people often get sidetracked by vanity and personal ambition.

When Curt finished, he closed the book and looked around at the gathering, thoughtful and smiling.

"I want to thank all of you for coming today, to share this special moment with these members of our community," he said. "I'm not going to preach a sermon today. I'm sure I can get an 'amen' to that." There were a few chuckles that skittered through the crowd. "There is, though, a bit of biblical guidance of which I want to remind you. When our Lord Jesus walked here on earth, the religious people of his day didn't like him. Now, they weren't bad people or evil people. They were good people. But they didn't understand Christ's mission. They said to themselves, 'How can he claim to be a servant of God, when all his friends are the dregs of society? They're all beggars and thieves, adulterers and prostitutes, swindlers and confidence men.'"

"Now, Jesus let them talk among themselves. He didn't change what he was doing. He didn't try to cultivate a finer circle of friends. He told them. 'Healthy people don't need a doctor! I haven't come here for the good godly people, I've come for those that need me.'"

"Now, I know my congregation," he said. "You are good people, righteous people. You're trying to follow the example set for you. But I want to ask you, this week, to think about, pray about, expanding your circle. Make friends with some of the people Christ would have chosen."

As they bowed their heads for benediction, Emma thought about Curt. He had surprised her. As a minister, she'd thought him to be a competent mailman. She'd thought him a nice guy, good enough for her sister. But she hadn't seen him as he truly was, a leader in his community. She found herself having more respect for him. And questioning her own abilities as a witness to human interactions. Maybe she'd grown soft in these summer days waiting tables at Bitsy's. She'd become so much a part of Warbler Lake, that she was no longer looking in. She didn't want that to happen.

Once the prayer was finished, the dinner on the ground began almost immediately. There were hungry, happy adults and jostling kids, and goodwill being spooned up as easily as potato salad.

As Emma was served up her plate of chicken and biscuits, she vowed to keep her eyes peeled and her brain engaged.

She found a seat in the last row of picnic tables. Except for the empty seat across from her, the table was full of teenagers. Emma might as well have been invisible for all the attention they paid to her. It was a perfect perch to watch what was happening around her. And there was plenty to watch.

There was the usual stuff, young parents trying to wrangle their children into actually eating before starting to play. The Dempseys quietly holding hands under the table. Flora Krebs swapping fishing stories with Newt Barker. Miss Welborn being doting grandmother to little Natty.

And there were some less than usual as well.

Pastor Curt had Nadine by the arm and he was going person by person, table by table, introducing her to the town that knew her all too well.

"Have you met Parker's mother?" he said to first one person and then another.

"This is Nadine Graves, Parker's mom."

Emma raised an eyebrow, impressed. Some people were less than delighted to meet her, but nobody was rude. Nobody refused to speak to her or shake her hand.

Emma smiled as she began conjuring up a field note about

tribal outcasts, but lost her train of thought as Katy and Sean headed in her direction. They stopped to talk to everyone they passed and everyone talked to them. It was like they were the most popular kids in high school. Except this wasn't high school. And they weren't kids. They were hardworking business persons, parents and neighbors. Katy had certainly found a home in this community and she was bringing Sean into it as well. Emma didn't know what that might mean for them or for her. But because they were content with it, she was trying to be that way, too.

They stopped at the table in front of Emma.

"We're taking our plates over to Mrs. Bullock's house," Katy told her, indicating the dish covered with aluminum foil that Sean held. "Her knee was bothering her a lot this morning, so she stayed home. We thought we'd share some of this lunch on her front porch."

"That sounds like a nice thing to do," Emma said.

Katy nodded. "It was Sean's idea. He and Mrs. Bullock are great buddies."

Emma agreed and encouraged them to have a nice time. She started to ask if Katy wanted her to keep an eye on Josh, but glanced over to see he and Brianna chatting amiably with Gwen.

"Okay, tell Luella I said hi," Emma told them.

"We will."

The two walked down the shoreline. They were happy, clearly happy. Emma had tried to deny that, but she no longer could. She didn't know how it could possibly work out between the two of them, and with the custody fight still hanging over their heads, but in the past few days, since their return from St. Louis, it seemed certain that it would. They both seemed eager and excited to make a go of the B & B, and Katy's conviction that Sean would never take Josh from her seemed more realistic.

Emma's attention was drawn back to the crowd when Gus Gous-whelter and his daughter-in-law, sitting at separate tables and engaged in separate conversations, paused to throw verbal darts at each other.

The snarl of contention was apparently the high quality of Birdie's cooking.

"For company and strangers, she makes these light-as-air biscuits," he said. "But if it's me, living every day in my own house, she just puts some spongy store bread on the table. That's what she thinks is good enough for me, store bread."

Birdie's eyes narrowed and her lips thinned to one horizontal line.

"If a man just sits around all day," she said to the people at her table, but loud enough so that anyone within twenty yards could hear. "If he just sits and does nothing but take up space, then who would want to cook for him?"

"The space I'm taking up is space that belongs to me," Gus complained loudly. "If I put a roof over your head, the least you could do is manage some decent vittles for me to eat."

Birdie angrily rose to her feet. "You selfish, loudmouthed old man," she said. "Every bite of food you put in your mouth is furnished by Hiram's hard labor. He don't ask you for thanks, 'cause he's not that kind of man, but the least you can do is shut up your complaining."

"Don't you tell me to shut up, woman!" Gus hollered. "I ain't some pantywaist that would let you push me around. I'll say what I want, when I want and in my own house whenever I want."

"You're not in your house, old fool," Birdie answered back. "You're at a church picnic. Is your old-timer's brain so befuddled you don't know where you are?"

"I know damn well, where I am."

"Dad! Stop!"

His son Hiram suddenly appeared between them, his face as red as a beet and his visage angry.

"Dad, we don't curse at a Sunday school picnic," he told the old man.

Behind him, his wife huffed and shook her head. "That old man is just a disgrace."

"Birdie! Sit down and hush up!"

Normally soft-spoken Hiram's angry order was so unexpected, everybody in the park quieted. You could have heard a pin drop and Birdie wordlessly took her seat.

"I am sick to death of this," Hiram announced. "It's bad enough that I have to hear it every day of my life. But you two don't even have enough shame to keep your differences out of the public park." He looked around at everyone who was looking at him. "On behalf of my family, I apologize."

There were murmurs throughout the crowd; people tried to look away. But he wasn't finished.

"Dad?" Hiram spoke more quietly. "Do you want Birdie and me to find our own place?"

Gus sobered. "I can't live in that house by myself," he admitted.

"Then if I'm going to stay, so is Birdie," Hiram told him.

"I don't like her," Gouswhelter stated flatly.

Hiram shook his head. "You don't have to like her," Hiram said. "But because she's my wife, you have to treat her with respect." He half turned to face Birdie. "And because he's my father, you're going to do the same."

Neither said anything.

Gus went back to eating. Birdie busied herself by cleaning off the table. Hiram wandered back to his seat and the crowd politely pretended that nothing had happened.

Under what she hoped was a poker-faced demeanor, Emma was chuckling to herself. Both of them had been badly in need of a time-out for a good long while.

From far across the tables, her gaze met Gwen's. Emma knew

the two might never have anything else in common, but at that moment they were both seriously stifling the nervous giggles. Then the moment was gone as Latt touched Gwen's arm. She looked up at him and smiled. Emma raised an eyebrow at that. She didn't know if she should worry that her lawyer was getting too chummy with the plaintiff, or be pleased that the bait producer/lawyer could manage enough charm to co-opt the opposition.

As Emma watched them for a couple of seconds, she casually began to take in the people around them. When she didn't spot the face she expected to see, she widened her search. Everyone was talking and chatting as she scanned face after face. He wasn't among them. She rose to her feet, eyeing the playground in the distance. She caught sight of Parker standing around in a group of older kids. Neither his sister nor her best buddy were nearby.

Emma left her chair and took a couple of steps forward before she caught sight of something at the very edge of her vision. She glanced in that direction, the direction of the shoreline. She saw Brianna standing alone, waist high in the lake. Gazing down, her hair soaking wet and clinging to the back of her neck, she was desperately looking for something in the water.

The hairs rose on the back of Emma's neck.

"Josh!"

Emma wasn't sure if she had screamed the name or heard it on somebody else's lips. She was running. And she wasn't alone. A surge of people were rushing to the lakeside. It was less than a hundred yards, but at this moment it seemed like miles. Spurl Westbrook somehow managed to arrive ahead of her. He jerked Brianna out of the water.

"We were playing baptism," Emma heard her explaining. "We were playing baptism and then he didn't come back up."

Emma rushed out into the water. She bent down, rushing her

hands across the bottom of the water, frantically seeking the child that was so dear to her. The lake was suddenly alive with people doing the same. Through the roaring of her own blood in her ears, Emma could hear a hundred voices calling Josh's name. Emma couldn't see them. All she could see was the empty water just in front of her. The lake was so big and Josh was so small.

Emma lost a shoe. She hadn't realized she was still wearing them. She quickly stepped out of the other and kept moving. As the water got deeper and deeper, it was harder to search the bottom. Finally she dived down. Swimming, fully dressed and in a straight skirt, was harder than she'd imagined. And the influx of people into the lake had stirred up the mud until visibility in the brown water was almost none. Still she ran her hands along the bottom arm's length by arm's length, resisting the need to go up for air although her lungs were screaming. How much more urgent was Josh's need for oxygen?

Suddenly, she heard something. She didn't know how she could pick up one sound among all the others, but the tenor was somehow different. Immediately Emma pushed off from the rocks. She had barely broken the surface when she heard the echoes of shouts.

"They've got him, they've got him."

Emma swam quickly to shore watching Pearly Ross and J. T. Metcalf dragging the little body to the water's edge. When she got close enough to stand up, she did. Making the slow trudge through the water as quickly as possible, her eyes were glued upon the circle of bodies, some squatting, some standing around her nephew. She couldn't see Josh. There were too many people in the way.

When she was finally out of the lake, she hurried to his side.

"Let me through," she demanded as she pushed through the crowd. "Let me through."

On her knees at her side, she could almost wish they had kept her back. Little Josh lay on his back, unresponsive. His lids were open wide, but his eyes had rolled back in his head, only the whites showing. His skin was a strange, inhuman blue. His head had been tipped back unnaturally and Newt Barker had pinched his nostrils closed. He leaned forward and breathed into Josh's mouth. Somewhere above her Emma heard Curt's voice, praying. The sound didn't comfort her. Emma began to shake. It was as if she were cold, but she wasn't cold. Her heart was pounding, her whole body quaking out of control. Tears were coming out of her eyes, but her head was shaking so badly that they were sprinkling all over her face. She put her hand over her mouth. She could feel the screams building up inside her. She didn't know if she could hold them in. She was losing control. She was losing control.

Just then she felt an arm slip around her shoulder. Katy was beside her. Emma was supposed to protect and take care of her. She was supposed to see that nothing bad ever happened to her. But she couldn't protect her from this. She was helpless. And if she couldn't cope, how would her sister?

Amazingly, Katy was not shaking, she was not crying, she seemed complete calm. She watched Newt doing the CPR for just a moment and then she reached over and grasped her son's hand.

"Joshua Dodson, you get back here right now!"

Her voice, firm and unwavering, carried the full authority of motherhood. And from wherever the child was at that time, he must have heard it.

Immediately, Josh's body heaved upward. A terrible, horrific sound came from his throat followed by copious amounts of vile-smelling water shooting up out of his mouth like a fountain.

Newt turned the boy on his side and more water poured out. He was choking and gasping. The crowd around him was alternately startled and cheering and praising.

Josh caught sight of his mother and burst into tears. She gathered him into her arms and rocked him as if he were a baby.

Nadine showed up with a blanket and Katy wrapped Josh in it. Sean squatted beside them, holding them both in his arms, one hand stroking his son's wet hair.

Emma glanced up then to see that just beyond those huddled around Josh, a circle of townspeople were all holding hands. The clothes of each and every person were drenched at least waist high with water. They'd all been in the lake, they'd all gone after Josh. Everyone was joined together. The ancient Mr. and Mrs. Dempsey. Waymon Riley. Pricy and Noodle Metcalf. Harriet Welborn. Flora Krebs. All three of the Gouswhelters—Gus and Birdie didn't even seem to realize their hands were clasped. Pearly Ross was there. And Latt Meicklejohn. And they'd all prayed with Curt for Josh to breathe in life again.

Newt was talking to the boy, asking him questions about where he was, who he was, what day he thought it to be and what he'd been doing. Apparently assessing damage to the child's brain.

"He seems all right," Newt said to Sean. "But you'll need to take him to the hospital and let a doctor check him out."

Sean nodded.

"How did this happen?"

The question came from across the little circle of intimates from Gwen. It was accusatory and angry and directed at Katy.

"I thought with all of you here, someone would keep an eye on him," Katy said.

Gwen's eyes narrowed. "Did you ask someone to look after him?"

"I…no, I…" Katy's face went pale, immediately stricken by guilt. It ripped through her like a knife.

She glanced over at Emma. "I meant to ask Emma, but I got distracted and I forgot."

Emma realized that, of course, that's why her sister had deliberately come up to her and told her where she was going. Of course, it was her intention to leave Josh in her charge.

"I would have been watching him," Emma explained to Gwen, feeling equally to blame. "But he was with you and Latt. I assumed that he was with you."

"Nobody ever said a word to me about keeping track of the child," Gwen told her, clearly shocked that anyone would think that she had fallen down on the job. "I didn't even realize that his mother had walked off and left him."

"It's all my fault," Parker piped in. "I always look out for Brianna when my mom's busy. But I was just thinking about myself and let her and Josh wander away."

"No, Parker," Nadine assured him. "You're seven, you're not expected to be responsible for the children. I'm the one who should have had my eyes on Brianna."

"But I dragged you away," Curt said. "With all the adults standing around here, we should all have been watching."

"Blame is not the important thing," Sean said, effectively stopping the discussion. "We need to get Josh to the hospital. Mother, we're taking your car."

Bitsy's Wisdom 29

Bitsy's Wisdom 29: Controlling temperature in the pit smoker can be tricky. If you get a good, efficient fire going, then all you have to remember is getting plenty of air makes it hotter, pinch that off and it cools down quick.

The light sparkled on the water like diamonds. The sound of it lapping against the sides of the little boat she sat in had a musical quality to it, almost like wind chimes. Gwen was in a dream. And as she gazed at the rocky beach in the distance, she knew it was, but in a way that was so pleasurably real.

A gnat brushed her cheek and she pushed it away.

On the shore she saw Garrett and she called out to him and waved. He looked good, strong and healthy, happy. Much different from the last time she'd seen him. And it had been such a long time since she'd seen him. He began to come toward her. At first she was shocked to see him walking on the water, but then she remembered that he was dead and thought, "Oh, sure, I suppose spirits could do that." He was dead and not subject to the laws of the earth, so it was perfectly natural that he could accomplish such a feat. But as he neared the boat she realized he was not Garrett, but Sean.

The gnat landed on her face again; she shook her head to get it off.

Her heart was in her throat as she watched her son taking one careful step after another upon the water, whose smooth-as-glass surface had now roughed up with whitecaps.

"Sean," she called out to him. "What are you doing? You can't walk on water."

He laughed and shook his head. "Of course I can, Mother," he agreed. "The lake is only two inches deep here."

The gnat had grown into a giant dragonfly and was no longer content just to land on her skin, but was walking down her face and the length of her throat. She swatted at it. The movement brought her fully awake to find herself not in the little boat, but in her little bed in the tiny lake cabin. And the annoying gnat turned out to be Lattimer Meicklejohn, sitting on the side of her mattress, trying to wake her by caressing her face.

"What the devil are you doing in here?" she asked.

He shrugged and answered with a grin, "The door was unlocked."

"There are no locks at Gouswhelter Lake Cabins," she pointed out, unnecessarily.

"My point exactly," he said. "Curt brought by my mail this morning and I just couldn't wait any longer for you to get up."

She glanced around, looking for her watch. "What time is it, anyway?"

"It's nearly eleven-thirty," he said. "And I know an important chairman and chief executive officer, like yourself, wouldn't want to sleep till noon, even when she's on vacation."

Gwen sat up in bed and carefully patted the sleep out of her eyes, careful not to do anything to encourage wrinkles. She didn't see people in the mornings before she was dressed, groomed and fully made-up. Being caught barefaced and in dowdy cotton pajamas should have embarrassed her. But the level of her comfort with Latt was off the scale. For some reason, when she was around him, the facts of her age, appearance, reputation or confidence level never seemed to be a problem. She supposed it was because she didn't care what he thought. Or perhaps it was because he didn't care about those kinds of things.

He handed her a little clutch of wildflowers, tied together with a piece of ribbon.

"Oh?"

"Thought you might need a touch of sunshine in your morning," he said.

"Thank you, I do," she agreed.

"Late night?" he said. "At least I know you weren't out tying one on."

She smiled. "Not hardly."

"What time did you get back from the hospital?"

"About 2:00 a.m.," she said. "The emergency room was about the size of my kitchen, Josh was the only patient, and it still took ten hours to get out of there."

"An ER is an ER even in the country," he said. "The urgency is to get you there, once that happens the getting taken care of and getting home is as slow as molasses."

She nodded.

"I don't have to ask how Josh is," Latt said. "Because I've already seen him this morning out playing in the backyard at Bitsy's. He's jumping around and yelling like nothing ever happened."

Gwen smiled.

"I think yesterday was the scariest moment I ever lived," she said. "Even when Garrett had his heart attack, I didn't feel like so much hung in the balance. It's really kind of crazy. Six weeks ago I didn't even know that child. Now the idea of losing him is more than I can bear."

Latt was smiling at her, but his expression was serious. He leaned forward and planted a kiss on the corner of her mouth.

Gwen was caught completely off guard.

"What was that?" she complained.

He shrugged. "A lot of things," he answered. "Part thank-you, part I admire you, part I'm so glad to have this adversaries thing behind us."

"What are you talking about?"

"I got my letter this morning," he said.

"Letter?"

"From your lawyer," he answered.

"You got a letter from my lawyer?" Gwen was a little surprised. She hadn't heard from David since the venue change. She assumed that he was busy. She'd meant to call him for a progress report, but had just not gotten around to it. "Has he got the date?"

"The date?" Latt frowned. "What date?"

"The hearing date, silly," Gwen answered. "What else is there?"

Latt's frown deepened and he leaned away from her. "His letter was to inform me that you are withdrawing the petition for change of custody."

"Withdrawing?"

"Yes, withdrawing," Latt said. "No muss, no fuss, no day in court."

"No, that's impossible," Gwen said. "I'm not giving up custody. My God, after what happened yesterday, I'm guaranteed a win. Josh nearly drowned in her care."

"In her care? The whole town was there, including you and Sean."

Gwen shook her head. "Katy has custody, so it's her responsibility. If he was with me, none of us would even be at this lake," she replied. "It may not seem fair, but that's the way the legal system works."

"I know exactly how the legal system works," Latt said. "That's why I try to avoid working in it as much as possible."

Gwen huffed derisively. "Throwing away your talent and your education so that you can live the life of some Hicksville hippy is certainly your choice to make. But you can't believe that it garners any points with me."

"As if I would want to garner points with some stubborn, over-controlling, stuffed-shirt female CEO who can't let her own son be with the woman he loves because it might reflect badly on her."

Gwen's sharp intake of breath was as much for hearing how unflattering she appeared in his version of the truth, as it was for having her own confession, made in confidence, used against her.

"I'm a mother trying to do the best for my son and my grand-son," she declared. "You and Katy and the people who live around this dumpy, has-been resort may be satisfied with your petty, in-significant little lives, but Sean and Josh and I, we can do better."

He rose to his feet.

"I'm not here to argue with you," he declared. "The petition has been withdrawn and I got notice of that this morning. If you want to yell at somebody about it, yell at your own lawyer. I'm not paid to listen to you."

Latt turned and walked out the door, slamming it hard behind him.

Gwen was so furious she jumped to her feet, ran over to the door and slammed it again, even harder. And then once more for good measure. She made a very unladylike hand gesture toward his retreating back. And once he'd gone around the bend of the lake path, she cursed aloud.

She stomped across the floor and jerked up her PDA before remembering, no towers. She almost slammed it back on the table, but just managed to stop herself and set it down gently.

Gwen couldn't imagine what kind of stupid screwup had precipitated David Faneuf withdrawing the custody petition. But the sooner she straightened it out, the sooner they'd get the process back on track.

She threw off her pajamas and headed for the shower. She was done with this place, she decided. She'd been here long enough to establish a relationship with Josh and she'd accumulated enough evidence against Katy to make her look bad in court. There was nothing more she needed to do and nothing more she wanted to do. As soon as she talked to David, she was coming back here to pack up. She and Sean could be home by dinnertime.

The water poured down on her and she thought about the time she'd spent here. Yes, she'd relaxed a lot, laughed a lot, but that was to be expected. It was her first vacation in years. And it was easy for a person to be lazy when there were no cell phones or Internet access. She would go back home and get to work. She'd stop thinking so much about family connections and personal relationships and concentrate on running a business. The lawyer would get the custody agreement changed. She was still certain of that. It would take longer. Josh probably wouldn't be able to start school in St. Louis, but he'd be living there by Christmas for sure.

Out of the shower, she dried her hair in the miserable, half-bent-over method that she'd perfected in the cabin's one plug-in bathroom. She carefully applied her makeup and passed up the casual blouses and capri pants that had become her uniform at Warbler Lake for a tailored summer pantsuit. She opted for open-toe pumps over her comfortable espadrilles and gathered up her things and headed out to the cemetery. She spotted the flowers that Latt had brought her and picked them up, too. She let the screen door slam behind her. The sound brought back unpleasant memories and she sighed. Gwen liked Latt better as her friend than as her critic.

She stopped at Sean's cabin, but he wasn't there. She figured that he must be at the restaurant. At least this summer had improved his work ethic.

She walked up to her car, but she wasn't able to get away quickly. Old Gus waved her over and asked about Josh.

"I haven't seen him yet this morning," Gwen said. "But I heard that he's feeling fine."

Gwen hoped she wouldn't be obliged to say more, but Birdie and Hiram joined the old man on the porch.

"We heard you get in really late last night," Birdie told her. "I guess they didn't keep him in the hospital?"

"We brought him home," she said. "The doctor gave him some prophylactic antibiotics to take care of any potential lung infection, but he thinks he'll be fine."

"That's wonderful," Hiram said, and the other two nodded agreement. "He's a sweet little boy, I'm sure you're very proud of him."

"Yes, I am, thanks," Gwen said. "I've got to go."

She got into her car and got out of there as efficiently as possible, managing all the niceties of local custom. As she drove the now-familiar circuitous route across the ridge and up the side of the mountain, she planned her day. After she straightened things up with David, she'd call Myra. She couldn't imagine what the management team must be thinking about her not even calling to check in on a Monday morning. But she'd be back home tomorrow. She'd get up to speed on everything in the company in a day or two and have everything running back to her liking within a week.

She parked at the cemetery, grabbed up her load of papers and equipment and walked across the ground. Gwen was swamped with a strange sense of melancholy. She had been coming to this quiet secluded place of the dead for weeks now. She'd spent so many mornings among these stones that she knew that she would miss them. And she never planned to be in this place ever again.

At Bitsy's grave she dropped the bunch of wildflowers that Latt had brought her and then walked toward Carlton Bullock's bench. As she sat down she remembered his widow's joke about the old man looking up her skirt and laughed aloud.

She was actually smiling when she got David Faneuf on the phone. Everything could be straightened out. She was certain of it.

"Good morning, Mrs. Dodson," he said. "I'm surprised to hear from you."

"I meant to call earlier in the week to see how things were going," she said. "But this morning there's some confusion that I need you to address. Lattimer Meicklejohn, my daughter-in-law's lawyer, received a letter saying the petition had been withdrawn. I can't imagine how such a mistake could have happened."

There was a very long silence on the other end of the line.

"Ah…" David hesitated. "I…I didn't realize that you were un-aware, Mrs. Dodson," he began. "Mr. Dodson contacted me last week and withdrew the petition."

"Mr. Dodson?"

"Yes, Sean," Faneuf confirmed. "It is *his* petition, after all."

"Why on earth would he do that?"

Another silence followed.

"I truly don't know," David said. "He didn't offer any specifics and I didn't feel as if it were my place to ask. I told him that I be-lieved, even with the venue setback that we had, our case was very winnable and I expected notice of our court date very soon. He said that it was moot and to withdraw, so that's what I did."

Now Gwen was the one who was speechless. She just sat there, holding the phone, trying to get her mind around what to say. Sean had gone behind her back and thrown a wrench in all her machinations. It was infuriating, but more than that, it was inexplicable.

"Perhaps you should talk to Sean," David suggested gently.

The sympathy in the man's tone so infuriated Gwen it was all she could do not to hang up on the man. Instead, she fell back on professionalism, almost always the perfect refuge.

"All right then, thank you so much," she said. "Have a nice day."

She pressed her thumb on the red dot that ended the connection.

Bitsy's Wisdom 30

Bitsy's Wisdom 30: It's useless to use a knife on a barbecued butt. If it's cooked right, just pull it apart with your fingers.

Sean flipped the two burgers he still had on the grill and tossed a handful of onions on the side. It had once been suggested that on his tombstone it would probably read *Five Billion Served,* but he didn't mind. He liked the restaurant business, he always had. As a kid he'd loved to hear the stories about his dad's first burger joints. The old bread truck with its open-out windows. And the first drive-in out on the highway. His dad had known his customers and had spent every day trying to make something good that they might like. That was his love, his art.

Dodsonburger made a very good product. It was a quality, full-size hamburger with all the fixings. And you could get one in Kansas City that tasted exactly like the one you bought in St. Louis or Springfield or Joplin. Consistency was good. People liked food that they could depend on. And when they wanted a Dodsonburger, they ought to be able to find one. But there weren't going to be any Dodsonburgers at Bitsy's Bait & BBQ.

Sean opened some buns and lay them out on the high side of the griddle away from the grease. Then he tossed the onions slightly and smashed down the two meat patties. Nothing that he ever made here would be uniform, everything would be unique. That's the way you ran a restaurant that catered to regulars, you couldn't allow them to get bored.

That was the plan, the one that he and Katy had hatched out together. They would run this place the way Bitsy had and no one would ever get bored.

He thought about the photograph hanging in the dining room of a young woman full of life and eagerness. She had found a life of happiness in this modest little business, and Sean and Katy would, too.

Sean scooped up the buns, squirted them with mustard and then added the meat with the browned onions on top, a leaf of lettuce and a slice of tomato. He set the completed burger up on the shelf and hit the bell.

He was back to scraping down the griddle. Fortunately, he'd discovered that he could clean it up after lunch and it would still be in very good shape by the end of the night. Hamburgers were a highly popular item on their lunch menu. He was just glad that the barbecue had turned out to be so popular in the evenings. And they were hoping to add a barbecue sandwich at lunch. He and Katy were very optimistic about the future.

"Where is Sean!"

He heard the angry utterance coming from the dining room and paused in midmotion. He recognized his mother's voice. And he even knew what it was about.

A minute later she pushed through the kitchen door, with Katy right behind her.

"Sean Garrett Dodson, explain yourself!"

Sean struggled with the inappropriate desire to laugh. It was not a funny moment. But he was struck by the consistency of her reaction. This was exactly how his mother would have confronted him for using crayons to draw on his bedroom wall, building a skateboard ramp in the driveway or spending his entire allowance at the video arcade.

His mother had not changed. But he had.

Sean didn't get nervous. He didn't get defensive. He didn't get mad. He glanced over at his wife. Her expression was all sympathy. He tried to telegraph the message *everything will be fine,* because he knew that it would.

"I've withdrawn my petition for custody," he answered his mother simply. "I told the lawyer that it was no longer necessary, and it's not."

"You just withdrew it, willy-nilly, without even consulting me?"

"It wasn't your petition, Mother," he said. "It was mine."

His mother's mouth thinned to one line. She started to speak and then hesitated, glancing toward Katy.

"Does she have to be here?"

"No, I'll leave," Katy offered.

"You can stay," Sean told her. "This concerns you, too."

His mother appeared disgusted with that decision and let him know with an upraised eyebrow, but she didn't bother to argue.

"There was no reason to give up on this case," Gwen told him. "We were winning."

"Winning was never my goal," Sean explained. "I just wanted to see more of Josh."

Gwen nodded. "And to see that he was brought up in better circumstances and with better opportunities."

"The circumstances and opportunities here are fine," Sean said.

His mother vehemently disagreed. "In St. Louis we can give Josh a fine private school education, music, culture and all the benefits of wealth and a position of privilege in society."

"Those things are nice, Mother, but they are no guarantee of happiness or success in life."

She gave a huff of pure frustration. "Do you want your son to grow up in some greasy restaurant kitchen, raised by a distracted, part-time mother who can only pay attention to him when she doesn't have customers waiting? That, or she has to hand him off into the care of strangers, whose background you may or may not know while she tries to make certain the rent will be paid on time? Is that the kind of life you want for your son?"

She seemed to think the answer was obvious. And it was to Sean as well. He smiled.

"It's the kind of upbringing I had, Mother," he said. "I don't think it's such a bad way to grow up. I never regretted a minute of it."

His mother was momentarily speechless. Sean took the opportunity to tell her something that he thought she ought to hear.

"Mother, I love you," he said. "I know that you made a lot of sacrifices in your life to make things better for me. I appreciate that. I know that you love me and none of your maneuvering or manipulations were ever meant to hurt me, or even to hurt Josh. I know you want the best for me, but I am a grown-up man. I make my own decisions for better or worse. I forgot that for a while, but I remember it now. You may not agree with my choices, but at this point in our lives, if you want to continue to have a relationship with me, you'll have to butt out and keep your opinions to yourself."

His mother's face was pale and she looked as hurt as if he'd slapped her. He felt badly about that. He hoped that over time he'd be able to make it up to her. But right now, this was the way it had to be.

"So you're just going to walk away," she said. "You're just going to leave Josh here to be raised by her."

"No."

The word hung out there for a moment. His mother frowned, confused.

Sean reached out his hand toward Katy, and when she clasped it, he pulled her to his side and slid his arm around her waist.

"Josh is going to be raised by both his parents," Sean said. "Katy and I got married again last week when we were in St. Louis."

From the other side of the pass-through window Sean heard a little screech of delight.

"They're remarried," he heard Emma repeat to the customers in the dining room. "They remarried last week."

It was not until that moment that Sean realized how public their private family argument was in this place.

"We're husband and wife," Sean said to his mother more quietly. "We're going to stay here and raise our son and run this business together."

"What about Dodsonburger?" she asked him. "It's your inheritance, your legacy."

"Mother, that's your company," he said. "More than it was Dad's, more than it would ever be mine. You've put your heart and soul into that corporation and you should continue to do with it exactly as you see fit. I don't want to be a corporate office guy. My favorite part was always the day-to-day running of a restaurant. I can do that here. Yeah, I know the place will never be mine. It belongs to my wife. But that's another great thing I learned from you. How to work for a woman boss."

Bitsy's Wisdom 31

Bitsy's Wisdom 31: Aesop's fables give grasshoppers a bad reputation. But in the dog days of summer on Warbler Lake, those lazy green fiddlers are your best bait choice.

News of the wedding spread among the customers and neighbors of the Bait & BBQ faster than tacky gossip at a quilting bee. Katy and Sean decided to have a small reception at Bitsy's over the Fourth of July weekend. They had never had any public gathering for their first wedding, but now they both felt that they had more to celebrate. And flag waving and fireworks seemed to perfectly reflect their feelings.

Chick, O.O. and Theon made the trip from East St. Louis to spend the weekend, enjoy the celebration and give advice and assistance as Sean barbecued his first whole hog.

The beautiful piece of meat weighed almost one hundred and fifty pounds. It took nineteen hours of cooking, which kept them up most of the night before. But the men, along with the neighbors and friends drifting in and out, seemed to enjoy the long stories and jokes that kept everybody awake and having a good time all night long.

Chick declared there would be enough pork and fixings to feed five thousand. Fortunately not that many showed up. But nearly everyone in and around the Warbler Lake community was there. Plus, they'd sent handwritten invitations to all of Sean's former buddies and their families from Ladue as well as the friends of the Dodson family from in and around St. Louis.

To Katy's complete surprise, they were actually able to get in touch with her mother and stepfather. The two were already planning to spend the long weekend driving their tired old rusted RV from Florida to Minnesota. They actually seemed pleased to detour out of their way to show up in the Ozarks. Katy's mother had gone completely hippie, including tie-dyed clothing, no makeup and waist-long braids. She was funny, she liked Sean, and she was delighted with the grandson she'd never seen.

"I can see why you love this place," she told Katy, gesturing out toward the lake and the mountains. "It's just gorgeous here."

Katy gazed at the landscape and nodded.

"It is pretty," she said. "But that's not why I love it. It's home for me and my family. I knew the minute I saw Bitsy's photograph that we could be happy here."

"Well, you do seem to be happy," her mother said. "And I hope that you always are."

"Nothing can guarantee that," Sean told her. "But we'll be together, and we've been apart long enough to appreciate what a gift that is."

Also located and invited was a distant cousin of Bitsy's. Patrick McGrady and his family had never met Bitsy nor been to her place, but his wife had run across the "feelers" Spurl had put out on a genealogy Web site when Bitsy died. When he'd called up, Katy had immediately invited them to the reception and was not completely surprised when they decided to come.

She'd packed up all the photographs in the small bedroom upstairs. That had seemed the thing to do when she'd moved Josh into that room as his own. His new wildlife wallpaper and fishing-theme bed linens just didn't go with frames full of smiling people he didn't know. They deserved to find a new home among the bits of family that Bitsy had left behind.

"I've made you a copy of this one," Katy said to Patrick, indicating the photo of bathing-suited Bitsy holding up the fish she'd caught. "It's been in the dining room of the B & B since it was new. I can't imagine the place without it."

The man nodded. "It should stay here with you," he said. "It's great to know the old gal lives on in this place."

Of course, one person who was not living on in the place was Emma. As soon as she heard that Katy and Sean were back together again, she made arrangements to get out of the small bedroom and into her own quarters. She rented a room from Mrs. Bullock. The old lady who'd lived alone in her big house for so many years seemed perfectly amenable to having a "boarder," as she described it.

"That's really great," Katy said. "And close. I thought you'd probably get a cabin at Gouswhelters'."

"I thought about it," Emma said. "But I worried about the long term. They close those cabins up in the winter. There is heat, I guess. If you want to have a fire in the fireplace all day. But without those open windows, it would be like living in a cave."

Katy frowned. "But you don't need to worry about winter. You'll be off to college by fall," she said.

Emma shrugged. "Not this year," she said.

"But you've been thinking about it, planning for it, saving for it."

Her sister looked sheepish and didn't answer. Katy pressed.

"Tell me," she said. "I'm not some silly teenager that you have to protect from real life. Why aren't you going?"

"I spent my money," Emma said.

"On what?"

She hesitated only a moment before she answered. "I used it to pay Latt for being our lawyer."

"Oh."

"Now, don't get all weird and feeling bad about it," Emma said. "I just barely had enough for a semester, anyway. I was happy to do it and everything has worked out great. There'll be plenty of years to go to college. And this place has more than its share of strange tribal culture for me to study."

Katy had laughed at the little joke and pretended that Emma's sacrifice was just one more that she was willing to make for her family. But it worried Katy nonetheless and she spoke to Sean about it.

"I wish we could give her a raise or set aside some money to pay her back," she said.

"Well, we can pay her back eventually," Sean said. "But there's not really anything we can do for her now."

Katy felt bad. She felt guilty. But Sean was right. Bitsy's was doing okay, they were paying their bills and keeping the lights on, but it would take several good summers to amass college money.

With no solution in sight, Katy reassured herself that everything in her sister's life would work out exactly as it was supposed to.

Katy enjoyed meeting many of the new people in her husband's old life. His high school buddies were as strange as high school friends can sometimes be. But they seemed genuinely happy for him, and their wives, all dressed in chic designer casuals, were polite to Katy, if not welcoming her into their inner circle.

She especially liked seeing the corporate people from Dodson-burger. Her experience with them during her first marriage to Sean had been limited. But they all seemed like bright, caring people, eager to get the layout of Sean and Katy's new venture.

She got into a long conversation with Pete's wife, Lila, surprised to discover that the woman, now a stay-at-home mom, had a degree in archeology.

"I still try to go on one dig every summer," she told Katy. "It keeps me engaged in what's going on. So when the time gets right, I'll feel comfortable about getting back into it."

"My sister is interested in anthropology," Katy told her. "I guess they don't do digs."

"Oh, sure they do," Lila said. "Not digs, per se, but they do have volunteers engaged in doing grunt work for projects. She should contact the university about that."

"Emma doesn't have a degree like you do," Katy said.

"It's not required to be of help," Lila said. "Most of the volunteers are just interested amateurs."

Katy was so excited. Surely they could manage for Emma to be off volunteering for a few weeks every year. Katy was eager to tell her sister about it right away. But Emma seemed to have disappeared from the party. Katy checked all the edges of the crowd, expecting to find her out there looking in. After failing to spot her anywhere, she went looking to find her. As she walked, talked, visited and searched, it took several minutes before she finally located her sister.

Emma was sitting all alone on the steps to the apartment. She had a letter in her hand and tears in her eyes.

Katy's own heart was immediately in her throat.

"What's happened?"

Emma was so choked up she couldn't answer. She handed the paper to Katy.

Dear Emma,

Please find the enclosed check for the money that you gave me for Katy's legal defense. Because things were settled so quickly and so amicably, I've decided to forgo any fee. I've also included the remaining monies in the college account of my daughter, Cassandra. The funds, saved from regular paychecks from the day she was born, have just been sitting around drawing interest since she passed away fourteen years ago. She didn't live long enough to complete her education. I'm sure she would be so pleased to see that you are finally going to be able to complete yours.

Good luck and don't disappoint either of us.

Latt

Katy glanced at the amount on the check and gasped.

"One hundred and sixty-seven thousand, eight hundred twenty-two dollars, and forty-seven cents! Oh, my God!"

Emma was still crying.

"Is this really happening?" she asked Katy. "Am I really going to get to go to college at last?"

"Yes, you are," Katy said.

"Can I accept this?" Emma asked. "It's his daughter's money. He probably shouldn't give it to me."

"Of course you can accept it," Katy said. "You will accept it. You've accepted every burden and every responsibility that's ever been thrown at you. Now you're going to get some good fortune. And you deserve it. You deserve it so much."

The two sisters hugged. They both cried and then laughed, wiping each other's tears.

"We've got to find Latt and thank him," Emma said.

Katy agreed and they were off into the huge crowd of congratulatory friends and family, looking for their favorite bait producer.

The crowd was festive. Out on the beach, Spurl and his wife, Vivy, with the help of Miss Welborn, had the children in a big circle teaching them to play Drop the Handkerchief. It was a totally new game to most of them and they loved the excitement of the chase.

She spotted Chick and O.O. with their grandson, Theon, in the crowd. They were the kind of friendly, never-met-a-stranger people who fit in everywhere they went.

Emma and Katy's stepfather, Larry, was swapping stories with Pricy Metcalf.

Katy excitedly told her mother the news about Emma.

She nodded. "I knew you'd make it," she said to her oldest daughter. "I never knew how, but I had complete confidence. We're so happy for you kids, and so proud."

"Thank you."

"Your place looks mighty fine," she said. "Larry and I were just saying that it would be nice to have a port of call somewhere to come home to once in a while. This might be a good place for us."

"I think it might be good for you," Katy agreed. "And it would be even better for us."

She excused herself when she caught sight of Old Crank in his wheelchair. She hurried up to greet him.

"Well, hey there, hunk-a-sugar," he said. "You get prettier to look at every gall-darn day."

"I didn't know you were back from your rehab facility," she said.

"Got home yesterday," he told her. "And here's my babydoll, you're a sight for sore eyes yourself."

Katy glanced over to see Emma had come up behind her.

"You look as mean and crazy as ever," her sister said. "When are we going to see you back in a boat on that lake?"

"I'm sure those fish have been missing me," he said. "I dang sure have been missing them."

Other people came over and engaged the old man in conversation.

Katy saw Curt and Nadine sitting together on a bench. They were smiling and talking. Baby Natty was asleep on Curt's chest.

"Hi," she said, walking up to them.

Katy saw Nadine guiltily jerk away her hand from Curt, who held it. Her cheeks blushed vivid red.

"Have you seen Latt?" she asked, ignoring their obvious discomfort.

"I saw him at the gas station yesterday," Curt said. "He was headed out of town."

"Out of town?" Katy was disappointed. "You mean he's not coming today?"

"No, he'll be here," Curt said. "He said he had to go to the city to pick up something for the party."

"The city?" Katy questioned. "What would we need from the city?"

"I hope it's not champagne and caviar," Emma said. "Champagne just doesn't taste right with barbecue. And caviar." She shook her head and tutted. "This crowd would be thinking we're trying to feed them stock from the bait shop."

They all laughed. Emma shared her good news and good fortune. Nadine and Curt both wished her well.

The two sisters made their way back into the crowd. They spoke a polite word with Newt Barker. Accepted compliments on the party from Flora Krebs. They nodded to Luella Bullock, in deep conversation with Gus Gouswhelter. They talked and laughed and visited with neighbors. And they stood listening as Waymon Riley entertained on guitar.

"You know, Katy," Emma said. "Now that I know I'm really leaving, I may even be a little sad to go."

Katy hugged her.

"You can go around the world a hundred times, sis," she told her. "But you can count on me to always be here with a place you can call home."

At that moment Katy caught sight of two familiar faces edging into the crowd. Lattimer Meicklejohn had arrived with a "ladyfriend" on his arm. She was a city woman, chicly dressed, wealthy, cultured, but in this community she fit right in. Everyone she passed greeted her with familiar welcome.

"GramMarr!" a little voice rang out. Josh came rushing through the crowd at full speed, friends and family hurriedly getting out of his way. His eyes were bright, his smile was nearly ear to ear, and with full confidence of being caught in midair he leaped into her arms.

She laughed and hugged the boy tightly and placed a kiss atop his dark curly hair. "I've missed you," she said.

"I've missed you, too," Josh said. "I told Mr. Latt that it just wouldn't be a wedding resumption party without you."

"Reception," she corrected him. "A wedding reception. Or resumption, I suppose."

Sean came and grabbed Katy's hand. Their eyes met and in that one glance he communicated his heart, *I love you, Katy, so don't get scared, don't hang on to resentment, she's my mother and she's always welcome.*

Together they crossed the distance between Gwen Dodson and themselves.

Sean kissed her on the cheek. "Thanks so much for coming, Mother," he said. "It's really good to see you."

Gwen smiled at her only son and ran a loving hand down his cheek.

"You look good," she told him. "All this sunshine and fresh air is doing wonders for you."

"Maybe it's married life," he said. "I think it suits me."

Gwen turned slightly and she and her daughter-in-law were eye to eye.

Katy took a deep breath and gave a determined smile. "Yes, thanks for coming, Mrs. Dodson. Josh is right, it's good to have you here."

"You must call me Gwen," she said. "We're family."

Katy could never say who made the first move. If she had reached out, or if Gwen had opened her arms. But at that moment the two strong women who loved Sean Dodson embraced.

It was a start.

Readers' Ring

We hope you enjoyed this wonderful book by Pamela Morsi. Overleaf are a series of discussion questions that you might find interesting. It is our hope that these questions enhance your enjoyment of this book.

Readers' Ring Questions for
Bitsy's Bait & BBQ

1. Starting over in a brand-new place is a fantasy for a lot of people. Can we ever *really* start over?

2. Cultural differences, like those Katy and Emma faced moving to the Ozarks, range from interesting asides to insurmountable obstacles. What strategies work best in learning to live among people who are not quite like us?

3. Katy was relatively young when she got married. Sean was older, but less prepared to take on that commitment. What factors determine our level of readiness for marriage?

4. Emma put her own goals aside to help Katy achieve hers. Was she a saint or an enabler?

5. At one point Katy explains to Sean that she hasn't talked to Josh about his father because she doesn't know what to say about a parent who is absent by choice. What should she have said? Sugarcoated truth or brutal honesty?

6. Gwen was disappointed with her son's choices, so she tried to pressure him into changing them. Where did she cross the line from "tough love" to meddling?
7. The inhabitants of Warbler Lake were seemingly ordinary people but Emma liked to observe them as if they were an unfamiliar native tribe. How can our perception of people change with the perspective by which we view them?
8. Gwen is a truly toxic mother-in-law. In reading the story from her point of view, did any of her machinations make sense? Would you try to intervene if you thought your child was picking the wrong life partner? How would you have handled Gwen if you were Katy?

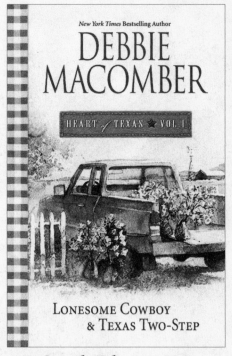

THE EXTRAORDINARY DEBUT NOVEL BY
DEANNA RAYBOURN

A PSYCHOTIC MURDERER IS ABOUT TO MAKE HIS ONE MISTAKE: UNDERESTIMATING LADY JULIA

SILENT *in the* GRAVE

Available wherever hardcovers are sold.